ALRENE HUGHES wa[...]w up in
Belfast and now lives [...]r of the
Manchester Irish Writ[...]y have
been published in a[...]. She
was an English teac[...]writes full
time. *A Song in My Heart* is the fi[...]rt in her bestselling
trilogy of novels that consists of *Martha's Girls* (2013) and
The Golden Sisters (2015), both published by Blackstaff Press.
The trilogy was inspired by a scrapbook of concert programmes
and newspaper cuttings about her mother and her aunts, the
real Golden Sisters.

A Song in my Heart

ALRENE HUGHES

THE
BLACK
STAFF
PRESS

Acknowledgements

My heartfelt thanks go to Patsy Horton, managing editor at Blackstaff Press, and her team for their belief in the first book, *Martha's Girls*, and for encouraging and supporting me to complete the trilogy.

Thanks also to: Michael Faulkner for his editing; Carolyn Baines for all things musical; Dr Sara Farrell for all things medical; the Deruchie family for 'Clemmie'; and special thanks to Heather Hart for everything.

Once again, I acknowledge Brian Barton's academic insight combined with natural storytelling in his book *The Blitz: Belfast in the War Years*.

Last, but not least, thanks to the grandchildren of Martha's girls: Adam, Dan, Rebecca, Andrew, Daniel. The books were written so they would get to know our family and the city they called home.

Many of the characters and incidents in this book are fictional, but the Goulding family did exist, the historical events are accurate and the Golden Sisters did sing.

Published in 2016 by Blackstaff Press
4D Weavers Court
Linfield Road
Belfast BT12 5GH

Typeset by KT Designs, St Helens, England

Printed and bound by CPI Group UK (Ltd), Croydon CR0 4YY

A CIP catalogue for this book is available from the British Library

ISBN 978 0 85640 973 8

www.blackstaffpress.com
www.alrenehughes.com

This book is dedicated to the
people of Belfast

Chapter 1

Martha carefully hung the dress on the kitchen door and stepped back to admire it. Mrs McKee was indeed a skilled seamstress: the skirt, cut on the bias, would swing with any slight movement and the tiny darts on the bodice would emphasise a trim waist and flatter a full bosom. The fine lawn material had used up all their clothing coupons, but it would be worth it to see Pat walk up the aisle in the pale lavender gown, so perfect against her ivory skin and rich auburn hair.

Martha had only to add the finishing touch – a design of intertwined leaves and petals to embellish the scooped neckline. She cleared the table and set out needles, scissors, thimble, skeins of embroidery thread and a bowl of milky pearls from an old necklace, all carefully washed and polished. Finally, she laid the dress on the table and began to mark with a pin the centre of each pearl flower.

The morning wore on and, with each pearl stitched in place, Martha gave thanks that her daughter had found a good man in Captain Tony Farrelly for, Lord knows, Pat deserved some happiness after all she'd been through.

★

Peggy was late for work, but it wasn't her fault. How was she to know that half the US Army would be driving up Royal Avenue in convoy with policemen on point duty stopping the traffic at every junction to let them through? Mr Goldstein would no doubt roll his eyes and tut under his breath when she arrived at the music shop, but she would explain that she had left the stationary trolley-bus and walked all the way from York Street past the GIs who waved and whistled at her and never stopped once, but only smiled in acknowledgement.

Goldstein was in the shop window putting up a poster to promote his new idea. 'Sheet Music Library' it read. 'Don't buy, borrow.' He was clearly in a good mood and did not mention that she was half an hour late. 'Peggy! I want you to sort out all the old or dog-eared sheet music that nobody wants to buy, but might pay tuppence to borrow.'

Peggy stared at the dozens of sheet-music boxes and her heart sank.

Goldstein went on, 'There's a shortage of paper so the price of sheet music has increased. This is our contribution to Make Do and Mend.'

'Why would anybody pay for grubby bits of paper?'

'You have no head for business, Peggy. They're not buying paper, they're buying music as sparkling as it ever was, taking home the score and lyrics to enjoy and then they can bring them back and borrow something else. Just like books in a library.'

Peggy rolled her eyes. 'Where's Esther? Can't she sort it out while I serve the customers?'

'I've just sent her to the *Northern Whig* to place an advertisement for our concert at The Grosvenor Hall a week on Saturday and guess what?' Peggy shrugged her shoulders and Goldstein went on, 'The Golden Sisters will be top of the bill.'

Peggy's mood changed in an instant and she clapped her hands in delight. She had pushed for top billing for so long and at last she and her sisters would be the stars of the show. She couldn't wait to see the look on Pat's and Irene's faces when she told them and they could hardly complain if she arranged some extra rehearsals to learn some new songs, could they?

★

2

Just beyond the city centre, in Short Brothers & Harland aircraft factory, Irene had already done two hours' work. Throughout the morning the heat from the rivets and the smell of solder and grease had built up inside the fuselage of the Stirling bomber and, although dinnertime was only half an hour away, Irene could stand it no longer. She pulled off her mask and climbed down the ladder with all the speed she could muster and crossed the factory floor. There was an angry shout from the foreman, but she ignored him and headed for the toilets out in the yard. This was the pattern of her days: late-morning sickness; afternoon weariness; unsettled nights. It didn't help that her mother reminded her daily that being a riveter was no job for any woman, let alone a pregnant one.

When the hooter sounded for the dinner break she made her way to the canteen for dry toast and tea. Macy, the only American working in the factory, would have been easy to spot even without her stars and stripes turban, and Irene went to join her.

'Hey girl, how you doin'?'

'I'll be all right when I've eaten this.' Irene kicked off her shoes and put her feet up on the chair opposite. 'I'm into the fourth month. Surely it can't last much longer. If it does I'll get the sack.'

'They won't let you go – there aren't enough riveters as it is.'

'That's as maybe, but my mother or Sandy will probably nag me into leaving anyway.'

'Have you heard anything from Sandy lately?'

'Just a note to say he's still waiting to hear if he can get leave for Pat's wedding, but he's not hopeful.' Irene lowered her voice. 'There's so much going on at the base in Enniskillen, something to do with protecting the Atlantic convoys. It's bursting at the seams down there with American and Canadian air crews and their planes, not to mention the RAF.'

'If he does get leave, he might ask you to go back there with him.'

Irene raised an eyebrow. 'He can ask all he likes, but I'm not living in a tin hut or a pokey cottage in the back of beyond!'

Martha embroidered all afternoon, neat little rings of petals in primrose yellow around each pearl, and as she did so she thought of

William Kennedy and how, if not for a cruel twist of fate, it might have been him that Pat would be marrying on Saturday. Pat had always had a fondness for him and working together had drawn them close. But it wasn't to be. Martha shuddered at the thought of the hell Pat went through when she and William were caught up in the Dublin bombing. His death had plunged Pat into a nervous breakdown so severe that Martha had feared her daughter would never recover. Even now, she felt a sense of amazement at how Pat had fought against a despair that frequently overwhelmed her. Then, God bless him, Tony Farrelly came along.

There was a tap on the window, the back door opened and Betty from next door cooed, 'It's only me.'

'Come on in,' said Martha, slipping the needle into the back of the neckline. 'I was just going to put the kettle on.'

'Well, would you look at that.' Betty examined the embroidery. 'So delicate. You've a quare talent, Martha, so you have.'

'Ach, it's nothing more than patience and good eyesight.'

'Well, I've neither so that's my excuse. But wait till you see what I've brought you.' She felt in the pocket of her apron and pulled out a rope of pearls. 'The catch is broken, but I thought you might need a few more for decoration.'

'Oh Betty, that's great. I was only just thinking it would be nice to have a few more flowers round the three-quarter-length sleeves.'

'Will you have time to do it?'

'I think so, everything else is ready. All that's needed now is the signed permission forms from Tony's commanding officer.'

'Permission forms?'

'Aye, apparently that's how it works. An American soldier can't just marry; he has to fill in a lot of forms. They wanted to know all about Pat, checking up I suppose.'

'There'll be no problem there then,' said Betty. 'They'll soon see what a grand girl she is.'

Pat was seething. Why, today of all days, did she get stuck in a meeting when Tony was waiting outside for her so that they could go to the jeweller's together?

Half an hour late, she ran down the steps of Stormont Buildings hoping he was still there. She needn't have worried. He was leaning against the jeep and she felt again that somersault of her heart at the sight of his dark crew cut and broad shoulders beneath the well-pressed GI uniform. She ran towards him, and he caught her in his arms and swung her round.

'Thought I'd been stood up there for a while, Patti.' He laughed.

'I'm so sorry I'm late.' The words tumbled out of her. 'There's been such an argument about the evacuees. You know most of them have come back home to Belfast, but nobody's checked up on their welfare. They couldn't decide who was responsible. I wanted to tell them we're all responsible, but of course I'm only a clerk. In the end they said we'd have to meet again tomorrow.' She paused for breath and noticed the concern on Tony's face. 'Oh, am I too late? Is there still time to go for the ring?'

He kissed her cheek. 'Don't worry. Hop in and we'll head into town and you can tell me all about your evacuees on the way.'

Tony swung the jeep in a wide arc and drove down the long avenue towards the wrought-iron gates at the bottom of Stormont Hill.

'The problem is that so many homes were destroyed in the bombing and a lot of those still standing aren't fit to live in. A lot of children don't bother to go to school any more and most of them don't get enough to eat.'

Pat talked and Tony listened. 'I can't help thinking that the children would have been better off staying out in the country until the houses were made habitable. But then you wouldn't want to keep children away from their families any longer than necessary …'

Tony pulled in to the kerb and stopped the engine.

Pat looked around. 'Are we stopping here? I thought we were going to Queen's Arcade?'

'We'll go in here first,' said Tony. 'It's quiet and there's something we have to talk about.'

'A public bar?'

'Come on, it's okay, you'll see.'

The dimly lit interior was pungent with the smell of porter and, as her eyes adjusted to the light, Pat took in the elaborate surroundings. The walls were covered with decorated tiles, and ornate lanterns of stained glass were suspended from the ceiling on chains. Along one side there was a row of mahogany booths complete with doors to conceal the drinkers within and from which wreaths of smoke rose upwards to linger over their heads.

Tony found an empty booth and ushered Pat inside. Almost immediately a waiter appeared to take their order, and as soon as he had gone, Pat took one look at Tony and knew something was wrong.

'What's going on, Tony? What's happened?'

His eyes never left her face as he reached out for her hand and whispered, 'I'm so sorry, Patti, but we can't get married.'

It should have been a shock, but it wasn't. In fact, ever since Tony had asked her to marry him, there had been a tiny dark corner in Pat's mind filled with the fear that it would never happen. But even though she had half expected something to go wrong, devastation overwhelmed her. 'Tell me,' was all she could say.

'My commanding officer was called to London three days ago. That happens sometimes and usually he's back within forty-eight hours, so I wasn't worried. But it turns out that the order has been given for us to leave Northern Ireland. You know we've been on alert, ready to move any day now. Well, the first contingent left Belfast this morning on their way to England for final training before deployment overseas. My division is next to go.'

'But you're still here; we could get married before then.'

Tony shook his head. 'He left before he could sign the papers. I haven't got the permission to marry—'

'But someone else could sign them, couldn't they?'

'Patti, that ain't how it works and right now we're just getting ready to ship outta here.'

'We'll go to the registry office in the morning—'

Tony shook his head. 'No, it can't be done, you have to see that. I'd be court-martialled for marrying without permission.'

And Pat felt a clawing fear that in this confined space in a public bar her future had been snatched from her. She clung to him and his embrace was so strong she felt his anguish too. When he spoke again it was as though he knew her darkest thoughts. 'Patti, my darling, this is not where it ends for us. We knew I would have to leave soon and I hoped we would be married first, but nothing – nothing – is going to change how I feel about you.' He lifted her chin. 'I love you so much.'

'But what if something happens to you? I couldn't bear it.'

'Oh Patti, I know the heartbreak you went through when William died, but I swear I'll come back. You won't be left alone a second time.'

'You can't say that. Nobody knows what's going to happen. You're a soldier!' Pat's voice had risen steadily.

'Stop it!' Tony gripped her arms. 'I will not die. This war will end and I'll be back to marry you. You have to be strong, Patti, you have to believe me.'

'I want to, I really want to, but—'

'Look, there's still time to go to the jeweller's like we planned and we'll buy the ring anyway. It'll be like a pledge.'

Pat shook her head. 'The last thing I want now is a ring. It would be tempting fate.'

'Okay. Okay.' Tony wiped a tear from her cheek. 'But as far as I'm concerned, Patti, I am your husband.'

Pat took his hand from her cheek and brought it to her lips. 'And I'm your wife,' she whispered.

They left the Crown Bar and walked through the gathering dusk to the City Hall and as they walked they talked about the future they would have together. Tony told her again about his home town. 'I know a little fixer-upper a few blocks from the ocean: wraparound porch, big magnolia tree in the backyard. You'll love it. It's been empty a while, but I'm gonna write my sister to find out if it's still for sale. I could put down a deposit.'

They sat on a bench close to Victoria's statue, just a girl who cried a little and her GI who comforted her and tried to make her laugh. They held each other and kissed and talked and talked.

Slowly the moon rose and Pat forced herself to ask, 'When do you leave?'

'Tomorrow early.'

'You need to get some sleep then,' said Pat and she stood to go.

He caught her hand. 'Stay a bit longer, please.'

'It's time, Tony.'

He knew that too. 'I'll drive you home.'

'No, I'll be fine.' She reached up and put her arms around his neck and saw all the love in his eyes and at that moment she believed absolutely that they would be together. The world would not be so cruel as to take him from her.

He held her in his arms and kissed her tenderly, the sweetest of sorrows. 'I love you,' he whispered as he let her go.

She held back the tears and smiled. 'I'll be waiting for you.' Then she turned and walked away.

In the late afternoon, Martha dug up some carrots, parsnips and potatoes and gave thanks again that Betty's husband Jack had helped her clear an area of the back garden last year to grow vegetables. He had given her fruit bushes too and advised her to leave the brambles at the bottom of the garden to multiply in the hope of a good crop of blackberries. 'There's a lot to be said for Digging for Victory,' Jack had told her. 'It'll make your rations go much further.'

She had a big pot of stew on the range: the bit of beef skirt with the vegetables, along with the wheaten loaf she had baked, would fill the girls up after their days' work. As usual, Sheila was first home. Working in the office meant she finished half an hour after school ended and it didn't take her too long to cycle up Cliftonville Road from the Royal Academy. She was no sooner in the door than the complaining began. Martha could have set her clock by it.

'I'm fed up with that place, so I am. That woman has it in for me, you know.'

'What's she done this time?'

'Just because I didn't finish the filing from yesterday she said I should have come in early this morning. She forgets I didn't get it finished because she had me checking her bookkeeping. Then to put the tin hat on it she was showing off her new clothes and saying wasn't it a pity I only had the one skirt to wear to work.' Sheila took the lid off the saucepan and sniffed. 'Is it stew again?'

'Now don't start, Sheila. That's good nourishing food.'

'I'm not complaining. I'm that hungry I could eat a horse and the wee boy on it.'

'That's all right then, because I got the last horse in the butcher's.'

Sheila's eyes widened. 'It isn't, is it?'

Martha laughed. 'Praise be to God, we haven't come to that … yet. Now get the table set – you're not the only one coming home from work starving.'

They didn't wait for Pat to come home before eating. 'Sure, she'll be a while choosing the ring,' said Peggy.

'Tony might take her somewhere for her tea afterwards,' Irene suggested.

'And then they'll go for a walk and hold hands and she'll look into his eyes and he'll—'

'That's enough, Sheila,' said Martha, but the girls were already giggling and Martha let them be.

'Did you get Pat's dress from Mrs McKee?' asked Peggy.

'Indeed I did and I finished the embroidery as well. It's upstairs, I'll fetch it down when Pat comes in. That's if she doesn't have Tony with her. We wouldn't want him to see it before the wedding.'

After tea they sat in the front room round a meagre fire of some sticks and a shovel of coal dust and listened to the wireless. They were laughing so much at Tommy Handley and *It's That Man Again* that they didn't hear the back door. Martha caught a movement out of the corner of her eye and realised Pat was standing in the doorway. 'Ah, you're home at last,' she said and looked past her. 'Is Tony not with you?'

'No,' said Pat, 'he had to go back to base.'

'Mammy, can we see the dress now that Pat's back?' asked Sheila.

'Away and get it then. It's on my bed.'

Pat slowly unbuttoned her coat and Martha was struck by how weary she looked. 'Here I'll hang that up, Pat. You go and sit near the fire. Have you had anything to eat?'

'No, sure I'm not that hungry.'

'Well, did you get the ring?' asked Irene, but Pat didn't seem to hear her. At the sound of Sheila running down the stairs, all eyes turned towards the door. She burst into the room and held the lavender dress up against her, holding the skirt out and swaying to show it off.

Irene and Peggy were on their feet at once examining the dress, feeling the soft material, admiring the embroidery and commenting on how beautiful it was. It was a moment before they realised that Pat hadn't moved. 'Do you like it, Pat?' asked Irene.

Pat caught a sleeve and her fingers traced the embroidered leaves and petals and stroked the pearls. 'It's beautiful. I'm glad it's finished.'

'Just in time,' said Martha, and laughed. 'Why don't you try it on and we'll check the hem length?'

'No, I couldn't do that.'

'It'll only take a few minutes.'

Pat leaned back in her chair and closed her eyes. Her face was drained of expression. 'There's no need, it'll be a long time before I get to wear it.'

'What do you mean? The wedding's on Saturday,' but even as she spoke, Martha knew there would be no wedding. The tears that escaped from Pat's closed eyelids were proof enough of that.

Pat sighed. 'The Americans have started leaving already; Tony goes first thing in the morning.'

No one spoke – there were no words to comfort someone who had lost her first love in a bombing only to have her second sent to fight days before their wedding. Pat wiped her eyes with the heel of her hand and looked at the sadness on the faces of her family.

'We will get married,' she told them. 'This war can't last forever and Tony'll come back for me, I know he will.' She managed a smile. 'Would it be all right if we didn't talk about it now?'

'That's fine,' said Martha, 'just you sit there quiet, love. Sheila, take the dress back upstairs. Now, Pat, could you manage a bit of wheaten bread?'

Later, the conversation turned to the Grosvenor Hall concert and Peggy's eyes lit up. 'I've got such good news, you'll never guess. We're top of the bill and, Sheila, you're to open the second half with two songs. In fact, we could start rehearsing right now, if you like?'

'Well, maybe not tonight, Peggy,' said Martha, with an almost imperceptible nod towards Pat.

Peggy's face fell. 'Oh Pat, will you not want to sing at all, after what's happened?'

Pat's tone was icy. 'I may have lost my voice once before, but this is not the same at all. I'll be singing in the concert, don't you worry!'

When Martha locked up and went upstairs to bed, she didn't switch on her bedroom light or draw the blackout curtains. Instead she went to the window and gazed upwards at clear skies and a full moon – a bomber's moon. It was nearly eighteen months since the city was last bombed and she was thankful that the searchlight of war had swept elsewhere. Around midnight she awoke in panic and turned to see the lavender wedding dress, a ghostly shadow on the wardrobe door, and understood that fear comes in many guises.

Chapter 2

The girls were laughing as they came from the cold November night into the Grosvenor Hall, but as they entered the auditorium, with its sea of wooden chairs and huge stage, they fell silent.

'I can't believe we're back here again,' said Irene. 'Our first big concert – remember how nervous we were?'

'First days of the war,' said Pat softly. 'If we'd known then what lay ahead of us …'

'All the concerts to come, singing with George Formby, Glenn Miller—'

'I was thinking of three years of war, Peggy. The bombings, the deaths—'

'But we're still here, Pat, still singing and tonight we're top of the bill.'

'Come on you two.' Irene linked her arms through theirs. 'Let's go and see who else has arrived.'

'Do we get our own dressing room now?' asked Pat.

'Ha!' said Peggy.

There were already performers standing around backstage in costume and full makeup. 'It's a big cast tonight,' shouted Peggy over their excited chatter. 'These people will be in the first half and the second-half performers like us will just be arriving now so there should be space in the dressing room.'

'Did I just see wee Lizzie and her accordion?' asked Pat.

'Probably,' said Peggy. 'Mr Goldstein has brought together some of the original Barnstormers and the newer acts from the Stars for Troops show.'

It was even busier and noisier in the dressing room. 'Follow me,' said Peggy and she squeezed through the crowd.

'There's Davy the magician.' Irene waved at a bulky man in white tie and tails. 'I hope he doesn't get stuck in this crush or his poor doves will suffocate.'

At the back of the room were four coat-pegs and a mirror with a piece of cardboard stuck in the corner: 'Reserved for the Golden Sisters'. Pat shook her head in disbelief.

'Irene!' a disembodied voice screamed and a headdress that looked like a cascading fruit bowl came towards them through the crowd.

'Oh my God, Macy, what are you wearing?'

'My Carmen Miranda costume. What do you reckon?' And Macy swivelled her hips to show off her vibrantly coloured skirt, caught up at the front to reveal her long, shapely legs.

Then she leaned in and whispered, 'Do you see the young guy in the South American costume – ruffles on his sleeves?' Irene nodded. 'My new dancing partner. Kinda cute, ain't he?'

'He looks about eighteen,' said Irene. 'Where did you find him?'

'Betty Staff's Dance School, of course. I taught him everything he knows,' she said, and she gave her deep-throated laugh and sashayed back to the boy.

It was Goldstein's custom to speak to the performers before curtain up, to rally his troops and inspire them to excel. Everyone squeezed into the dressing room and someone found Goldstein a crate to stand on. He straightened his dicky bow and cleared his throat.

'The Grosvenor Hall is where I saw the first fundraising concert of the war and I knew then that entertainment would be crucial in sustaining the morale of this city. And so it has been – even in the darkest days you have put aside your sorrows and fears to tread the boards. And I salute your courage.'

There were cheers from the company and after a moment Goldstein held up his hand. 'Tonight, we have some special guests in the audience – British Army top brass and an advance contingent of US Army officers replacing those who have only recently left, en route to North Africa. So, I ask you once again to raise the roof with your incomparable Belfast talent.'

The first half moved along at a good pace and Pete, the new compère, had the audience in stitches with his jokes. When Macy and her partner left the stage after their 'South American Way' routine to the sound of cheers and wolf whistles, Pete quipped, 'Haven't seen that much fruit in one place since before the war. We'll be raffling it off at the interval!'

Backstage, Pat was applying Sheila's makeup. 'This is a big stage, with strong lights,' Pat told her. 'Large sections of the audience are quite a distance from you so everything needs to be emphasised.' She stood back and studied Sheila's face. How her little sister had changed over the past few years. The schoolgirl had grown into a beautiful young woman. Her face was less round, her cheekbones more pronounced, though not so much as Peggy's, and there was a softness about her features. Hers was a gentle beauty.

Pat applied the foundation and rouge, then used shadow to enhance Sheila's almond-shaped eyes and added mascara, before sweeping a dark pencil under her lower lashes to extend the outer corners. With Sheila's chestnut hair and the striking kingfisher blue dress she would be wearing, Pat decided that a strong red lipstick would be the dramatic finishing touch.

'There you are – a Hollywood starlet if ever I saw one.'

While Sheila and Pat were occupied, Irene thought it might be a good idea to have a quiet word with Peggy. 'Just come out here a minute,' said Irene and they went out into the corridor. 'Do you think Pat'll be all right? You don't think she could lose her voice again like she did when William was killed?'

Peggy shrugged her shoulders. 'Who knows? She's been putting a brave face on it since Tony left but … Oh, I don't know … She managed the rehearsals, but there's something missing, isn't there?

Take the Gracie Fields solo, "Wish me Luck". All those difficult high notes – it's a song made for her range, but all she does is complain about it. She's just not got that vitality about her at the moment and, I'm telling you, that has an effect on her singing.'

'If only she'd had a letter from Tony it might have lifted her.'

'He's not been gone two weeks. That's hardly enough time to settle in his new billet and I'm sure his first priority wasn't to get out the Basildon Bond.'

Irene nodded towards the dressing room. 'The tension's already building up in there, so we'll just need to keep her calm.' She hesitated, choosing her words carefully. 'Peggy, are we still singing the same songs we agreed on?'

'What do you mean by that?'

'It's just that sometimes—'

'What!'

Irene could sense Peggy's temper fraying. 'Well, you know sometimes when we're on the stage you, maybe for a very good reason, change your mind and play the introduction to a different song, and we have to—'

'Oh, for goodness sake,' said Peggy, 'the songs we rehearsed are the songs I will play,' and she stomped off.

'That's grand,' Irene shouted after her, 'but will they be in the right order?'

The Golden Sisters, Irene, Pat and Peggy, stood in the darkness of the wings dressed in their polka dot blouses and slim black skirts, listening to the compère introduce them.

'And now, ladies and gentlemen, these three Belfast girls have been singing their way through the war in the concert halls, dance halls and army camps. Tonight they're top of the bill at the Grosvenor Hall, so please welcome on stage Belfast's answer to the Andrews Sisters – our very own Golden Sisters!'

They ran on to the stage smiling at the warm applause. Peggy went straight to the piano and started the introduction to 'Zing went the Strings of my Heart', while Irene and Pat went to the microphone and swayed to the music. So far so good, thought

Irene and she glanced over at Pat. Please God, let her be all right, let her sing, and in that split second Pat turned to her and winked and they came in right on cue. It was clear that the excitement of being on stage had restored Pat's sparkle and, as usual, the strength of her voice carried her sisters along in their harmonies.

As the act at the top of the bill they had a longer set of eight songs with a staggered costume change halfway through. After the third song Irene and Peggy left the stage, leaving Pat to sing the Gracie Fields number. It was to be a celebration of those going off to fight, and Peggy had choreographed it to the second. The front row of the audience had been given flags to wave and Pat was to lead them up one aisle and down the other with everyone singing the chorus, finishing with Pat back on stage for the spectacular ending of high notes.

Backstage, Irene was getting changed. 'Oh no,' she said. 'These trousers.'

'What is it?'

'They won't fasten.'

'What do you mean? They fitted you before.'

'That was a month ago. I'm another month pregnant now.'

'Never mind,' said Peggy. 'We took the waist in to fit you, remember? We'll just let out the stitches. I've got some scissors—'

The tannoy, that allowed those in the dressing room to hear what was happening on stage, had fallen silent. Peggy's hand went to her mouth. 'Something's wrong – Pat should be singing by now.' They listened with bated breath, and then there was the sound of footsteps and Pat clearing her throat and finally speaking softly into the microphone.

'I'm supposed to sing a song now about leaving the ones you love and being happy and positive about everything. Well, a lot of young men have been leaving lately to go and fight and I'd like to tell you what it feels like to be the one left behind.'

And without any accompaniment she began to sing. 'I'll be seeing you, in all the old familiar places ...' and her voice had such purity of tone and emotion that a stillness passed over the audience and seemed to move backstage, along the corridors and into the dressing room to settle on the performers.

'I'll be looking at the moon, but I'll be seeing you ...'

Pat sang her heartbreak and the rapturous applause when the last note faded showed that all who heard her felt it too.

By that time, Irene and Peggy had changed into US Army uniforms for their medley of American songs and, as Pat came offstage to get into her uniform, Peggy couldn't resist a comment. 'So much for sticking to the programme, not to mention all those wasted rehearsals!'

'Well, what do you always say, Peggy? Oh yes, that's it – I changed it for something much better.'

After the finale, Goldstein was full of praise for his company and described Pat's impromptu change to the programme as 'inspired', adding that the Gracie Fields number might still get an airing in a future concert.

He then invited the sisters to join him at the Grand Hotel where he was meeting some of the British Army officers for a nightcap. 'They will no doubt want to discuss concerts for the troops,' he said, 'and it is always helpful to have some performers there.'

The lounge at the Grand Hotel on Royal Avenue, with its large sofas, winged armchairs and subdued lighting, was popular with Belfast's prominent citizens and high-ranking British officers late at night. The latter were easily spotted not only by the khaki they wore, but by their loud English voices.

'Over here, Mr Goldstein!' A tall, well-built officer was on his feet, having seen them coming through the revolving door. He held out his hand. 'Major Archie Dewer, Coldstream Guards, so glad you could join us, we were just about to order some drinks.' He was speaking to Goldstein, but his eyes never left the girls. 'My, my, how lovely that you've brought along some of your wonderful performers. All sisters, yes? Now let me work it out ...' He looked from girl to girl. 'You must be Sheila. Your Billie Holiday songs were thrilling.' He had the cut-glass diction of a BBC announcer but without the formality. 'Then we have the Golden Sisters. I know your names from the programme, but which name suits which sister?' He pretended to consider then said, 'You look like a Peggy to me.'

'No, I'm Irene.'

'Then you must be Peggy.'

'No, I'm Pat.'

He turned to the final sister. 'At last I've found you, Peggy.' He took her hand and brought it to his lips and, of course, Peggy giggled. 'Now all of you, sit where you like, there's plenty of room,' he said, and still holding Peggy's hand he led her over to the sofa and sat down beside her.

The conversation focused on a plan for an evening's entertainment in the officers' mess at British Army Headquarters. The major explained, 'We'll have a good dinner, Mr Goldstein – you're welcome to join us for that – followed by a show featuring a few of your performers such as these lovely girls and perhaps that striking-looking dancer. What do you think?' Archie Dewer leaned back and slid his arm along the top of the sofa in the direction of Peggy.

For a moment Goldstein seemed to be weighing up the major and when he spoke, his tone was cautious. 'We don't normally do such intimate evenings,' he explained. 'I have always worked on the principle that the shows should be seen by as many people as possible, particularly ordinary ranks in the military.'

Archie Dewer smiled. 'Absolutely agree, old chap, must look after the squaddies. Thing is, the CO is not that keen on entertainment – doesn't want the men going all soft and sentimental. However, if he were to see the quality of your show, I think he might be persuaded, particularly if I tell him that the Americans are keen to have you for themselves.'

Goldstein thought for a moment. 'Maybe I could put together a small group for such an evening, if I was sure that it might lead to shows for a wider audience. Can I suggest you call on me at my shop next week to discuss the matter?'

'Splendid! I'm sure it will prove to be a mutually beneficial partnership,' he said, and his hand on the back of the sofa touched Peggy's shoulder and squeezed it.

The coffee and brandy arrived and soon the officers were entertaining the girls with stories about London during the Blitz. Then, when Goldstein spotted an acquaintance at the bar and went to talk to him, Archie suggested that it was very warm in the lounge and asked Peggy if she would care to step outside for some fresh air. She knew he had been over-attentive and had a tendency to touch but, perhaps because he was older, she found in him something charming and sophisticated.

She smiled demurely and looked up at him from under her lashes. 'Maybe just for a few minutes.'

Outside, Archie took a gold cigarette case from his tunic pocket and flipped it open. 'Can I offer you …?'

Peggy was about to tell him that she didn't smoke, but something made her think that it would be unfriendly to refuse. Besides, she had seen so many films in which the leading man had offered a cigarette to a woman he had just met, and had always thought how romantic that was. She took a cigarette and held it to her lips. The lighter flared and she leaned towards the flame. Her cigarette glowed, and she stepped back and watched as the flame illuminated his face: dark eyes, thin moustache, strong jaw. He could have been a matinee idol.

'I was very impressed by you tonight, Peggy. You're very talented.'

'Do you think so?'

'Oh yes, my dear, I have an eye for these things, you know. I'm often at the West End theatres.' He paused and tapped the side of his nose. 'I've connections there.'

Peggy's eyes widened. 'Really?'

'Oh yes, and I tell you, I know real stage presence when I see it and you have it in handfuls. Would I be right in saying that, even though you're so young, you're the force behind the Golden Sisters?'

Peggy was flattered. 'Well, I'm actually twenty-one, but you're right, I do organise most things, score the harmonies, run the rehearsals, decide on costume …'

Archie nodded knowingly. 'I knew it. And am I also right in thinking that your boyfriend is very proud of you and perhaps a little possessive?'

Peggy was taken aback. 'Oh, I don't have a boyfriend.'

Archie took a step towards her and she found herself unable to meet his gaze, so embarrassed was she to admit such a thing. She felt his arms encircle her and draw her close, knew that he had kissed the top of her head. She closed her eyes and, wrapped in his strength, she was surprised at how her heart quickened.

Then suddenly she was released and she looked up into Archie Dewer's smiling face. 'You're beautiful, Peggy,' he said, 'and very soon you will have someone to love you.'

Chapter 3

Goldstein was in an unusually good mood when he opened up the music shop the following morning. For a start there was his appointment at eleven with a family on the Malone Road interested in purchasing an upright piano for their daughter who, they explained, had shown considerable talent since she started having lessons. In Goldstein's view, a house on the Malone Road was no place for an upright, whereas a baby grand would bring the family pleasure even if the child never played it.

Then there was the *Northern Whig* under his arm. The Grosvenor Hall concert had received a splendid review from the theatre critic who praised not only the quality of the performances, but the 'inspired' production and directing. Goldstein sipped his morning cup of tea and read sections of it aloud for the benefit of Peggy and Esther.

'He even makes special mention of Pat's solo performance: "deeply moving, not a dry eye in the house". She'll be delighted to hear that. You should buy a copy of the paper on the way home, Peggy, keep it for the scrapbook.'

Peggy said nothing.

Just before lunchtime, Peggy was up the stepladder searching for a box of gramophone needles when the shop bell rang. Esther was at the counter and Peggy heard her say, 'Can I help you?'

'Yes, I'm looking for Mr Goldstein.' The voice was unmistakable. Peggy turned round quickly and the stepladder rocked; she tried to right herself and snatched at the shelf above her. She screamed as the ladder fell to the floor leaving her hanging by one hand, but there was nothing to grip. She closed her eyes as her fingers slipped off the front of the shelf.

Archie Dewer caught her in his outstretched arms and held her fast. She opened her eyes and there he was, laughing at her. She struggled to be free, but he carried her away from the ladder and the fallen boxes and set her down in the middle of the shop. 'My, my Peggy, do you throw yourself into the arms of all your customers?' She was about to protest at his presumption, but he had turned away to pick up the bouquet of white, long-stemmed roses he had dropped in his rush to reach her as she fell. 'These are for you,' he said with a flourish.

Peggy could feel the deepest of blushes spreading across her chest and upwards to the roots of her hair. 'Thank you … thank you.' She was covered in confusion. 'I mean for catching me.'

'You're welcome.'

'Oh, and for the roses. Thank you.'

'You're welcome.'

Peggy tried to regain her composure. 'Er, this is Esther, Mr Goldstein's niece.'

'A pleasure to meet you,' said Archie and shook her hand. 'And Mr Goldstein is … where, exactly?'

'Oh, he's out,' said Peggy. 'He'll probably be back in an hour or so.'

'Good, I'll have some lunch and call back later.' He turned to go, then hesitated. 'I say, would you care to join me?'

Peggy excused herself to collect her coat from the office, and nodded to Esther to follow her. 'Best not to tell your uncle I've gone to lunch with Archie. I don't think he likes him very much.' She quickly refreshed her makeup and brushed her hair, then checked the seams on her stockings and turned up the collar on her fuchsia blouse. 'How do I look?'

'Elegant as always,' said Esther.

The Carlton Restaurant was quite the most stylish place to have lunch in Belfast. It had been only marginally affected by rationing in that two courses were served instead of the three available pre-war. Peggy had never eaten there in her life. Nor had she experienced the feeling of superiority she had as she came into the dining room on the arm of her distinguished-looking companion. Of course, the uniform helped. She could tell it was no standard issue, but had been tailored to fit the major's large frame and the coloured ribbons on his chest told of his no doubt illustrious military career.

Seeing the major again in daylight and across the table, she assessed his looks. His skin had a tanned appearance, as though he had spent some time overseas. There was grey in his dark hair, but she liked that. A few lines around his eyes, yes, but they were beautiful brown eyes and maybe the lines were because he smiled so much.

Archie looked up from the menu and caught her staring at him. She blushed again.

'Shall I order for us?' he said, and Peggy nodded.

The table d'hôte lunch was roast beef followed by apple tart and was by far the best meal Peggy had ever eaten. Even better was the company – she had never known such sparkling conversation.

They were still chatting as they walked back up Royal Avenue.

'You actually saw Duke Ellington perform?' Peggy said in amazement.

'Yes, back in thirty-three at the Palladium – astonishing sound.'

Suddenly someone stepped out in front of them and there was a flash.

'What the hell?' shouted Archie. 'Damned street photographers!' He grabbed the man and pushed him away. Then, as if nothing had happened, he turned to Peggy. 'As I remember, the singer was a young woman called Ivie Anderson, lovely voice.'

They were almost at the music shop when Peggy stopped. 'It's probably best if I go in first and you follow me in a minute. I'm not sure Mr Goldstein would approve of me having a leisurely lunch at the Carlton.'

Goldstein had just finished serving a customer when she came in.

'Oh, you're back,' said Peggy brightly. 'Did you manage to sell the baby grand?'

The look on his face told her that he hadn't. 'Where have you been?' he asked. 'Esther and I have been rushed off our feet.'

'I'm sorry, I met a friend in Woolworths who was at the concert. They were telling me how much they enjoyed it and we got chatting, you know?'

'I do know, in fact I saw you with your friend. Not in Woolworths, as it happens, but in the Carlton, enjoying the roast beef.'

Peggy blanched. 'You saw me?'

'You and Major Dewer, a man twice your age, there for all the world to see. I nearly choked on my dinner. What were you thinking of? What would your mother say if she knew?'

At that moment, the shop bell rang and Archie strolled into the shop, his hand outstretched as he greeted Goldstein. 'Glad to see you again, sir. I wonder if now is a good time to discuss the supper show in the officers' mess?'

Goldstein turned puce with anger, but said nothing. Archie looked at Peggy, who gave a quick shake of the head. 'Perhaps now is not a good time, Mr Goldstein.' Archie turned to go.

'Wait. Follow me,' said Goldstein, and disappeared into his office. Archie glanced at the girls again and, with a bemused shrug of his broad shoulders, turned and followed Goldstein. The raised voices lasted a good five minutes, followed by half an hour of comparative silence, before Archie emerged from the office and, without a backward glance, marched with full military bearing across the shop, stopping only to open the door and to close it gently behind him. Peggy had opened her mouth to speak but thought better of it.

Within a few minutes Goldstein emerged and Peggy, who was expecting another telling off, was surprised at the smug expression on his face. 'I have come to an arrangement with the major,' he explained. 'A small group will perform at a dinner in the officers' mess before Christmas.' He handed Peggy a piece of paper. 'I want you to contact the performers I have chosen and ask them to attend a rehearsal on Sunday.' He walked back to his office, then turned and added, 'We have also agreed that in the New Year the full company will take part in a series of concerts at various camps.'

Peggy glanced at the scrap of paper and breathed a sigh of relief – the Golden Sisters were on the list. She would get the chance to see Archie Dewer again.

Pat stared up at the gable end and noted how it bulged, as if at any moment it would collapse into the rubble at its base. A tin street sign hung from the wall by a single screw and she tilted her head to read 'Eliza Street'. Frankie Reilly lived here with his parents; now all she had to do was find him. The idea had come to her the previous night as she lay awake worrying about the evacuated children who had returned to the bombed areas. In the end she asked herself, 'What would William do?' Her clever, caring William who had worked tirelessly in the Ministry of Public Security worried all the time about the safety of the people of Belfast and the lack of anti-aircraft guns and searchlights and shelters. His words came back to her. 'I have to be out there to see for myself what's going on. Then I can do something about it.' Yes, that was the answer – she needed to see what was going on. She had been involved in bringing them back into the city and knew their names, their ages and where they lived. Now she would see for herself whether they were safe and she would begin with Frankie Reilly.

Beyond the gable end, every house bore the scars of the bombing. Some were missing slates; some had no roofs at all, only charred timbers. But if the flapping clothes on makeshift washing lines were to be believed, the ground floors were still inhabited. There were craters here and there exposing bits of shattered pipes and towards the end of the road there was a standpipe where a woman in a headscarf and wearing a man's overcoat that was far too big for her, was filling a bucket with water.

'Hello,' said Pat, 'I'm looking for number fourteen – the Reilly family?'

'Are you now?'

'Do you know which house that is?'

'Are you from the bru? For if ye are, ye'll find no men round here have any work.'

'No, I'm not from the unemployment bureau.' Pat realised that anyone who looked like they'd come from the authorities would get nowhere asking questions. 'No, no, I'm from the church.' A white fib could do no harm. 'I'm just seeing if there's anything we can do for the family now that Frankie has come home.'

The woman looked Pat up and down and must have taken her at her word. 'Just down there on the left, green door, windies boarded up.'

There was no answer to her knock, but she heard the excited shouts of children coming from an alleyway at the end of the row of houses. There she found half a dozen boys playing a frantic game of football with a rolled-up bundle of rags. At that moment, a boy kicked the ball high in the air over the head of the goalkeeper and Pat, standing behind him, jumped up and caught it.

'It's a goal!' shouted the striker.

'No it isn't, she saved it.'

'She's not in your team, ye eejit.'

'It doesn't matter, she still saved it. Well done, missus.'

Pat handed the ball back to the smiling boy. 'Do you know Frankie Reilly?' she asked.

'Aye, I do,' he said.

'And where would I find him, do you know?'

'He's right in front of ye.' He laughed.

Frankie was a sturdy boy, with a healthy colour to his skin, and his clothes were decent enough. Then Pat looked beyond him to where his friends waited to resume their game and she was struck by the contrast. They looked, as her mother would say, like a good feed would kill them – gaunt and pasty-looking, their clothes threadbare.

'Will you take me to your mother?' asked Pat.

He hesitated, the laughter gone. 'Am I in trouble?'

'No, not at all.'

He kicked the rag ball in the air to his friends and nodded for Pat to follow him.

'Why are you not at school?' asked Pat.

'Sure, none of the boys round here go very often and I've been helping Mammy since I came back. I've a new sister now, you know.' He pushed open a gate and led her through the backyard into his house.

It was freezing inside and dimly lit. There was no fire in the grate and the only light came from the lower half of a sash window, the upper part having been replaced with cardboard. A woman sat in an armchair, her eyes closed, a baby asleep in a drawer on the floor at her feet.

'Mammy, wake up, there's a woman here to see you.'

Mrs Reilly opened her eyes and at the sight of a stranger in the room she jumped up.

'It's all right, don't get up,' said Pat.

'I'm sorry, I was just … haven't been getting much sleep with the baby. Are you from the education? Frankie's not long back and I've been meaning to send him to school but—'

'Don't worry, I'm not from the Education Committee,' said Pat, and she introduced herself and explained that she worked at Stormont and had been involved in bringing the evacuated children home. 'I'm just visiting some families to see how the children have settled in now they're back.'

Mrs Reilly swept her hand round the room. 'This is hardly the sort of place you could settle in to, is it? But Frankie's glad to be home, aren't you son?' She ruffled his hair. 'And I'm glad he's home too, for I sorely missed him.'

'He's looking well,' said Pat.

'Aye, he is, but …' She sighed.

'But what?'

'How long will that last? He's been well fed and cared for by the family that took him in. To tell you the truth, I couldn't believe the size of him when he came home. How long's it going to be before the weight starts dropping off him? We haven't the money …' She shook her head. 'Sure, we're living hand to mouth for God's sake. And would you look at this place. How long is it since we were bombed and the landlord's never set foot here? The roof's gone, we've no running water and we only light a bit of a fire at night to

27

cook our tea. I tell you, I wish to God Frankie had stayed in the country.'

In the murky late afternoon, Pat caught the bus home and through the rain-splattered windows she saw the grey streets and buildings and the grey people going about their miserable lives. And she thought of the mothers like Mrs Reilly all over the city who needed help, and the knowledge that there was none to be had made her shake her head in despair.

Pat was soaked when she got in, but the kitchen was warm and her mother helped her out of her wet coat and handed her a towel to dry her hair. 'You're home early, aren't you?'

'I was out of the office this afternoon visiting a bombed area near the Markets. Oh Mammy, you wouldn't believe how some people are living.' She told her about Frankie and his family. 'It would break your heart, so it would. And the worst of it is, there's nothing being done to help them.'

'Was that not what your department was supposed to be doing?'

'There's no money for anything, sure. Nothing has happened in all the time I was away working with the Americans. The evacuees are home now and what have they come back to? Bomb sites and living in one room. What hope have those children got?' She slumped into the armchair next to the range.

Martha hated to see Pat so despondent, but today she knew she had something to put a smile on her face.

'I've something to cheer you up,' she said and reached for a letter propped behind the clock on the mantelpiece.

Pat recognised Tony's handwriting right away and looked heavenward. 'Thanks be to God.'

'You see, I told you he'd be fine,' said Martha.

Pat opened the envelope carefully and quickly scanned the first page. 'He's been on intensive special training somewhere remote by the sounds of it. Now that's finished he says he doesn't know when he'll get the chance to write again. You know what that means, don't you? He'll be shipped out soon. This'll be the letter he was allowed to write before being posted.'

'You don't know that.'

'Of course I do, it's exactly what he told me would happen. What he's saying is a bit vague, but he knew he couldn't explain in detail in a letter because it would be censored. I just didn't think it would take so long to hear from him. There's talk of the Americans being sent to North Africa, you know. But look, he's written me three more pages and they won't be about his posting.'

Martha peeled the potatoes then chopped the scallions and every now and then looked up to see Pat smiling as she read and re-read her letter. It was a worry that Tony would soon be on active service and she hoped that Pat's nerves would hold through the long separation.

By the time the potatoes were boiling, Martha had come to the conclusion that Pat needed something to focus on, something that would take her out of herself.

'You know, Pat, you could push to get help for those families.'

'Ach, Mammy, I'm sure better people than me have tried, but there's just so much that needs to be done.'

'Then why not start with Frankie's family or even his street? You're good at organising and getting things done.'

'But there's no money.'

'It's not about money.' Martha was warming to the idea. 'Make do and mend they say. It's willpower that's needed, not money. Find some of that and you'll begin to see things happen. Did you say he lives near the Markets?' Pat nodded. 'Then you should talk to Aunt Kathleen; he's probably one of her pupils.'

Chapter 4

Cyril Wood had been a civil servant for over thirty years and he prided himself on his ability to spot a good clerk with potential for promotion. Patricia Goulding was one. She'd worked with young William Kennedy and he often spoke about her sound judgement. Then she kept the Americans in line, even turned a run-down dance hall into a successful services club. It was good to have her back in his department and causing a bit of a stir.

Her one-page memo on his desk was concise and outlined a seemingly modest, but potentially bold, strategy. He took his pen and scrawled across the top of the page, 'Approved'. He'd give her a month and see what progress she could make. He just hoped it wouldn't ruffle feathers.

Pat sat at her desk staring at a list of ideas to help families in bomb-damaged areas and realised that she had certainly bit off more than she could chew. How could she make landlords mend roofs and windows, or the corporation fix water pipes and sewers? She only had a month to get things moving and Christmas would eat into that time. And then she realised, Christmas wasn't a problem – it was an opportunity. She couldn't fix the big things, but she could make sure that Frankie and his street had a good Christmas. She quickly made another list, put on her coat and caught the bus to the city centre.

When Pat walked through the door of the American Red Cross Services Club it felt like coming home, everything was so familiar. But there was sadness too. This was where she and Tony had spent so much time creating a club for American soldiers. The colour of the paint in the entrance hall, the light fittings, even the size and position of the handsome reception desk, brought back every discussion, every decision they made. She didn't recognise the soldier who greeted her, but why would she? It was two months since all the GIs she knew had been sent overseas.

'Hi ma'am, can I help you?'

'I was hoping to speak to the officer in charge.'

'He's kinda busy at the moment, but if you wait here … Who shall I say—'

'Patricia Goulding.' But there was no flicker of recognition from the soldier, and the excitement and confidence she had felt when she left the office quickly evaporated. She waited. People came and went and each time the door to the ballroom swung open Pat moved a little closer to catch a look inside. Eventually, she could bear it no longer.

Beyond the doors, the sight of the beautiful Canadian maple dance floor brought her close to tears. She remembered the day it was finished, the day she and Tony had danced on it – the first people ever to do so. She recalled how he kissed her … could almost feel the soft caress of his lips. It was where he had proposed. The tears pricked her eyes.

'Patti, Patti Goulding! Gee, is it really you?' An American officer she didn't recognise was crossing the floor towards her to introduce himself. He was very tall with blond hair. 'Captain Walters,' he said and shook her hand. Pat looked into his pale green eyes.

'I've heard so much about you and Captain Farrelly,' he said, 'and how you got this club up and running. Now, what can I do for you?'

★

When Irene clocked in at Short Brothers that morning, she felt the worst of the morning sickness was behind her. She had managed to get through each day this week without being sick and this morning, at last, she had enjoyed a proper breakfast of egg, bacon and fried bread – the first time in months she had eaten her share of the ration.

Macy was already standing up on the fuselage when Irene came on to the factory floor and she called down to her, 'Hey, you've got colour in your cheeks for once.'

'I know,' shouted Irene, 'I feel great!' and she ran up the steps. As she neared the top she suddenly stopped. Macy must have seen the look on her face because she shouted, 'What is it? What's the matter?'

Irene laughed. 'Oh my goodness, the baby did a somersault. That's the weirdest feeling ever!'

'Are you okay?'

'Yes, but remind me not to run up any more ladders.'

The morning wore on and the heat and the fumes built up in the carcass of the plane as Irene, Macy and the other riveters concentrated on combining the precision of their work with a sense of urgency. They had been told often enough that every plane built brought the end of the war closer. With half an hour to go to tea break, Irene became aware of the throbbing in her head, and minutes later her vision blurred. She pulled off her mask and called to Macy, 'I need some fresh air,' but she only made it as far as the top of the ladder before she dropped to her knees and vomited on to the floor far below.

In the factory sick room the nurse, a fierce-looking woman with carrot-red hair, stood in front of Irene with her hands on her hips and delivered the nastiest, most unsympathetic medical advice Irene could ever have imagined.

'Now, listen you here, you're no use now in that job. You're a liability, so you are. I'm sending you home right now and if you want to carry on working, show up in the morning and we'll put you back on skivvying duties – down on the ground, sweeping up.'

'But I'll be all right. It's just because I ate a fry for my breakfast and I haven't been used to that lately.'

'For God's sake, woman, the cause of yer problem isn't a fry! It's the baby you're expecting. Now, get yerself straight home and don't forget to clock out.'

'But it's pay day. I need my wages.'

The nurse shrugged her shoulders. 'You can ask at the office if you like, but you won't be paid for today, you know.'

Irene knocked on the door of the wages office and went inside. There was a counter with a grille and beyond that she could see the office workers at their desks. Irene rang the bell on the counter and waited. Eventually, a smartly dressed woman appeared.

Irene gave her name and explained, 'The nurse says I'm to go home. Could I have my week's wages, please?'

'No wages are paid out until late in the afternoon, you know that.'

'Yes, but I won't be here then and I need—'

'We haven't even made up the pay packets yet.'

'But I've just been sick, you see. I'm expecting a baby and I need my money …' Irene held back the tears.

At that moment the door opened and Macy came in. She took one look at Irene's face, drew herself up to her full height and turned to the woman. 'I've been sent by Mr McVey, head of the Stirling team; he worried about one of his riveters.' She nodded towards Irene. 'He's sending her home because she's ill and he wants her to get better real quick. Told me to get on over here and make sure she gets her money straight off, including payment for the hours she's worked this morning.'

'Well, we wouldn't normally do that. The wages aren't ready yet—'

'Yeah, yeah, Mr McVey knows that. Says he'd be much obliged if you would make an exception. He wouldn't want one of his best workers to lose out.'

The woman hesitated.

'He'd have come over himself,' said Macy, 'but you know how busy he is. He said you'd be just the person to sort it.'

'Mr McVey said that?'

'Oh yes. Do you want me to tell him you can't sort it?'

The woman thought a moment. 'Wait here, I'll see what I can do.'

Ten minutes later Macy walked with Irene to the factory gates. 'Make sure you rest up when you get home and maybe call the doctor.'

'I'll be fine,' said Irene. 'Can you believe Mr McVey? Sending you over like that?'

Macy said nothing.

Irene glanced at her. 'No, you didn't …'

Macy laughed and put her arm round her friend. 'Hey, aren't you one of his best workers? Weren't you entitled to the money you earned?'

Irene threw back her head and laughed. 'You've got some nerve, Macy!'

Irene was foundered by the time she got home. The biting north wind went right through her coat and it felt like it was eating into her face as she walked from the bus stop to Joanmount Gardens. She came round the back of the house into the kitchen and went straight to the range to warm herself, but the fire was out and the room felt even colder than outside.

'Mammy,' she called.

There was the sound of movement above her then footsteps on the stairs. Martha came into the kitchen and Irene shook her head in disbelief at the sight of her mother wearing her coat and scarf and carrying a bucket and scrubbing brush. 'What are you doing?'

Martha raised the bucket. 'What does it look like? I'm cleaning the oilcloth upstairs.'

'In your coat?'

'Aye, it's freezing in here.'

'You can say that again. Why haven't you lit the fire?'

'Because I'm saving the wee bit of coal we've got left. I keep my coat on and do the housework to keep warm. Anyway, why are you here in the middle of the day?'

'I was sick again and the nurse sent me home. I was all right, but she just wouldn't listen.'

Martha shook her head. 'What have I been saying to you for weeks? You should never have gone to work there in the first place and you should certainly not be doing that riveting job. What kind of work is that for a woman and a pregnant one at that?'

'Don't start on that all again, Mammy. It's a good job and I'm learning a trade. I can earn good money.'

'And for how much longer, tell me that? I've said all along you shouldn't be climbing ladders.'

'They said I can go back to skivvying for a while.'

'And then what?'

'I don't know!'

'You don't know? What sort of ridiculous nonsense is that?' Martha shook her finger, her voice rising. 'By God, Irene, the one thing you do know is that you'll be a mother soon. That'll be your job and God help you then!'

'Aye, aye, I hear you.' Irene hadn't the strength to argue. All she wanted was her bed. She had barely the energy to climb the stairs, remove her shoes and creep under the eiderdown still wearing her coat.

She must have slept a couple of hours and woke up warm – thanks to a hot water jar at her feet – and very hungry. She could hear voices downstairs and then Sheila's laughter.

Irene came into the warm kitchen and the smell of broth made her mouth water.

'Ah, you're up then,' said Martha. 'Would you like something to eat?' It was as though their previous conversation had never happened. Irene sat at the table and listened to Sheila chatter on about some mishap at work and Martha filled a bowl with broth and put it in front of Irene along with a slice of plain bread.

'Now then,' said Martha. 'I've been down to the chemist, told him how you were and he's made up a tonic for you.' She shook the bottle, poured a tablespoonful and held it out for Irene to swallow. 'Good, you'll have another one before you go to bed.'

That evening, when the blackout curtains had been drawn, Martha settled down with an old copy of the *People's Friend* that Betty had given her and left the girls to chatter about the officers' mess dinner and show.

'We were lucky to be chosen,' said Peggy. 'There are only six acts and the Golden Sisters and Sheila are two of them.'

'Why would you think we might not have been chosen?' asked Irene. 'We were top of the bill last time.'

'Plain as the nose on your face why Mr Goldstein might not want us there,' said Pat.

Her sisters turned to her and Pat looked at their blank faces in disbelief.

'Because he doesn't like Archie Dewer, of course.'

'What's Archie Dewer got to do with it?'

'Who is Archie Dewer anyway?' said Martha, suddenly interested.

'Do you think he's a bit of a ladies' man, Pat?' asked Irene.

Pat bristled. 'It's not what I think; it's what Mr Goldstein thinks. You know how he likes to look after his performers.'

Peggy spoke up. 'You've no idea what you're talking about. Mr Goldstein and Major Dewer had a perfectly friendly meeting at the shop to decide on the most suitable acts.'

'Don't be so naive, Peggy,' said Pat. 'The man has sugar daddy written all over him.'

'What's a sugar daddy?' asked Sheila.

'We'll have none of that talk here,' said Martha. 'Now, who is this Archie Dewer?'

'Ach, Mammy, he's just the person in charge of concerts to entertain the troops,' said Peggy. 'He's a major, very well-spoken, has connections in the London theatres. It'll do us no harm to keep on the right side of him ... professionally, I mean.'

'Hmm,' said Martha. 'Well-spoken or not, he sounds more like the sort of character you should give a wide berth to.' And with that she went and fetched the tonic bottle. 'Another dose of this, Irene, then away to your bed and we'll see how you are in the morning.'

'I think I'll go up early as well,' said Peggy.

Upstairs, Irene lay awake thinking of Sandy and how much she missed him. She longed to feel his arms around her and his soft Scottish voice telling her that everything would be fine.

In the next room Peggy sat up in bed, staring at the picture of her and Archie walking together along Royal Avenue – she looking up at him, he smiling down at her. What a handsome couple they made. Well worth the five shillings it cost her, she thought.

★

After a week of skivvying duties and a whole bottle of tonic, Irene was still as exhausted as she had been when she was a riveter on twice the wage. The following Monday, she came down to breakfast and her mother took one look at her and sent her back to bed. 'This has gone on long enough, my girl. It's time to get the doctor out.'

The doctor arrived late morning, immediately diagnosed anaemia and prescribed bed rest and iron tablets. Outside the bedroom door he explained to Martha, 'We'll see how she is in a week, but it'll maybe be a month before she's past the worst of it. She needs to get her strength back, so feed her up – plenty of liver, if you can get it, good for the blood.'

Irene stood listening behind the door, then crept back to bed and turned her face to the wall. Her silent tears wet the pillow. She cried because she was tired and her clothes didn't fit, but most of all she cried because she was useless. She'd lost the job she loved and couldn't even do the one she hated. Then she remembered the concert on Saturday at the officers' mess and let out a howl of frustration. She didn't need bed rest, she needed her life back.

Chapter 5

The security around British Army Headquarters was tight. Goldstein and the performers had their signed passes ready, but it still took almost half an hour for the bus to clear the two checkpoints. Once through, they followed the drive and caught sight of the impressive Georgian mansion – not even the rows of Nissen huts covering the extensive lawns could detract from its size and grandeur.

'Are you sure you're all right, Irene?' asked Peggy. 'We could have managed with Sheila singing your harmonies.'

'I'm grand,' said Irene. 'I just felt so much better this afternoon and I know there hasn't been time for Sheila to rehearse. It's just easier for me to do it.'

'You told Mammy you were coming with us?'

'No, she'd already gone to the McCrackens, but she did say this morning how much better I looked.' Irene gave a nervous laugh. 'Must be all that liver.'

The mess entrance was flanked by sentry boxes and in front of each stood a guardsman resplendent in greatcoat and bearskin, his rifle shouldered. Goldstein led the way and they passed into the entrance hall. The sight that met the performers was dazzling. The officers in their different dress uniforms – scarlet, dark blue, bottle green – filled the room with colour.

Major Dewer had obviously been watching out for them and went quickly to Goldstein and shook his hand. 'Good to see you again, sir,' he said, and briefly glanced at the performers. 'I hope you and your artistes will join us for a cocktail before dinner.'

Peggy was surprised that Archie didn't acknowledge her, but maybe as the organiser of the event he had a lot to do. Besides, she and her sisters and, of course, Macy were soon surrounded by several young officers who explained that they had been given special duty for the evening as escorts. They brought them cocktails and, when the gong sounded, each of the female performers went in to dinner on the arm of a handsome young guardsman.

The ballroom of the original house had become the officers' mess, but it was easy to imagine what it looked like before the army took up residence. Oil paintings still hung around the room and the chandeliers still sparkled. The tables were set with silver cutlery, crystal glasses and fine Sèvres china. The regimental silver centrepieces, the pride of each regiment, had been polished until they gleamed. Peggy scanned the room looking for Archie and spotted him at the top table with the high-ranking officers, all bedecked with gold braid and ribbons. Next to him sat Goldstein. She willed Archie to look at her, to acknowledge her in some way, but there was never a glance. So she let herself be charmed by the young officers and laughed at their jokes.

The chaplain said grace, the dinner began and the courses of rich food came and went. At times Peggy had no idea what she was eating, but it all tasted so good and was so plentiful that she felt she must have eaten a week's rations for a family of four. In between courses there were toasts to the different regiments and their heroes that had them all up and down in their seats. As the evening wore on, Peggy tired of her escorts who, having drunk so much, behaved like silly little boys. Worst of all, Archie never looked in her direction. Not once. Finally, they toasted His Majesty and a short interval was announced, after which Goldstein's troupe would sing for the supper they had just enjoyed. Archie would have to look at her then, when she was on stage, but she had no intention of looking in his direction. Oh no, not even a glance.

A room off the entrance hall had been set aside for the performers to get ready, but as they walked towards it Peggy heard someone softly call her name. She looked around, but could see no one. Then a door opened and a hand reached out and pulled her inside. Archie closed the door and leaned back against it, and drew Peggy towards him.

'Ah, Peggy, my dear, how beautiful you look tonight.'

She pushed him away. 'What do you think you're doing?'

'Thought I might steal a kiss from my favourite Golden Sister?' His eyes were bright and there was the smell of whiskey on his breath.

'Well, you know what thought did.' She had no intention of letting him get away with ignoring her all evening, and turned her back on him and walked further into the room. The walls were lined with bookcases and the air smelt of musty leather and paper. She took down a volume, read the spine – *Vanity Fair* – and opened it, pretending interest. Without turning round she said, 'You ignored me – never looked at me once. I had to sit with those boys and listen to their nonsense.'

'I thought you'd enjoy their company. They're handsome and charming, don't you think?'

She wanted to say, 'I'd rather have been with you', but she sensed him behind her and then his hands were on her fingers where they held the book. They moved up her arms to her shoulders. His touch was electrifying and she sighed softly and went to turn towards him, but his hands stopped her and he ran his fingers down the contours of her body. She breathed deeply as his hands slid around her tiny waist and onwards over her hips.

'Listen carefully, Peggy.' She felt his breath on her skin. 'I've told Goldstein that I will not become involved with you, so he mustn't suspect anything. We don't need him interfering, do we?'

Peggy moved her head slowly from side to side.

He went on, 'These things should be savoured, not rushed.' His cool lips were on her neck. 'I will come and find you when I can and slowly, slowly, we will be together.'

He turned her towards him. 'When you're on stage tonight, I'll be thinking of what it felt like to touch you. But you mustn't even look in my direction, you understand?' She nodded. 'Now, promise me you won't tell anyone about us.'

And she looked up into his dark eyes, now so serious. 'I promise,' she said.

Goldstein accepted a large cigar from Major Dewer and wondered whether he had been wrong about the man. Dewer had kept to their agreement and had shown no interest in the female performers, beyond commenting on their talent. And his own fears that a concert in such an intimate venue with a small audience would not be a success were equally unfounded.

Having eaten an excellent dinner and enjoyed the finest single malt, Goldstein leaned back in his chair and considered a future in which his troupe of performers would go from strength to strength. There would be big productions for British and American troops as well as intimate supper shows, such as the one tonight, for other organisations. Best of all, any money raised would alleviate the plight of the people of Belfast who had suffered so much and continued to need help. He blew a ring of blue smoke towards the ceiling and contemplated the words 'impresario' and 'philanthropist'.

The finale brought rapturous applause and the Commanding Officer of British Forces Northern Ireland spoke of his appreciation, and his delight that his men would soon be seeing an extended version of the show. He then brought the evening to a close by explaining that one of the performers, Patricia Goulding, was raising money to bring some Christmas comforts to a group of children in an area of Belfast that had been badly bombed. He was sure that everyone would want to contribute something to such a good cause and he was passing round a hat – a bearskin, of course – so they had better dig deep.

It was well after midnight when they boarded the bus for the trip back to the city and within minutes most of the performers, full of good food and drink, were nodding off. Peggy was too excited to sleep after her encounter with Archie and was going over the evening in her head, when suddenly a thought occurred to her and she nudged Pat. 'Hey, you never said anything to me about having a whip-round for some children. When was that discussed?'

'During the interval.' Pat gave her a stern look. 'Round about the time you disappeared. I asked Mr Goldstein if it was possible that the officers might like to make a donation. He couldn't find Major Dewer to discuss it, so he asked the CO and he agreed right away.'

Peggy thought it wise to let the conversation drop, but Pat didn't let it go.

'Where were you anyway? You had barely enough time to change into your stage clothes and collect your thoughts before we were on.'

'Oh, I was just chatting, you know, with those guardsmen.'

'Don't lie to me, Peggy. You were with the dashing major, weren't you?'

'I was not. Anyway, he's not my type.'

'Of course he isn't,' said Pat, then added, 'he's far too old and creepy.'

Peggy opened her mouth to argue, thought better of it and said simply, 'I couldn't agree with you more.'

The girls went round to the back door and found the key under the scrubbing brush. Inside, the house was dark and silent. They took off their shoes and crept up the stairs, one behind the other, but as the first girl reached the landing the light came on and there was their mother, in her thick felt dressing gown and wearing a hairnet.

'Oh Mammy,' said Sheila, 'we've had a great time. You'd never believe the dinner we—'

'Away on with you. Sure, I'm not interested in all that nonsense. Now get to your beds,' she said, and the girls slunk past her. Irene was last in line and Martha stepped in front of her. 'You,' she said, 'in here now!' and Irene followed her mother into her bedroom.

Martha glared at her, shook her head as though she was lost for words and, when she finally found them, her voice was full of anger. 'Are you right in the head?'

'Mammy, I'm telling you, I'm fine. I've been lying in bed for a week, doing nothing and all I've done tonight is go for a bus ride and sing a few songs. Where's the harm in that, for God's sake?'

'Don't you blaspheme at me. You could have undone everything we've tried to do this last week to get you well again.'

'But Mammy, I couldn't let them down, could I?'

Martha shook her head in disbelief. 'It was agreed that Sheila would take your place.'

'I know, but the sound isn't right with Sheila's voice.'

'Ach, it would have done rightly. Sure, it wasn't the Belfast Empire, was it? But you know what? It wasn't about your sisters, was it? It was about you doing what you want. And the worst of it all is that you defied me. You waited until I was out of the house and away you went.'

Irene sat on the bed and stared at the floor. She knew there was some truth in what her mother was saying, but the fact remained that she felt so much better after her week resting and all she had wanted to do was sing.

'I meant no harm. It's just … Oh, I don't know.'

'It's just what, Irene?'

'I feel like bits of me are disappearing – my job, the singing, being a wife. Soon there'll be nothing left.'

Martha felt her anger drain away and she sat on the bed next to her. 'But there'll be a baby and you'll be a mother; that's more important than anything. The toughest job you'll ever have.'

'Tougher than riveting?'

'By a country mile.'

'But I'll have to give up the singing, won't I?'

'Irene, you can't have everything. You've made choices and, make no bones about it, there's no walking away from a family.'

Irene covered her face with her hands but Martha reached out and took them away. 'Look at me,' she said, and Irene raised her head. 'Remember how excited you were when you found out you were expecting – how happy we all were? I still feel that, so do your sisters; a baby brings joy to everyone. Of course, your life will change, because you'll realise that your child is the most precious thing you'll ever have and the love you have for it will last your whole life.'

Irene looked down at her hands cradled in her mother's. 'Is that how it was for you, Mammy?'

'Yes, Irene, that's how it *is* for me.'

When Martha opened the curtains the following morning it was barely light, but she could make out the heavy clouds over Cave Hill. With a bit of luck she might get to church and back before the rain set in. She left the girls still sleeping, but she'd expect them to go to the evening service. If they could sing for the army they could certainly sing for God.

She put a thick cardigan on under her coat, to keep the heat in, and stood in front of the hall mirror to put on her Sunday hat. Maybe it was a trick of the light, but there in the glass was her mother's face, weary and disappointed. Was it the lot of mothers to hope that their daughters would somehow be more than they had been? But the truth of it was that her girls would do whatever they wanted and she could do little to protect them from their mistakes.

After breakfast the girls left the dishes where they were and sat round the table. 'There's no getting away from it,' insisted Peggy. 'It's time we sorted out what's happening with the Golden Sisters.'

'Has Mammy put you up to this?' Irene was on the defensive, certain that her sisters had overheard some of the conversation she'd had with her mother the previous night.

'She didn't need to,' said Peggy. 'It's obvious you won't be able to carry on for much longer. Mr Goldstein's already planning lots of new concerts and that'll mean we'll be out two or three nights a week, probably travelling further afield. And to be blunt, Irene, you won't be able to do it.'

'I could sing for a while longer. There's nothing wrong with my voice.'

'But you can't fit into the costumes and I can't imagine you carrying on with your lindy hop routine, can you?'

Sheila laughed and Irene glared at her. Then Pat spoke up. 'We need to consider the options without anyone getting upset or angry. Agreed?'

Her sisters nodded.

'There are no concerts actually arranged yet and it's only two weeks till Christmas. So it'll probably be a month at least before the first concert. Now, Irene, even if you were able to do a few it wouldn't be long before you had to stop. The baby's due in March and who knows when you'll be singing after that.'

Irene couldn't deny Pat's logic and sat expressionless, staring at the tablecloth.

'Option one,' said Pat, 'is that we just forget about the Golden Sisters for a while. Sheila, you could still sing solo and Peggy you'd carry on as Mr Goldstein's assistant director. Me, I wouldn't mind taking a rest from performing; I'm very busy at work at the moment.'

'But we're one of the best acts – Mr Goldstein relies on us,' said Peggy, 'and you know I really think we're on the verge of something big.' The words tumbled out of her in a desperate plea to save the Golden Sisters. 'We could make a name for ourselves, maybe get an agent. I know someone who's well connected with London theatres and … who knows?'

They stared at her in disbelief. Pat was the first to speak. 'Peggy, what are you talking about? Your head's turned. Even if Irene was able to sing, it's time that you faced up to the fact that we've only ever been three girls from Belfast who do a bit of singing to entertain people, that's all. And sooner rather than later, this war will be over and we'll go back to singing in the church choir and concentrating on earning our living.'

'But it could happen – you can't predict who might get a break in show business.'

'Aye, and pigs might fly,' said Pat, 'but right now we need to stick to the problem we have.'

'I could try again to get the harmonies right and maybe take Irene's place,' said Sheila.

Peggy shook her head. 'Mr Goldstein didn't think your voice suited the Golden Sisters' style the last time we tried it, when Pat couldn't sing. Anyway, you're better off keeping your own spot in the show.'

'Then what about just you and Pat – a duo might work,' said Sheila.

'No,' said Peggy. 'The sound would be too thin for the songs we sing. We'd need a brand new repertoire and that would take months to sort out.'

'Are there any more ideas?' asked Pat, and their blank faces said it all. 'Well, that's it then.'

The girls fell silent, each contemplating life without the Golden Sisters, the excitement of performing, the applause, the fun – all gone.

When Martha arrived home from church soaked to the skin, they were still sitting at the table, dirty dishes untouched and the fire in danger of going out.

'Heavens above, what's the matter?' she said. 'You look like you've lost a pound and found a ha'penny.'

'We've been talking about the Golden Sisters and it looks like we'll have to stop singing,' said Pat. 'We can't carry on without Irene.'

At that moment Irene, who had been silent throughout, began to cry in great gulping sobs as though her heart would break. 'Getting married, having a baby – I've spoiled everything!' she said, and ran from the room.

Martha called after her, 'Come back here love, don't be silly.' But there was already the sound of footsteps running up the stairs. Martha didn't follow her. She had no right to comfort Irene, for hadn't she just sat in church and prayed to God that all this singing nonsense would come to an end?

Chapter 6

The ballroom in the American Red Cross Services Club had been transformed. There were Christmas decorations of brightly coloured crepe paper strung across the room and giant paper bells dangled from the light fittings. A twelve-foot Christmas spruce, hung with coloured lights, filled the room with the scent of pine. Trestle tables were set with plates of sandwiches, biscuits and bottles of lemonade. A dozen GIs, who had volunteered to make sure the party was a success, stood ready.

As three o'clock approached, the sound of excited children's voices in the entrance hall grew louder and louder.

'Well, Patti, it's almost time,' said Captain Walters. 'Are we good to go?'

'Just one more thing,' said Pat. She lowered the needle on to the record and seconds later the sound of 'Jingle Bells' filled the room. The doors to the ballroom were thrown open and a hundred excited children rushed inside.

While the children enjoyed their party with the GIs, the parents were served tea and doughnuts in the library. Pat waited anxiously in the entrance hall, and at precisely the time agreed Aunt Kathleen arrived, looking every inch the headmistress, in a well-tailored coat and trilby hat with an ostrich feather.

'Thank you so much for coming Aunt Kathleen, I'm very grateful to you for agreeing to speak to the parents.'

'No need to thank me, Pat, I've been trying to get these children back into school for so long without success. When you wrote to me with such a sensible proposal, I was delighted to come.'

'They're upstairs now. I'll just tell them about the donated Christmas meal and the children's clothes then you can have the floor.'

There was a bit of a stir when Kathleen came into the room as several of the parents recognised her, but she went to stand at the back while Pat addressed them.

'Thank you for bringing your children to the party. We know that times have been hard for families in your area and we wanted to see if we could help make Christmas a bit better for you all.'

A woman put her hand up. 'I'm sorry, but can I ask who you are and why you're helping us?'

'I work at Stormont,' said Pat. 'We're trying to improve things for the children in the areas that were bombed.'

A man standing in the corner called out, 'Who's "we"? Seems odd to me – suddenly Stormont wants to help. When has the government ever bothered about us before?'

'I don't know about that,' said Pat, 'but I do know that there are plenty of people who want to help, like the American and the British Armies based here. As well as today's party you'll be able to take home food to cook for your Christmas dinner and the Belfast Society for Jews has donated boxes of good quality second-hand children's clothes.'

'And what about after that?' the man challenged her. 'We'll be right back where we were – on starvation rations in freezing houses.'

'Now, Sammy, just hold on a minute.' Frankie's mother was on her feet. 'To my way of thinking, we should be thanking this woman.'

'Ach, what do you know? A few sandwiches and party games for the kids – you're easy pleased.'

'I know that she's the first one come to my door and offer to help my childer and, yes, I'm pleased about that.' There were nods of agreement.

'Look,' said Pat, 'I'll make sure that the people in charge know how bad things are for you and if you let me know what you're short of, I'll try to get it for you. In the meantime, this Services Club has offered to do more to help your children and I've invited Miss Goulding, Headmistress at May Street National School, to come along to explain it to you.'

Kathleen was nothing if not direct. She told them, 'Parents have a decision to make every day – shall I send my children to school to receive an education? Or shall I let them roam the streets getting into mischief and growing up ignorant?' She scanned the room, her face stern. 'So your house has been bombed. Surely you don't want to compound that misfortune by adding to it a child who can neither read, nor write, nor reckon up?' The parents avoided her eye, looking at the floor or their hands. 'No, of course you don't.' She went on, 'Immediately after the Christmas holiday I will expect to see all children back at school and attending every day. I'm sure no other incentive is needed, but the American Forces and the Red Cross who run this club have said that during January they will provide free hot dinners at our school for your children.'

Pat and Kathleen took the parents back to the ballroom just in time for the arrival of a special visitor. Captain Walters made a fine Santa Claus, if a little on the lean side, wearing a splendid red suit and carrying a huge sack. Every child was given a toy and a bar of chocolate to take home for Christmas Day.

Pat looked at the children. If their smiling faces were anything to go by, the party had been a huge success, but it was only a drop in the ocean. Frankie and his friends would have a good Christmas, but would they go back to school?

'They will,' said Kathleen.

'How can you know that?' asked Pat.

'Because we'll make sure they do. I've an idea that might work. Look, can you come to my house the day after Boxing Day?'

'Of course, but even if we persuade your pupils, what about

all the other Frankies out there – the ones who don't go to your school?'

'One step at a time, Pat, one step at a time.'

The rain was lashing the windows when Martha crept downstairs early on Christmas Day morning, and her heart sank at the thought of the miserable day that lay ahead. It was difficult enough to make a Christmas out of nothing with shortages and rationing, but it was the girls that worried her the most. Pat was missing Tony and Sheila was unhappy in her work. Then there was Irene struggling with the changes in her life while Peggy, contrary as ever, was elated one minute and snapping at everyone the next. Martha knew too that there was another reason they were so miserable – soon Mr Goldstein's concerts would begin and this time there would be no Golden Sisters on the bill.

Be thankful for small mercies, she told herself. Hadn't Bridie McManus, her Dungannon friend, sent a goose to grace their table – not many of those to be found in Belfast – and she was pleased with the gifts she had made for the girls.

Soon the goose was in the oven and a pan of porridge, enough for all of them, was bubbling gently on the range; and to Martha's surprise, the girls came down for breakfast in good spirits. By the time they were sharing gifts, it was clear that everyone had made an effort with their presents and she was chiding herself for doubting the spirit of Christmas.

Martha had made each daughter a pair of gloves with some fine two-ply wool she'd had since before the war. She wasn't used to knitting on four needles, but soon got the hang of it. Then she had turned her hand to rag rugs made from cut up old clothes, one for each bedroom.

The only awkward moment was when Pat opened a package that had come from America. Inside was a small box and a letter from Tony's sister explaining that he had asked her to buy the present and send it to Pat. There were squeals of delight from Sheila and Peggy when Pat opened the box to reveal a gold bracelet. 'I'll give the Yanks one thing,' said Peggy, 'they know how to treat a girl!'

And Irene, who had just opened a card from Sandy with a postal order inside, looked wistfully at Pat's beautiful present.

Martha caught the look and said quickly, 'Oh, I nearly forgot, I've got something else for you, Irene,' and she handed her a bulky, loosely-wrapped, present. Irene opened it and held up the garment inside. It was a dress, of sorts, large and olive green. 'It's a maternity dress,' said Martha. 'You're going to need it as you get … bigger.' Irene continued to stare at the present as Martha went on. 'You recognise it, don't you? It's your dress, but I've stitched in an extra panel on each side to make it bigger and dyed it all the same colour.'

Sheila started to giggle. 'It looks like a tent, so it does.'

Martha turned on her. 'Don't you be so cheeky.'

'It's all right, Mammy,' said Irene. 'Thank you.'

'Right then,' said Martha. 'Time for church, I think.'

The girls groaned.

'Ach, Mammy, it's pouring rain,' said Peggy.

'No matter, it's Christmas and we're going to church.'

'I'm not going,' said Irene. 'I'm not walking all that way.'

Martha was about to insist, but thought better of it. 'Well, maybe you could peel the vegetables while we're out.' But Irene wasn't listening; she was still staring at the dress.

Christmas dinner surpassed everyone's expectations. For weeks beforehand Martha had worried that it would be a meagre affair, but the goose was delicious and the vegetables from their garden filled them up.

'Are you going to finish that?' Peggy pointed at the food left on Irene's plate.

'No, I've had enough. You can have it.' She pushed the plate towards Peggy.

'You will not,' said Martha. 'That's good food, Irene, and you need to keep your strength up. I've told you before you're eating for two now.'

'I don't want it.'

'Nonsense, get it down you.'

'I'll be sick if I eat any more.'

'Oh, for goodness sake.' Martha snatched the plate and scraped the leftover food on to Peggy's plate.

Later, as they sat in the front room listening to the wireless, Martha slipped away and returned just in time for the King's speech, with cups of tea and a Christmas cake.

Pat laughed. 'Where did you get that? I thought there was a war on.'

'There is, but sure haven't I been saving up the points coupons for some treats – the cake's got dried fruit and treacle in it – and when the visitors come we'll have a box of sugared almonds and glacé fruits to share.' And the whoops of delight drowned out the striking of Big Ben on the wireless.

As always, Betty and Jack from next door, and Mr Goldstein and his niece Esther came to share Christmas evening with Martha and her girls. It had been the pattern every Christmas since Martha had lost Robert. She well remembered the day in 1939 when Mr Goldstein had arrived unexpectedly and had brought with him his niece who, that very day, had arrived in Belfast after escaping Poland and the Nazis. Esther had been so distressed she couldn't speak, and it was clear from her appearance that she had been through a terrible ordeal.

'I don't know how to help her,' Goldstein had told Martha, 'so I've brought her to you.' And Martha had taken charge of the frightened, starving girl; run her a bath, found her clean clothes and persuaded her to eat.

And now here she was tonight, the picture of health, standing in Martha's sitting room playing Mozart on her violin accompanied by Peggy on the piano.

When Esther had finished, Jack sang 'Hark the Herald Angels Sing' with gusto. Then Peggy called her sisters to the piano to sing a new song, 'White Christmas', that they had been practising just for the occasion and everyone enjoyed it so much that they sang it again and by the third rendition everyone was singing along. Martha watched Irene's animated face as she sang; it was good to see her happy. If only she'd worn the maternity dress and not those awful jumble-sale trousers and a man's shirt that had seen better days.

Later, when the talk turned inevitably to war and the situation in

North Africa, Martha slipped away to get the supper ready and by the time she returned with tea, sandwiches and cake, the topic of conversation had moved on.

'The Golden Sisters are my best act,' Goldstein was saying. 'You can't give up.'

'But Irene can't carry on.' Pat shot a look at her sister, who sat motionless. 'At least not for a while.'

'There is a way,' said Goldstein.

'You mean Sheila? We've discussed that, but she has her own spot and we can't expect her to sing in the Golden Sisters as well. And anyway, you said last time that the sound wasn't right with Sheila singing.'

'No, I am not suggesting Sheila should step in,' said Goldstein, 'I agree she should be a separate act. I have another idea . . .' He paused and looked at the faces turned towards him.

'Well, what is it?' asked Peggy.

'I will do what any director would do given these circumstances. I will hold an audition.'

There was a rush of voices, loud and protesting.

'You can't do that!'

'It's not fair.'

'It'll never work.'

Goldstein held up his hands. 'You need to be professional about this. I am sure we can find someone who has the voice, looks and personality to become a Golden Sister.' He addressed his words to Peggy and Pat. 'It is the only solution if you want to carry on singing.'

Martha glanced quickly at Irene and her heart sank. Minutes ago she had seen her daughter singing and looking happier than she had been in weeks and now her face was drained. 'What do you think, Irene?' she asked.

Irene's face was devoid of expression. 'I don't think anything. It's got nothing to do with me any more.' She stood up. 'I'm going to bed now.'

Chapter 7

It was still dark when Irene left her bed, got dressed and tiptoed out to retrieve the small case from the cupboard on the landing. She hesitated outside her mother's bedroom door, listening. There was no sound. Had there been, she might have been tempted to explain what she was doing, but she knew it was better to slip away and avoid a good talking to that might have weakened her resolve and sent her back to bed.

In the kitchen she took the note from her case and put it on the mantelpiece behind the clock. There were a few sandwiches and a piece of cake on a plate from supper and she wrapped them in a tea towel and put them in her handbag. Then she tied her headscarf in a turban, picked up her belongings and slipped out into the chill of the morning.

She wasn't sure whether there would be any buses running into town so she set off walking and hoped to flag one down if it passed her. What she did know was that a bus to Enniskillen would leave Belfast at nine. She had last made the journey in July to visit Sandy at the Castle Archdale RAF base.

He wouldn't be expecting her, of course, and the chances were she wouldn't be able to stay on the base, but she would find lodgings.

54

She needed to be with him now more than ever. There was nothing for her at home any more. She couldn't face skivvying at the aircraft factory; her sisters had made it clear she couldn't sing with them; and her mother had no patience with her at all. It was so clear in her mind now. Sandy had always wanted her by his side, but time after time she had been selfish, choosing to stay in Belfast for her work and her singing. Now they would be a family – just her, Sandy and the baby.

The dawn crept slowly across the sky as she walked; there were few people on the road and no bus passed her. By the time she got to the station she was exhausted and greatly relieved to see the Enniskillen bus with its engine running. She climbed on board, glad to rest and, once the bus set off, she stretched her legs across the empty seat beside her and fell fast asleep …

She was backstage in a dressing room and she heard the five-minute call for the Golden Sisters. Peggy and Pat had already gone to stand in the wings and she rushed to join them. In the corridor it was pitch black and she lost her bearings. She held her hands out in front of her as she walked until she felt the heavy stage curtain. She had only to find the opening, but the curtains were heavy and as she pulled at them they twisted and fell, enveloping her. Out of the dark a hand gripped her shoulder …

'Wake up, miss.' The conductor was shaking her gently. 'That's a quare sleep you've had.'

Irene rubbed her eyes and looked out the window to see a street dusted with snow.

'Are we in Enniskillen?'

'Indeed we are.'

'Do you know if there's a bus would take me as far as Castle Archdale?'

'Don't know,' said the conductor, 'I've only ever come this far, before going back to Belfast.'

Irene heaved herself up and groaned as she felt a deep ache in her side; she knew at once that the baby had been lying awkwardly.

'Are you all right, miss?' He took her case.

'Aye, just a bit of a cramp. I'll ask someone about the bus.'

'Well, you look after yourself now,' said the conductor, 'and watch these footpaths – they're slippy.'

There was no one about. The shops were shut and no doubt the good people of Enniskillen were at home by their fireside with their families. Irene pictured her mother with that hastily written note in her hand. She would have been so angry when she read it and full of harsh words about her eldest daughter's stupidity. But now that several hours had passed, Irene knew she would be worried and desperate to know that she was safe. The tears pricked Irene's eyes, but she had come so far that she had to carry on and she comforted herself with the thought that she would soon be with Sandy. She remembered the food in her bag and crossed the road to a little war memorial and sat down to eat and think. She wasn't sure of the distance to Castle Archdale. The last time she had been there Sandy had met her off the bus and taken her to the base on his motorbike and it didn't seem so far. There were still a good few hours of daylight left and, after her sleep on the bus, she felt she could walk there. With a bit of luck, someone with a car or, more likely in these parts, a horse and cart, might stop and give her a lift.

Soon she had left the town behind and found herself on a road with hedgerows on either side, but no footpath, and every now and again she passed a row of cottages or a lane leading to a farm. At first she made good progress, but after an hour or so her legs began to tire and she was aware of the baby lying heavy. At last, she spotted a bus shelter in the distance and fixed her eyes on it, promising herself a rest when she got there. The first specks of snow were beginning to fall and by the time she reached the shelter they were sticking to the front of her coat. She set the case down inside and flexed her arm and fingers to relieve their aching stiffness, then carefully lowered herself on to it. The snowflakes were bigger now, swirling in front of her and covering the road. What was she doing in the middle of nowhere in such weather? She had never felt so alone. She closed her eyes and prayed, 'Please God, let me get to Sandy.' As if in reply, there was a low rumbling sound and she looked up to see a lorry coming down the road towards her. It was headed in the opposite direction, towards Enniskillen, but she struggled to her feet and waved and shouted. As it drew level she saw the RAF emblem on the door and the blue uniform of the driver as he beeped the horn and waved back at her. Then she was looking at the back of the lorry, fast disappearing into the snowy landscape.

She pushed aside her disappointment and set out again with renewed hope. The lorry would certainly have come from the base so it couldn't be that far off. The snow had eased off a little, but it lay on the ground deep enough to seep into her shoes and soon her feet were like blocks of ice. A mile or two further on and she knew that her energy was draining away; just putting one foot in front of the other took so much effort. In the gathering darkness she came to a crossroads with an old stone marker. Enniskillen, back the way she came, four miles. Straight ahead Castle Archdale – no, it couldn't be – six miles!

She'd been so stupid and angry about everything. All she had thought of was running away from her mother with all her interfering and her sisters who wouldn't let her sing. Now look where that had got her. Soon it would be dark and no one would be looking for her, no one knew where she was. And in the morning, when it was too late, they would find her …

She sat once more on her case and tried to make her brain work, but her eyelids were closing and she felt herself drifting. Suddenly the baby kicked out and jolted her awake. Her mind cleared and she knew that she must not fall asleep. She needed to get on her feet and walk, for surely somewhere along this road there must be a village or even a solitary house where she could ask for shelter.

She set off again, determined not to give in and, to keep her mind focused, she sang under her breath, 'Come on and hear, Come on and hear, Alexander's ragtime band.' Then after that, song after song from the Golden Sisters repertoire, and as she sang she recalled the excitement on stage, the sound of applause, and slowly some of the energy of performing found its way into her weary legs and her frozen feet.

She had no idea how far she had walked when she became aware of a noise far behind her. It sounded almost musical and coming closer. Voices carried on the still air. Closer still and she half-imagined the haunting melody of 'Silent Night'. Then she heard the drone of an engine and she turned to see a lorry coming up behind her. As it slowed, her heart leapt to see on the door the familiar red, white and blue circles of the RAF.

'Hello there, love.' An English accent. 'What you doing out in this weather?'

'I'm trying to get to Castle Archdale. My husband's there.'

'Well, you'd better come on board then. Can't leave an airman's missus on the side of the road, can we?' He jumped down and took her case, nodding for her to follow him to the back of the lorry. 'Right you lot, shove up,' he shouted. 'We've got an extra passenger here – a young lady – so mind your Ps and Qs.'

And then there were hands reaching down and pulling her up into the back of the lorry and, as her eyes adjusted to the dim interior, she saw that there were as many as twenty men sitting on the floor. They made room for her and one of the men took off his greatcoat and draped it round her shoulders. At that moment someone began to sing 'Silent Night' and, as lorry moved off, the entire contingent joined in.

At the base, the driver dropped off the men and took Irene to the headquarters in the castle, where she waited in the entrance hall while the driver went in search of someone who could help. He returned with an officer who wrote down Sandy's name, rank and squadron.

'Can I see him now?' asked Irene.

'That might not be possible,' said the officer. 'He could be anywhere on the base and if he's currently on duty he'll have to remain at his post.'

'I understand. It's just that I've come from Belfast and I need to see him.' Irene's voice cracked with emotion.

The officer stared at her, weighing up her clothes and the battered suitcase. 'Wait here,' he said.

He returned five minutes later with a nurse. She was smiling and spoke quietly to Irene.

'Hello, I'm Ethel, what's your name?' she said.

'Irene, but I'm fine, I don't need a nurse. I just want to see my husband.' Irene struggled to keep her voice steady.

'I know, and someone has been sent to find him. Come on, you can wait with me upstairs in the sick bay.' As she followed the nurse, the elation Irene had felt when she arrived at Castle Archdale began to seep away to be replaced by an anxiety that made her heart thump. She was cold, too, and by the time they arrived at the sick bay, her teeth were chattering.

'Goodness,' said the nurse, 'how long were you out in the cold?'

'I don't know exactly. I got off the bus in Enniskillen about dinnertime and then I started walking—'

'You walked from Enniskillen!'

'Not all the way – maybe five miles – then the lorry came by and gave me a lift.'

'Heavens above, you must be freezing. And you're expecting, I see. When's the baby due?'

There was just enough time to say 'March' before the nurse put a thermometer into Irene's mouth. Then she filled a kettle and set it on the little stove in the corner. 'First things first – we'll get you a hot drink and into bed with a hot water bottle. Raise your body temperature. I'm sure you'll want something to eat as well.'

All Irene could do was nod.

In no time at all she was in her night clothes and lying between crisp white sheets with one hot water bottle at her feet and another by her side. The scrambled egg, toast and tea was the best she had tasted in a long time. 'I'll check your temperature again in half an hour and maybe Sandy will be here by then too. Now why don't you just have a wee doze.'

And Irene thought it would heaven to just close her eyes for a while.

It was the noise outside the door that woke her; someone calling her name then raised voices. She was awake immediately and already climbing out of bed when Sandy burst through the door. If she had expected a romantic reunion with her husband after all these months, she was to be disappointed – she could see from his face that he was far from pleased.

'What are you doing here?' he said.

'I've come to see you …' She sounded pathetic.

'Why didn't you tell me you were coming, instead of showing up here in the back of a lorry?'

'They gave me a lift—'

'They found you on the side of the road in a snowstorm!'

'I just wanted to see you … I, I needed to …'

Ethel had followed Sandy into the room. Now she stepped between them. 'Irene get back in bed, please.' Then she caught Sandy's arm and said softly, 'Why don't you sit down and talk to Irene and I'm sure she'll explain why she's here.'

Sandy took a deep breath. 'I'm sorry, I was told to come to the sick bay. I didn't know what to expect.' He turned to Irene. 'I thought something had happened to you.'

Ethel set a chair next to the bed. 'Sit down, Sandy. Irene, you should explain how you came to be here. I'll be outside the door if you need me.'

When Ethel had gone, Irene said simply, 'I just wanted to be with you. I don't want to be at home any more.'

Sandy folded his arms and sat back in the chair. 'Well, you've changed your tune. You've never wanted to leave Belfast before.'

'Yes I have – I went to live with you at the Ballyhalbert base, didn't I?'

'And how long did that last? Three months? Then when I was posted to England you went straight back home.'

'I wasn't going to go to England.'

'So you didn't want to be with me then. And I've been at this base six months and you made it clear you didn't want to come here either.'

'But you said not to come because you were working all the hours God sends.'

'That's true, I am, and I've to be on duty in half an hour.' Sandy leaned forward. 'Irene, if it was possible for you to be here, I would have moved hell and high water to have you with me. But it's not practical. Even if I could find somewhere for you to stay off-base, I couldn't look after you properly.' He stood up. 'But you know what really upsets me? You just turning up now out of the blue. You didn't even tell me you were coming. Instead you set off in the middle of winter and ended up at the side of the road. What would have happened if that lorry hadn't come past?' He raised his arms in exasperation. 'God, Irene, you're five months pregnant. What were you thinking of?'

And the realisation of what she had done and what could have happened struck Irene like a slap on the face. She had been rash beyond comprehension and she shuddered at her recklessness in putting herself and, more importantly, the baby in danger. There was no way to undo what she'd done, but the worst of it was that Sandy didn't want her either. She turned her face from him. There was nothing more to say.

Martha didn't often have a lie-in, but that morning after the Christmas night get-together she allowed herself the luxury of turning over in bed to steal an extra hour of sleep. The girls would no doubt linger much longer in their beds knowing that, by the time they got up, their mother would have a good fire going and that Boxing Day breakfast would be an Ulster fry – a rare treat.

Two hours later, Pat came into the kitchen to find her mother sitting at the table, deep in thought. She glanced at the unwashed dishes and the dead fire. 'Are you all right, Mammy?' she said.

It was a moment before her mother answered. 'Hardly,' was all she said.

'What do you mean hardly? Are you not well?'

Martha held out the letter. 'Irene's gone.'

'Gone where?' Pat took the letter and scanned it quickly. 'Oh, she's gone to Sandy.'

'Why on earth would she do that, do you think? How many times has she said she wouldn't live in the back of beyond on an Air Force base? And now when she's expecting and needs to be here with her family, she sets off on a dark winter's morning to travel to the other side of the country. Answer me that.'

'It's simple,' said Pat. 'She wants to be with her husband.'

'But to leave now?'

'Can you not see, Mammy?'

'See what?'

'That there's nothing here for her. Soon she won't be able to work

61

and, worse, she won't be singing again for a long time, if at all. Right now, Sandy is what she needs.'

'No, you're wrong, Pat. She needs us to take care of her now and once the baby's born I'll be able to help her. You need family to bring up a child.' Martha stood up. 'I've been sitting here thinking about what to do and I've decided. I'll get my things together and go to Enniskillen to make sure she's safe and to tell her she's to come home with me.'

'No, you will not,' said Pat firmly. Martha opened her mouth to protest, but Pat held up her hand. 'You will not interfere between Irene and her husband. She's nearly twenty-five and she can make her own decisions.'

'But it's not the right decision. I have to talk to her.'

Martha was close to tears and her daughter's voice softened. 'Mammy, let her be. It's time now to let go.'

And Martha pressed her fingers against her eyelids to stop the tears from falling as she realised that Irene had slipped away, not only from her home, but beyond her mother's reach.

Chapter 8

Irene slept soundly and woke up around nine when it was just coming light. Her first thought was of all the trouble she had caused and the angry look on Sandy's face when they had argued the previous night. The thought of making the journey back to Belfast filled her with dread, but there was no way she could stay at Castle Archdale.

By the time Irene had washed and dressed, Ethel had arrived for her shift. 'How are you feeling today?' she asked.

'I'm fine. I'll get myself ready now and go back to Belfast. What would be the best way to get to Enniskillen to catch the bus?'

'Now just hold on a minute,' said Ethel. 'Don't you want to stay here?'

'How can I? Sandy said last night there'd be no quarters for me and anyway he doesn't want me here.'

'Ah, but you don't know what he's going to say today.'

'It'll be no different, I can tell you. He probably won't want to see me at all.'

'I think he will,' said Ethel. 'I've just been talking to him. He's downstairs waiting for you.'

'He wants to see me?'

'Of course he does. You're not the only one who feels bad about last night. Anyway, he has something to show you. So wrap up warm.'

Sandy was standing in the entrance hall dressed in his Air Force greatcoat talking to an airman; by the flashes on his flying jacket, an American. Irene hesitated and stood a little way off. They were in good humour, laughing and shaking hands, and she felt a rush of pride watching them. Surely with men like these working together, the war would soon be won. What right had she to distract Sandy from the important work of protecting the Atlantic convoys?

The first time she met Sandy on that beach in Stranraer she had thought he was handsome. Seeing him now in his own environment she admired him for his bravery and his honesty and she could not have wished for a better man, or a better father for the child she was carrying. And at that moment she was struck by the depth and intensity of her love. As she watched, the pilot gave Sandy a hearty slap on the shoulder and, with a quick wave, headed for the door. She went to Sandy then and he turned to her, the smile disappearing from his face.

She looked at the floor, overcome with remorse. 'I'm so sorry for what I've done, Sandy, I shouldn't have come ...'

'Och, Irene, I'm the one who should be sorry. I shouldn't have spoken to you like that.' He put his arms around her and when he spoke his voice was no more than a whisper. 'It was because I couldn't bear to think that I might have lost you and the baby.' He looked down at her, his face full of concern. 'Tell me you're all right?'

'Yes, I'm fine.'

'Come on, I want to show you something,' he said. 'It's a bit of a walk. Can you manage that?'

Outside the sky was blue and clear and the hardened snow cracked under their feet as they set off from the main buildings and headed down a narrow road bordered by leafless trees. Sandy pointed out the NAAFI and workshops and stores along the way and when they rounded a corner, there in front of them were perhaps twenty planes on a pebbled beach, and beyond them several more bobbing gently in a huge expanse of water that sparkled in the morning sun.

'What is this place?' asked Irene.

'We're part of Coastal Command. These planes patrol the North Atlantic protecting convoy ships from attack by German U-boats. Without them there would be very few supply ships getting through and we'd have even less food than we do now. That pilot I was talking to just now nearly lost his life last night when there was a problem with his instruments. We guided him down, talked to him and gave directions over the wireless so that he could land in the pitch darkness.' He pointed to the planes. 'They're flying boats – Sunderlands and Catalinas. They take off and land on the lough.'

'Yes I know,' said Irene.

'Of course. Shorts – I should have remembered.'

Irene's face lit up. 'The Sunderlands are built in the hangar next to where I work on the Stirling bombers. They're beautiful, aren't they?'

'Yes, but they're not easy to fly,' he said, and he took her hand. 'Come on then, we'll go down to the jetty, there'll be a couple taking off soon.'

'Did you know the Sunderlands are flush-riveted?' Her eyes lit up. 'Do you think they'd let me take a look?' Sandy looked down at her and laughed.

'You mean that, don't you?'

'Of course. It's my trade.'

'Know what I think? You're too pretty to be a riveter.'

As they stood on the jetty, the first of the flying boats lumbered out into the middle of the lough, turned south and roared past them, its engines at full throttle and its fuselage sending out a great plume of spray behind, and Irene watched in awe as it lifted from the water. She had seen them often enough on the ground, but had never imagined what they would look like in action.

The plane made a slow right turn as it climbed, and they watched as it grew smaller in the western sky. The silence it left behind was profound, and neither of them spoke as they retraced their steps to the NAAFI. Then Sandy said, 'Let's go in and get warm.' The sound of conversation and the smell of bacon greeted them as they came into the warmth and one or two airmen called out to Sandy.

He waved at them, but didn't join them. Instead, he led Irene to a table in the far corner.

'Are you hungry?' he asked.

'Starving.'

They ate bacon, egg, sausages and toast, washed down with mugs of scalding tea, and chatted about the base and its British, American and Canadian squadrons. When they'd finished, Irene tried to tell him that she understood the base was bursting at the seams and that the shifts Sandy worked were long and arduous. 'I had no idea how important this base was and I understand you're all working round the clock. I shouldn't have come, I know that now, but I'm so glad I've seen you. I'll go back to Belfast this afternoon so you don't need to worry about me.'

Sandy leaned across the table and took her hand. 'I'm not sorry you came. It made me realise how much I've missed you.' He brought her hand to his lips and kissed it. 'What would you say if I told you there might be a way that you could stay?'

Irene's eyes widened. 'How?'

'There's a place not too far from here. It would just be for you, I'm afraid. I have to stay on the base, but we'd be able to see each other when I get time off. If you like I could take you there now. That is, if you want to see it?'

'Oh, yes please.' Irene felt her spirits lift for the first time in months.

Sandy hesitated. 'Would you be all right to ride pillion?'

'Of course. How did you find somewhere for me to live?'

'I didn't. Your friend Ethel told me about this place.'

They rode for fifteen minutes down a narrow lane until they came to a house set back from the road. 'Are they expecting us?' asked Irene.

Sandy was about to answer when the door opened and a girl of about five, with a shock of ginger curls, ran out and went straight to Irene and took her hand. 'Hello, I know who you are,' she said.

'Do you?' Irene smiled.

'Aye, you're Irene and my name's Susan. Are you coming to stay with us?'

At that moment a young woman, wearing a wrap-around apron

and with a baby on her hip, came to the door. 'Now, Susan, don't you be rushing at people,' she said, and called to Irene and Sandy: 'You're very welcome. Come on in.'

The kitchen was cosy and they were met by the smell of fresh soda bread cooling on a rack. In front of the range there was not one but two wooden clothes horses covered in freshly washed nappies. 'Sit yourself down,' said the woman and nodded at the battered horsehair settee. 'You'll both take a cup of tea in your hand, won't you?' While the kettle boiled she told them that her name was Dorothy and she was Ethel's sister. Her husband was serving in the Royal Inniskilling Fusiliers. 'God knows where,' she added. Then she explained how Ethel had come home after her shift the previous night and talked about Irene and how she would have to go back home because there wasn't a room to be had anywhere.

'Well, says I to her, sure haven't we a spare bed upstairs in your room and a wee bit of money for the board and lodging would come in very handy.'

Irene had to listen carefully to catch what Dorothy said in her strong Fermanagh accent.

'Says she, "Would you not mind if Irene came to stay with us?" "Mind?" I said, "Why would I mind? It'd be great to have some company while you're off doing your nursing." Would you like to see the room?'

Dorothy led the way up the steep stairs and the baby, still on her hip, laughed and gurgled at Irene all the way up. 'He's a happy baby, isn't he?'

'Aye, our wee Johnny has a lovely nature, so he does.' As if to prove it, the baby kicked his legs in excitement and gave Irene the biggest smile she'd ever seen.

The room was under the eaves, but there was enough space to move around. Along with the two single beds, covered with patchwork quilts, there was a wardrobe and a dressing table.

'How much would you charge?' asked Sandy.

'I was thinking two pounds a week including meals,' said Dorothy.

'Hmm,' said Sandy as he looked around the room, while Irene smiled shyly at Dorothy.

'Well,' said Dorothy, 'sure I'll leave you here so you can think about it.'

When she had gone, Sandy said, 'I'm sure you'd be fine here, but you need to think seriously about whether you really want to be away from Belfast and the family.'

Irene opened her mouth to speak, but he held up his hand. 'Take your time, because the last thing I want is for you to be unhappy. I won't be with you as much as I'd like and I don't want you complaining that you're lonely because, I'll tell you now, I can't be worrying about you when I've work to do.'

Irene sensed the mixture of frustration and concern in his tone and knew this was the moment when she had to choose and that, once made, the decision would be irreversible. It would change her life completely. But it wasn't about her any more; it was about her husband and their child. Her mother and her sisters would always be there for her, but soon she would have a new family and she would be the one to make it work.

She reached up and put her arms around Sandy's neck. 'I know now that all I want is to be with you and the baby. I'll be happy here, don't worry.'

Sandy's broad smile said it all. 'Irene, I know this is a big decision for you and I'm so happy.' He kissed her tenderly. 'I love you so much and I promise you we'll come through this war and we'll settle down in our own house – you, me and the baby.'

Chapter 9

In the cosy parlour of Kathleen's large Edwardian terraced house on the Cregagh Road, Pat and her aunt sat making plans to ensure that as many children as possible returned to school after the Christmas break.

'You don't think the promise of a free dinner will be enough?' asked Pat.

'Oh, the parents who were at the Christmas party might have been convinced, but lots of them weren't there. Besides, plenty of the children will wake up to a cold and miserable day in January and decide they'd rather stay in bed and the parents will let them.'

'So what do we do?'

Kathleen took a sheaf of pages from a large envelope, split it in two and gave one half to Pat. 'These are the names and addresses of the pupils who attend May Street School. I think we should do some canvassing – knock on doors to persuade parents to send their children to school.'

'But what if they already send their children?'

'Simple, you just say that's grand and could they pass on the message to other parents. In these communities people know each other so well and soon they'll be talking about what's happening with the free dinners and everything.'

'But what about the children who don't go to your school?'

'Ah, you don't know how children's minds work, Pat. If we can set the ball rolling to get our pupils to come to school, it won't be long before other children in the area follow suit. The last thing they want is to be left behind with fewer and fewer friends to play with on the streets. You've heard of the Pied Piper, haven't you?'

And that was the plan. They had one week to persuade as many parents – mostly mothers – as possible to send their children to school. Pat arranged with Cyril Wood that she could sign in at the office every morning before going out to canvass. 'If you can restore some normality in the education system in that area of the city that'll be a start, but don't get your hopes up,' he told her.

Pat decided to start with Frankie to make sure he would be attending. His mother, Trixie, invited her in and, when she explained why she was there, Trixie interrupted her. 'Oh, don't you worry, Frankie'll be there. You can't wait can you, Frankie?'

Frankie nodded, but then Pat asked, 'What about your friends? Will they come, do you think?'

Frankie shrugged his shoulders. 'Some said they would, but some won't bother I don't think.'

Trixie tutted. 'What's the matter with people? It's like they've lost their way altogether and just accept this terrible state of affairs. The way I look at it is this. Let's get the childer sorted right now, then we'll get pushin' for the runnin' water and a decent roof over our heads. You know what I think?' Trixie didn't wait for an answer. 'You should contact the *Belfast Telegraph* and get them to write about these childer not goin' to school. The headmistress was right – education is what'll set this city to rights after the war. In the meantime, I can promise you I'll go round everyone I know in this area and I'll tell them to make sure they send their childer to school next Monday.'

When Pat met Kathleen after a day walking the streets they compared notes. The response had been mixed but, like Trixie, several women said they would spread the word. Pat wasn't sure that would have any effect, but Kathleen was heartened by what she had heard.

'Look at it this way,' said Kathleen, 'when we started this morning there was only you and me and now there are all these women out there prepared to tell others about the importance of education. Reminds me of another time when women got together. I was about your age then and standing shoulder to shoulder with other women was so exciting. We didn't change the world, but we did enough to give women a sense that they could make a difference. Maybe we've forgotten that over the years, but in here' – she touched her heart – 'maybe we still have that power. I've a feeling our time will come again.'

Pat hadn't intended to mention Trixie's suggestion of going to the *Telegraph*, but hearing Kathleen talk of change and power she wondered if it might not be a way to reach other women whose children weren't going to school.

Kathleen's eyes lit up. 'Yes, of course, it's exactly what we should do – harness the power of the press. Emmeline Pankhurst knew all about that.'

'Emmeline who?'

'I'll tell you all about it sometime.'

Kathleen telephoned the deputy editor there and then, and she and Pat met the following morning outside the front door of the famous sandstone and red-brick building on Royal Avenue. 'I knew the man when he was a cub reporter,' said Kathleen. 'He'll write a good piece for sure.' The deputy editor listened carefully when they explained what they were trying to do and he made copious shorthand notes as they talked. He seemed quite shocked by the number of children not in school and asked about the role of the Belfast Education Committee. Kathleen told him she had written to them several times about the problem, but there had been no response. Finally, he made sure he had spelt their names correctly, noted their official titles and assured them he would write the report immediately and that it would appear in the late edition of the paper.

The following morning when Pat signed in at work, she was told to report to Cyril Wood immediately. She knocked on his office door and waited for him to call 'Enter'. He was leaning back in his chair smoking his pipe and on the desk in front of him was a copy of the *Belfast Telegraph* with the headline in large black letters: 'CITY SCHOOLS EMPTY'.

'What's the meaning of this?' he demanded.

'I didn't say the schools were empty.'

'No? Well, what exactly did you say?'

Pat could feel her heart race. 'I said there were too many children from bombed areas not attending school. I said their lives had been disrupted and it was time to get them back in school so they could get an education.'

'Very laudable, Miss Goulding, but what concern me are your remarks about the Belfast Education Committee, several members of which have telephoned me this morning demanding to know why a clerk in the Ministry of Public Security had seen fit to damn the city's entire education system.'

Pat was horrified. 'I didn't do that.'

He leaned forward and set his pipe on the desk, turned the newspaper towards Pat and put his finger on one line.

'*Miss Goulding explained, "As far as I can see the Belfast Education Committee do not seem interested in the missing pupils."*'

Had she really said that? Weren't they Aunt Kathleen's words? She felt the anger rise within her. Never mind who said it. It was true!

She looked Cyril Wood straight in the eye. 'The fact remains that if we can persuade at least some parents to send their children to school, that'll be a good thing, won't it?'

'The committee want you stopped,' he said.

Pat's face fell. Was he going to dismiss her? 'You agreed that I should do what I could to improve the lives of the children,' she said.

'Yes I did, but I'm going to have to suspend you from duty for a week to let all this fuss with the Education Committee blow over. Now go home and say nothing more to the newspapers. We don't want any more trouble between the Stormont government and Belfast Corporation, do we?'

By the time Pat arrived at Aunt Kathleen's house her anger had been replaced by a stubborn defiance that not even the thought of losing her job could shake. Kathleen must have been watching for her because she threw open the front door before Pat had opened the gate. Her face was flushed with excitement and she said, 'Pat, you'll never guess what's happened. I've had schools from all across the city telephoning me to say they're going to follow our lead. Operation Pied Piper has begun!'

Within half an hour both Pat and Kathleen were back on the streets knocking on doors.

Chapter 10

Pat and Kathleen stood in the January drizzle and stared at the almost empty yard of May Street School. Just a handful of children were gathered inside the gates, while teachers watched from the classroom windows. It was almost nine o'clock and Kathleen had the brass bell ready in her hand to ring the start of the school day. 'I can't understand this,' she said, 'by this time we would certainly have had more children arriving. Do you think—'

'Listen,' said Pat.

'What?'

'It's music ... sounds like a bugle.'

And as they listened other bugles joined in. Then came the sound of tramping feet. Left right, left right ...

Pat ran across the yard to the gate. Now they could hear the sound of children singing. 'Pack up your troubles in your old kit bag ...' Round the corner they came, a whole procession, led by a band of American soldiers, and bringing up the rear was a catering corps truck. The children came to a rather shambolic halt in the yard and when the song ended and the bugles were silent, Captain Walters from the American Services Club stepped forward and saluted Kathleen. 'They're all yours now, ma'am.' Kathleen rang the bell for all she was worth and the children lined up class by class then marched into their lessons.

Pat shook Captain Walters' hand. 'How on earth did you do that?'

'Old army trick,' he said. 'We were coming here anyway with the catering truck so we thought we'd drive round the neighbourhood and play the "Reveille". If it can get lazy troops out of bed it can sure as hell shift kids.'

At that moment there was a clicking sound and Pat turned to see a man taking their photograph and she realised with a start that she was still holding the captain's hand.

The following morning Pat returned to Stormont after her one-week suspension and went straight to Cyril Wood's office. He looked up as she came in, but didn't speak and went back to reading a memo. Eventually, he put it down and with a stern face said, 'You should have done what you were told and spent the week at home; that way you'd still have a job in my department. Instead of which you ploughed ahead and now' – he paused for effect – 'you're on the front page of the *Telegraph* with the Americans, cocking a snook at the Education Committee.'

Pat felt her stomach turn over. 'But lots of children went back to school yesterday and there'll be more today. Other schools are starting to do what we did and now there's milk and bread being donated to feed the children. Surely that's a good thing, isn't it? Why should I lose my job for trying to help people who have nothing?'

'Pat, I've been asked not to discuss this with you. You're to go right away to the Ministry of Commerce offices – they're expecting you.'

'The Ministry of Commerce? Why there?'

Cyril Wood shrugged his shoulders. He had known Pat Goulding would cause a stir, but he hadn't expected her time in his department to end like this.

Commerce had been one of the smallest ministries before the war, but after a slow start to war work it had found its feet and now ranked as the most important in the government. As Pat followed the signs down long corridors to the far side of Stormont Buildings she presumed she would arrive at a pokey office where a miserable clerk would have her cards ready and that would be the end of her career in the civil service. As she walked, both her pace and her sense of injustice quickened. 'How dare they,' she said between clenched teeth.

Pat took a deep breath and pushed open the door marked 'Ministry of Commerce' and was surprised to find herself in a large airy room with a high ceiling where several men, clearly senior civil servants, were working at their desks. A woman approached her.

'Are you Patricia Goulding?'

'Yes.'

'Please follow me.'

Another corridor, carpeted this time, and another door. The woman knocked and when a voice called 'Come in' she ushered Pat inside. A tall, rather distinguished-looking man with a moustache was standing in front of an elegant plaster fireplace, on either side of which was a high-backed brocade armchair. He came towards her and shook her hand. 'How do you do, Miss Goulding? Basil Brooke.' He indicated the chair. 'Please sit,' he said, and sat down opposite her. His piercing eyes examined her and she wondered if she was expected to say something. It wasn't every day she found herself in the office of a cabinet minister. After what seemed an age he said, 'So you're the young woman who set the cat among the pigeons.'

'I beg your pardon?'

'You've given the Education Committee and Belfast Corporation a bit of a pasting, not to mention our own Ministry of Education.'

Pat was determined to defend herself. 'Sir, I'm sorry but I didn't mean to cause trouble, I was just trying to—'

'I know what you were trying to do. I read the papers and as far as I'm concerned Belfast Corporation deserves to be made to look incompetent. They should have done something about the missing pupils months ago.'

Pat hadn't expected that response. 'So why am I being dismissed?'

The minister laughed. 'Is that what you think?'

'Why else am I here?'

He went to his desk and came back with a newspaper and handed it to her. There was a large picture of the children marching into school and in the corner was a small insert of Pat shaking hands with Captain Walters. She blushed at the sight of it.

'I hope you don't mind me asking, sir,' she said, 'but why am I here exactly?'

He smiled. 'Fair question,' he said, and nodded at the newspaper. 'Miss Goulding, far from dismissing you I'd like to offer you a new position in my ministry.'

'But—'

Sir Basil held up his hand. 'Let me explain. I think you're the person I need to ensure the success of an important project I'm working on. You've shown excellent organisational skills as demonstrated in the setting up of the American Red Cross Services Club and the drive to get children back to school. But equally important are your contacts and sensitivity when dealing with the Americans.'

Pat felt relieved and flattered in equal measure, but slightly worried too as she had only just got going with the plans to help people in bombed areas. 'What exactly does this project involve?' she asked.

Sir Basil leaned back in his chair and stretched his legs out in front of him. 'There is to be an event to mark the first anniversary of the arrival of American Forces in Britain, right here in the city where they first came ashore. I want you to join the small team already working on the proposals. Your brief will be to liaise with the Americans. I want them to be impressed by the organisation of the event and you will report directly to me. We have less than a month to stage a celebration of which Belfast can be proud.'

Pat was not averse to working with the Americans, but still had a nagging doubt about leaving unfinished business. 'At the end of the month, what'll happen to me?' she asked.

'We'll cross that bridge when we come to it, shall we?'

Chapter 11

Martha knew it was a mother's lot to see one child contented only to find another had become the opposite. So it was with her daughters. Irene had written a lovely letter saying that she had found a place to stay near Castle Archdale with a family. She was feeling well and the food was good and plentiful. Sheila too seemed much happier and had stopped complaining about her work at the Academy. She had even volunteered to do some overtime. Pat had been living on her nerves with the project to get the children back to school. Thankfully her efforts had paid off, and she had since moved on to some big project with the Americans. But then there was Peggy, who had become even more snappy and agitated as the day of the Golden Sisters audition approached.

'Now don't forget, Mammy, we won't be home till quite late,' she reminded her mother before she went to work on the morning of the auditions. 'They won't start until after the shop is closed and goodness only knows how many people will show up. We could be inundated.'

'And Pat's meeting you at the shop, so there's only me and Sheila for tea?'

'Yes, Pat and I will have to agree on the right person.'

Martha raised an eyebrow. 'Agree, eh? Well, that'll be a first.'

Business had been slow in the shop and the time seemed to drag. Goldstein had spent most of the day in his office, only leaving it to spend a couple of hours at his club. But Peggy and Esther whiled away the time talking about the sort of person who would make a good Golden Sister.

'We need someone with a sense of style,' said Peggy. 'A bit of class, you know?'

'That would be good,' said Esther, 'but she must have a great voice too, yes?'

'Goes without saying, but it must be a voice that suits our repertoire and most of all it has to blend with our voices. That's why in the audition they'll have to sing by themselves and then with Pat and me.'

'Sounds terrifying,' said Esther.

'And so it should be,' said Peggy. 'It's not easy being a member of the Golden Sisters.'

Half an hour before closing time, the shop was already filling up with young women waiting to audition. Esther was given the job of taking their names while Peggy looked on, examining each new arrival: the confident and the nervous; the pretty and the plain; the well dressed and the shabby.

Pat arrived just before six. 'It's a good turnout,' she said to Goldstein.

'Indeed it is. We should find someone tonight. Right Peggy, I think we'll get started with the solo singing and after that we'll decide who should go home and who should stay to sing with you two.'

As one hopeful girl followed another, Goldstein, Peggy and Pat made notes and in most cases it was easy to spot those who were not suitable almost as soon as they stood in front of them. Sometimes it was to do with their presence, sometimes it was the quality of the voice. It wasn't hard to agree on the six girls who would go on to the second audition.

Goldstein read out the names of those who had not been chosen and thanked them for coming. Then he announced that there would be a ten-minute break before the next stage of the audition when, in turn, they would sing 'Don't Sit Under the Apple Tree' with the two Golden Sisters.

Pat was chatting with Peggy at the piano when she heard the shop bell ring and looked up to see Sheila in the doorway with a young man. 'Well, I never,' she said and Peggy followed her gaze.

Sheila was flushed and smiling as she introduced her companion. 'This is Charles – he works at school.' He was tall and thin and it occurred to Peggy that his clothes were certainly those of a schoolmaster. Pat, however, noticed that he was nervous, and from the way he looked at Sheila it was clear he was quite taken with her.

'Have you chosen someone yet?' asked Sheila.

Pat explained what was happening. 'It'll all depend on how they sound when they sing with us. But Mr Goldstein says if they're not good enough we'll have to carry on looking.'

'Are you going to stay?' asked Peggy. 'You could tell us what you think.'

'Oh, I wouldn't have a clue,' said Sheila. 'We'll just stay at the back there and listen.'

It was one thing to prepare an audition piece and deliver it to a good standard, but quite another to weave complex harmonies as a member of a trio. Pat and Peggy had sung together since they were children and their performances were instinctive. Added to that, there was the overall look of the three girls together to be considered.

One by one, the girls did their best: some managed the harmonies but didn't look right; others had the glamorous looks but their singing didn't blend well; and some had neither one thing nor the other. Throughout, Goldstein's face gave nothing away and when the last girl had sung he asked Pat and Peggy to join him in his office to make their final decision. At that moment there were raised voices at the back of the shop.

'But you have to do it.'

'I ... I don't think I can—'

'I'm telling you. You must!'

Goldstein had noticed earlier that Sheila and a young man had arrived to watch the auditions and, at the sound of their voices, he went to speak to them.

'My name is Goldstein,' he said to her companion. 'And you are …?'

Charles stood up and offered his hand. 'My name is Charles, sir, and I think Sheila should sing for you.'

'She doesn't need to sing. I know her voice very well and it's not quite right for the Golden Sisters.'

'I think you'll find it is.' Charles seemed to have found his confidence.

Goldstein was sceptical. 'And how would you know that?'

'Because I've trained her to sing the harmonies and I think you'll find she is exactly what you're looking for.'

Goldstein turned to Pat and Peggy, but they looked as puzzled as he was.

'Is this true?' he asked Sheila.

'Yes,' she said softly.

'Well, this is highly irregular, but if the ladies who have auditioned don't mind, I'd like to hear Sheila sing with the Golden Sisters.'

Sheila stood at the piano next to Pat, and Peggy played the intro to 'Apple Tree'. At the end of the third bar, Pat turned to Sheila and smiled encouragement. But a minute later Goldstein shouted, 'Enough of that. Now sing "Chattanooga Choo Choo" please.'

Again Peggy played the intro, the sisters sang and Goldstein listened intently. When they had finished, there was a spontaneous round of applause from everyone there. Goldstein, Peggy and Pat went to the office to discuss what they had heard.

Martha enjoyed the quiet evening on her own with her knitting and the wireless and only occasionally went upstairs to look out for her girls coming up the road. She told herself that Sheila must have gone to watch the auditions, but she would have words with her for not coming home for her tea first.

When she heard them coming round the side of the house talking and laughing she went into the kitchen to take their dinners out of the oven.

'Well then, did you find a singer—'

Martha stopped in her tracks. There were her daughters, all smiles, and with them a young man clearly embarrassed at finding himself in her kitchen.

There was an awkward silence before Pat took control. 'Mammy, this is Charles Turner. He's a music teacher at Belfast Royal Academy.'

Martha looked from the young man to Pat and back again. 'Mercy me!' she said, 'are you the new Golden Sister?' And all at once her daughters were looking at each other and laughing. Charles turned scarlet and tried to explain. 'I just went along to the audition with Sheila.'

'And before he knew it,' said Peggy, 'he was' – she couldn't get the words out for giggling – 'he was … one of us!'

Martha shook her head at the silliness of her daughters, but it was infectious and she couldn't help but smile. When the laughter subsided and the girls had wiped their eyes, Martha asked, 'So who did get the job?'

There was no reply and no one met her eye.

'Well?' she said. 'You must have found somebody.'

'It's me, Mammy,' said Sheila.

'You? But I thought—'

'Charles helped me. He taught me how to do the harmonies.'

Martha saw the way Sheila looked up at him under her eyelashes and asked, 'When did that happen?'

Charles spoke for her. 'Oh, mostly after school; we'd listen to the Andrews Sisters records and practise singing along with them. Sheila just needed a bit of advice and support. That's why I went to the audition. I don't think she would have sung if I hadn't gone with her.' His face lit up with the happiest of smiles.

'Is that so?' said Martha, giving him a hard stare, and Peggy, sensing the way the conversation was going, tried to explain.

'There were plenty of other girls at the audition but honestly, Mammy, when we had heard them all sing …' She shook her head.

Pat felt the need to add her bit: 'Sheila only sang at the very end and Mr Goldstein said nobody came close – she was perfect.'

To everyone's surprise Martha said, 'Well, I suppose if that's the way of it, you might as well sit down and have something to eat. You're welcome to join us, Mr Turner.'

It was a Friday afternoon and Sheila had been walking down the corridor past Charles' classroom when she heard him call her name. She had turned to see him coming towards her. 'Sheila, I've been thinking … and you can say no if you want. Er … do you want to … would you like to … go for a bike ride on Sunday?'

Would she like to? It was all she had thought about these last few months – a date with Charles Turner. 'Yes, that would be very nice. Where should I meet you?'

Okay, so they weren't going to the pictures or a dance, but Charles had asked her to meet him at a certain place, the Waterworks, at a certain time, two o'clock, to go for a bike ride, and that definitely counted as a date in Sheila's book.

She washed her hair the night before with coal tar soap and rinsed it with vinegar to make it shine, then went to bed with her head in curlers. Pat lent her a pair of stockings, warning her not to bother coming home if she laddered them. Peggy lent her a lipstick and powder compact and told her not to use them until she was out of the street and her mother's sight. Sheila had been nervous and a little embarrassed about telling her mother she was meeting Charles, but her mother had raised no objections and simply asked where they were going and when she would be back.

'I can't believe Mammy didn't stop me from going or give me a lecture about how to behave,' Sheila told Pat.

'It's because she's met him already and, if he's a school teacher, sure he must be trustworthy,' said Pat. 'Anyway, I think she likes him.'

Charles was waiting for her at the gates of the Waterworks public park. He was wearing a mackintosh and a college scarf, and his black bicycle had a box fastened behind the saddle. She waved at him and he watched her as she freewheeled down the hill towards him, smiling all the way.

'I thought we could ride towards Cave Hill,' he said. 'It might be a bit steep in places, but we can stop whenever you like. What do you think?'

'I think that's a good idea,' she said, and they set off riding side by side through the park.

'What happened there?' asked Charles as they rode past a huge crater filled with stagnant water.

'It was the Easter Blitz,' said Sheila. 'They say the Germans made a mistake. When they saw the Waterworks on their map they thought it was a reservoir and if they destroyed it there would be no water to drink.'

'There are so many bomb sites, aren't there? It must have been terrible in the city during the Blitz.'

'It was very scary and every night you went to bed, well … you just never knew. When the alert sounded you took shelter. You'd listen to the explosions wondering if a bomb was going to drop on your head.'

'Did you go into an air-raid shelter?'

'No, we went under the stairs. It was a bit cramped. One time we went up Cave Hill and we could see right across the city. It looked like everywhere was in flames. Of course, that was all before you came to Belfast.'

'Yes, I was still in Armagh with my parents. I only came to Belfast just before I started at the Academy in September.'

'And where do you live now?'

'I've lodgings with a nice family in Fortwilliam Park.'

They left their bicycles at the bottom of a narrow lane that wound up the hill. Charles took a string bag from the box on his bike and held it up. 'I've got a bit of a picnic,' he said.

It was colder up here and they saw their breath in the air as they climbed. Above them the outcrop of the hill loomed dark against the sky and after twenty minutes on the well-worn path they came to a sheltered area beneath some trees. There were boulders, flat and large enough to sit on, and here and there the ashes of small fires.

'You wait here,' said Charles, 'and I'll collect some wood for a fire.'

Left alone, Sheila wondered whether going to watch a film might not have been more sensible. But before long, the little fire was burning away and Charles poured her a cup of tea from his thermos flask and offered her a bloater paste sandwich. She watched him closely as he talked, noticing how his dark hair flopped over his forehead and every now and again he'd push it back slowly. He told her how he had had come to the city to teach. The previous music master, like several other teachers in the school, had enlisted and the headmaster, a second cousin of his father's, had written to Charles to ask if he would fill in until the end of the war.

'I've been involved in music all my life, playing the organ in church and the cello in a string quartet. I was hoping to study music after the war, and in the meantime I was teaching the piano. But when the chance to teach in Belfast came along, I jumped at it.'

'Do you like teaching?' Sheila asked.

His eyes lit up. 'Oh yes. I can't believe I get paid for spending my days talking about and listening to music and, best of all, helping people to play an instrument.'

'Or sing.'

'That's right.' He laughed and Sheila felt her heart beat a little faster. 'You know, when I found out you were a singer, I knew why I'd been drawn to you the first time I saw you ...' Now there was a twinkle in his eye. 'That and the fact you're the prettiest girl I've ever seen.'

Sheila looked away, uncertain how to respond.

'I'm sorry. I don't know why I said that.'

She heard the nervousness in his voice and looked up to see that he was biting his lip. Instinctively, she changed the subject. 'So tell me – how does someone who plays the organ and cello know so much about the Andrews Sisters and close harmonies?'

'It's my secret vice,' he said. 'American swing, especially when sung by three girls in close harmony.'

When the fire died down and the wind picked up, they both knew it was time to go. The path was uneven underfoot and when Sheila slipped for the second time on the loose stones it was the most natural thing in the world for Charles to take her hand. When they got back to the bikes, they stood and talked some more, reluctant to leave the seclusion of the lane.

'Did you mean what you said before?' asked Sheila.

'What, about you being pretty? Yes, I did. You know I did,' he said, and he drew her into his arms. 'I'll say it again. You are the prettiest girl I've ever seen.' He brushed his lips against hers with the softest of touches. Then he laughed. 'But I'm bound to think that – I'm from Armagh!'

Sheila looked away.

'Hey, I'm only teasing,' said Charles and with a sudden urgency he pulled her even closer and kissed her full on the mouth. The closeness of him and his lips pressing on hers was all she wanted for ever and ever.

Chapter 12

Since the supper concert for the British Army top brass, Peggy had heard not a word from Archie Dewer. At first she had expected him to call into the music shop, then she thought he might be waiting for her after work one evening. What had he said? 'I'll find a way for us to be together.' How those words had thrilled her; but eventually she had come to the conclusion that he had either been sent to fight, or he was quite simply a liar. It didn't matter, she told herself, because now Harry Ferguson had sent her a lovely letter from his training base in England telling her how much he loved her and how the war would soon be over and he'd be coming home. So she had no need for Archie, had she?

It was one of those bitter January days when the east wind blew up Belfast Lough into the city to whip around bare legs and threaten to lift skirts. Peggy left the shop and headed towards Robinson & Cleaver's to spend her dinner hour looking at lipsticks on the cosmetic counter. She had gone just a few yards when someone touched her arm and she turned to see Archie smiling down at her. 'Ah Peggy, my dear, I've found you at last.'

'Found me? It's you who disappeared, not me. I'm at the music shop every day.'

'A figure of speech, no more. I've been so busy, but you were always in my thoughts.' He nodded in the direction of the Café Royal. 'Let's pop in out of the cold.' He took her arm and propelled her across the street.

They sat at a window table and when the waitress arrived Archie ordered a pot of tea and two slices of Madeira cake. 'It's lovely to see you again, and looking radiant as ever,' he said.

Peggy could see the twinkle in his eye and knew he was flirting with her, but she was in no mood to play along. 'I expected you to be in touch with me before now,' she said, and pouted in her displeasure.

'I've been waiting for the right moment and looking for the right place to spend time with you.' He passed her some cake. 'As a matter of fact, I'm free on Saturday night and I know a very good hotel where they have a dinner dance. Do you like to dance, Peggy?'

'I might do.' She took a bite of cake and stared out of the window.

'I bet you have a beautiful gown to go dancing?'

Peggy thought of the midnight blue organza dress hanging in her wardrobe and tried to suppress a smile.

'And I wonder if you ever sweep your hair up in a chignon to show off your exquisite neck ...' He reached out and ran his finger from her cheek to her collarbone.

She had no idea what a chignon was, but his touch was electric. His eyes were full of laughter and there was a knowing look on his handsome face.

'Say you'll spend Saturday night with me, Peggy.'

She drank some tea and thought about Harry's letter. She took another bite of cake and imagined what it would be like to go to a hotel dinner dance and all the while Archie watched her and waited. Eventually, she patted her lips with the napkin and said, 'Well, you'd better be a good dancer.'

Peggy knew that her mother would want to know all the details: where exactly was the dance; what time she would be home; and, most importantly, who she was going with. Any one of those questions answered honestly would result in her being forbidden to go at all. On the other hand, a dance at the YWCA – a bastion of respectability – would still bring questions, but the chances were she would be allowed to go.

'There's a crowd of us going,' she told her mother. 'No, I won't be too late, provided the buses are running on time.'

On the Saturday morning before she left for work, Peggy reminded her mother that she wouldn't be home for her tea. 'We'll have something to eat then go on to the dance,' she told her.

'You must have money to burn. Going out for your tea – I never heard the like.'

'Ach, Mammy, it's what people do these days,' she said, then ran upstairs, collected her dress in its box and was out the door and away down the street, leaving her mother busy in the kitchen and deploring, no doubt, the extravagant habits of her daughters.

It being Saturday and the Jewish Sabbath, Peggy was alone in the shop all day. She opened a little later than usual so that she could hang the ball gown on the back of the office door to let the creases drop out. All day she chose her favourite dance records and played them louder that Mr Goldstein allowed, imagining what it would feel like to dance with Archie. She closed the shop as normal at six and an hour later she was standing outside in her ball gown. She caught her reflection in the shop window: face like a Max Factor model and hair swept up like Olivia de Havilland.

The look on Archie's face was just what she'd hoped for and as she got into the car, he leaned over to kiss her cheek and whispered in her ear, 'You take my breath away.'

He drove over the river and out along the south shore of the lough. 'Where are we going?' she asked.

'The hotel's out in the country towards Bangor.'

'I didn't realise we'd be going so far.'

Archie laughed and put his foot down and the car roared away. 'It's not far, don't worry. We've got the whole night ahead of us.'

The hotel was off the main road at the end of a long drive. The entrance hall looked like it had seen better days, but as they entered the ballroom Peggy couldn't help but admire the tables, set with crystal glasses and silver cutlery and capturing some of the hotel's pre-war grandeur. The room was full of well-dressed couples, mostly businessmen with their wives. As they waited to be seated, Peggy was aware of eyes darting in their direction and some outright stares at the sight of the tall, uniformed officer and the dark-haired girl in the striking midnight blue and silver dress. They were shown to a table for two and Archie immediately moved his chair closer to Peggy.

'Have you ever had champagne?' he asked.

'Oh yes – lots of bubbles – lovely.'

'My goodness, quite the woman of the world, aren't you?'

'Not really. I drank it once, a long time ago.' And she smiled at the memory. Sipping champagne with Harry Ferguson – how long ago it seemed.

'You look … wistful.' He reached for her hand. 'Are you sad?'

'No, it's a nice memory.'

'Tell me about it.'

And it seemed the most natural thing in the world to talk about the French restaurant, the champagne and the midnight drive on that first date with Harry.

'And where is he now?' asked Archie, his voice soft and comforting.

'He's in the army and I don't know when I'll see him again.'

'Well,' said Archie, 'I'm not Harry, but I know how to make a beautiful woman happy … if you'll let me.' He kissed her cheek. 'Will you let me?'

She looked into his handsome face and his laughing eyes, and nodded.

The meal was a poor affair of overcooked meat and watery vegetables, but Archie was such good company that Peggy didn't notice. He told her about London: the theatres, restaurants, art galleries. 'You'll have to come and visit me after the war,' he said. 'You'd love it. We could have dinner at the Dorchester, followed by a West End show, then drinks at the Ritz. Would you like that?'

Peggy was enthralled. 'Oh Archie, could we really?'

And right there, surrounded by all those stuffy, middle-aged people, Archie leaned towards her. 'Of course we could, my darling,' he said, and kissed her full on the lips.

Eventually, the meal was cleared away, the lights dimmed and it was time for dancing. Archie led her on to the floor. He was probably the tallest man she had ever danced with and certainly the most skilled. Peggy knew a good dancer needed a combination of precise steps, a finely tuned sense of rhythm and the confidence to be creative. Archie had all of these, but by the time the first dance, a waltz, had finished, Peggy knew he had something else – an instinctive sense of his partner's body. He held her a fraction more closely than she had ever been held and used the lightest of touches to blend her body with his. It felt like heaven.

The dances came and went: foxtrot, quickstep, tango, quick waltz, slow waltz, and all too soon it was time for the orchestra to take a break. Archie and Peggy reluctantly returned to their table. Archie ordered more champagne and Peggy went to find the ladies' powder room. She spotted the sign and went through the door into a little vestibule. She was about to pull open the next door, when she heard a woman's voice from inside.

'A British officer, I ask you. He's old enough to be her father. I've a good mind to complain to the management – these wee Belfast girls are a disgrace.'

Peggy hesitated. Should she walk away or brazen it out? But she'd done nothing wrong. Why couldn't she go out dancing – where was the harm in that? She pulled open the door and swept in to face the women. She was calm and her voice was steady: 'You're entitled to your opinion of course, but let me tell you that this Belfast girl is the Assistant Director of Entertainment responsible for organising Entertainment National Service Association concerts and I'm here tonight with the major to decide whether this hotel is suitable for a white-tie ball to raise money for war charities.' She paused to let her words sink in before adding, 'But as far as I can see, the clientele would be inappropriate for the military top brass.'

The women looked at each other, uncertain how to respond. One of them, a plump woman in a puce-coloured, 1930s-style gown flushed the colour of her dress. The other opened her mouth as if to protest then thought better of it. Peggy stepped aside and they went quickly past her, muttering about how anyone can make a mistake. Peggy rinsed her hands in cold water and stared at herself in the mirror. Despite her sharp words to the women, their assumptions had hurt her deeply. Archie was older, but that's why he was so sophisticated and so attentive. No one, not even Harry, had ever made her feel so self-assured and attractive as Archie did. She powdered her nose and reapplied her lipstick and looked at herself from side to side in the mirror. How could anyone mistake her for one of those sugar daddy girls?

The first dance after the interval was a slow waltz to the tune of 'I Only have Eyes for You' and Peggy's head was light with champagne and the romance of the song. She melted into Archie's arms and felt blissfully content as his kisses caressed her neck. The room disappeared from view as he softly sang the refrain and Peggy wondered if this was what it felt like to fall in love. She thought she loved Harry, but this … this was … and she moaned softly as she tilted her head for Archie to kiss her again.

Without warning her head began to spin and her legs gave way. Archie held her upright, guided her back to her seat and knelt beside her. 'Looks like you've had a bit too much champagne,' he said. 'What about a bit of fresh air? Maybe that'll make you feel better?'

As soon as the frosty air hit Peggy her head began to clear. Archie suggested, if she was up to it, that a short walk would help and he took off his tunic and put it round her shoulders.

'I'm so sorry.' Peggy was close to tears. 'I've spoilt everything.'

'Hush, my lovely girl, you'll be right as rain in no time,' he said, and he pulled her to him and stroked her hair.

She shivered and looked up at him, her cheeks wet with tears. 'Maybe we should leave – it must be late.'

'Nonsense, you'll be fine. Tell you what, why don't we go up to the room now and we'll get you warm and cosy?'

It was a moment before she shaped his words into some sort of sense.

'What room?'

Archie took the strand of hair that had escaped from her chignon and tucked it behind her ear. 'Our room,' he whispered, 'where we'll spend the night together, just as I promised.'

Peggy's eyes opened wide with fright, her mind suddenly putting together all the signals she had misinterpreted. Peggy gasped in horror. How could she have been so naive? She pushed him away. 'I never meant to stay all night. I'd never do anything like that.' But he held her fast. 'Don't be frightened. I promise you it'll be wonderful – you and me.'

'I want to go home!' Peggy shouted.

'But when we were dancing, I know you wanted to be with me; I could see it in your eyes.' He bent forward to kiss her as he had done before.

She turned away from him. 'Let me go!' she cried and suddenly she was free while Archie stood, hands by his sides, with a look of bewilderment on his face.

'I made a mistake,' he said. 'I thought you … Never mind – I'll take you home.'

'Don't bother. I'm not getting in a car with you,' she said, and in her shame she turned and ran down the drive, away from the lights of the hotel and into the darkness.

The gravel under her feet was uneven and she had just gone over in her high heels when she was caught in the sweep of a car's headlights. She struggled to get back on her feet, determined not to get in his car. Her heart was thumping, and she began to run. The car caught up with her and there was the sound of the window being wound down.

'Leave me alone!' she yelled.

The car drove a little way past her and stopped; a dark figure got out of the passenger side. 'Well, my dear, I feel we have both made mistakes tonight.' The voice was familiar. It was the woman in the puce dress from the powder room. 'Please, do get in the car. My husband and I will see you get home safely.'

It was a while before Peggy's heart stopped racing and even longer before she realised that she still had Archie Dewer's tunic over her shoulders. Never mind, if he was court-martialled for being inappropriately dressed when he got back to barracks, he had only himself to blame.

Her rescuers dropped her at the end of her street and as she passed an alleyway she stepped into the shadows, removed Archie's tunic, rolled it up and dropped it in a dustbin.

Chapter 13

The celebration of the first anniversary of the landing of American troops was a great success. The massed bands of the Royal Ulster Rifles and the Royal Irish Fusiliers led the march-past of American military personnel through the city centre to the grounds of the City Hall, where a small monument commemorating the event was unveiled. The following day, Sir Basil Brooke sent for the team who had liaised with US officers and Belfast Corporation to ensure its success. He was clearly delighted. 'Excellent work,' he said. 'Better than I thought possible. Don't know if you've seen the *Belfast Telegraph* this morning?' He proceeded to read from the paper. '"*The most brilliant spectacle to be staged in the British Isles since the outbreak of the Second World War.*" Magnificent. That will show Westminster what we can do.'

The team filed out of his office, but Pat lingered. 'Excuse me, Sir Basil,' she said.

He looked up from the newspaper. 'Yes?'

'I was seconded to the team to liaise with the Americans about the parade, sir. Can I return to my position in the Ministry of Public Security?'

Sir Basil looked taken aback. 'Why would you want to go back?'

'Because I was working to help people in bombed-out areas.'

'Out of the question,' he said. 'I'm responsible for dealing with the Americans and I need you on my team.'

'But the families are desperate. The water and electricity supplies still haven't been restored to some areas.'

Basil Brooke gave her a hard stare. 'As far as I'm concerned you're staying here. However, this is the Ministry of Commerce and strictly speaking those services come under my jurisdiction. I would be prepared to give you the authority to work with the water and electricity boards when you're not needed to deal with the Americans. What do you say?'

A week later, Pat was back in Sir Basil Brooke's office.

'I want you to arrange something, but I'm not quite sure what,' he said. 'Last night a Flying Fortress bomber on its way from England to the United States made an unscheduled stop on the airstrip at Nutts Corner. Engine problems, apparently. The plane was carrying the Supreme Commander of Allied Expeditionary Force in Europe, General Dwight Eisenhower. It'll be twenty-four hours at least before a replacement part arrives. Eisenhower is a man who never sits still and he's asked if he can tour Belfast docks to see the facilities there, no doubt to ascertain how effective we can be in supporting American warships. As the minister in charge of these facilities I will accompany him.'

'Do you need me to arrange this?' asked Pat.

'No, that was done late last night and they're expecting us there in a couple of hours. No, it's what happens after that. I want to take this opportunity to show the Americans what Ulster commerce is capable of, not just now, but after the war. The American dollar, military and civilian, is exactly what we'll need to expand our industries. From the moment I meet him until he gets back on that plane I want him to see us in a favourable light. I'll take care of the commerce aspect, but I need you to get the rest of it right. Get on to your contacts among the American officers and find out everything you can about him – what he likes to eat, what sort of people he might enjoy meeting, anything that might entertain him or make him feel at ease with us while he waits for that plane.'

Pat thought quickly. It would be best if, after touring the docks and factories, Eisenhower could relax. She knew that Sir Basil was regarded as a bit of a live wire personality-wise, and socially he was regarded as good company. Suddenly she realised why he was wearing his uniform; he was a military man at heart, having fought in the Great War, and no doubt he had worn it today to let Eisenhower know he was not simply a politician, but a man who understood the nature of war.

'I think we should bring him back here to Stormont for the evening,' said Pat. 'Every American officer has been impressed by its grandeur. We'll lay on a good meal and provide some entertainment based on his tastes. Invite maybe half a dozen military men to join you. What do you think?'

'Yes, yes, that's it. Give him an enjoyable evening in the company of men like himself. Just the job. Right, off you go and get it done. We'll be gone most of the day, but send a despatch rider to find me with the evening schedule as soon as you have it.'

The first thing Pat did was to ring Captain Walters at the American Services Club. 'I need you to tell me everything you know about Eisenhower,' she said.

By late afternoon the arrangements were almost complete. The top US Army chef had arrived with the ingredients for Eisenhower's favourite meal and was already in the Stormont kitchen beginning preparation. The military guests had been selected, the room was prepared and finally Pat received a message from one of Eisenhower's aides-de-camp informing her that the Supreme Allied Commander had a passion for Mozart. She rang Goldstein straight away. 'We've a special guest at Stormont tonight who's very fond of Mozart. Could you get Esther here by seven o'clock to play for him and Reuben, of course, to accompany her?'

The room chosen for the intimate evening was perfect. At one end there was a large marble fireplace above which hung a painting with the Giant's Causeway in the foreground and, in the background, rolling Atlantic waves. There were large Chesterfield sofas upholstered in dark blue leather and several matching armchairs. On the mahogany side tables there were Waterford crystal lamps glittering with light. There was also a large sideboard with decanters and a cigar box, a baby grand piano and, finally, a circular dining table at the far end of the room set for eight. Perfect.

Pat had just enough time to wash her face and comb her hair before the guests began to arrive. She was so glad she had chosen her pale grey woollen dress to wear to work that morning. It was a flattering A-line shape with glossy black buttons and a scalloped collar. Yes, it did make her look like a civil servant, but a stylish one nevertheless.

The first guests began to arrive and Eisenhower's aide introduced himself. 'I hope you got my message okay about the opera?'

Pat's heart began to race. 'Opera?' she said. 'The message said Mozart.'

'Yeah, Mozart, he wrote opera, yeah?'

'Well, yes, of course he did, but he wrote lots of other things as well.'

'You don't say. Talented guy.'

Pat could have screamed, but at that moment Goldstein arrived with Esther and Reuben. She took them to one side and thanked them for coming. 'It's a supper for Eisenhower and he loves Mozart, but ...' and she explained the misunderstanding about the opera. Goldstein shrugged his shoulders. 'No matter,' he said. 'I have never met a lover of Mozart's operas who did not also enjoy the rest of his music. Esther and Reuben have a good range of Mozart in their repertoire and this will be a wonderful experience for them to play for such a prestigious audience.'

'Excuse me,' said Reuben, his voice heavily accented. 'When I was music student in Warsaw I accompany my friend.'

'Yes,' said Goldstein, 'I know you have a wide repertoire.'

'My friend was soprano.'

Goldstein looked from Reuben to Pat and back again.

Pat saw the look in his eyes. 'I don't think—'

'You could do it. Just two arias would be enough,' Goldstein insisted. 'What about the ones you've sung at weddings?'

Pat thought for a moment. The last thing she wanted was to make a rash decision that she'd end up regretting. On the other hand she was responsible for ensuring Eisenhower enjoyed his evening and would have the best possible impression of Northern Ireland. 'I'll need to think about this,' she said. 'Esther, Reuben, do you want to get set up now? You'll be playing while the guests have a drink, but you should leave when they sit down to dinner. Then you'll return for a short session afterwards.'

She turned to Goldstein. 'It's disappointing, but I think we should just forget about the arias.'

Undeterred, Goldstein asked, 'You said there was a second session?'

'Yes, after dinner when they have cigars and brandy.'

'Well, let us see what we can do between now and then.'

And at that moment Sir Basil Brooke entered the room, followed by General Eisenhower. Esther, with Reuben accompanying her on the baby grand, began to play Mozart's violin sonata No. 21.

Outside the room, Goldstein tried to persuade Pat to sing. 'We will have a run-through and I will listen.' Pat shook her head. She had not sung a Mozart aria since before she joined the Barnstormers. Of course, she had sung all those duets with William, but for her to stand alone … No, it was quite impossible.

Soon, Esther and Reuben returned from the first session buoyed up by the kind remarks from the guests. 'General Eisenhower said he is really looking forward to hearing the arias later,' said Esther.

'What?' Pat was appalled. 'Who told him there would be arias?'

'Somebody … I don't know who he was … An American officer, I think.'

'Well Pat, it looks like you are going to have to sing after all,' said Goldstein, and he smiled smugly.

Faced with little choice, Pat warmed up her voice and ran through the two arias. What was it Mammy always said? 'You can only do your best and don't forget to smile.'

When the meal had been cleared away and the men had settled down with cigars and brandy, Reuben and Pat returned to the room. Pat stood with one hand resting on the piano and, as she faced the uniforms with rows of ribbons and pips, she saw Sir Basil Brooke raise an eyebrow in surprise. Reuben played the opening bars of 'Dove Sono' and Pat drew on all her experience as a performer to convey the unbearable sadness of the Countess in *The Marriage of Figaro*. At first she kept her eyes on the Giant's Causeway on the wall in front of her, but soon she played the role to the audience. Eisenhower at one point closed his eyes and was listening intently. With the final note hanging in the air, Pat stepped back and bowed, then raised her head to warm applause and smiling faces.

The second piece, 'Alleluia', was livelier and more uplifting. Pat, with growing confidence, made good use of the acoustics. Reuben, too, added more to the overall sound that filled the room. At the end the guests stood to applaud and there were shouts of 'Bravo!' and to Pat's amazement Eisenhower came over to her and shook her hand. 'I really enjoyed that. Thank you so much.'

And as Pat left the room Sir Basil caught her eye and mouthed, 'Well done.'

Chapter 14

'Are you sure this dress looks all right? I think it might be a bit old for me.'

Peggy gave an exasperated sigh. 'Look, Sheila, I wore this dress to the Floral Hall when I was your age. It's not too old for you – it's just a bit more sophisticated than you're used to.'

Sheila frowned at herself in the mirror. She did like the pattern of pink rosebuds, but she was worried about the neckline. 'It's not too revealing, is it?'

'Not at all, it's a sweetheart neckline and the little cap sleeves are just lovely. Trust me – it's a dress for dancing.'

'Maybe it needs something around the neck and shoulders, like a scarf?' suggested Pat.

Peggy dismissed the idea. 'No, too fussy, but pearls might work,' she said, and quickly found hers hanging over the dressing table mirror. 'There now, how's that?' she asked as she fastened them round Sheila's neck.

'It looks better and I can wear my own pearl earrings. The ones from a couple of Christmases ago, when I had my hair cut short?'

'Now, Pat, over to you for the makeup,' said Peggy, 'while I go and find Irene's dancing shoes.'

As Pat made up her face, Sheila could feel the excitement building inside her – her first real dance and a proper date with Charles on her seventeenth birthday. Oh, they'd been on quite a few Sunday bike rides. They'd ride somewhere, find a bit of shelter from the wind or rain, eat the bloater sandwiches then cuddle and kiss for a while before setting off back home. When she had first suggested doing something else, he'd looked disappointed then begrudgingly said they could go to the pictures next time. They arrived halfway through *In Which We Serve* and stayed in their seats after the credits to watch the first half, mentally piecing together the two halves when they left. Knowing the ending somehow killed the drama – a bit like the date itself.

Sheila had been determined, therefore, that her birthday would not be a let-down. So when he asked what she would like to do to celebrate, she had told him she wanted to go dancing.

Makeup done, Sheila had just stepped into Irene's dancing shoes when there was a knock at the front door. She could hear her mother's voice inviting Charles inside. Sheila took one final look in the mirror and went to put on her coat.

'Ah, no,' said Peggy, taking the coat from her. 'You go down and I'll bring the coat. First impressions count, you know. Better if he sees you looking all glamorous. That's what he'll always remember – not the dowdy coat.'

As they left, Martha couldn't resist popping upstairs to watch them walk down the street. They were holding hands, and what a grand couple they made. Her first thought when she had opened the door to Charles was that he looked so prosperous in his Harris tweed overcoat. Well, they don't come cheap. And by all accounts he was from a good family, albeit from County Armagh. Our Sheila might just land on her feet here, she told herself. A handsome man with good prospects – what more could she want?

The crowded bus emptied at Bellevue and the atmosphere was good-humoured as everyone made the steep climb up the steps to the gardens and on to the Floral Hall. It was an oddly shaped building and, as Sheila and Charles passed through the doors into the bright tangerine entrance hall to queue for the cloakroom, they marvelled at the modernity of it all. Having handed in their coats, they hurried into the dance hall and, although Peggy had described it to her, it surpassed what she had seen so far. It was like plunging into a dazzling deep blue and golden cave. The room, a complete circle, was edged with a thousand seats, with the dance floor in the middle and, above it, a glass dome.

Sheila never dreamt there could be such a place in Belfast; it must surely belong in some exotic foreign land. Yet here she was, glimpsing another world, and that wasn't all. Here was Charles holding her hand, soon they'd be dancing, and it was her seventeenth birthday.

They managed to find seats at a table with two other couples. Charles went to the bar and came back with glasses of lemonade and while they sipped they listened to the band and watched the dancers for a while. 'Come on,' said Sheila, 'let's have a dance now.'

'I'm not much of a dancer, you know,' said Charles.

'It doesn't matter, as long as we can shuffle round the floor.'

It was a quickstep, quite lively. Charles seemed a bit unsure when he took her in his arms and she waited for him to catch the beat and lead her round the floor. He set off at a lurch and they almost collided with another couple. He tried again and managed to get going in a straight line. He caught her toes a couple of times; then she realised he wasn't turning at all with the flow of dancers and soon he was cutting across other couples. They came inevitably to the edge of the floor, he stopped and attempted to go back the way they had come.

Sheila said, 'Charles, we have to follow the other dancers in a circle round the floor.'

'Can't do that,' he said.

'What do you mean you can't do it?'

'Never learned,' he said. 'I warned you I'm not a dancer.'

'Look, I'll lead,' said Sheila. 'So just relax and I'll guide us round and you try not to stand on anyone's feet, especially mine.'

They made it back to the table and Charles looked a bit shamefaced. Sheila shook her head. 'Why didn't you tell me you can't dance?'

He shrugged. 'I thought I'd manage it when I got going. I didn't think there'd be so many people. I'm a bit better at the waltz. I think.'

The girl sitting next to Sheila, who had clearly been listening to their conversation, gave her a nudge. 'You could have a dance or two with my fella if you want. I don't mind.'

'Oh no, that's all right, I'm fine—'

'Ach, away on with ye. What's the point of comin' to a dance if you don't get to dance?' She laughed and turned to her partner. 'Jamesy, give this wee girl a turn round the floor.'

'No really, it doesn't matter,' Sheila protested, but Jamesy was already on his feet and holding out his hand. She turned to Charles who looked away. What was she to do? The band had changed tempo for the next dance – the jitterbug, her favourite. She let Jamesy lead her on to the floor and they went for it – the newest dance craze to cross the Atlantic. She'd learned how to do it at the American bases when she was singing and she was pretty sure that between them, she and Jamesy cut quite a rug.

She returned to the table flushed and laughing, and soon she was chatting to Sadie and Jamesy and their friends Albert and Doreen. Charles seemed happy enough to be in their company, but Sheila noticed that he hadn't much to say. Later, when Sadie passed round a cigarette packet, Charles shook his head and said, 'We don't smoke.'

'Are you sure you don't want one? I work at Gallaher's. Get them free, so I do. What about you, Sheila? Why don't you try one?'

Sheila had always thought women who smoked looked self-assured and she often thought she would try one sometime, so why not now? Without a look at Charles she took the cigarette and put it to her lips. Between them, Jamesy and Albert made sure Sheila got plenty of dances. Of course, every time there was a waltz she tried to get Charles on to the floor, but each time he refused. Then out of the blue he took her hand and whispered, 'Come with me.'

He led her away from the dance floor, through the tangerine

entrance hall, and out into the night. 'Where are we going?' she asked. 'What about my coat?'

'Hush,' he said and they went down the steps towards the gardens at the front of the hall. By the light of the half moon, Sheila could make out shimmering water, a path and benches where couples, having escaped the dance hall, were kissing and courting. Charles pulled her on to a bench under the shadow of a tree and wrapped his arms around her. 'I'll keep you warm,' he said and kissed her fiercely, holding her so tight she could hardly breathe. She pulled away from him. 'Charles—'

'I'm sorry, Sheila, I couldn't stand it any longer, watching you dancing with those strangers. I had to take you away so that we could be alone.'

'It's just dancing, Charles, it doesn't mean anything. It's just a bit of fun.'

'I know, I know,' he said, 'but I want to have you to myself. There now, rest your head against my shoulder.'

Sheila relaxed into the cradle of his arms and closed her eyes. He traced the outline of the little cap sleeves on her dress. 'I think of you when I play my cello,' he told her and his voice soothed her. His finger played across the sweetheart neckline as he hummed a melody and she felt herself drifting. 'Some nights I dream I play you,' he said, and bent his head and kissed her softly. 'Sheila … open your eyes.'

She could barely see his face in the shadows, but she could hear the intensity in his voice. 'My darling,' he said. 'Will you marry me?'

Sheila couldn't sleep. Her head was full of images, sounds and sensations: the loud music; the crowds of people; the company of strangers. But most of all it was Charles' touch – trailing his fingers over her skin, his mouth on hers – that stopped her heart and made her sit bolt upright in bed. Then his words would come again: 'Some nights I dream I play you.' Strange words to thrill her. Then the panic would begin. She had gone to the Floral Hall to have some fun and had come home with a proposal of marriage. She hadn't known what to say to him, but Charles had been so understanding. 'I know you're only seventeen and I want you to take your time and think about it. I love you so much and I think maybe you love me too?' His voice lifted in expectation, but she couldn't say the words he wanted to hear. 'Of course, we couldn't marry right away,' he hurried on. 'We'd wait until the war is over and I qualify as a teacher.'

It was still dark when she heard her mother creeping downstairs to get the range going. It was Sunday morning so she would let them have a lie-in until it was time to get ready for church. Sheila thought about going down to tell her mother about Charles' proposal, but something stopped her. She looked across at Peggy fast asleep, then got up and went into Pat's bedroom, sat on the bed and shook her gently.

Pat shrugged her off. 'Go away,' she said. 'I'm asleep.'

'I need to talk to you,' Sheila whispered.

Pat opened one eye. 'It'd better be important; waking me up at this hour on a Sunday.' She turned over and propped herself on one elbow.

'It's about Charles,' said Sheila and she told Pat about the proposal, leaving out the kissing and courting in the gardens, of course.

'Do you love him?'

The same question she had been asking herself all night. 'I think I do.'

'But you're not sure?'

'Yes, yes, I do love him.' There, she'd said it. 'I was just taken by surprise.'

'Has he said he loves you?'

'Yes.'

'And did you believe him?'

Sheila thought about his fierce kisses and his desire to have her all to himself. 'Yes, yes, I'm sure he loves me.'

'Go back to bed for now,' said Pat. 'Don't say anything to Mammy or Peggy just yet. We'll have our breakfast and go to church as usual; that'll give you a bit of time to think. Then when we come home, the four of us could talk about it. What do you think?'

Sheila nodded. 'Could you tell Mammy? I don't want …'

'That's fine, I'll explain to begin with, but then you'll need to speak up for yourself. It's your future we're talking about after all.'

Throughout Pat's explanation about the proposal, Sheila didn't look anyone in the eye, but sat twisting her fingers in her lap. When Pat finished, the girls instinctively waited for their mother to speak first.

'Hmm,' was all Martha said and she continued to stare at her youngest daughter, noticing the flush of embarrassment on her neck. The first time she had met Charles Turner, Martha had taken to him – hadn't he good manners and, by all accounts, good prospects? She had dared to hope that Charles might take an interest in Sheila, but this sudden proposal was unexpected, unsettling. She was only seventeen after all.

'Do you think he really meant to propose?' she said, 'or was it something he just came out with … in the heat of the moment?' Almost at once Martha regretted her choice of words. Sheila's face turned bright red and Martha herself flushed.

'He meant it all right,' said Sheila, 'but he said he didn't want an answer right away, he wanted me to think about it carefully, said I should talk to my family.'

'I see' – Martha paused again – 'and it would be a long engagement?'

'Yes, we'll both be working at the Academy and saving up. It'll take him a while to qualify so it could be three years.'

'Are you sure you really love him?' asked Peggy. 'Don't forget all those other boys out there that you haven't met. You could find someone else – someone even better.' The others looked at her, unsure of her point. 'What I mean is, you haven't known him that long to be sure he's the one.'

'I've known him six months. Irene hardly knew Sandy at all when she married him,' said Sheila.

Martha wasn't sure that helped the argument. 'What do you think, Pat?'

'I think Charles Turner is a nice boy, but in the end, Sheila, it's you who has to decide whether or not to marry him.'

Peggy didn't know what to think about Sheila's proposal. On the one hand, she wanted her little sister to be happy, but on the other she was worried that Sheila was far too young to properly judge whether Charles was the one for her. Sheila had no experience of men and their slippery ways. Mammy might think he was a good catch, but she didn't know much about the modern man either. Anyway, it would be foolish of any daughter to marry on the recommendation of their mother.

When Peggy arrived at work on Monday, she discussed her misgivings with Esther while they dusted every instrument and wireless in the shop. 'If she loves him she should marry him,' said Esther. 'I tell you, I wouldn't hesitate for a moment if Reuben asked me to marry him.'

'But what about all the other men out there? He might not be the best of the bunch and then you're stuck with him.'

'It's funny, isn't it,' said Esther. 'Irene's married, Pat's engaged, and soon Sheila will be too. Just think, it could end up with just you and your mother.' Peggy turned, duster in hand, to stare at Esther who was busy polishing a flute, and delivered a quick smack to the back of her head.

Mr Goldstein was in his office on the telephone, organising several Barnstormers' concerts for the newly arrived British Army regiments. He wandered into the shop mid-morning and informed them that he was expecting someone to discuss the arrangements. He gave them a stern look and told them the visitor must be shown into the office immediately.

Peggy had just put the latest Glenn Miller on the gramophone and was humming along to the music when the door opened and there stood Archie Dewer, smiling broadly.

'Ah, Peggy, Esther – my favourite shop girls.'

Esther giggled and Peggy glared at him. 'You've got a nerve coming in here,' she said.

'Not at all – I'm expected I believe.'

'Of course,' said Esther. 'My uncle says you're to go straight in.'

But instead of going to the office, Archie crossed the shop in a couple of strides to Peggy and whispered in her ear. She ignored him, but he just laughed and headed for Goldstein's office.

At dinnertime, Peggy said she didn't feel so well and would go for a walk to clear her head. The Café Royal was packed when she went in, with a mixture of businessmen, wealthy women with their shopping and army officers. She saw him immediately, towards the back, smiling and waving at her as though they were the best of friends. The table was small and very close to other diners, no doubt chosen so that she wouldn't dare to say what she wanted to say to him. He stood up and bent to kiss her cheek, but she turned away and sat down. Sitting opposite him, her first thought was that he was more handsome than ever; then she noticed there were extra pips on his shoulders.

'Been promoted, have you?' she said.

'Ah, yes. A good excuse to buy a new uniform, not that I needed an excuse you understand. No, in fact it was a necessity. Can you believe it – some blighter stole my tunic?' He lowered his voice. 'What did you do with it, by the way?'

Peggy tried hard not to smile.

He put on a stern voice. 'It's a criminal offence to steal an officer's uniform. I could have you arrested.'

'Attempting seduction by plying a girl with champagne is a worse offence in my book,' said Peggy.

He acknowledged the point with a wry smile. 'But there were mitigating circumstances, your honour.'

'Were there indeed? Maybe you'd care to explain.'

Archie leaned across the table. 'The girl was so very beautiful that I lost my head. I meant no harm. I made a terrible mistake and I promise never to do anything like that again.'

Peggy sighed and shook her head.

Archie went on, 'And can I say, given another chance, I would make it up to her.'

At that moment a waitress appeared with a menu and he flashed her a smile. 'Two cups of coffee and two of your splendid toasted teacakes, please.' He turned back to Peggy. 'Well, what's your verdict? Am I a condemned man about to have his last meal of teacakes?'

The thing about Archie Dewer, thought Peggy as she walked back to the music shop, was that you couldn't stay angry with him for long – he was such good company. He was clever and funny and he made her feel that she was the only person in the world that he wanted to be with. Oh, she hadn't let him off lightly. She made him promise that there would be no repeat of his low, louche behaviour and she only agreed to go to the Grand Opera House with him to see *Me and My Girl* if he did everything she told him to.

Sheila sat in a cafe just round the corner from the Royal Academy, and waited for Charles to arrive. No one at the school knew that they had been spending time together over the past few months and Charles had been keen to keep things that way. He had instructed Sheila to leave for her dinner at twelve and make her way to the café and he would follow her ten minutes later. She was very uneasy about giving him an answer to his proposal in such a public place, but he had assured her that, whatever she decided, he would respect her wishes.

She had hardly slept the night before with everything spinning in her head. Charles was a lovely, gentle person and she didn't doubt for a minute that he loved her – his kisses and caresses told her that. But marriage was for ever and, now she'd found Charles to love her and take care of her, there would be no need ever to fall in love again. That morning she had eaten her breakfast porridge thinking she would say no, on the bus to work she thought she might say yes, but as the morning wore on she panicked and had no idea what her answer would be.

She smoothed the tablecloth and rearranged the condiments and watched the door and decided. She'd tell him she needed more time. And suddenly he was there, coming towards her with his lovely smile. He touched her shoulder and her heart missed a beat. He slid into the seat opposite her looking so nervous.

'Tell me,' he said. 'Tell me quickly.'

And she took his hand and the words tumbled out. 'Yes, Charles, I'll marry you.'

Chapter 15

Throughout the bleak winter of 1943, the Battle of the Atlantic raged, and on the shores of Lough Erne the flying boats came and went by day and by night. Flying hundreds of miles out over the ocean, their mission was to protect the convoys of ships from attack by German U-boats. Losses among Allied ships, with their precious cargo of food and fuel, mounted and the greatest fear was that the country would be starved into submission.

New squadrons of British, Canadian and American pilots and crew arrived and the camp at Castle Archdale grew and grew. Ground and air crews slept in shifts with little respite from the gruelling routine.

Irene, only a few miles down the road from the base, saw less and less of Sandy. Occasionally, he would turn up at Dorothy's house on his motorbike to spend an hour with her. But each time, he looked more and more exhausted and had little to say beyond asking her how she was and sitting with her, his head on her shoulder and his hand stroking the bump that was their unborn child. But on one of his visits, just two weeks from Irene's due date at the end of March, he seemed much brighter. They lay on the bed together and Sandy told her that he would be allowed to leave the base to come and see her and the baby once it was born, provided he could get someone to cover his shift. He was so excited.

'I don't mind if it's a girl or boy, but if it's a girl I hope she takes after you, because you're beautiful. I don't tell you that often enough, do I?'

Irene smiled. 'And I hope he or she will be clever like you.'

'You know, when the war's over the first thing we'll do is visit my family way in the north of Scotland. You'll meet them all and I'll show you round the town. Och, it's only a wee fishing port ...'

'Do you miss it?'

'I didn't used to, but now I have you and soon the baby will be here, I don't know – it seems so important now.' He laughed. 'Of course, you won't understand a word they say, but that won't matter. They'll love you as much as I do.'

Irene had made her decision to stay in Fermanagh knowing full well that she wouldn't see much of Sandy, but she counted herself lucky that Dorothy was such good company and the two of them had become firm friends. She also learned a great deal about looking after children. She bathed them, changed nappies, sang and played with them and became more and more excited at the thought that soon she would be nursing her own child.

A week before the baby was due, the doctor, an elderly man with not a hint of a bedside manner, called on Irene and spent quite a while feeling the way the baby was lying, tutting every now and again. Irene watched his face for any clue as to what was going on. Eventually, he spoke. 'Now here's one with no hurry to see the light of day.'

'What do you mean?' Irene hardly dared ask.

'Breech, missus, breech.'

'I don't understand.'

'The baby's head is up and its legs are down. So it'll be coming feet first if we can't persuade it to change its position.' He shook his head. 'Trouble is there's not a lot of room for manoeuvring.'

'Will it matter if it comes feet first?'

He looked at her as though she was daft. 'Let's just say it wasn't the way God intended babies to be born.'

Irene was frightened now. 'So what's going to happen?'

111

In reply, the doctor took off his jacket and hung it behind the door. 'I'll have to try and persuade it to move,' he said, and rolled up his shirt sleeves. The next ten minutes were quite simply the worst of Irene's life as the doctor tried to manipulate the baby, grasping and pulling at unseen limbs, pushing upwards, twisting downwards, until her stomach was heaving.

At last the doctor stood back, sweat rolling down his face. 'It's no good,' he said. 'You've a stubborn one there – it's just not for turning.'

Irene could feel the panic rising in her chest. 'What's going to happen? How will it come out?'

'Well, maybe the manipulation I've done might give it a bit more room and it'll turn of its own accord. There's a week until the confinement date, so there's still time.' He took his jacket from behind the door and put it on. 'I'll call again in a few days.'

When he had gone, Dorothy came upstairs to find Irene lying on her back, her face wet with tears. 'What in God's name is the matter?' she asked.

'He said the baby's the wrong way up. He tried to turn it round.'

Dorothy was very calm. 'Breech, is it?'

'Aye,' said Irene, 'he said it might turn itself, but what'll happen if it doesn't?' and she reached out and grabbed Dorothy's arm.

'Now then, there's plenty of time yet,' said Dorothy. 'Sure, I've known women have a breech birth and everything was fine. What you need is a strong cup of tea.'

When Ethel came home from work, she sat Irene down and explained exactly what it meant to have a breech birth and reassured her that the majority of breech babies either turned or were born naturally and, failing that, there were other procedures that would be explained to her if they were needed.

Irene lay in bed that night listening to Ethel across the room snoring gently and waiting for sleep to come. She cradled the baby's shape with her arms and prayed that the child would be safe. 'I wouldn't mind about dying,' she told it, 'if it means that you will live.' And, as if in answer, she felt a knee or an elbow move across her stomach from one side to the other. Maybe the child was turning already. Then there was another sensation, one she had never experienced, and she knew exactly what it was.

She got out of bed and walked across the room to wake Ethel. 'I think the contractions have started. What should I do? Ethel, what should I do?'

'Just stay calm, Irene. Now tell me, have you felt them before now?'

'I've had a few twinges, but nothing as strong as this.'

Over the next two hours Ethel monitored Irene's contractions as they increased in strength and frequency and when she judged that her labour was sufficiently advanced she said, 'Right, I'm going to leave you for a moment to speak to Dorothy. She'll fetch the doctor; he'll be here in no time.'

It was nearly an hour before Dorothy returned, not with the doctor but in an RAF staff car.

'What's going on? Where's the doctor?' asked Ethel.

'He was called out to somebody with a heart attack. I didn't know what to do so I ran to the base at Castle Archdale thinking they'd come with their ambulance and take Irene to hospital. But there's some sort of emergency – something to do with a plane coming down. All hell's broke loose there, but thank God one of the senior officers was being driven to the military hospital at Necarne and he agreed to stop off to pick up Irene. The car's outside.'

Ethel helped Irene to her feet. 'Time to go,' she said. 'Your baby's going to be delivered by an American, so it is.'

Irene lay on the back seat of the car with her head on Ethel's lap, while they sped along the pitch-black country lanes for what seemed like an eternity. She had no idea whether they were driving so fast because of her condition or whether there was another reason to do with the plane. In any event, she was terrified.

The car screeched to a halt behind two military ambulances and bright light spilled from the front doors of the hospital, in defiance of the blackout. Medical personnel were carrying stretchers out of the ambulances and running into the building. The senior officer had already left the car, leaving Ethel and the driver to support Irene as she walked into the deserted entrance hall.

'Where is everyone?' Ethel asked the driver.

'A Sunderland came down with ten crew on board. They were returning to base when one of the engines froze and it flipped upside down. Pilot managed to right it, but it crash-landed in a peat bog over near Belleek.'

Just then a nurse crossed the hallway and Ethel ran after her. 'I've a pregnant woman here gone into labour – a breech birth. Her contractions are coming fast and she's going to need help.'

The nurse shook her head. 'I'm sorry, we haven't anyone to see to her at the moment. Staff are dealing with the airmen who have just arrived – most of them are in a bad way. We're trying to get all medics in from their billets.'

At that moment there was a groan from Irene and she doubled up as another contraction began.

'Have you at least a bed she can lie on?' Ethel pleaded.

The nurse was torn between rushing off to where she was needed and her desire to do something to help. 'Through that door.' She pointed. 'Second room on the left, there's a bed there and I'll send someone as soon as I can, but I warn you it might be some time.'

As part of her nursing training Ethel had witnessed several births and read all she needed to know to pass her exams, but she had never delivered a baby on her own, breech or otherwise. She made Irene comfortable, checked her blood pressure and prayed that someone would come soon. There was another contraction – a ten-minute interval this time – and when it passed Irene slumped back on the bed. Ethel found a cloth and rinsed it in cold water and wiped Irene's face, arms and hands, then encouraged her to lie back to conserve her energy for the next one. Shortly after, there was the sound of a commotion in the hall and Ethel, now desperate for help, rushed out of the room. Two young men wearing leather jackets, one with a motorcycle helmet in the crook of his arm, were standing inside the door and a doctor was speaking to them about the plane crash. Then he said to one of them, 'I need you urgently in the operating theatre; get scrubbed up quick as you can. As for you' – he turned to the second man – 'there's a woman somewhere in the hospital about to give birth in the middle of all this mayhem. See if you can find her and do what you can.'

'She's in here,' shouted Ethel and the man, who didn't look more than twenty-five, followed her into the room where Irene was clearly having another contraction. He took one look at her and began pulling off his motorcycle gear, asking questions as he did so.

'Time between contractions?'

'Five minutes,' answered Ethel and she gave him an update on Irene's blood pressure.

'You a nurse?'

'Yes, at Castle Archdale.'

'Head engaged?'

'No, it's breech.'

Ethel saw him swear under his breath, but by the time he was stripped to his medic greens his voice was calm and reassuring as he spoke to Irene.

'What's your name?'

'Irene,' she answered, her eyes wide with fright.

'Well, Irene, I'm Doctor Dennis Morello, United States Medical Corps, and I think your baby will be born before too long. What I need is for you to listen carefully and do what I tell you. Okay?'

And Irene just had time to nod before another contraction wracked her body.

Dr Morello spoke quickly to Ethel. 'Outside here, end of the corridor – a storeroom. Grab everything we'll need for a breech birth, and bring oxygen.' He turned again to Irene. 'The baby's legs are coming.'

Everything happened so quickly after that. The body came and the doctor told Irene, 'Listen carefully, I'm going to do a manoeuvre now to deliver the head.'

Chapter 16

It was pension day and Martha was up early to get her housework done before the post office opened. She had been meaning to black-lead the range for a while, but she'd put it off until a good morning with plenty of light, so she could see what she was doing. By nine o'clock the range gleamed shiny black and it took no more than ten minutes to run a damp cloth over the floor. She washed her face and hands, combed her hair, put on her hat and coat and set off. The postmistress, a stout woman with a cast in her eye, was always pleasant enough and this week she asked again as she had for the past three weeks, 'Any sign of that grandchild of yours coming yet, Mrs Goulding?'

'No, but sure it'll come when it's good and ready,' she said, and she took her ten shillings pension and put it in her purse, before adding, 'maybe by the next time I see you.'

Martha's favourite shop, Joan's Wool and Haberdashery, was a fair walk down the Oldpark Road and she never failed to feel a wee rush of excitement as she pushed open the door and went inside to the sound of the bell ringing. There was a whole wall of little wooden cubbyholes containing shanks of wool, each one a different colour, from the darkest near the door across the whole spectrum of colour and finishing with white near the till. In the middle of the shop was a sturdy table with knitting pattern books neatly set out and a couple of chairs where customers could sit while they browsed the Fair Isle and Aran, the V-necked pullovers and the lacy cardigans. Joan herself was to be found by following the click, click of the needles to the large armchair behind the counter where she spent her days knitting to order for women who had money to burn.

Joan looked up as Martha came in and greeted her with, 'Did you manage to finish that wee matinee coat with the fancy pattern?'

Martha gave a little smile of pride. 'Indeed I did. Wouldn't let it beat me, so I stayed up till two in the morning.'

'Well, I hope this child appreciates all that's been done for it. Now, what are you after today?'

'I'll need a yard of quarter-inch yellow ribbon to finish off the coat and the bootees,' said Martha, 'and I was wondering maybe about a shawl for the christening.'

'Ach, there's some lovely patterns, so there is. The crochet ones are best and they don't take as long.' Joan began leafing through one of the pattern books. 'There you are,' she said, 'the three-ply wool in white makes it look fine and delicate; better than you'd find in Arnott's,' and she added, '– if it hadn't been bombed, of course.'

'I'm not sure about the white,' said Martha. 'Shows all the dirt, doesn't it?'

'Traditional christening shawl we're talkin' here – family heirloom,' said Joan. 'Wrap the child in it a few hours for the service then put it away in brown paper for the next one. Think about it, your handiwork could still be in use for your great-grandchildren.'

Martha paused then, for she had never imagined such a thing. And before she knew it she had bought the pattern and six shanks of soft white wool and couldn't wait to get back up the Oldpark to start.

When she came in the back door she put the kettle on and, while it boiled, she sat at the table to look again at the pattern. Then suddenly she was on her feet, through the front room and out into the hall. She'd forgotten to look to see if there was any post. A single letter lay on the mat. She recognised Irene's writing immediately and took it through to the kitchen. She set it unopened on the table while she made her tea and all the while her heart was racing – for this letter might be the one to change their lives.

The neck end of lamb simmering on the range filled the kitchen with a mouth-watering meaty smell. The blue potatoes still in their skins were boiling away and the carrot and turnips were ready to be mashed. Sheila was the first home and she was setting the table when Pat and Peggy came in.

'Smells good, Mammy,' said Pat.

'Been out spending your coupons and pension have you?' Peggy laughed.

'Never mind making fun, you should be grateful you're coming home to food on the table. There's plenty of people who aren't as well fed or looked after as you. Now, sit yourselves down.'

Martha wouldn't dream of telling them about Irene's letter until they had eaten. Decent food was hard to come by and needed to be appreciated. Besides, Irene's letter and the news it contained would cause such uproar that the food would most certainly be forgotten and allowed to go cold. Instead, she let the girls chatter about their day as they usually did and kept the letter in her apron.

'There's been a lot going on today at Stormont with the big noises,' said Pat. 'Meetings behind closed doors, government ministers you hardly ever see coming and going in their grand cars. Word is the prime minister might resign.'

'What, Andrews? Sure, why would he go when he's got the best job in the country?' said Peggy. 'Plenty of money for telling other people what to do.'

'I think he's too old,' said Pat. 'We'd be better off with Basil Brooke, if you ask me.'

'Oh, here we go, Pat Goulding leading the charge for Brooke again.'

'I'm telling you, Peggy, he's the only one in the building talking about rebuilding this city and looking after those that have nothing.'

'Oh, spare us the politics again. Now I'll tell you something interesting. Mr Goldstein's going to start booking three shows a week instead of two. There are more servicemen in Northern Ireland than there's ever been and, because there are no bombing raids for the moment, people are going out to be entertained. He gets requests from all over the place for the Barnstormers to perform. He'll be on the lookout for new acts and he's already told Esther and Reuben they'll have a permanent spot in the show.'

'That'll be because they played so well for General Eisenhower.'

Peggy rolled her eyes, but Pat went on, 'Maybe he might want me to sing a few arias. Did I tell you what the general said to me?'

'Yes!' said Peggy and Sheila in unison and Martha added, 'Several times. Now finish eating and I'll tell you my news too.'

The table was cleared and Martha took the letter from her apron.

'It's from Irene, isn't it?' shouted Sheila. 'Has she had the baby? Has she, Mammy?'

Martha looked at the anxious faces of her daughters and nodded. Instantly, they were on their feet, jumping up and down, screaming and laughing and hugging each other. Then the questions: 'When? … What is it, a boy or a girl? … Is Irene all right? … When's she coming home?'

Martha tried to keep calm and dabbed her eyes a little. 'It's all in the letter, so it is, but Irene can tell it better than me.' And she took the letter from the envelope, smoothed out the pages and began to read. Truth be told, she knew every word by heart, so many times had she read it since she opened it that morning.

Dear Mammy, Pat, Peggy and Sheila,

The baby has been born. A boy. He's the most beautiful child I've ever seen. He was born in the early hours of Monday at the Necarne hospital. It's an American hospital and an American doctor delivered him. I didn't have him at home because there was a complication called breech birth, but the doctor knew how to fix it.

When I went to the hospital there was a big emergency because a plane had crashed and everybody was helping with the air crew, but the doctor stayed with me. Sandy came to see me and the baby as soon as he could. He couldn't get away earlier because of the crash. I waited until he arrived to name the baby. He is called Alexander after the brave pilot in the plane, and Dennis after the doctor who delivered him.

Alexander Dennis weighs 7 pounds and has blue eyes and lots of black hair, but my friend Dorothy says that all babies have blue eyes at first. I have to stay in hospital for a week then I'll go back to Dorothy's. I wish you could all see Alexander. Maybe someone can come and visit me.

Yours truly, with love from
Irene
xx

When everyone had calmed down, the talk of Irene and the baby continued.

'Mammy, I think you should go and visit Irene right away,' said Sheila, and Pat and Peggy agreed.

Martha desperately wanted to go, but she hesitated. 'It's an awful long way to Fermanagh and I don't know where I could stay. Sure, Irene's living with people and I don't think they'd have the room for me?'

'Look,' said Pat, 'Irene's in hospital for the best part of a week. Why don't you send a letter tomorrow and ask if you could come and visit her once she's out of hospital? I'm sure there must be somewhere you could stay.'

'And you could give her all the things you've knitted for the baby and we could buy a present for him and you could take it,' said Sheila.

'What do you think, Mammy?' asked Pat.

And Martha said simply, 'I think I'd like to see my grandson.'

Martha quickly answered Irene's letter, asking if there was anywhere she could stay, and a week later she stepped off the train on to the crowded platform at Enniskillen station. Irene had replied that she could stay at Dorothy's house if she didn't mind it being a bit cramped. She added that they were quite a way out of the town but that Davey, their neighbour, would pick her up from the train station.

The people milling around were loaded up with just about anything that could be raised or cultivated: a man had a bale of hay on his shoulders; a woman carried a wicker basket with live chicks inside. There were crates of onions, cabbages and turnips stacked on the platform. A pedlar went by with all his wares hanging from two stout poles.

Good grief, thought Martha, it's as bad as the Twelfth of July. How on earth would she recognise the fellow they said would collect her? She squeezed through the crowds and emerged at the front of the station. The street outside was just as busy and then she heard someone call her name. A man was waving at her from across the street. 'Mrs Goulding,' he shouted, 'over here!' She crossed the road to where he was standing by a horse and cart and with a touch of his cap he acknowledged her, then laced his hands for her to climb up on to the cart.

'How did you know it was me?' she asked when he joined her.

'Ach, sure, you can tell a city woman easy enough among all these country folk,' he said. 'Anyway, you're carrying a suitcase and not something you've bought on market day.' And he took the reins and clicked his tongue and the horse trotted off away from the crowds and out of the town.

Davey was easy company. He told her his farm was close to Dorothy's house and, seeing as he was coming into Enniskillen anyway to bring vegetables, fish and rabbits to the market, he was happy to have company on his way home. Something about him reminded Martha of Vincent, a farmer she had met in Dungannon when Sheila was evacuated there. Maybe it was the ruddy cheeks or the soft country lilt of his voice that set her at her ease on the long road to Castle Archdale.

The late March afternoon was drawing in when they turned on to a narrow lane and followed it up an incline to a faded white cottage with a steep thatched roof. They were still a good way from it when the door flew open and Irene ran out to greet her, laughing and hugging her. Martha saw at once how Irene had filled out, which was a good sign after having a child, and what's more her skin glowed with health. She thanked God that her daughter was looking so well.

Martha came into the house and, as her eyes adjusted to the dim interior, she saw a good-sized room with an open fire and smelled the turf. She was introduced to Dorothy, a comely girl with a toddler on her hip and her little girl holding on to her mother's skirt. 'You're very welcome, Mrs Goulding. I hope you'll take us as you find us, we're not very grand,' she said shyly.

'Never you worry yourself,' said Martha. 'I'm just glad to be here and it's very good of you to put me up.'

'Come on, Mammy.' Irene grabbed her arm. 'Come and see Alexander, he's upstairs. Bring your case and I'll show you where you're sleeping.'

Martha's heart was palpitating. She never thought she would feel the excitement of this moment so physically. The room under the eaves was just catching the rosy light of the setting sun and next to one of the beds was a wooden crib. Irene bent down and lifted the baby out, speaking softly to him. 'Look, Alexander, someone very special has come to see you.' And she brought the little bundle in a blanket to show her mother.

Martha gazed upon the most perfect little face. Did she know this face? Something there was familiar: the almond-shaped eyes; the tiny Cupid's bow mouth; the fine bones of his tiny fingers. He was a stranger newly arrived in the world, but she did know him and his focused look told her that he recognised her too. Irene passed the child to her mother. Martha had no words to express her feelings. It was enough just to look at him. Irene was talking about the birth and his sleeping and feeding, but Martha just gazed at his face and whispered, 'Hello, Alexander, I'm your gran.'

Chapter 17

With their mother still away in County Fermanagh, the Easter weekend gave the girls the opportunity for long lie-ins and the chance to skip church altogether on the Sunday. They got up around twelve and Sheila made a pot of porridge for them all.

'You can tell the weather's going to be good,' said Pat. 'We should make the most of it and go out somewhere for the day.'

'Do you remember that Easter when we went to the Waterworks and rolled our eggs and went on the boats?' said Peggy.

'Ach, you wouldn't want to go there now – it's a mess after the bombing,' said Sheila. 'What about Bellevue, or Bangor?'

'They'll be packed out for sure,' said Pat.

'I know where we can go,' said Peggy. 'We'll get dressed up and go down town to the Wings for Victory day. It'll be like a carnival, so it will, with plenty going on and we could treat ourselves to our tea after.'

In the centre of Belfast there was a vast empty space where shops and businesses had once stood, but after bombs fell in 1941 it had been cleared and was now known as Blitz Square. As they got off the bus, the girls heard the sound of a military band playing a Sousa march and saw in the distance the sun glinting off the planes lined up in the square.

'What does it mean, "Wings for Victory"?' asked Sheila.

'They're trying to get people to buy National Savings bonds, then they'll use the money to build more planes,' said Peggy.

'And it's planes like these that are keeping the Nazis at bay,' added Pat. 'People say they'll win the war for us and I think they will – in the air. But if you ask me, as time goes on, it'll be armies on the ground that'll put an end to this war.'

First they went to look at a Stirling bomber. Sheila stared in amazement: 'Is this the plane that Irene built?'

In reply, there was a familiar laugh from the cockpit and they looked up to see Macy's face staring down at them.

'Sure is!' she shouted. 'Why don't you climb up and take a look inside?'

One by one they climbed the steps, holding their skirts close around their legs, and at the top Macy reached out and helped them into the fuselage. She was dressed in her working clothes – trousers, checked shirt and turban; so different from the glamorous costumes she wore for the Barnstormers' concerts. 'I'll give you the tour of Belfast's finest,' she said. Sheila hung on Macy's every word, asked about the tools she used, touched the rivets, and gazed in awe at the cockpit instruments. 'It's incredible,' was all she kept saying. When they left Macy, Sheila decided she wanted to see inside every plane on display, but her sisters were content to wander around in the sunshine.

Pat noticed that the cathedral next to Blitz Square was open and people were going in and out. She'd never been in the cathedral, though she had walked past it many times. A sign at the door invited people to come in to pray for an end to the fighting and for the safety of all those serving in the war. She pulled open the door and stepped inside. She was amazed at the interior: the vast, arched roof supported by stone pillars soared high above her. She marvelled at the huge stained glass windows filling the space with light. Why had she never before been inside this beautiful building right in the centre of her city?

She walked the length of the nave, past people praying, and on towards the altar. How grand it all looked with the choir stalls, the altar, the pulpit topped by a gold eagle. Oldpark Presbyterian was nothing like this. She sat in a pew and allowed the peaceful atmosphere to wash over her. She prayed for all of those fighting in the war and pictured Tony's face in her mind's eye, imagining him in the heat and dust of North Africa. 'I'm here,' she whispered. 'Keep safe, my love.' Over and over the same words. 'I'm here, keep safe, my love.' She sat completely still with just his face and these words in her head until she believed he had heard her. She didn't know how long she sat there, but slowly she became aware of the coolness of her tears on her cheeks. It was time to go, but she knew she'd return.

She walked back down the nave towards the entrance and caught sight of an American uniform. The officer stood up and moved along the pew towards the aisle. 'Hello Patti, how you doin'?'

'Captain Walters, what a surprise.'

He fell into step alongside her. 'I came to look at the planes,' he said. 'They kinda reassure you, don't they? Then I saw the church was open and I thought it would be something to come in and say a prayer. It's a mighty fine church.'

'It is,' said Pat. 'It almost makes me think that God might be right here to catch our prayers.'

'Don't doubt it, Patti. He's here all right.'

'You must have a strong faith.'

He smiled. 'Southern Baptist – lapsed though, since I came over here. Might think of coming on a Sunday morning.'

Pat stopped walking. 'Captain Walters, can I ask you something?'

'Sure, fire away, but please call me Joe.'

Pat gave a quick smile to acknowledge his attempt to put her at her ease and went straight to the point.

'The North African campaign – will it be over soon?'

'Well, I really can't say …'

'Captain Farrelly's with the 34th and it's been a while since I've had a letter. I just wondered …'

He took a moment to measure his words. 'We're on the move pushing towards Tunis, I hear. Word is it's going well.'

'Thank you so much,' said Pat. 'I just needed …'

He touched her elbow. 'Patti, if there's anything I can do for you, you've only to ask.'

'You're very kind,' she said and they walked out into the sunshine.

Pat found Peggy at the makeshift stage where a band was playing and lots of people were dancing in the sunshine. She had already danced with quite a few people and had promised dances to several more, but the afternoon was drawing on and they decided to head to the NAAFI canteen set up in the square.

'Where do you think Sheila's got to?' asked Pat.

'Well, judging by the interest she's been showing in the planes, she's probably at the controls of one right now, looping the loop.'

'Over the Channel in a Spitfire as we speak!' said Pat, and they laughed.

Sheila joined them. 'What's so funny, you two?'

'Just making fun of you as usual,' said Peggy.

Pat noticed Sheila had some papers in her hand. 'What's that?' she said.

Sheila's face was suddenly animated. 'I've just been talking to this woman about the WAAF.' She held up the papers. 'And she gave me all this information. It sounds great.'

'The WAAF?'

'Women's Auxiliary Air Force. It's like the RAF but for women.'

'We know that,' said Peggy. 'They're the ones with the unflattering uniform, guaranteed to make them look like sacks of potatoes.'

'It's not that bad,' said Sheila. 'The hat's nice.'

Peggy wrinkled her nose. 'Nice? It looks like a mob cap with a peak.'

Sheila ignored her. 'Anyway, they're recruiting. The only trouble is I'm not quite old enough to join yet, but she says I can apply now if I want and I'll get my call-up papers in a few months.'

Her sisters looked at her as if she was mad. 'You can't join the Forces,' said Peggy.

'Yes I can. What's to stop me?'

Pat realised the conversation was racing out of control. 'Just slow down a minute, Sheila. There are two very good reasons why you can't join the WAAF. Number one, you've already got a good job at the Academy and number two, you're engaged to be married.'

'And why would you walk away from a very good life to join the Forces and be sent to God knows where?' Peggy added.

'Because I want to do something that helps bring this awful war to an end. Pat, you're always going on about your job; how you pushed the Water Board to get supplies connected after the bombing and how you organised free school milk. I don't want to sit in an office and file things for the rest of my life. I want to get out there and do something.'

'But what about Charles?' said Pat. 'You can't leave him now – you've only been engaged two minutes.'

'Why can't I? We aren't getting married till the war's over anyway. So I'll just tell him that I'm joining up. Look at it this way, he's a man and if he said he was going off to fight, nobody would bat an eyelid, would they?' Sheila looked at her sisters expecting a comeback, and when they said nothing she threw her hands up in triumph. 'There you are. You see my point, don't you? I've made my decision, I'm applying for the WAAF and nobody, but nobody, is going to change my mind.' And she stomped off.

Pat and Peggy watched her go, stunned at the conversation they'd just had. Eventually, Peggy shook her head. 'You realise there's another reason why she can't join the WAAF, don't you?'

Pat's face was blank.

'Because that'll be the end of the Golden Sisters.'

Pat looked at her in disbelief. 'The Golden Sisters. Is that all you can think of? Never mind that – what's Mammy going to say?'

Chapter 18

Martha lay on the truckle bed under the eaves listening to the little noises her grandson made as he woke. She could tell that Irene was still sleeping by the sound of her breathing so she got up, dressed quickly and went to the crib. Alexander's eyes were open and his mouth moved as if he was speaking to her. Martha picked him up, wrapped the blanket around him and carried him downstairs. Over the past month it had become their morning routine, an hour when he was all hers. She changed his nappy, gave him a bottle and all the while she talked to him. He was an intelligent child – she'd seen that in his eyes the first time she saw him. Of course, he didn't understand the words, but he was soothed by her voice and knew that he was safe and loved. She rocked him in her arms or carried him around the room and all the while she would tell him stories about his family: his mother, his aunts, his grandfather and the great city where they lived.

She told him that on the morning of his christening they were going to church and lots of people would come to see him. Aunt Pat would be there because she was going to be his godmother and his gran had made a beautiful shawl just for him – a family heirloom. She laid the child on her lap, his head resting on her knees as she gazed at his beautiful face. The thought of leaving him was a physical ache that brought tears to her eyes.

She had tried so hard to persuade Irene to bring the child home where he belonged. She had pleaded, argued and wept but Irene, stubborn as ever, wouldn't be moved. Oh, she could see the way of it, she understood Irene's decision. 'This is my family now – Sandy, Alexander and me,' she had said, but the words had cut Martha to the quick.

Martha always knew Sandy was a good man, and over the past month when she saw him with Irene and Alexander she could see the love in his eyes. He would be watching Irene with the baby and she would look up and catch him looking at her and right then Martha knew that Irene and the baby didn't need her.

She had decided that she would leave after the christening and travel back to Belfast with Pat. 'Ach Mammy, why don't you stay a bit longer?' Irene had said, and Martha knew that she genuinely meant it, but it was time for her to go.

The christening was held in Enniskillen Methodist Church in the centre of the town, an imposing building with a portico of four elegant columns. Little Alexander, in his much-admired shawl, didn't cry when the water from the font was trickled over his head. Pat had brought gifts from everyone, including a silver napkin ring from Aunt Kathleen engraved with the baby's initials. She also brought a camera, borrowed from Jack their next door neighbour, and she used up the whole film taking photographs of Alexander and the guests.

On the train home, Martha stared out the window and said very little. Pat thought it best to let her be for a while, but after half an hour she had to say something.

'Mammy, you can't be upset about Irene living in Fermanagh. You know that, don't you?'

'I'll be upset if I want.'

'You can visit her again, maybe in the summer.'

'I know that – I'm not stupid.'

'You need to think about yourself more. You've looked after all of us so well … I'm just saying there are so many things you could be doing, that you'd enjoy doing, without the worry of us.'

Martha looked at Pat as if she was mad and went back to gazing at the passing countryside. Pat could feel the tension emanating from her mother and said no more. Shortly after that, the train slowed as they came into a station and the guard walking the length of the platform shouted, 'Dungannon'. Martha watched the people get off then suddenly she stood up and grabbed her bag from the luggage rack.

'What are you doing?' asked Pat.

'I'm getting off.' She leant out of the window and opened the carriage door.

'You can't get off here.' But Martha was already on the platform and walking away. 'I'll come with you!' Pat shouted after her.

Martha stopped dead in her tracks and half-turned towards her daughter. 'No, you won't. I'm doing something I'll enjoy for once.'

'What? What are you going to do?' said Pat, and at that moment realised where her mother was going and sank back into her seat. The stationmaster closed the carriage door, blew his whistle and waved his flag, and the train pulled out of Dungannon station.

Up the hill and into the square, everything was just as Martha remembered it. Hard to believe it was two years ago that she had come to the town as a stranger looking for her daughter. How desperate she'd been that day. Sheila had been evacuated from Belfast and because of a series of misunderstandings Martha had heard nothing from her, and all attempts to find her through the authorities had failed. Frantic with worry, Martha had travelled to Dungannon and found Sheila, alive and well, living with the McManus family. Now here she was again in front of their shop, Frank McManus and Son, High Class Butchers and Slaughtermen, and memories of that bittersweet summer she and Sheila had spent with the family filled her head.

She had kept in touch with Bridie McManus, writing every few months, and their friendship had grown. Indeed, Bridie finished every letter with an invitation to come and stay with them again.

Do something you would enjoy, Pat had said. Well, she had only to cross the square.

Rose, Bridie's daughter, was in her usual place behind the counter and glanced up as the shop bell rang. Not a regular customer this woman in a felt hat, carrying a suitcase. Then she looked again. 'My goodness, is it you?' she shouted and ran from behind the counter to shake Martha's hand. 'Is Sheila not with you?' Without waiting for an answer she called out, 'Ma! Come and see who's here.'

The door at the back of the shop leading into the house opened and Bridie McManus, a large woman with a laboured gait, filled the doorway. 'Lord bless us all, Martha Goulding as I live and breathe. Come on in,' she said and led the way into the warm, cluttered kitchen. For a moment Martha was at a loss to explain why she was there. How could she turn up on the doorstep and expect a family to put her up? But she needn't have worried. Bridie saw the suitcase. 'Ah, you've come to visit us at last, have you? How long can you stay?'

'For a couple of days, if that's all right?'

'Of course it is. Stay as long as you like, if you don't mind being in that wee house out in the yard. Remember, where you and Sheila slept? It'll need a bit of a clean but—'

At that moment, there was the cry of a baby from upstairs. 'That'll be Celia awake,' said Rose. 'I'll go and get her.'

Martha's eyes lit up. 'So you're a grandmother at last, Bridie.'

'Indeed I am and what about your Irene?'

'She has a wee boy, Alexander, born in Fermanagh a month ago. I've been down staying with her and I was on my way back to Belfast when I decided to come and see you.'

'Ach, I'm so glad you did. Both of us grandmothers now and plenty to catch up on. Tell you what, away you across the yard and get yourself settled while I see to the baby and make us somethin' to eat.'

The little whitewashed cottage was exactly as Martha remembered it. Just one room: hard earth for a floor; an open fire and next to it a bed. A place of her own for a while and time to think through the turmoil in her head.

Later, the two women sat in front of the fire with cups of strong tea and thick roast beef sandwiches, the like of which Martha hadn't seen since she was last in Dungannon and staying in a butcher's shop. While Celia dozed on Bridie's ample bosom, they talked about their grandchildren and before long Bridie, her head on one side, looked hard at Martha.

'God, it must have been a terrible wrench for you to leave that wee boy.'

Martha opened her mouth to deny the suggestion. It was not in her nature to share personal feelings, but the tears pricked her eyes when she tried to speak and it was a sob that escaped her lips. Bridie let her be and sat quietly. Martha wiped her eyes and gave herself a bit of a shake.

'I'm sorry, Bridie, I don't know what's the matter with me. But you're right, saying goodbye to the child was hard.'

'I know. Sure, you'd want to be a part of their lives and not be so far away.'

Martha stared at the fire. The turf shifted and sparks flew and died. 'They don't need me,' was all she said.

'Oh, they do need you, but not the same as before. They have to make their own way and they want you to be watching and proud of what they can do for themselves. And if something's not right, sure it'll be you they'll seek out for help, mark my words.'

Martha sighed. 'When I left Fermanagh, I didn't know what to do; I was at my wits' end. I couldn't face going back to that house of mine and the cooking and the cleaning. That's all those girls want me for. They're out all the time gallivanting here, there and everywhere with the singing, coming home in the dead of night and me lying there for hours worrying like an eejit.'

'I'm telling you, Martha, what you need is a wee break in the country with good food, good company and nobody to think of but yourself.'

Together they washed the dishes and the talk turned to Sheila. 'Ach, she's a great wee girl,' said Bridie, 'and no trouble at all to keep. We missed her when she went, Dermot especially.'

'They were a bit sweet on each other, weren't they?' Martha smiled.

'And now you're telling me she's engaged.'

'Thanks be to God for small mercies,' said Martha. 'She was a bit unsure, but in the end she took my advice. Young fellows like Charles don't come along very often. He's training for the teaching you know, musical too, and he dotes on our Sheila.'

'Well, there you are now, that's something to please you. Talking about good prospects, you've not asked me about me brother?'

Martha could feel the heat rising inside her and she hoped it wouldn't send one of those awful hot flushes across her face. 'I … I was just about to ask. How is Vincent?'

Bridie laughed. 'Would you believe it, he's courting a woman, a spinster, close to his age. She's a nurse at the cottage hospital, met her when he cut his hand badly on the flax.'

Martha picked up two plates and concentrated on drying them, not daring to look at Bridie who carried on chatting about the nurse. Martha heard not a word; she was too busy pushing aside an emotion she didn't recognise, but which threatened to overwhelm her. She couldn't let Bridie see her cry again, especially not over Vincent. Dear God, she thought, what's the matter with me? But the memory of that day with Vincent when he took her out in the pony and trap flooded back. She had known that he had feelings for her and she let herself be kissed, let him confess his love. But her heart had been too set in her widow ways and she couldn't respond. She had cherished that memory ever since, that feeling of being loved, but now it was spoiled and he loved another.

'Our Vincent had a bit of a notion for you, didn't he, but sure that wasn't to be. You're a Belfast woman through and through, Martha. You'd never have settled in the back of beyond.'

Chapter 19

In those early days of May, Martha fell into a routine to fit around the McManus family. She would wake early in her cottage and cross the yard to make a batch of soda bread for their breakfast. After that she would go for a long walk, striking out towards some neighbouring village and returning at dinnertime. She offered to serve in the shop so that Rose could spend more time with Celia and, after a few days learning the cuts of meat and how to use the bacon slicer, she was behind the counter each afternoon. In the evenings she sat a while with Bridie talking and doing a bit of sewing and went early to bed. With each day that passed, Martha felt her agitation and tendency to tears fade. She wrote to her girls to say she was fine and enjoying her visit to Bridie's and told them the weather was good, so she might stay another week or so. She almost added an instruction to make sure the house was cleaned and the vegetable garden weeded, but she didn't.

She began to think of the morning walks as a sort of spring cleaning of her mind – each aspect of her life like a room – discarding things no longer needed, polishing precious things and rearranging it all to make it seem fresh and new. One morning she sat on a low hill with a view across to the Sperrin Mountains and sifted through her thoughts about the war – the hardships and sadness and fear – trying to make sense of what she and her family had been through. They had come a long way and they weren't through it yet, but since the Americans joined the fight it was clear that the war would be won eventually. Life would return to normal, they'd have enough to eat, coal to keep them warm, decent clothes to wear.

On some walks she'd think of her daughters and try to put away her frustrations with them to concentrate on everything that she loved and admired about them. In her mind, she'd step back and look at them. Aye, they were good girls, right enough. And what of herself, what should she let go of? What did she have to cherish? Did her life need to be rearranged?

On a perfect morning, with a huge blue sky and the sound of birdsong, she stopped to lean on a five-bar gate and take in the land that stretched for miles on either side of the hawthorn hedgerows. Little hills, drumlins, sat like pebbles scattered across the landscape, with a patchwork of tiny fields undulating up and over them. Martha opened the gate and walked through the green shoots of unripe oats. Close to the edge of the field stood a magnificent sycamore tree. She realised she knew this place, had been sitting underneath that sycamore when she first met Vincent three summers before.

Bridie was right about Martha, of course. She would never have settled on a farm, never have left her girls for a man. She knew that herself when he courted her; knew the moment he declared his love that she would say no. But Vincent's love and that igniting of desire within her was something to be cherished – it was the first time since she was a young woman that she had felt such a yearning.

Martha was happy to admit she had always been a woman who was plainly dressed, some might say a little old fashioned. When she left Belfast to visit Irene, Peggy had insisted she take something 'a bit dressier', as she put it, for the christening. She tried on a few of the girls' dresses and finally decided on a cotton print with soft green leaves. It had a revere collar, like a blouse, a thin belt and the skirt was slightly flared.

'My goodness,' said Pat when Martha tried it on, 'it takes years off you.'

'Not mutton dressed as lamb?'

'No, of course not – it's suitable for a woman of your age. I'd tell you if it wasn't.'

And Martha had enjoyed wearing the dress for the christening, and the compliments she received. Now, she had an opportunity to wear it again to a hooley – a going-away party for Bridie's nephew who was leaving to work in America.

'It's a chance to say goodbye to the boy,' Bridie told her. 'Who knows when he'll be back, if ever. There'll be a bit of food and a few drinks. It'll be great craic.'

The house was a good size, double-fronted with a garden out the back. There were already lots of people there when they arrived and many of them acknowledged Martha. Some recognised her as the woman from Belfast who had stayed with Bridie before, while others knew her from serving in the shop. They were such friendly people, with plenty of chat and good humour, that she felt quite at home. There was a fine spread of food and Bridie's husband Frank had brought a big ham and a side of roast beef to carve. Martha spotted Vincent and went to say hello to him. He seemed a little shy, but she asked how he was and he told her that he was grand and was walking out with a lady.

'I know – Bridie told me and I'm really happy for you, Vincent.'

'Will ye come and meet her?' he said. 'She's out in the garden.'

Mary was a bonny-looking woman with a ready smile and it was clear she was smitten with Vincent. Martha could plainly see their happiness at finding one another and she wished them well. It didn't sadden her that she had no one – instead it warmed her heart to know that Vincent had found someone who would return his love.

The music began and, like all good hooleys, there was plenty of dancing and Martha didn't want for partners. If her daughters could have seen her dance the jigs and reels, heard her laughter as she was spun faster and faster, they would have been amazed. Never mind a different dress, a different outlook on life had taken years off her.

Soon it would be June and Martha began to wonder whether the grass in her garden would be knee high and whether the honeysuckle had climbed over the lean-to shed filling the evening air with scent. She loved being in Dungannon, but she missed her girls and now it was time to go home.

The night before Martha left she sat with Bridie in the kitchen drinking tea, the two of them putting the world to rights. 'Unsettled times we're livin' through,' said Bridie. 'And the young ones'll bear the brunt of it. But you can't tell them anything. They think we know nothin', but sure haven't we seen it all before?'

'You want to save them from making the same mistakes we did,' Martha said, 'but you can't, can you?'

They sat in silence a while nursing their tea, then Martha looked up and said, 'Do you still read the tea leaves, Bridie?'

'Aye, sometimes.'

Martha handed Bridie her empty cup. 'There you are, then. What can you see for me?'

Bridie rotated it three times, turned it upside down on the saucer and waited a few seconds. Then she took the cup and studied the patterns of tea leaves on the china.

'I see a friend, maybe an acquaintance, and death surrounds this person. They need your help.' Bridie frowned.

'What is it? What can you see?'

'No more than that, but be careful, Martha. Trust your instincts.'

As Martha came up her garden path, the unmistakable sound of *ITMA* on the wireless floated out through the open window – 'Shall I do you now, sir?' said Mrs Mopp, followed by howls of laughter so clear that Martha could distinguish the individual laughs of her daughters. She knocked on the window and watched the surprise on their faces when they saw her. Sheila was first on her feet to open the front door, but Pat and Peggy were close behind and then they were all laughing at once and Martha kissed and hugged each daughter. 'Mercy me,' she smiled, 'coming in the front door of my own house. It must be a special occasion.'

'Will I make you something to eat, Mammy?' said Pat. 'Egg on toast and I've a slice of my bacon ration left you can have.'

'That'd be lovely,' she said, and handed Pat a string bag. 'Put this somewhere cool, will you? It's full of the sort of food you won't have seen in a while that Bridie gave me. Oh, and there's an apple tart too so we can all have a slice of that.'

There was so much to catch up on, beginning with the concerts. 'Sheila's been great, every bit a Golden Sister,' said Peggy. Pat talked about the election. 'So exciting – you know that Basil Brooke's the new prime minister?' Then Sheila shyly held out her hand to show her beautiful engagement ring, and Martha was overwhelmed with the happiness of it all.

'And what about you, Mammy?' said Pat. 'What have you been doing?'

Martha hardly knew where to start. 'I've had such a good time,' she said. 'I worked in the butcher's shop, went on long walks and met lots of lovely people. I even went to a hooley and danced till I was exhausted.'

'You look so well,' said Peggy.

'And happy,' said Sheila.

'Why didn't you stay a bit longer?' asked Pat.

'Ach no, it was great, but it was time to come home. Sure, I missed my own bed,' she said, and they all laughed.

'And did you miss us, Mammy?'

'What, miss you three? Away on with you!'

Chapter 20

In the summer, a second wave of American Forces began arriving. The GIs disembarked from ships and aeroplanes and travelled on trains and in trucks and jeeps to camps right across Northern Ireland. These soldiers had never seen military action, but they were about to undergo extensive training for a campaign, still in the planning stage, that all hoped would be the beginning of the end of the war.

Goldstein was delighted to see the influx of Americans and wasted no time in making an appointment with Captain Walters, who was in charge of entertainment for the troops. The Barnstormers' concerts for the British Army were always well received, but there was something special about the American audiences that made Goldstein think of Broadway, and the motion pictures.

After his lengthy meeting he rushed back to the shop, eager to tell Peggy and Esther his news. There were two customers being served and it was all he could do to stop himself from interrupting them. Instead, he paced the shop wishing for the first time in his life that his customers would go elsewhere.

When they finally left, he closed the door behind them and turned the card hanging in the door to read 'Closed'.

'Such news, such news I have!' he said, his Polish accent thickening with excitement. 'A Hollywood star is coming to Northern Ireland with his entourage to entertain the American troops. The good news is he is short of female acts to bring some glamour to the biggest show at the Langford Lodge base and I have been asked to provide them. The one thing I have learned about performances for GIs is to give them what is familiar, something to remind them of home. So I think the Templemore Tappers, Macy and, of course, the Golden Sisters would fit that bill exactly.'

'Who is it? Who's the Hollywood star?' asked Peggy.

'Bob Hope, star of *The Road to Morocco*.'

'A comedian ...' Peggy sounded a bit disappointed. 'Is he bringing Bing Crosby and Dorothy Lamour with him?'

'I do not know,' said Goldstein. 'To be on the bill with one film star sounds like a great opportunity to me, but as usual, Peggy, there is no pleasing you.'

By the time Peggy arrived home that evening she had come round to the view that performing on the same bill as a film star was precisely the sort of achievement that would enhance the reputation of the Golden Sisters. When she told her sisters there were squeals of excitement.

'Even better than the George Formby concert,' said Pat.

'Imagine, a real Hollywood star. I loved *The Road to Morocco*,' said Sheila.

'Mr Goldstein says we'll probably be asked to learn a few new song and dance routines. He says the rehearsals will start next week and the show will be at the end of July. Who knows, we could be discovered and go to America to be in Bob Hope's next film.'

Martha tutted.

The first rehearsals for the Bob Hope show took place on a warm Sunday afternoon in early July at Betty Staff's dance studio. The plan was that ten Templemore Tappers, three Golden Sisters and one Macy would rehearse as detailed in a letter from Bob Hope's stage director. Their final rehearsal would be the day before the show when the American cast would arrive and there would be technical and dress rehearsals.

'This will be the most challenging show you will ever do,' Goldstein told them. 'We will be expected to fit in with a cast we have never met, to perform routines we have rehearsed in isolation.'

'So we won't have our own spots in the show at all?' asked Macy.

'No, that is not how it will work. They want some link to *The Road to Morocco* so we will be looking at the songs from the film for the Golden Sisters and some Moroccan-style music for the dancers. I have some records we can use. The idea is to have some interaction with Bob Hope; he likes to get on stage and crack some jokes, and that might be while you're performing.'

'Wow,' said Macy, 'that's a tall order you got there.'

'It certainly is,' said Goldstein, 'and I will have to rely on you quite a bit, Macy. You have worked wonders with the Tappers in the past, so I am going to ask you to start work right away on the choreography for their routine. Then I'll work with you on your solo dance. Golden Sisters, you get started on "Moonlight Becomes You" and try to make it more upbeat than in the film.' He clapped his hands. 'We have the rehearsal space for the next eight hours. Let's get started.'

With the girls out for the rest of the day, Martha took herself down the road to visit her cousins the McCrackens, who had a grocery shop on Manor Street. It felt good to be out walking on such a lovely summer's day and, as she passed some of the big houses on the Cliftonville Road, she admired the neat gardens and the flowers all in bloom. The shop was closed, of course, and the blinds had been pulled down to protect the stock from the sunlight, but she rapped sharply on the front door and waited for someone to come through from the back of the house. There was no answer at first, but on her second knock she could hear some movement. Slowly the locks and bolts were undone and a pale-faced Aggie peered round the door.

'Oh Martha, it's you, thank the Lord. Come in, come in.' Martha was surprised to see Aggie looking so anxious – normally she was full of smiles – and then she noticed that her arm was in plaster of Paris.

'What on earth's happened to you?'

'Just lock up for me there, would you? Then come through and I'll tell you all about it.'

Aggie fetched some homemade barley water from the cold press and they sat at the table sipping their cool drinks.

'Now, what's the story?' said Martha.

'It was stupid, so it was, my own fault altogether. I should never have gone out in the pitch black, I tell you, but here's me thinking I've only to cross the yard and put my hands out in front of me till I come to the privy door. Well, how was I to know that John had left crates of empty lemonade bottles in the middle of the yard? I caught this auld calliper of mine on the edge of a crate' – she slapped the metal brace on her leg – 'and down I went. Tried to break the fall with my hand and ended up in the Mater Hospital.'

'That's awful, Aggie. You know, the number of times I've heard of people getting injured in the blackout. Sure, there's been people run over and killed.'

'The broken arm's not the worst of it.' Aggie leaned closer to Martha. 'I'll tell you the rest, seeing as those ones aren't here.'

'John and Grace, you mean?'

'Aye, John's ragin' because I can't serve in the shop with him. Says he can't manage on his own and we'll either have queues out the door, or we'll lose customers altogether. Then he starts on Grace, telling her she'll have to give up her job at Robb's to help him.'

'And what did Grace say to that?'

'I'll give her her due, she stuck up for herself. Said she wasn't giving up a good job that she enjoyed doing. The two of them stood in this kitchen after church this morning and went at it hammer and tongs. Says he, I'm your brother, head of this household, and you'll do as I say. Says she, I'll do what I like, and she put on her coat and left.'

'Where are they now?'

'John's out at a Bible reading and Grace …' Aggie hesitated. 'You know, working in Robb's department store is Grace's life. It gets her out of this house and she's well respected there. She has a life outside these four walls where she's meeting people: customers and colleagues. Grace has friends.'

'Where is she, Aggie?'

'Maybe I shouldn't tell you this, Martha, but Grace has a friend. He's the manager of the shoe department. She meets him every Sunday afternoon.'

'And John doesn't know, does he?'

Aggie shook her head. 'He'd forbid it, call it sinful. He'd probably lock her in her room if he found out ...' Aggie pursed her lips as if to keep the anger inside, but clearly she couldn't. 'It's not fair that she'll lose her job and her friend, but that's what's going to happen and I'm at my wits' end because I keep thinking it's all my fault.'

'Now, you listen to me, Aggie. None of this is your fault. If John hadn't left those crates out, you wouldn't have fallen in the first place. But even if we call that an act of God, he still has no right to dictate what his sisters can and can't do. Just wait till I see him, I'll give him a piece of my mind.'

'Oh, please don't say anything to him, Martha. You know what he's like. He'll dig his heels in and we'll all be damned.'

'Well,' said Martha, 'maybe you're right, but there's more than one way to skin a cat. When he gets home, you just tell him that I'll be round first thing in the morning to serve in the shop and I'll do that until your arm is mended. Oh, and you can tell him I'm fully trained on the bacon slicer.'

The month Martha had spent in the butcher's in Dungannon had been a pleasure: spending the day talking to and serving all the different customers, the weighing and wrapping, the reckoning and giving change. She had loved it all. And the McCrackens' grocery shop was, if anything, a step up. There were so many things that people could ask for and she had to know where to find each item and learn the prices, not to mention knowing about the different foods on ration. And as each day passed, she learned much more than how to keep shop.

Martha was no stranger to hardship – she could remember the twenties and thirties – but the desperate people coming through the door of McCrackens' shop were enough to break her heart.

That first day serving, Martha watched the women, some with just a handful of coppers, trying to buy something to make a meal. She lost count of the number of women coming in with barefoot children, their clothes threadbare, who looked ground down with the strain of living.

When John locked the shop door at the end of the day, Martha went home with a heavy heart and thanked the Lord that she had three girls in decent jobs and a home untouched by the bombing.

Chapter 21

The pavement outside Goldstein's music shop was crowded with his performers, all in a high state of excitement as they waited for the transport to arrive.

'I'm so nervous,' said Sheila. 'I just want to get there and get it over with.'

'Don't think of it like that,' said Pat. 'Keep calm and tell yourself it's just another show.'

Peggy laughed. 'Yes, except this one's got Bob Hope in it.'

'You're making me worse,' said Sheila. 'I'd have been all right if we'd actually been able to rehearse with him like they promised. It's not going to be easy on stage with him if we've never had a run-through.'

Goldstein interrupted. 'I will speak to the director as soon as we get there. There will be plenty of time to sort out a quick rehearsal. Ah, here we are ...' The US Army truck pulled up in front of them and the Tappers, the sisters, Macy and Goldstein climbed on board.

Langford Lodge, close to Lough Neagh, was a huge American base for the servicing of planes. The mess hall where the concert would take place was already set up. There was seating for five hundred, gantries of lights and a stage with a banner proclaiming 'Bob Hope – Tonight'.

In the makeshift dressing room the girls got into their costumes and were putting on their makeup when Goldstein came in looking annoyed. 'Listen, please,' he said. 'I have some bad news. Bob Hope has been delayed, which means that there will be no time for the run-through. The director has decided that you will be in effect the warm-up acts. So you will be able to perform, but of course all the interaction with Mr Hope that we rehearsed will be impossible.'

There were audible sighs of disappointment. 'But the whole point was that we'd be performing songs from *The Road to Morocco*. Now we'll be doing it without the star from the film.' Peggy sounded cross as much as disappointed.

'None of the time we spent getting everything right will be wasted,' said Goldstein. 'You will sing the songs as we rehearsed them and I do not want to see anything less than a superb performance from all of you.'

The Templemore Tappers opened the show to cheers and wolf whistles that threatened to drown out the music, but the excitement and enthusiasm of five hundred GIs brought out the best in them. Their smiles were wider and their high kicks higher and, when they finished the routine, the applause and whistles went on and on until the compère walked on to the stage and pretended to shoo the Tappers off.

'What about that, guys?' he shouted. He held up his hands for silence and went on, 'If you like that, you're gonna love this. A beautiful woman all the way from Queens New York; put your hands together for Macy!' The music began and from the wings a long, shapely leg appeared and as the audience watched the leg kicked in time with the first dramatic chord. On the next chord an arm appeared and the hall filled with the music of a North African souk. A striking figure emerged, tall and willowy in shimmering red and gold gossamer, and swirled across the stage. On her head she wore a jewel-encrusted turban from which there hung a veil covering the lower part of her face. She extended her arms and with the smallest of movements she made the veils hanging from her wrists shake and, without breaking the rhythm, she pulled each one away and let it fall. The music quickened and now it seemed that every part of her body was in motion, shimmying and writhing. The bracelets on her arms and ankles rattled and the veils of gossamer that hung from her body lifted and fell as she moved. With a sweep of her arm she caught the veil across her middle and there was a gasp from the audience as her gyrating belly was revealed. She moved towards the front of the stage and turned her back to the audience. Her long red hair swished from side to side as her body swayed in a wide arc. She pulled the veil from across her chest and spun round to face the audience, exposing a brassiere covered in gleaming jewels, and the whistling and cheering erupted. She moved sideways across the stage and back again, leaving two more veils on the floor. Now the men were on their feet, drawn by the fluid, sensuous movements. Time and again she dipped and rose, never breaking the endless rhythmic shaking of her body, until the music slowed and her hands, intertwining like a temple dancer, moved upwards and pulled aside the veil to reveal her beautiful face. The applause was deafening.

Pat, Peggy and Sheila were standing in the wings as Macy came off stage shivering with excitement. 'Great audience, but so loud,' she whispered, then added, 'Bob Hope's here, I saw him as he came in at the back of the hall.'

'He's here!' Sheila gasped.

'Never mind that,' said Pat. 'Macy, go and get covered up – you can relax now.'

When she had gone, the girls waited while the compère told a few jokes and the GIs calmed down. Soon it was their cue. 'Hey guys, we got three more lovely ladies for you now with a couple of songs from *Road to Morocco*. So give a big welcome on stage for the girls with the golden voices – the Golden Sisters!'

The girls, one behind the other, with a hand on the shoulder of the sister in front, began singing the opening line 'We're off on the road to Morocco' from the wings, and then walked on stage swaying from side to side just as Bob Hope and Bing Crosby did when they were riding a camel in the film. When they reached the microphone they went straight into three-part harmony. They were halfway through when they noticed some movement in the audience. Soldiers were standing up to get a better look, pointing at the stage and laughing. The girls carried on singing, never letting their concentration or their smiles slip, until they were aware of another voice joining in. They turned to see that Bob Hope had joined their line-up. He winked at them and began swaying alongside them – out of time – then he took Sheila's hand and danced her round the stage, and all the time the GIs were roaring with laughter at his antics.

When the song finished Bob Hope took his bow along with the girls, although he turned it into an awkward curtsy and Pat had to help him up. He looked at them and demanded, 'Own up, Crosby, that disguise doesn't fool me. Which one are you?'

'None of us,' said Peggy. 'We're the Golden Sisters.'

'Where you girls from?'

'Belfast.'

'Belfast, Maine? Geez, you're a long way from home. Say is that Macy girl a friend of yours?' They nodded. 'Any chance you could get me a date?' They shook their heads. 'What you singin' next?'

'"Moonlight Becomes You",' said Peggy.

'How about I start it off, then you can join me with all those fancy bits you do to make it sound like we're in a Broadway show?'

The music began and Bob Hope serenaded the girls, making wisecracks about the lyrics. Then he nodded to the girls to join in, but by the third verse he was off waltzing with Pat, leaving Peggy and Sheila to sing, only returning to the microphone for the final lines and to take a bow with the Golden Sisters.

He waved the girls off stage and held up his hand for the men to settle. 'Before we go any further, the CO here at Langford Lodge asked me to tell you word has come in from the guys over there in Sicily that the US Seventh Army have taken Palermo. Just walked right in there and took the place!' And the five hundred GIs were on their feet, cheering and whistling and stamping their feet.

At the party after the show to celebrate the end of Bob Hope's trip to Northern Ireland, everyone was in high spirits. There was plenty to eat and drink and music for dancing. Bob Hope said a few words about his time on the road, touring army bases all over Europe and North Africa, that had them in stitches. He finished by saying, 'It's been a real pleasure to work with you guys from Belfast and I gotta say, "Thanks for the Memory …"' As he sang, he changed the words to make it about Northern Ireland and working with 'Goldstein's Girls'.

Goldstein had arranged for them to leave at midnight for the long trip back to Belfast, but when the time came, Macy was nowhere to be seen. Eventually, Goldstein spoke to the director who explained that she was talking privately to Mr Hope and he would go and find her.

Macy appeared, flushed and laughing. 'Gee guys, I didn't realise the time. That Bob Hope is somethin' else when it comes to making people laugh. You'll never guess what's just happened.'

'We shall save the guessing until we are on the road, shall we?' said Goldstein and he hurried them out to the waiting lorry. When they were on their way, Peggy chirped up, 'So, Macy, tell us about your … what was it … your meeting with Mr Hope?'

Macy gave her deep laugh. 'Yeah, he wanted to tell me how much he enjoyed my dancing. Said he'd have given me a part in *The Road to Morocco* if he'd known me back then.'

'He must have been quite taken with you,' said Peggy sharply.

'He sure was.' Macy gave a little satisfied sigh. 'That's why he asked me to join his show. Wants me to go travelling with him – pretty much round the world, to the American bases.'

There were gasps of astonishment from the rest of the girls.

'Well, fancy that,' said Peggy.

'And are you going to do it?' asked Sheila.

'Nope, that's why I'm on this truck going back to Belfast. There are planes to be built and I'm a riveter. Hoofers are two a penny.'

The morning after the concert, Pat and Peggy went to work as usual but, it being the school holidays, Sheila had a lie-in. Around nine, the sound of things being moved about downstairs woke her up and she put on her dressing gown and went to see what was going on. In the front room the furniture had been moved out from the walls and her mother was on her hands and knees behind the piano with a floor cloth, washing the skirting boards.

'What are you doing, Mammy?'

'What does it look like I'm doing?' Her mother's voice was shrill.

'Sure, this place needs a good clean, but there's not a one of you would notice.'

Sheila knew there was no point in saying anything when her mother was in that kind of mood – best to leave her be – and she squeezed past an armchair and climbed over the settee to get to the kitchen. She made some bread and jam and went to sit at the table. It was then she noticed a brown envelope. Her throat tightened as she saw the Royal Air Force stamp and her name and address underneath. She hadn't expected it so soon; she thought she had plenty of time to—

'Well, are you not going to open that?' Martha stood in the doorway with a bucket in her hand.

'Mammy I …' But Martha had already crossed the kitchen to the back door and by the time she had emptied the dirty water over the garden, Sheila had ripped open the envelope. It was, as she suspected, her Women's Auxiliary Air Force call-up papers.

'Are you going to tell me why the Air Force are writing to you?' Martha was at her shoulder.

Sheila held out the letter to her mother and watched anxiously as she read it.

'I was going to tell you, but I didn't … I didn't think it would come just yet.'

Martha's face was a mixture of bewilderment and anger. 'Is this true? You're being called up?' Her voice was rising steadily. 'How can that happen? There's no conscription here.'

'I'm not being conscripted – I enlisted.'

'Enlisted!' Martha stood with her hands on her hips, her face like thunder. 'Let me get this straight. You've enlisted in the Forces without telling me?' She shook her head in disbelief. 'Dear God, what did you do that for?'

'Because I want to do something worthwhile; to go out in the world and do something that really matters.'

'What kind of nonsense is that?'

'It's not nonsense. It's what I want to do.'

'But working in a school matters and – I never thought I'd hear myself say this – entertaining the troops matters. Anyway, you're far too young to be in the Forces.'

'No, I'm not. That's why they've called me up.'

'Now, you listen here, my girl, you go and see these people today and tell them you've changed your mind. They can't make you join up.' And she threw the letter on the table.

'I'm not doing that.' Sheila's voice was defiant.

'Of course you are, or you'll feel the back of my hand.'

'It's my decision. I'm old enough to make up my own mind.'

'Ach, what do you know? You're only seventeen. I can't believe you would go and do this without asking me.'

'You weren't here – you were away in Dungannon.'

'But I've been back weeks. Why didn't you tell me?'

'Because I couldn't face all this shouting that I'm getting from you now.'

Martha slumped into the chair opposite Sheila and covered her face with her hands. Her mind raced this way and that, but at every turn all she saw was disappointment and heartbreak: her daughter posted who knows where; living in camps; exposed to all kinds of danger. She could be in a plane being shot at. Here in Belfast she'd be safe and she had a good job in the Academy and … Suddenly Martha looked up, her eyes wide.

'What does Charles say about you joining up?'

Sheila looked away.

'Oh my goodness.' Martha was horrified. 'You haven't told him, have you? Dear God, what is the matter with you?'

'I meant to tell him, I really did, but he is always making plans for us. He goes on and on talking about when we're married … I haven't the heart to tell him.' She began to cry.

'Well,' said Martha, 'maybe that's for the best, because you won't be joining this ridiculous WAAF nonsense.'

'But I've got the call-up papers – I have to go. I want to go.'

Martha thumped the table. 'You're going nowhere, my girl, because I forbid it.'

Sheila was on her feet in an instant, eyes blazing. 'I don't care what you think – you can't stop me. I'm going to do this, do you hear me? I am!' And she pushed past Martha and ran upstairs to her room and slammed the door.

Martha went to the foot of the stairs and shouted, 'Over my dead body. Do you hear me? Over my dead body!'

Martha was due at the McCrackens' shop before noon that day to help with the lunchtime trade and to allow John to go to the wholesalers in the afternoon. She took her time getting ready and tried to calm herself, but she was still seething when she got off the bus at Manor Street. She bid a curt good morning to John, put on her apron and went behind the counter. The lunchtime trade was brisk with workers coming out of the linen mills and she was soon distracted by the customers. The rush eased off around two and, when John left, Aggie called out from the back kitchen, 'Lock the door now, Martha, and fetch a pan loaf and a tin of bully beef for our dinner.'

Martha made the sandwiches while Aggie sat, nursing her plaster cast, recounting the latest in the story of Grace and the shoe department manager.

'I tell you, Martha, we've been to hell and back. John went to his ARP meeting last night and it seems one of the men there remarked that it was very nice to see Grace walking out with a man last Sunday afternoon.'

'Oh no,' said Martha. 'What happened?'

'Well, we're sitting here quiet, Grace and myself, when John comes through that door like a man possessed, shouting that she's a disgrace, deceitful and all kinds of awful things.' Aggie shuddered at the memory. 'And before you could say Jack Robinson, he had the whole story out of her – how long they'd been seeing each other and the man's background. Poor Grace was in pieces and when she told him that the man was divorced … let's just say all hell broke loose.'

'That's terrible. Poor Grace.'

'That wasn't the worst of it,' said Aggie. 'He says to her, "I forbid you to have anything more to do with this man." But Grace came right back at him and asked how she could manage that if he works in the same shop. "Self-control," says he. "Either that or I'll see to it that you never go back to that job." Grace asked him how he could stop her. "I'll lock you in your room if I have to," he said.' Aggie took a handkerchief from her apron pocket and wiped her eyes.

'What happened then?' asked Martha.

Aggie shook her head. 'Grace was no match for him. He's forbidden her from having any contact ever again with the man. What else can she do, if she wants to keep her job?'

'I know he's in a different department,' said Martha, 'but she'll still see him every day, won't she? She might even start walking out with him again.'

'She never will,' said Aggie. 'He made her swear on the Holy Book that she wouldn't and Grace would never—'

'No, you're right, she would never break a promise sworn on the Bible.' Martha was overwhelmed by the injustice of it. 'Now every day in work she'll see him and never be able to speak to him. What a cruel, cruel thing to do to your own flesh and blood.'

All afternoon as she served in the shop, Martha thought of Grace and how she had so little control over her life that John could step in and forbid her to make her own decisions. It seemed so unfair. Grace wasn't too old to fall in love. But she was old enough to know what she wanted.

On the bus home, Martha sat next to a young woman nursing a toddler dressed in a gingham dress. The little girl was lively and wouldn't settle. In the end, the mother allowed the child to bounce up and down on her knee. Soon she was laughing and pointing out the window, turning every now and again as if to say, 'Look what I can do.'

'She's awful wilful,' said the mother.

Martha nodded. 'Aye, they always are.'

The house was empty when Martha got home, but she saw immediately that the kitchen had been cleaned, and on the draining board there were pans of peeled potatoes and carrots and a dish with liver soaking in milk all ready to be cooked.

She went upstairs to change her clothes and the smell of lavender polish met her. She looked in each bedroom: beds neatly made; no clothes on the floor; dressing tables cleared of clutter. There was no sign of Sheila.

She lay on her bed for a while and tried to bring some order to her thoughts. She didn't want Sheila to join the WAAF, but she shouldn't have lost her temper. The best thing now would be to persuade her not to throw away what she had.

The liver was sizzling in the pan and the potatoes and carrots bubbling away when Pat and Peggy arrived home from work.

'Where's Sheila?' asked Pat.

Martha stood with her back to them, frying the liver, deep in thought.

'Mammy, did you hear me?'

Martha turned and stared at them.

'What is it? What's the matter?' said Pat.

'Did you know that Sheila has enlisted?'

For a moment they stared at her then flashed a look at each other. Neither of them spoke.

'You did,' said Martha. 'You knew and you never said anything to me.'

'Sheila's joined the WAAF?' Peggy was incredulous. 'We didn't know she'd actually signed up.'

Pat tried to explain. 'She talked about it, she had the papers, but we told her not to do it.'

'Why didn't you tell me about this?' Martha demanded.

'You were in Dungannon. She never mentioned it again. We thought she'd forgotten about it.'

'She's your wee sister – you're supposed to look after her.'

'You can't blame us. She did what she wanted ...' The side gate rattled and they looked up to see Sheila come past the window.

By the time she came into the kitchen all conversation had ceased and the atmosphere was charged with tension. Pat and Peggy didn't meet her gaze.

'I'm putting the tea out now,' said Martha.

Sheila crossed the room. 'I don't want any.'

'Sheila, please sit down and have your tea.' Martha didn't raise her voice. 'We'll not waste good food.'

Sheila hesitated, then shrugged and joined her sisters at the table, and Pat tried to ease the awkwardness by talking about the Bob Hope concert and the party afterwards. When they had eaten Martha said, 'We'll leave the dishes for now. We need to sort out this WAAF business.'

Sheila's eyes flitted from her family to the door as though looking

154

for an escape route. 'There's nothing to sort out. I'm going,' she said.

'So you've actually signed up?' asked Pat. 'Why didn't you tell us?'

'Because I knew you'd try to talk me out of it like you did when I got the papers and I can tell you now, I'm not changing my mind.'

Pat persisted. 'And you have your call-up papers?' Sheila pulled the letter from her pocket and gave it to Pat to read.

'I'm not going to shout, Sheila,' said Martha, 'but I need to say my piece. I can't be certain, but it seems to me that this war is slowly coming to an end and it's very unlikely that we'll be bombed again. You have a good life at the moment with your job and Charles and your singing and I don't want you to throw all that away to be sent into danger. I want our family to stay together. That's why I'm asking you not to go.'

'Now you're asking me? You said you'd forbid me to go. You said I was too young.' Sheila was on her feet. 'But you can't control my life, do you hear? I'll make my own decisions.'

Martha put her hands over her ears as if to shut out the anger in Sheila's voice. How could she, the sweetest and gentlest of her girls, speak to her mother like that? But the cruel words lodged in Martha's brain.

Peggy caught Sheila's arm. 'That's enough. You can't speak to Mammy like that.'

Pat said quietly, 'Sit down, Sheila.'

Sheila hesitated.

'Please,' said Pat and after a moment Sheila sat down, folded her arms and stared straight ahead.

Pat took a deep breath and began, 'We just want to make sure you've thought this through. What does Charles think about you joining up?'

'She didn't tell him,' said Martha.

'That's where you're wrong,' said Sheila. 'I've been with him all afternoon and I've told him I'm joining up.'

'And what did he say to that?' asked Pat.

Sheila seemed to calm herself and when she answered her voice was measured. 'He said I should go if that's what I want. He loves me and he's going to wait for me. This war will end, but more people need to join the fight if that's to be sooner rather than later.'

Pat listened to the argument, but then she turned to Sheila and asked, 'Did you read all of this letter they sent you?'

'Of course I did – it says I've to report to Ballykelly Camp in two weeks' time.'

'What about this last bit at the bottom where it says, "*Parent or guardian signature required if enlisted is under eighteen*"?' Pat slid the letter across the table.

'What?' Sheila grabbed the letter and hastily read the bottom line. 'It can't be!'

'I'm afraid it is,' said Pat.

Sheila didn't move, didn't speak. They watched her for some sign of her thoughts, but her expression was one of confusion as she read and reread the final part of the letter. Eventually, Martha spoke. 'Well, there's an end to it now, so I'll leave you all to wash the dishes and tidy up in here.'

Martha went straight to her bedroom and, even though it was a lovely evening, she closed the blackout curtains and went to bed. She could hear the muffled voices of the girls talking, but she had no desire to go over the arguments again. The night was warm and she was restless, sleeping on and off until the sound of the house martins outside her window told her it was dawn and she got up to make herself a cup of tea. The call-up papers, now screwed into a ball, were still on the table.

While the kettle boiled, she watched a family of blue tits chase each other in and out of the lilac tree, and wondered whether they were squabbling or playing. She took her cup outside and wandered up and down the borders, stopping now and again to admire the flowers – lupins, roses, lilies. In the little vegetable garden she checked the stakes on the peas and pulled up a cabbage and some onions to make a broth. And all the while she thought of John McCracken and how he had forbidden his sister to make her own decisions about her life. It was cruel and she knew Grace would never forgive him. He was a good man at heart and she understood why he had behaved as he had towards Grace, but there was no getting away from the fact that he was wrong.

She went back to the kitchen and carefully smoothed out the WAAF call-up papers.

Chapter 22

Pat had bought Sheila a small case made out of waxed cardboard, which was cheap enough and light to carry. She wouldn't need that many clothes anyway, because she would spend most of her time in uniform.

Peggy advised her, 'Always keep your compact and lipstick in your pocket so that you can touch up your makeup, and make sure you tell them you want a close-fitting uniform or you'll end up like a frump.'

'It's not a fashion show,' said Pat.

'I'm just advising her to look her best. I tell you, that WAAF uniform is a disaster.'

York Street Station had been severely damaged by the Blitz of 1941 two years before and the remains of the once grand building amounted to no more than three walls and a tarpaulin roof over the ticket offices. There were crowds of people, many of them in uniform, milling around when Sheila and Martha arrived. 'You wait here, Mammy, while I hand in my railway warrant to get a ticket.' Martha watched her go and marvelled at how self-assured she looked, a young woman making her way in the world. She had been right to sign the call-up papers, but that didn't stop the churning in her stomach every time her mind conjured up some new disaster that might befall her youngest daughter.

Sheila had wanted to say her goodbyes at home, but Martha would have none of it. 'Don't argue with me – I'm coming to see you off. Lord knows, you'll be soon enough on your own.' Martha was glad she had come to the station because there were things she wanted to say. Things she should have said long ago ...

'Hello, Mrs Goulding.'

Martha was startled to see Charles Turner standing next to her, looking anxious.

'Has Sheila gone already?'

'No, no, she's getting her ticket. She didn't say you were coming to see her off.'

'Ach no, that's because I didn't tell her I was coming. But I had to ... well, I just needed to see her, you know?'

Martha wasn't best pleased. She had wanted this time alone with Sheila. She knew fine well that Charles must have had the same idea, but she didn't care – mothers came before fiancés in her book.

'But I'm seeing her off,' she said.

Charles looked bewildered. 'I just want to see her, that's all.'

Then Sheila was there. 'What are you doing here, Charles?' No smile, no softness in her voice.

'Could we ... ?' He looked at Martha, who raised an eyebrow.

'I'll get myself a platform ticket,' she said and walked away, just far enough to keep them in sight. Charles was talking quickly, his eyes searching Sheila's face. She listened, but made no reply. He touched her arm and she didn't respond. His shoulders slumped and he looked away from her, his face full of misery. Then Sheila was speaking but, whatever it was she said, it didn't alter Charles' expression. Martha watched as he took Sheila in his arms; there was no parting kiss, just a sad farewell before he walked away.

Sheila said nothing when Martha joined her, but it was clear some of the excitement at leaving had left her. They went on to the platform where the train was waiting, carriage doors open, but they still had time to say goodbye.

'Do you remember the last time you went away, when you were evacuated?' said Martha.

Sheila nodded. 'It was a strange feeling leaving you all and not knowing where I'd end up and who I'd meet.'

'Does it feel like that now?'

'A bit, but I'm older and I'm going because it's what I've chosen.'

'Sheila, about Charles—'

'Leave it be, Mammy.'

The last thing Martha wanted was for these precious moments to be awkward. Hadn't she spent ages thinking of the right thing to say to Sheila?

'You know we're going to miss you so much and we're really proud of you.' Martha attempted a smile.

'I know, Mammy, and I'll miss you. I'll write to you every week I promise.' There was a shrill whistle and the guard walked up the platform towards them, a flag in his hand. 'I'll need to get on now,' said Sheila, and she picked up her case and hugged her mother.

'Look after yourself and keep safe,' said Martha. 'You know I love you.' But her final words were drowned by another blast of the whistle and the sound of slamming doors.

Sheila pulled away from her. 'I have to go,' she shouted and ran towards an open carriage door. Safely inside, she leaned out the window and waved to her mother. There was the deafening sound of steam being released as the train began to move and Martha watched it take her youngest child into the unknown, leaving her behind, bereft and diminished.

The journey from Belfast to the far northwest of Northern Ireland was slow, with several stops at small towns on the way. There were no signs on the platforms, but as the train drew to a halt a stationmaster would appear and call out the name. Even though Sheila had listened carefully at every stop, she began to panic that she had missed her destination. Sharing the carriage with her was an elderly gentleman, who had his head in a newspaper, and a well-dressed young woman with long blonde hair.

'Excuse me, have I missed Ballykelly Station?' she asked the girl.

'Oh, I was just thinking that myself.' Her voice was high and quick with an accent Sheila had only ever heard on the wireless.

The man looked over his paper and said, 'Next stop – a few minutes.'

'Are you going to Coastal Command?' asked the girl.

'I don't think so,' said Sheila. 'I'm going to the Air Force base. '

'Same thing,' she said. 'So you must be a WAAF then.'

'Well, I will be when they give me the uniform,' said Sheila.

The girl laughed, a high-pitched tinkling sound, and held out her hand. 'Jessica Cavendish, lovely to meet you.'

Sheila shook her hand. 'I'm Sheila Goulding. Are you WAAF too?'

'I will be when they give me the uniform,' she said, and she laughed again.

At Ballykelly Station they were surprised to see another four women alight from different carriages and join them on the platform. As the train steamed away, they stood for a moment in uncomfortable silence wondering what to do. They scanned the flat fields that ran across the landscape as far as the sea glittering in the distance, and listened to the eerie sound of corncrakes that shattered the silence. Then Jessica spoke up. 'I think perhaps we are all waiting for our transport to RAF Ballykelly. Is that so?'

And that was the cue for the six new WAAFs to get to know each other.

By the time they arrived at the base in the RAF lorry sent to pick them up, the girls had lost some of their anxiety. At least they knew that, whatever dangers or hardships they faced, they would be with other young women like themselves. They were met by an older woman who told them in a barking voice that she was Sergeant O'Dwyer. She took some time to get them lined up in formation, then marched them to some wooden huts close to the camp perimeter. Inside their hut, there were twelve iron bedsteads, and next to them were metal lockers. Half of the beds were made up with bedding and there were small personal effects on the lockers. Sheila and Jessica managed to get two vacant beds together at the far end. Next they were shown the 'ablutions block', a concrete structure with three toilets against one wall and three basins against another. They had just enough time to be appalled by the smell and the state of the facilities before Sergeant O'Dwyer dismissed them, saying she would be back for them in half an hour when they would be taken to base headquarters.

Back in the hut the girls sat on their beds and chatted. Sheila looked from girl to girl, struck by how different they were. There was Jessica, of course, who sat there looking around the hut, clearly appalled by her new home. Linda had the loudest voice and ginger hair. She told them she had worked in Woolworth's. 'Boring,' she said. 'I'm hoping for a bit of excitement coming here.'

Nell wore a neat grey costume and spectacles so Sheila wasn't surprised when she said she was a shorthand typist. Geraldine, a farmer's daughter from Tyrone, had the broadest smile. Barbara had peroxide hair and an English accent, but she sounded nothing like Jessica.

At headquarters an officer registered them, collecting their call-up papers and issuing them with identity cards; then on to the mess to eat. Sheila was not surprised by the quality or quantity of food she was served. She had eaten in mess halls many times when she was singing at camps, but some of the girls were amazed at the food they could expect from now on.

Having eaten, they reported to the quartermaster's store for their uniforms and kit. There were no measurements taken. Instead, the WAAF corporal in charge walked round each girl, then went into the store and came back with not only a uniform, but a huge pile of everything from knickers and bedding to a tin hat. When it came to Sheila's turn to be sized up, she remembered Peggy's advice.

'Could I have a small size?' she asked.

The corporal gave a humourless laugh. 'Of course, madam. I'll order you a bespoke uniform from Savile Row, shall I? Oh, wait a minute, I think there's a war on, isn't there? Looks like you'll get what you're given then.'

When every WAAF had collected their uniform and kit, the corporal told them, 'Don't forget you must post most of your civilian clothes back home. You won't need them again till the war ends.'

Jessica leaned in towards Sheila and whispered, 'If she thinks

I'm sending my silk underwear home, she's got another thing coming.'

Back at their hut, the girls, in high excitement, laid their uniforms and kit out on their beds. They were amazed to see that they would indeed be clothed entirely in uniform, including the regulation issue knickers, bras, vests and suspender belts.

Linda, the smallest of the girls, pulled the long blue drawers on to her head and jumped up and down on her bed. 'Look at me,' she shouted. 'I'm a WAAF, I'm a WAAF!' Barbara and Geraldine joined in and soon they were running round the hut shrieking while the rest of them tried to snatch the drawers from their heads as they ran past. Then suddenly Sergeant O'Dwyer was standing in the doorway with a face like thunder. She waited until everyone became aware of her presence then barked, 'Stand by your beds.'

She walked the length of the hut and back staring into each face. No one met her eye. 'There's a war on,' she shouted, 'and men and women of the Royal Air Force are serving and dying and you're making fun of their uniform. Tomorrow you will begin your basic training with a six-mile march. Normally, it would be three miles, but your disgraceful behaviour needs to be punished.' She paused to allow her words to sink in. 'Now get into uniform, you're due in the lecture room in twenty minutes. There you'll learn about the importance of discipline and the tests you'll sit tomorrow. Oh yes, and the rule about hair is that it mustn't touch your collar. So get it sorted.'

By lights out that evening Sheila was exhausted. The long journey from home, the strain of settling into such a demanding environment and the news that she would be taking an important test the next day, not to mention the six-mile hike, had left her wondering what she'd got herself into.

'Are you still awake?' Jessica whispered from the next bed.

'Yes, just about.'

'I've been trying to decide what will be worse – the test or the hike.'

'The march will be bad enough,' said Sheila, 'but the test is to decide what job we'll be doing for the rest of the war. I hope I don't get something like cooking or cleaning. It would be worse than staying at home.'

'Good heavens, I can drive a car, so I hoped I might be given the position of driver. Surely I won't be expected to do manual labour?' said Jessica. Sheila had never heard the term before, but she could hear the horror in Jessica's voice. They had only spent a few hours in each other's company, but already it was clear that they came from different worlds.

Sheila slept on and off through the night and towards dawn she was awakened by the sound of someone getting into the next bed. It had been empty when she went to sleep, but now in the dawn light she could see a girl sitting up in her regulation pyjamas brushing her hair. Sheila rubbed her eyes and yawned.

'Hi there, when did you get in?' The girl sounded American.

Sheila sat up. 'We got here yesterday afternoon.'

'New recruit?'

'Yes, there are six of us. We came on the train from Belfast. Have you just arrived now?'

'No, I've just come off my six-hour shift. This week I'm working all night and sleeping in the day.'

'What do you do?'

'I'm a plotter, work in the operations room. We plot the positions of all the planes and convoys and German U-boats.'

Sheila was amazed that a girl would be allowed to do such important-sounding work.

The girl went on, 'I'm Clemmie. What's your name?'

'Sheila. Have you been here long?'

'Oh, I came over from Canada about six months ago. Stationed in Lincolnshire then got posted here to Coastal Command. Hey, you taken your test yet?'

'No, it's today. I'm a bit nervous about it.'

'We could do with a couple more plotters,' said Clemmie. 'Maybe you'll be assigned to us. Are you any good at calculating? Quick and accurate, I mean.'

'Well, I'm quite good at reckoning up, but I don't think I could do anything like that.'

At that moment there was a banging on the door. 'That's it,' said

Clemmie, 'time for you lot to get up and for me to go to sleep.' And she flopped down on her pillow and pulled the blanket over her head.

The lecture room, where they had been the previous day for talks about the history of the RAF and the importance of discipline and respect, had been set out with six card tables. The girls took their seats and cast nervous sideways glances at each other as the first test paper was given out. Sheila did her best to complete this general intelligence paper in the half hour allowed, but the questions got more and more difficult as it went on and she didn't finish it all before the time ran out. Well, that's it, she thought. I'll probably end up with 'manual work'. The second paper was handed out and Sheila's hopes were raised a little when she read 'Mathematics' on the front. What had Clemmie said? Quick and accurate – that was it. Only ten minutes allowed for this test and Sheila was determined to do her best.

When they had finished, they stood outside the lecture room talking about the test as though they were still at school.

'I didn't understand some of the questions,' said Barbara.

'I didn't finish,' said Geraldine.

Nell looked worried. 'The maths was so hard.'

So much was resting on the results, but there was nothing more they could do. Sheila didn't tell them she had completed the mathematics test. She had worked fast, but in doing so she had probably made more mistakes than the others. No use worrying about it, they told each other, it would be a month before they would hear what job they would be assigned, but secretly Sheila already had her heart set on being a plotter like Clemmie.

The days flew by, filled with lectures, marches, square bashing, kit inspections; no wonder that at the end of each day they were exhausted. It didn't help that they were confined to barracks for the first month and had very little opportunity to mix with other service personnel. Towards the end of the third week, when the girls had started grumbling about interminable basic training and the fact that they were never given anything worthwhile to do, an event that brought home to them the dangers that airmen faced.

They had got used to the constant noise of planes taking off twenty-four hours a day to fly sorties over the Atlantic Ocean protecting convoys of ships from German U-boats. But one night in late August they were wakened by a shrill whining noise somewhere in the distance, followed by the sound of running feet and people shouting. A clanging bell cut across everything, as a fire engine raced past their hut. They ran out in their pyjamas and bare feet to stare up at the pitch-black sky. The fire bell was silenced, but the whining was louder now and there came the sound of an engine spluttering.

'Look! Look!' screamed Barbara and they turned to see a black shape low in the sky hurtling towards them. They threw themselves on the ground as the bomber just cleared their hut. It was a moment before they realised the spluttering and whining had stopped and in the deathly quiet they held their breath. The ground shook once ... twice ... three times. The fire engine's bell rang again as it chased the bomber, which had spun off the airstrip and careered across the fields beyond.

The following morning in the NAAFI there was plenty of banter about the escapade the previous night. The bomber crew were based at RAF Aldergrove, twenty miles away, and a miscalculation had led to them running out of fuel as they returned from an eight-hour patrol over the Atlantic. The crew had cuts and bruises from the rough landing, but they were in good spirits as the Ballykelly airmen shook their hands and thumped the pilot on the back to show their admiration for his skills in bringing the plane down safely.

'How could they run out of fuel?' asked Sheila.

'Oh, you'd be surprised,' said Clemmie. 'They might be chasing a U-boat and don't want to lose it so they stay in the air longer than they should.'

'Does it happen very often?'

'More often than you'd think, but most of them have just enough fuel to reach us. Not many end up with absolutely nothing in the tank.'

At the end of the month the six girls crowded round the noticeboard outside the lecture room, where the list of names and allocated jobs had been posted. Jessica got there first and whooped with joy. 'I'm a driver,' she shouted, 'how wonderful. I hope it's one of those huge lorries.'

Sheila was pleased for her friend. Most of the girls could probably turn their hand to any job they were given, but Jessica was a one-off. Nell, with her office skills, was assigned to clerical work. Barbara and Linda were in the kitchens. Sheila desperately hoped that she would get work that directly contributed to the war effort. Geraldine stepped back from the noticeboard and declared without much enthusiasm, 'I'm in the stores.' With her heart beating madly, Sheila searched for her name. There it was. Her eyes jumped to the next column where there was just one word: 'Plotter'.

Chapter 23

Peggy was late. It wasn't her fault – it was the weather. She was meant to be meeting Archie at the gates of the Botanic Gardens at two o'clock, but she couldn't decide what to wear. It was warm for September, but was it warm enough to leave the house in a cotton dress and cardigan? In the end, she chose her pale green dress and matched it with Irene's little box jacket with the three-quarter sleeves. Still she wasn't satisfied and then she remembered Pat's cream straw hat with the pleated brim.

Dates with Archie had been few and far between. He had explained that his new role at headquarters was very demanding and that he was at the beck and call of his commanding officer most of the time. No matter, Peggy was just happy to be with him whenever he could get away and she was glad she had the photo of the two of them on Royal Avenue to look at every night. Since the misunderstanding at the dinner dance, he had been the perfect gentleman, but sometimes in her dreams she felt again the passion of his kisses that night.

She could see him as she turned the corner, his back to her – so upright, so tall – her dashing major. She was at his side before he realised she was there and she slipped her arm into his. 'Hello, soldier, are you looking for someone to spend an afternoon with?'

He looked down at her and appeared to study her. 'I was supposed to be meeting someone. I think her name was Peggy but, alas, she hasn't arrived.'

Peggy tutted. 'What a shame, and you so handsome. We can't leave you lonely, can we?'

'No, but you'll have to be very nice to me, not like Peggy.'

She stood on her tiptoes and kissed his cheek and together they walked into the gardens.

There were people everywhere, dressed in their Sunday best, enjoying the sunshine. It might have been possible to forget that they had been at war for four years, had it not been for the number of people in uniform. Lately, a mood of optimism had settled over the city and there was talk of a new, even bigger wave of American troops coming to Northern Ireland. Forces were gathering, plans were being made and this war would be won.

Peggy and Archie strolled along a broad path lined with vividly coloured begonias towards the ornamental lake. Anyone watching would surely have thought they were lovers, so attentive was he, smiling and chatting and making her laugh. She gazed up at him, content to listen and adore. They sat for a while watching the sun sparkle on the fountain and listening to the splashing of the water. Archie had one arm across her back, the other across her waist. Peggy had her head on his shoulder, her eyes closed, enjoying the feel of his gently stroking fingers beneath her jacket. She could have stayed there forever.

'Come on, let's walk a bit further and see if there's someone selling ice cream,' said Archie. They found a cart next to the band stand with 'Mesci, Italian Ice Cream' written on the side in green, white and red.

'Due gelati, per favore,' said Archie.

Peggy looked at him in amazement. 'I didn't know you spoke Italian?'

'Ah, Peggy, there's a lot you don't know about me.'

'Why don't you tell me?'

Archie laughed. 'I wouldn't know where to start.' He took the ice creams and handed her one.

'You could start with how you learned Italian.'

They wandered past impressive specimen trees: redwoods, monkey puzzles and Japanese acers, while Archie explained that he had had an Italian nanny as a child. 'She mostly spoke Italian when we were on our own and by the time I was thirteen I had a good grasp of it. Then I went away to boarding school.'

'Your parents sent you away?'

'Of course, that's what happens in families like ours.' He shrugged his shoulders. 'It's what makes a man of you, they say, that and the army.'

By this time they had arrived at the most impressive sight in the park, the spectacular cast iron glasshouse. It towered above them; thousands of panes of glass reflecting the sunlight. Archie looked up in amazement. 'My word, it's the image of the famous glass house in Kew Gardens. My family home is just down the road from it.' He sighed. 'I used to go there such a lot with my ...' He stopped himself and shook his head as if clearing his thoughts.

'Let's go in and have a look,' said Peggy. There were two parts: the cool house, a long low building, and the Palm House, a high globe-like structure with a large curved section at ground level and a high dome to allow for the tropical palm trees.

Inside, the Palm House was hot and humid and the smell of damp earth and vegetation hung in the air. They followed the iron walkways past towering tropical trees, and flowering shrubs and cacti, several of which Archie recognised. 'I've seen mango trees like these in India. The fruits are the size of my hand, sweet and juicy. Those are proteas – they flower in South Africa.'

'You've been to so many places,' said Peggy. 'I've never been out of Ireland.'

'Don't worry, you're young,' he said, 'you've so much ahead of you,' and he stroked her cheek and bent to kiss her head.

But she wanted more, so much more. She reached up and put her hands around his neck, drew him towards her and kissed him with a passion she had no idea was inside her. His arms were round her and he pulled her body towards his so fiercely that she could hardly breathe. His lips were on hers, his hands caressing the backs of her thighs. Her breath quickened; there was nothing else in the world but his lips and his hands and her body.

Suddenly his lips were gone, his hands pulled back. She opened her eyes. The iron walkway was rattling with the sound of running feet and two children came round the curve of the building and stopped suddenly in front of them. Archie took her arm and whispered, 'I think we need to leave.'

They went outside and sat on a bench at the front of the Palm House. Peggy's face was flushed, her lips slightly parted. She didn't speak.

'Peggy, my dear, you're full of surprises.'

She couldn't look at him. Then he covered her hand with his. 'It's all right, you know. It's what happens when you're attracted to someone. It's how the journey begins.'

They sat a while in silence watching a boy with a kite trying to catch the wind. He ran this way and that and just when he thought it was about to soar it crashed to earth.

Archie reached out and turned her face towards his. Her eyes were downcast. 'Do you remember what I said when we were in the Café Royal after what happened at the dinner dance?'

Peggy shook her head.

'I agreed to do everything you tell me. That means that, although I'm older and I have more experience of the world than you do, when it comes to us, you are in control.'

She looked up, her eyes glistening. 'I think I'd like to go home now,' she said.

'Would you look at that?' shouted Pat. 'I've just seen my straw hat go past.'

Martha looked up from shelling her peas. 'What are you talking about?'

Pat pointed. 'There – on the other side of the hedge – my hat.' And as she followed it, Peggy emerged and walked up the path. Pat was waiting for her, hands on hips, when she came in.

'You stole my hat!'

'I didn't steal it. I borrowed it.' Peggy replied as if she had barely the energy to speak.

'In my book, if you borrow something without asking, it's called stealing.'

'Whatever you say, Pat.'

'And while I'm at it – that's Irene's jacket. Mammy, will you tell her she can't keep taking other people's belongings!'

Peggy ignored her and crossed the room, heading to the stairs.

'Where are you going? We're supposed to be rehearsing.'

'I'm too tired,' said Peggy. 'I'm going to lie down.'

Martha looked at her in amazement. 'Tired? Since when have you ever been tired?'

'Since I arrived home to such petty nonsense,' she said and swept out of the room, leaving Pat and Martha lost for words.

She put the hat and the jacket back where they belonged, took off her dress and, still in her slip, got into bed. Her mind was a whirlwind of thoughts and feelings and she couldn't pin any of them down for long enough to begin to piece together what had happened between her and Archie. One minute she was deeply embarrassed by what she'd done in such a public place, the next she thrilled again at the physical intensity his response had awakened in her. How could she ever face him again and how could she bear not to? What kind of girl would he think she was? She blushed to think what he would have assumed.

Peggy reached for the magazine she kept under her bed and took the photograph of her and Archie from between the pages. She traced his face with her finger and kissed him. This was so much more than she had ever felt with Harry. This was a love so fierce that she ached for him.

Much later, Martha crept upstairs to check on Peggy and found her fast asleep, her face to the wall. She pulled the bedspread over her bare shoulder and underneath was a magazine, and something else …

Martha was taken aback by the photo. The officer next to Peggy cut a striking figure, tall and good-looking, but he was no young lad wet behind the ears. Everything about him suggested a man in control. She could tell that the photo had been taken in winter so

Peggy must have known him for quite a while. But as she looked closer the real shock was not the man, but the expression on Peggy's face.

There was a time when Martha might have shaken Peggy awake and demanded to know who this man was. She might even have insisted he was too old for her and forbidden her to see him again. But instead she gently placed the photo back into the magazine and slipped out of the room.

Downstairs Pat was listening to the news on the wireless. 'The Americans have invaded mainland Italy,' she said.

'You think Tony's there now?'

'Probably – this will be the start of the next campaign. Sicily was just a toehold to launch an invasion in Italy. They need to get the Italians out of the war.' Pat fetched her school atlas. She knew from Captain Walters that Tony had been in Tunis in North Africa and at some point he would have boarded a ship. She traced the route across the Mediterranean to the island of Sicily, then on to the mainland and north towards Rome.

When Peggy came down for her tea she looked a lot brighter and later she and Pat rehearsed as they usually did on a Sunday. Goldstein had decided that there was no point in trying to replace Sheila after she joined the WAAF and had suggested to Pat that she should sing some Vera Lynn songs in the concerts, accompanied by Peggy. Neither of them was keen on the songs, but they were so popular with the audience that Pat, at least, had warmed to them.

'It's only because you get the loudest applause of the night,' Peggy had complained after their first performance. 'But of course it's not really for you, is it? It's for the sentimental lyrics and the fact that they can all have a good sing-song.'

Unlike her daughters, Martha liked the songs. They made her proud that her country had stood up to a tyrant and gave her hope that they would come through this war. She leaned back in her chair and hummed along, enjoying her own personal performance by her daughters.

'You're in good form tonight, Mammy,' said Pat.

'It's just lovely to sit here and be entertained.'

'It's "We'll Meet Again" next. That's your favourite, isn't it?'

Martha nodded and Pat said, 'Come on then, get up and sing it with me.'

'Ach, away on with you,' said Martha, but the girls didn't listen. They took an arm each and pulled her out of the chair. She tried to protest, but Peggy was already playing the introduction. Once Pat began to sing Martha joined in, softly at first, but when Peggy came in on the second verse all three of them sang it as though they were on the stage at the Grosvenor Hall. By the time they finished, Martha's face was flushed. 'Mercy me!' she said. 'I haven't sung like that in years.'

But Peggy was playing again, and they carried on with 'Tomorrow Just You Wait and See'.

It was after ten by the time they had run through the songs. 'I haven't enjoyed an evening aas much since I don't know when,' said Martha.

'I think I'll have a word with Mr Goldstein tomorrow,' said Peggy.

'What about?'

'Getting you signed up for the Golden Sisters – you're better than Sheila!'

And Martha couldn't stop herself laughing in delight. 'Aye, an ould woman like me is just what you girls need to show you how it's done.'

'You're not an ould woman, Mammy,' said Pat, 'and when you laugh like that you look lovely.'

When Pat had gone off to bed with the school atlas under her arm, Peggy sat picking out a tune on the piano. Martha watched her a while, then asked, 'Are you all right?'

Peggy swivelled round on the piano stool. 'Hmm … yes, I think so.'

Martha struggled to frame her words so that Peggy wouldn't fly off the handle. 'I don't want you to think I'm prying, but can I ask you something?'

Peggy was immediately on her guard. 'You can ask, but don't start shouting if I don't want to tell you.'

'I won't shout,' said Martha. 'I went up earlier, to see if you were all right, and you were asleep.' Peggy shifted uncomfortably in her chair. Martha went on, 'There was a photograph on the bed ... you with a man, a soldier. I wondered who he was.'

'I don't think it's any of your business and if I told you I'd never hear the end of it.'

'You don't have to tell me, Peggy, but I'd like you to. You're old enough to make your own decisions and I'm not going to stand in your way.'

Peggy was taken aback by her mother's words and wondered why she was being so measured and so calm. Perhaps now would be the time to tell her about Archie – especially if, as she hoped, their relationship was becoming more serious.

'His name is Archie and he's a major in the British Army. He's older than me and I like that because he's such an interesting person. I don't see him very often – he has a very important job.'

'I see – and do you like him better than Harry Ferguson?'

Peggy shrugged. 'I thought that Harry and I would end up getting married when the war was over, but I'm not so sure now. He's always let me down, you know. He never writes – '

'And what about Archie? Does he want to marry you?'

'No. Well, not yet. It's too soon to say but, Mammy, I really like him ...'

'Will you bring him home to meet us?'

Peggy gave a nervous laugh. 'Not yet, I don't want to scare him off,' she said, and stood up, aware that she had revealed quite enough already. 'I'm away to bed now. Night-night.'

'Night-night, love,' said Martha, but she couldn't stop herself from adding, 'but just be careful, Peggy, and don't let yourself down.'

When Peggy had gone, Martha sat a long while considering what she'd been told. This was a man with considerable authority and no doubt experience of the world. As to how old he might be ... by the look of him, he was certainly past thirty. She felt herself getting agitated, but what could she do? Peggy seemed quite smitten with him and would surely disobey any attempts to stop her seeing him. If only she could see the two of them together, then she'd know. If he came to the house she could get a good look at ... what was his name? Archie, that was it. Martha gasped. Wasn't that the one Pat had called a sugar daddy?

175

Chapter 24

Sheila's heart was racing as she took the slip of paper and noted the coordinates. Working quickly, she plotted the position on the huge map of the Atlantic Ocean pinned to the table that filled the operations room. She reached for the rake that, during the course of her training, had become an extension of her arm and used it to manoeuvre a grey cigar-shaped wooden block across the table. During her training she had been instructed not to think of the blocks as ships, planes or submarines, but as she stepped back she shivered at the thought that she had just moved a German U-boat several miles closer to a convoy of twenty Allied ships loaded with food, fuel and people. Clemmie, standing next to her, squeezed her elbow as if to reassure her. Sheila had completed her six-week training in the ops room and was now being shadowed by Clemmie, an experienced plotter, for a short time, after which she would be allowed to work independently.

Above the map table a wooden gallery encircled the room from where Coastal Command senior officers had a bird's-eye view of the ocean while they received situation updates, made their decisions and directed operations. Within minutes the coordinates of the response to the U-boat closing in on the convoy were in Sheila's hands and she turned a Liberator plane in its direction. Time slipped away and the many blocks on the map moved steadily over the ocean, but all eyes flickered towards the U-boat and the Liberator each time they were adjusted. The race was on and tension mounted as they waited to see whether the plane could destroy the submarine before it reached the convoy. Sheila had been on duty for five hours already, but she felt no tiredness; she was desperate to see the U-boat removed from the table and the convoy and the plane turn towards home. Then suddenly the coordinates for all three converged on the table. The clock high on the plotting room wall moved at a snail's pace: one minute, five minutes, ten minutes … There was a shout from the gallery and the room erupted into cheers … The U-boat had been hit and Sheila was instructed to remove the block from the table.

When they came off shift in the early morning Sheila and Clemmie went straight to the NAAFI, where everyone was in high spirits and the talk was all about the Liberator and its crew.

'Well, Sheila,' said Clemmie, 'how did that feel?'

'I can't describe it, my heart's still racing. I never thought I'd feel like this. Oh Clemmie, this is why I wanted to join the WAAF – to do something that made a difference, something to bring an end to the war.'

'Well, let's get something to eat then we need to go to bed, because we have to do it all again tomorrow.'

When Clemmie and Sheila had been on the night shift they would sometimes visit the little tea shop just outside the base in the afternoon. Most days it was crowded with RAF personnel, escaping the NAAFI to enjoy tea that wasn't stewed and soda scones baked the same morning. Clemmie would often meet her boyfriend Brad, a Canadian pilot, there when they were off duty. Sheila wouldn't normally have gone with her, but today Clemmie insisted. 'You can't lie on your bed all afternoon. Come on, it'll be fun.'

Sheila knew she should stay in the hut and write to Charles; he'd sent her three letters and she'd only replied to one. The trouble was that he could write about his love and how much he missed her – indeed he could make her blush with his passionate words – but try as she might she found it hard to express her own feelings. She jumped off the bed and grabbed her makeup bag. 'Give me five minutes.'

Brad was already there with another pilot when Clemmie and Sheila came in. He gave Clemmie a peck on the cheek then introduced his friend. 'This is Philippe, he arrived last week. We trained together back home; never thought we'd both end up in Ireland, let alone at the same base.' He turned to his friend. 'Philippe, this is Clemmie and Sheila.'

Philippe, leaning back in his chair with his flying jacket open, acknowledged them with a slight nod. His dark hair and olive skin gave him an exotic look, more Mediterranean than Canadian.

'Where were you based before?' asked Clemmie.

'RAF Aldergrove but, now that your runway's been extended, a few of us have transferred with the Liberators so we can be closer to the Atlantic.' Sheila was curious about his accent; she'd have to ask Clemmie about that.

'Yeah,' said Brad, 'and he's not been here a week and he's already bagged a U-boat!'

'Wow!' said Clemmie. 'That was you, last night?'

Sheila's eyes widened. This was the airman whose plane she had plotted, the one she had prayed would make it back safely.

'Call sign Panther,' said Clemmie. 'Hey, we were in the ops room – Sheila plotted your plane.'

Philippe, his eyes dark and striking, winked at Sheila. 'Looks like you brought me luck – merci.'

She blushed under his gaze and was glad when, at that moment, the tea and scones arrived.

Brad and Philippe talked of missions flown and narrow escapes and Clemmie happily listened and chipped in now and again. Sheila was conscious that she had very little to say and felt slightly intimidated by their easy banter and swapping of stories. So instead she surreptitiously studied Philippe. He was not particularly tall, but he was solid like a boxer and when he laughed he tipped his head back and his teeth were very white. His jaw was strong with a tinge of blueness as though he hadn't shaved. She wondered how old he was. Early twenties probably, yet he could fly that huge plane out over the ocean to—

'What do you think, Sheila?'

They were looking at her, expecting an answer, but she had no idea of the question. Clemmie came to her rescue. 'Next time we've all got Saturday night off we could go to the dance in the village. What do you think?'

Sheila hesitated. 'I don't know …'

'Oh, it'll be great fun – you've got to come,' said Clemmie.

'Okay, that's settled then,' said Brad and he stood up. 'We've gotta go, there's a briefing.' But as the two pilots left, Sheila thought she caught a look of irritation on Philippe's face, and he seemed to be having words with Brad.

'What was the matter with you back there?' asked Clemmie as they walked back to the base. 'You love dancing.'

'You've just fixed up a foursome and I'm not interested in going out with anyone. I'm engaged, remember?'

'Don't worry, we'll just be friends out together.'

'But you and Brad are a couple and we'll be the gooseberries. Did you not see the look on Philippe's face when he left? I don't think he liked the idea either. He's a bit strange isn't he? I mean he sounds strange.'

Clemmie laughed. 'He's French Canadian, that's why. I love his accent, don't you?'

Sheila shrugged.

Clemmie linked arms with her friend. 'You could get to know him, if you come to the dance.'

As it happened it was only two weeks later that Sheila went to the village dance and she didn't have to worry about Philippe because he wasn't there. In fact she knew exactly where he was because, just before she finished her shift, she had plotted the coordinates of his Liberator and moved it just beyond the coast heading west. Tonight there would just be Jessica, Clemmie and herself – a girls' night out – to celebrate Jessica's birthday and the first dance they had attended together since they arrived at the base.

Sheila felt completely different out of uniform. She was wearing the one decent dress she had brought with her, the rosebud print with the sweetheart neckline, the same one she had worn to the Floral Hall the night Charles had asked her to marry him. That all seemed so long ago. Now her world had changed beyond anything she thought possible and every day her was head was filled with convoys and planes and some days she hardly thought of Charles at all.

'Are you ready?' shouted Clemmie.

'In a minute.' Sheila took a last look in the mirror. In uniform they had to wear their hair off their shoulders, but tonight she left it loose and slightly flicked out at the ends. Her makeup was exactly how she would do it for the stage.

'Now all we need is the birthday girl so we can get going. Where is she?'

'Still in the ablutions, I think,' said Sheila and at that moment the door opened and Jessica came into the hut.

Clemmie and Sheila gasped at the sight of her. She wore an expensive, silk, off-the-shoulder cocktail dress in a rich ruby colour and around her neck was an amethyst necklace.

'Wow, you're going to raise a few eyebrows dressed like that,' said Clemmie.

'Oh, is this not what's expected on these occasions?'

'I can safely say that no one will be expecting that,' said Clemmie.

At the church hall, they paid their shilling entrance fee and went to the cloakroom. 'Let's start with a little cocktail, shall we?' suggested Jessica and she took a sizeable silver hip flask from her handbag and unscrewed the cup at the top. She filled it up and offered it to Clemmie who took a sip and started to cough.

'What kind of cocktail is that?'

'Well, it's whiskey,' said Jessica.

'Whiskey and what else?' Clemmie handed her back the little cup.

'Just whiskey, that was all I could get.' Jessica drank the remains, poured another measure and offered it to Sheila. 'Go on, try it, you might like it.'

Sheila took a sip and shuddered. 'Ugh, it's horrible.'

Once again Jessica finished it off, then poured another just for herself and drank it in one. 'Well, shall we go and mingle with the hoi polloi?' she said, and led the way into the hall just as the sound of 'I Don't Want to Set the World on Fire' blared from a crackling gramophone.

There were only a few couples dancing, while most of the men stood around talking and every now and again sneaking a look at the girls on the other side of the room.

'Not exactly the Ritz, is it?' said Jessica.

'Oh, it's early yet,' said Clemmie. 'There'll be more airmen in later when they've had a few drinks in the bar down the road. We can take it in turns to dance together until they get here.'

Jessica groaned. 'Why don't you two go ahead? I'd rather wait for a genuine Brylcreem boy. In the meantime, I'll be happy here with my friend …' She patted the flask in her bag.

The next record had a faster tempo and the two girls danced a quickstep around the almost empty floor and after that they had a few dances with the airmen. By eight o'clock the hall had filled up and the dance floor was packed. Sheila thanked the corporal with two left feet she had been dancing with and made her way back to their table for a rest. Neither Clemmie nor Jessica was there, but she soon caught sight of them waltzing past.

'Can you believe it?' A voice, honey warm, behind her. 'My guardian WAAF deserts me to go off dancing and, before I know it, my luck runs out.'

Sheila looked over her shoulder and did a double take because there was Philippe, not in his flying gear, but in full uniform as though he was going on parade.

'Why are you here?' she demanded. 'You should be—'

'Over the Atlantic? That's right, but only half an hour out we were hit by lightning – messed up the instruments. We returned to base pronto; bit hairy coming down.' He threw himself into the seat next to her. 'What have you to say for yourself, deserting your post?'

'I can't be on duty every time you fly.'

'Why not?'

In spite of herself, Sheila smiled and shrugged her shoulders. Philippe leaned forward. 'You know how superstitious flyers can be, don't you? I thought you and I were somehow connected.'

Sheila was on her guard. 'Why would you think that?'

'Because the funny thing is, when I met you, I kind of thought I knew you, like I'd seen you before.' He paused and studied her face. 'I got the same feeling just now, only stronger.' He reached out and lifted a tress of her long hair and let it fall. 'Do you know me?' he said.

Under the intensity of his gaze, she shook her head and lowered her eyes. Then he laughed and she looked up. The moment had passed.

'Hey, do you want to dance?' he asked.

'I ... I'm not sure ...'

'Come on, it's just a dance,' he said, and took her hand. It was a slow bluesy Ella Fitzgerald song, one of Peggy's favourites. They moved round the floor; it was hardly dancing at all, but Sheila didn't care. The song made her think of Peggy, Pat, Irene and, most of all, her mother and after all this time away she felt such a longing to see them again. She rested her head on Philippe's shoulder and let the mournful sound of the minor key bring her close to tears. When the music stopped she quickly thanked Philippe and walked off the dance floor, through the hallway and straight out into the night. It was pitch black, not a star in the sky. The cold air steadied her and she wiped her eyes, but then she sensed someone behind her. 'Who's there?' she said.

'My dancing wasn't that bad, was it?'

'No, no ... I'm sorry. It's just that I ... it's silly ... I suddenly felt so homesick. I don't know why, it just hit me.'

'Sometimes it happens like that – everybody gets it. Who have you got back home?'

'My sisters and my mother.'

'They must be proud of you, oui?'

'Oh, I don't know ... probably. My mother didn't want me to enlist.'

'No, neither did mine, that's the way it is. Heard you've a sweetheart too, is that right?'

'Yes, we're engaged.'

'Too bad.' She could hear the smile in his voice.

'And what about you?'

'Mother, father, brother and two sisters back in Montreal; used

182

to have a sweetheart too, but not any more. She found somebody else.'

'Oh, I'm sorry.'

'No need, I'm not sorry. Tell you the truth, when I got her letter it was a weight off my mind – not having to worry about a girl back home when I'm doing a job like this. Doesn't mean I can't have a dance or talk to a girl, just don't want to get involved, that's all.'

'So what was all that you were saying about knowing me?'

'Oh, it wasn't a chat-up line or anything. I don't know, maybe you remind me of someone.' He touched her hair again. 'That's to bring me luck.' He gave an embarrassed laugh. 'Hey, it's getting cold out here. How about we go back inside and talk some more?'

After that night, Sheila was surprised how often she would bump into Philippe. Whether in the tea shop, the NAAFI or the mess, he always looked pleased to see her and would ask about her family and how her job was going. Sometimes he'd touch her hair for luck and to make her laugh. Before long she found herself looking out for him and when they met his easy smile never failed to brighten her day.

Towards the end of October, when she was on her own eating breakfast after her shift, he came into the mess. He didn't see her at first so she watched him as he got coffee and toast at the counter and she found herself running her eyes over his broad shoulders and the dark hair curled tightly on his head. She waited for him to turn round and waved him over. By the time he sat down opposite her, his brief smile had been replaced by a serious expression.

'Hello.'

He nodded in reply.

'Are you all right?'

'Not really.' He was clearly annoyed. 'I've just been put on the roster to do a training flight later on this afternoon, something to do with parachute tests, instead of going on patrol.'

'Can you swap with someone?'

'No, you shouldn't ever do that.'

'Why not?

'Oh, it's a sort of superstition – you know what we're like. If you're on the roster, you fly the roster. But never mind me, how's my best buddy today?'

'Tired, ready for my bed. There was a lot going on last night. A U-boat was tracking a convoy, but then it disappeared into thin air. They were searching for it all night, but it must have slipped away.'

'Have you written to your mother and Charles, like you said you would?'

Sheila looked away. 'No – I'll do it today.'

Philippe gave her a stern look, but she could see his eyes were twinkling. 'You promise?' She nodded and he went on, 'Got a letter myself yesterday.'

Sheila waited, but he just sat there eating his toast. Eventually she said, 'Who was it from?'

He dusted the crumbs from his hands and took a drink of coffee before he spoke. 'From the girl back home, you remember the one who ...'

'Yes, I remember.'

A heavy silence settled between them. Sheila was shocked at how much she wanted to know what was in the letter, but how could she ask something so private, so delicate? Philippe swirled the dregs of coffee round his cup and didn't meet her eye. Then they both spoke at the same time: 'Why did she write to you?' 'She wants to make up with me.'

'Sorry,' said Sheila, 'what did you say?'

'I said she wants us to get back together.'

'Oh ...' Sheila felt his words churn her insides. 'Oh ...' she said again.

'Exactly,' said Philippe and the silence crept back into the space between them.

'What do you thing about that?' said Sheila at last.

'I don't know what to think. As far as I was concerned, she'd found someone else and, well ... I tried to get over her. In a way, I was glad not to have to worry about her, you know, if something happened to me. Then out of the blue there is this letter.' He stared into the distance. 'And I've no idea what to say to her.'

Sheila spoke gently. 'Do you want to get back together with her?'

He raised his head. 'People change,' was all he said, but there was confusion in his face and something else – a sadness maybe.

Sheila resisted a sudden urge to touch his hand. Instead she told him, 'Give yourself time to think about it. There's no rush, is there?'

'No,' he said. 'There is all the time in the world.'

Tired from her long shift, Sheila went back to the hut and wrote a letter to her mother then got into bed. It was still light outside, but that wouldn't usually have kept her awake. Then there was the cold wind blowing through a gap in the corner of the hut – she got up and put her greatcoat on top of the blanket. But there was no escape from the real reason she was wide awake after a six-hour shift. The truth was she couldn't stop thinking about Philippe and the girl who wanted him back. She couldn't blame her – he was such a nice person and good company – but how could she have been so cruel as to send a letter to a pilot serving overseas, rejecting him? It was even worse to write and upset him again when he had just got over her. Sheila yawned and curled up in a ball. Slowly she began to warm up and her heavy eyelids closed …

She slept the day away and woke up in the dark, cold and hungry. If anyone had come into the hut she certainly hadn't heard them, but it was surprising that no one was about. She braved the cold and went to the ablutions block to wash, then got back into her uniform and wandered over to the NAAFI. There was, as usual, no light coming from the building because of the blackout curtains, but there was no sound either. At this time it would normally be full of people having their tea and chatting to their friends. She pushed open the door and saw at once that it was indeed full of people, but the faces that turned towards her stopped her heart. Jessica rushed over to her and led her to the table where several of the girls from their hut were sitting. She could see that they had been crying and felt panic rise inside her.

'What's wrong? What's happened?' she asked.

'Sit down,' said Jessica and Sheila felt for the chair and lowered herself into it.

'There was an accident this afternoon,' Jessica explained. 'A plane clipped a telephone wire over behind the church and it crashed.

We've been waiting here for word of the crew, but we've heard there were no survivors.' Sheila closed her eyes tight, trying to hold back the tears, trying to make sense of what she had been told.

'Were they coming back from patrol? What was the call sign? I was probably plotting them early this morning.'

'No,' said Jessica, 'they hadn't been on patrol. They went out this afternoon on a training flight, something to do with testing parachutes.'

As soon as Sheila heard the words 'training flight' she let out a cry: 'Philippe. It's Philippe, oh no!'

Jessica got hold of her by the arms and spoke sternly. 'Listen, we don't know the names of the crew yet. Some of them don't even belong on this base. We're waiting to hear—'

Sheila tried to squeeze her words out between sobs. 'He told me this morning he'd been rostered for a training flight. He didn't want to go, said he couldn't get out of it. It's him, I know it is.'

Jessica could see the unsettling effect of Sheila's distress on everyone. Philippe was popular on the base and his name spread across the room in seconds. 'Sheila, you need to calm down. Come outside with me and we'll walk over to HQ to see if there's any more news.' And she took her by the elbow and led her out into the night.

'You were talking to Philippe this morning?' asked Jessica.

'Yes, he was annoyed about the switch to the training flight. If only he'd gone on patrol ...' Sheila's voice cracked and she began to shiver.

'Look, you've got to be very brave, Sheila. You know that, don't you? It was only a matter of time before one of these planes came down. I know you were friendly with Philippe, but it's not like he was your boyfriend or anything.'

'No, he wasn't,' said Sheila, 'but I liked him – he was my friend.'

Inside the HQ building Jessica spotted one of the squadron leaders she had driven many times. 'You wait here and I'll see if he knows anything.'

Sheila hadn't been inside HQ since that first day and she felt she shouldn't be there now. People were coming and going and she could see the effects of the grim situation they were dealing with on every face. In her head she said over and over, 'Philippe ... Philippe,' until she could bear it no longer; she had to get away. She rushed outside and ran and ran until she came again to the empty hut where she threw herself on her bed and let the darkness envelop her. When she could cry no more she brought to mind the image of him in the tea shop when they met, the first time he said she had brought him luck. Well, she wasn't lucky after all, was she? Then she remembered the impulse she had to touch him this morning; if only she had done so, maybe then she would have sensed he was in danger. If only she'd known ...

She sat up. Was that a noise? Someone was in the hut. Had they come to find her? She sensed someone searching for the light switch. 'Who's there?' she called.

The single bare lightbulb dangling from the centre of the ceiling came on, illuminating the central area, and beyond that Sheila could make out a shadowy figure coming towards the light. She held her breath.

'Sheila, are you in here?'

She gasped at the sound. The figure moved again and stepped into the pool of light and her heart stopped. Philippe! His face was pale and drained of expression.

'Are you here?' he called again.

She stood up and went towards him. 'Is it you?' she said.

'Yes. I'm here,' he said, and she ran to him and flung her arms around him.

'Easy, easy,' he said and held her while she wept. 'Come on now, I'm okay.' He stepped back and they were staring into each other's eyes.

'They told me the plane had crashed and everyone was dead,' said Sheila.

'Not my plane,' he said. 'After I left you this morning there was a sighting of the U-boat that disappeared off Donegal last night when you were on duty. They needed an extra plane out there and, because I was rested, they sent me on patrol.'

'But the training flight went ahead.'

'Yes, it was scheduled for late afternoon and by that time there were other pilots who were rested and able to do the training flight. I guess …' Philippe bowed his head a moment and when he spoke again his voice was just a whisper. 'I guess one of them would have volunteered to do it.'

'When did you get back?'

'I've only just landed. Walked into the NAAFI to get something to eat and they were all staring at me like they'd seen a ghost. Then Jessica told me you'd gone off on your own so I went looking for you. Came here as a last resort.' He gave a half-smile. 'And I'll tell you, if I get caught in WAAF quarters, I'll be for the high jump.' He touched her hair and winked. 'Come on, Lucky, let's go get something to eat before you go on night shift.'

Chapter 25

Oldpark Presbyterian Church was anything but welcoming that first Sunday of Advent. Martha had walked there in the bitter cold for the morning service, only to find it was even colder inside the church than out. There were no flowers to brighten the altar and seemingly no end to the sermon. The Revd Lynas had taken the theme of hope and twisted it and turned it to preach anything that came to mind and, by the end, all Martha could think of was, 'Abandon all hope ye who enter here'.

When the service was finally over she didn't linger to chat to anyone, but as she paused in the porch to put on her gloves someone behind her spoke her name.

'Martha, I wonder if I could have a private word.'

She knew exactly who it was; his country accent and commanding tone were unmistakable. She turned round to face Ted Grimes, but didn't speak or smile.

'Are you well, Martha?'

She shrugged her shoulders. If this man thought he could just accost her in church after his disgraceful behaviour, he was in for a rude awakening.

'I've been thinking about ye for a while so I have and, to tell you the truth, I need to get something off me chest.'

She weighed him up, with his RUC uniform, cap under his arm and his gun on his belt. Had the man no sensitivity, coming into a church like that?

'I want to apologise for all that misunderstanding with Irene last year. I was wrong. I know now that Irene was friendly with Theresa O'Hara, but I was wrong in thinking she had anything to do with her republican brother.' He paused as though expecting some acknowledgement from Martha. There was none. He shuffled his feet and tried another tack. 'Well anyway, I've wanted to say that for a while. The other thing is … ah … I thought you'd want to know that Vera isn't well, not well at all – looking bleak as they say.'

When Ted Grimes had accused Irene of withholding information about the whereabouts of an IRA fugitive and his wife, and threatened her with jail, Martha had severed all ties with him, despite the fact that they had known each other for years. She certainly had no desire to renew their friendship just because he'd made a half-hearted apology; but his wife Vera was another matter. She was a pleasant woman, would always ask about the girls when they met on the street and pass the time of day. God help her, she'd always been delicate, but Martha had no idea she was in a bad way.

'What's the matter with her?'

Her question was the trigger for Ted to pour out everything that he had come to say to her. 'It's her heart. Sure, she can hardly walk now, sleeps downstairs. It's her breathing too; sometimes she struggles for breath and time and again I think she's never going to catch it. Lately she's been asking about ye and wondering why ye never call round. She took a turn for the worse this last week and … I don't know … she wanted me to ask if you'll come and see her.'

Martha had nothing against Vera and she was sorry to hear she was so ill, but she didn't want to get involved with Ted ever again. 'I'll think about it,' she said.

'Well, I wouldn't leave it too long,' said Ted, and he took his cap from under his arm and set it firmly on his head and straightened the peak. 'Good day to you, Martha.'

★

When her mother had left for church, Pat quickly got ready in her Sunday clothes and slipped out of the house. She too was going to worship, but not in Oldpark Presbyterian Church – she was heading for the cathedral in the centre of town. She hadn't been there since the Wings for Victory day, when the grandeur and atmosphere had had such a profound effect on her and she had felt that Tony was somehow with her, even though he was far away in North Africa.

She knew from the wireless reports that his unit must now be somewhere in Italy, but there hadn't been a letter from him for almost three months and during that time she had felt that he was steadily slipping away from her. Maybe in the cathedral she would feel close to him again and, although she couldn't explain it, she had the feeling that he would somehow know she was thinking of him.

Not being a member of the congregation, she sat towards the back of the church when she arrived, but it wasn't long before every pew was full and the service began. The building itself was as impressive as she remembered it and the first sounds from the organ lifted her spirits as it filled the vast space with a rich, dramatic sound. The choir were wonderful: so well trained; such beautiful voices. The minister preached a lively sermon about love. But try as she might, she couldn't find the comfort she had experienced the last time she had been in the cathedral. That day she had believed that her prayers would be heard and that Tony was alive and well and thinking of her. But today she felt nothing and knew she had been foolish to come at all.

When the service ended the people filed down the aisle past her and she sat a while with her eyes closed, trying to gather her thoughts.

'Hello Patti. I didn't expect to see you here?'

She opened her eyes to see an American uniform and the smiling face of Captain Joe Walters.

'It's good to see you again,' he said and slipped into the pew in front of her.

Just hearing the American accent made her feel better. 'And you,' she said. 'How are you?' and she almost managed a smile.

Joe tilted his head to one side and studied her. 'I'm okay,' he said, 'but I'm not sure about you. Is there something wrong?'

Pat didn't answer right away. She couldn't possibly tell him that she was worried sick about Tony and had come to the cathedral for some sort of comfort or a sense that Tony was with her in spirit.

Joe took an educated guess and said, 'Have you heard from Tony lately?'

Pat shook her head.

'You mustn't worry, you know. Since they crossed on to the Italian mainland the situation is changing all the time and communications are not that good. Sometimes they're moving fast and letters probably aren't being written. Gee, even if they were, there isn't the time or the backup to run a mail service. Up till now it's been about advancing, but the weather's closing in and …' he paused, uncertain whether to go on.

'And what?'

He lifted his hands. 'Who knows, maybe they'll dig in for the winter, or the advance could be halted anyway.'

'What do you mean "halted"?'

Joe didn't answer.

'Tell me, I need to know.'

He gave a deep sigh. 'The mountain terrain is difficult and there'll be more resistance the further north they go. I can't really say more than that.'

'Thank you,' said Pat and she stood up to go.

Joe caught her arm. 'Hey, maybe this is the wrong thing to say, but … if you need someone to talk to, maybe explain things, you know I'd be happy to oblige any time.'

'That's really kind of you,' said Pat, and together they left the cathedral.

Later, it being Sunday, her mother drew the blackout curtains in the front room and lit a small fire so they could spend the evening listening to the wireless. Pat got out her atlas and studied the map of Italy, tracing the Apennine Mountains mentioned in the latest news report on the Italian Campaign. On reflection, she was glad she had gone to the cathedral because in a way she had connected with Tony. She had met Joe and he had been able to explain why there were no letters and, what's more, he was honest enough to tell her what was likely to happen. Her certainty that Tony would come through the war as he had promised was as strong as ever.

Shortly after seven there was a knock at the front door and Peggy went to answer it. There was the sound of a man's voice and Peggy answering. Martha tutted and shouted, 'You're letting all the heat out, Peggy! Who is it?'

The door opened and Peggy came back in, followed by a man with a cap pulled low over his eyes. Martha recognised the Harris tweed coat immediately. What was Charles Turner doing coming to her door on a dark Sunday night?

He quickly removed his cap and stood twisting it in his hands, and when Pat saw how nervous he was she said, 'Come and sit near the fire, Charles. It's a bad night isn't it?'

'Aye, it is.' His eyes flitted round the room and it was clear he was building up to saying something, but when he opened his mouth nothing came out.

'Are you all right?' asked Pat.

'Aye. Well, no … I wanted to ask if you'd heard from Sheila lately.'

'We had a letter a week ago, didn't we, Mammy?' Pat gave her mother a nod as if to say, you'd better deal with this.

'Yes, she wrote me a page like she does most weeks,' said Martha. By the look on Charles' face she deduced that he wasn't getting regular letters. She had feared that something like this might happen after seeing the way they had parted at the train station. Martha went on, 'Just general chat about life on the base. Nothing about her job, of course – that wouldn't be allowed.' Martha leaned forward in her chair. 'Am I to take it that she hasn't been writing to you?'

Charles nodded. 'Haven't heard anything for over a month – I just keep writing and I get nothing back.'

Pat and Peggy exchanged looks. This could be embarrassing for their mother and when she answered they could hear the annoyance in her voice.

'Well, I'm sorry to hear that. I think that's very remiss of Sheila.'

'I thought she might be having second thoughts about our engagement. She didn't say anything to you, did she?'

'Good heavens, no.'

'She could have met someone else.'

'Certainly not.' Martha was affronted. 'Right, I'll send her a letter tomorrow to ask her what's going on and why she's not been writing to you.'

Charles wasn't listening; he seemed to be lost in his own thoughts.

'I'll write to her,' said Martha again.

'I didn't want her to join the Air Force, you know. I told her that her place was with me, but she wouldn't listen. She'd got it in her head that she was free to do whatever she wanted – never a thought for me. I told her, you're engaged now and you don't have to prove anything to anybody.'

The Goulding women stared at him in disbelief.

'Now, just a minute,' said Pat. 'Sheila joined the WAAF because she wanted to do something that would help bring an end to the war and we're proud of her.'

Then Peggy waded in. 'Look here, our Sheila is free to do what she wants and the cost of an engagement ring doesn't give you the right to say otherwise.'

'If you'd decided to enlist, which of course you haven't,' said Pat, 'Sheila certainly wouldn't have stood in your way. She'd have supported you.'

Charles stood up. 'There's no conscription here and anyway I would never have left Sheila. But when she comes home at Christmas I'll have this out with her.'

'She won't be home for Christmas,' said Martha. 'Did she not tell you there's no leave from their base until they've been there six months?'

Charles swore under his breath and stormed out of the house, leaving the door wide open and letting the heat out and the freezing night air in.

The following morning, Martha posted her letter to Sheila explaining that Charles was worried that he hadn't heard from her and suggesting she should write to him. If it hadn't been for his outburst the previous night, her tone would have been a lot stronger.

When she came out of the post office she hesitated, uncertain whether to go straight back home or walk down the Cliftonville Road to Ted Grimes' house. The truth was she felt guilty about losing touch with Vera because of Ted's behaviour and, now that she was ill, it seemed petty not to visit her. She just hoped that Ted would be at work.

She stepped into the vestibule and knocked, but there was no answer. She tried the door and it opened. 'Hello,' she shouted, 'anybody home?' There was just enough light inside for her to see the heavy hall stand, no cap or gun there. Ted was out. 'Vera, it's Martha,' she called again and there was a muffled sound from the parlour. She pushed open the door and was met by stale air and the sound of laboured breathing. The curtains were closed and she could just make out the shape of Vera propped up in her bed.

'Is it you, Martha?'

'Aye, it is. I've come to see how you are.' She pulled up a chair. 'Ted tells me you've not been well.'

'The doctor says it's my heart, but the worst of it is I can't be walking anywhere, not even to the front door.'

'I'm so sorry, Vera. Is there anything I can do for you?'

'Ah, just sit a while, will you? I don't get much company at all. Tell me, how's those girls of yours?'

And Martha told her the news about each one: Irene's baby, Peggy and the major, Pat singing for Eisenhower and Sheila in the WAAF. 'Sure, I can hardly keep up with them,' she said.

'Right enough, it must wonderful to have those girls. We were never blessed with children as you know and when you're coming to the end of everything ...' She left the rest unspoken as she struggled to get her breath and, when she found it, her voice was stronger and more urgent. 'I worry about Ted. God knows, he's not an easy man to like and I'm sorry if he offended you in some way. But the thing is, Martha, you're one of the very few people he respects. He's no family in Belfast other than me and when I'm gone there'll be nobody.'

Martha became increasingly uneasy as Vera talked, and tried to steer the conversation in another direction. 'But Ted has his work, he's devoted to the police force and I'm sure he has good friends there.'

Vera shook her head. 'I'm not so sure. Men bury their heads in the sand when things are awkward. They've not much sense when it comes to feelings, wouldn't notice things like a woman would. All I'm asking, Martha, is that you keep a wee eye on him, no more than that.'

Chapter 26

'She's here, she's here!' screamed Peggy and she flew out the door and up the path to throw her arms around her sister. 'I can't believe you're here, Irene,' she said, 'and Alexander too,' and she peered into the pram.

Martha, still in her apron and with her hands covered in flour, was hard on Peggy's heels. She hugged her daughter. 'Is he asleep?' she asked and right on cue Alexander began to gurgle.

Irene laughed. 'Well, he was!'

Martha took control of the pram and together they went into the house. 'My goodness it's warm in here,' said Irene.

'Aye, that'll be the new paraffin heater, Mammy's pride and joy,' said Pat from the kitchen doorway. 'We'll all be roasted.'

'Now then,' said Martha, as she lifted a sleepy Alexander. 'We have to keep you nice and warm don't we, wee man?'

Peggy held out her arms. 'Give him to me, Mammy, you'll get flour all over him.'

Irene took off her coat and flopped down on the settee. 'That was such a long journey I thought I was never getting here.'

'Never mind, you're here now and for two whole weeks,' said Peggy as she struggled to get Alexander out of his winter coat, hat and mittens.

'It's going to be the best Christmas ever,' said Pat.

Alexander stretched and yawned and looked around him at the strange faces. Peggy jigged him on her knee. 'You're with your Aunt Peggy now,' she told him, but his face puckered and he began to cry.

'Ach, you're too loud, Peggy – you're frightening him,' said Pat. 'Give him to me.' And she took the child and walked with him round the room pointing out the piano with the bust of Tchaikovsky on top and the wireless and the china cabinet. 'There you are; he's happy with his Aunt Pat.'

'Only because you have an ample bosom for him to rest his head on,' said Peggy.

The next day Irene took Alexander to the aircraft factory to show him off to the women she used to work with. She arrived in time for the dinner break and went up to the canteen. Everyone crowded around her and Alexander was passed from one woman to another. They cooed over him and talked about his eyes, his hair, his tiny fingers while he was bounced on knees and lifted into the air. They pressed silver sixpences into his palm, 'for his moneybox,' they said, and Irene rescued them one at a time and put them safely away. Macy waited until everyone had held him and gone back to their dinner before cradling Alexander in the crook of her arm, where he promptly fell asleep.

'How the hell are you, Irene?' she said. 'How's things in the back of beyond?'

Irene laughed. 'I'm grand – going to Fermanagh was the best thing I ever did.'

'Never thought I'd hear you say that.'

'It's like Sandy and I have started all over again. He works so hard, but we get to spend time together when he's off duty and, now we have Alexander, I feel like we're a proper family.'

'You're very lucky,' said Macy.

'I am,' said Irene. 'And what about you? You look well.'

'Oh, I don't know. I'm just waiting for this war to end so I can go home.'

'I heard you got an offer from Bob Hope.'

'Yeah, maybe I'll go to California and turn up at his Beverly Hills mansion. Next thing you know, you'll be watching me on the screen at the Ritz.'

'I wouldn't be surprised,' said Irene.

'How's Sheila doing? Found a handsome pilot yet?'

'I don't think so, but Mammy's a bit sad that she won't be coming home for a while. There'd be room at the table for Christmas dinner, if you're not doing anything?'

Macy winked. 'I'm gonna be kinda busy – there's a sergeant major who's promised me a real good time over the holidays.'

If anyone at the base had asked Sheila whether she was homesick, she would almost certainly have said 'No'. She was too busy either working, sleeping or enjoying the company of her friends. But the truth was that sometimes when she went straight to bed after a long shift in the ops room, she couldn't calm her racing brain. So, instead of tossing and turning, she would imagine herself back home in Joanmount Gardens, sitting in the kitchen with her mother or listening to the wireless in the front room. Sometimes she would be with her sisters rehearsing for a show and she'd sing all the songs in her head until sleep overtook her.

As Christmas grew nearer, the NAAFI acquired a ceiling-high spruce bedecked with lights, paper decorations criss-crossed the room and the longing for home crept steadily into her heart. But in the end it was the letter telling her that Irene and Alexander would be in Belfast for Christmas that finally tipped her over the edge into a severe bout of homesickness.

'What's the matter with you?' asked Jessica as they sat together in the tea shop.

'Nothing really.'

'You've hardly spoken since we got here.'

'Oh, sorry, I'm just thinking about Christmas.'

'Christmas? It's going to be great fun with too much to eat and dances in the NAAFI and the village hall.'

'I know,' said Sheila, 'but I've been thinking about my family. It'll be the first time I've not been with them. I haven't seen my sister Irene since last Christmas when she went to Enniskillen, but she's coming home with her little boy and I really wish I could be there.'

When Clemmie arrived she took one look at them and said, 'I don't think I'll bother sitting with you two …'

'Sheila's homesick,' explained Jessica, 'and I think she's smitten me as well.'

'Oh, you'll get over it,' said Clemmie. 'This'll be my second Christmas away. I've not been home since I signed up. At least you're not three thousand miles away from your families. You might be lucky and get a bit of leave next year.'

Sheila shook her head. 'What I wouldn't do for a pass. A two-day one would be enough for me to get home for Christmas dinner even if I had to leave before the plum pudding.'

Clemmie smiled. 'Funny you should say that. Talk about singing for your supper – you could sing for your Christmas dinner.'

'What are you talking about?'

'They've just put up a notice about a talent competition next Saturday. The winner gets a two-day pass.'

'No, really?' said Jessica.

'Yeah, it's right there on the noticeboard. So, either of you a got talent you've been hiding under a bushel?'

Jessica laughed. 'Of course. I'll have you know I play the piano very badly. What about you, Sheila?'

But Sheila was staring into the distance, a strange expression on her face. 'I'm going to sing,' she said.

'Okay,' said Clemmie. 'Have you sung before, in front of an audience, I mean?'

'Ah … yes, yes I have, with my sisters and on my own as well.'

'Why didn't you tell us you could sing?'

Sheila shrugged her shoulders.

'So you're serious? You really want to do this?' said Jessica.

Sheila nodded. 'I'm going to win that two-day pass.'

They could see how determined she was. 'Do you want an accompanist?' asked Jessica.

'Oh, that'd be great. We'll need to practise a bit together.'

Jessica was suddenly excited. 'I say, we could nip down to the church hall, there's a piano in there. I'm not on duty until later. What about you?'

The church hall was empty when they slipped in and Jessica went straight to the piano, lifted the lid and played a few notes. Sheila stood at her side and Clemmie, happy to be the audience, pulled up a chair.

'What do you want to sing?' asked Jessica.

'I'm not sure yet. I'll run through a couple and you play along. Do you know "Stormy Weather"?'

'I'll do my best.' Jessica tried an introduction and Sheila began to sing.

The warm bluesy sound of her voice filled the hall and both Clemmie and Jessica looked at her in astonishment. How could such a powerful sound come from this slight, almost fragile, figure? Her voice, expressing such emotion, touched them so deeply that Jessica all but stopped playing to listen and Clemmie felt tears prick her eyes. When the last note had died away, they both squealed with delight, jumping up and down, hugging her.

'I can't believe you. How did you learn to sing like that?' said Jessica.

'Hey girl,' said Clemmie. 'I think that pass has your name on it.'

'Was it all right?' asked Sheila. 'I haven't sung for so long. I'll need to practise quite a bit.'

'Gosh, I think I'm the one who'll have to get practising,' said Jessica. 'I don't know if I can do you justice.'

Clemmie was suddenly serious. 'Sheila, why didn't you ever mention to us that you could sing like that?'

'I don't know. It's not something you go around saying to people, is it?'

Clemmie smiled. 'Well, I suppose not. Come on then, you said you had other songs, can we hear those as well?'

Sheila sang 'Blue Moon' in an upbeat, swing style, then 'Night and Day' just like Ella Fitzgerald and Jessica began to get a sense of Sheila's rhythm and phrasing.

'I think if you and I could get an hour or two of practice over the next week I could polish up the accompaniment,' said Jessica as they walked back to the hut. 'And we'll have to sort out what you're wearing.'

'And which song you'll sing,' added Clemmie. 'Maybe we should ask the boys what they think.'

Sheila stopped walking. 'Oh, I don't know about that. I don't want a fuss, with people asking me about it. I just want to sing one song on the night to try and win the pass.'

'What, keep it a secret?' said Jessica. 'Why would you want to do that?'

Sheila didn't know what to say. How could she explain that when she joined the WAAF she just wanted to concentrate on doing a good job? Singing was in the past, that's why she hadn't mentioned it to anyone. It was one thing to perform in Belfast for the war effort, but she couldn't help thinking that her new friends might just see her as a show-off.

'I … er … might get a bit nervous if people are talking about it. I'd rather just get up there and sing.'

'Oh, like a surprise – that could be fun!' said Jessica. 'Can you imagine their faces?'

On the night of the concert, the NAAFI was packed – every seat taken and plenty of airmen standing at the bar and around the edge of the room. At one end there was a makeshift stage with a piano and a microphone lit by a single spotlight. The WAAFs from the hut had got there early and pushed three tables together. Brad, Philippe and some of their air crew sat just behind them. As the noise levels rose and the excitement and anticipation built up, Sheila wished Pat could be there with her to calm her as she always did before they went on stage. She had never felt so nervous but, as the butterflies fluttered inside her, she remembered Pat's advice. 'Breathe deeply and don't worry about the song – it's there inside you just waiting to be sung.'

She relaxed a little and whispered to Jessica. 'Thank you for the dress. I love it.'

Jessica had insisted she should wear her cocktail dress and, as soon as Sheila stepped into the ruby silk, she knew at once how beautifully made and expensive it was. The amethyst necklace and matching earrings were Jessica's too. Sheila wore a cardigan draped round her shoulders to cover the top of the dress until it was time for her to perform.

At seven o'clock precisely, a leading airman known as 'Gift of the Gab Gerry' jumped on to the stage and, amid cheering and whistling, welcomed everyone to the Ballykelly Talent Show.

'What a prize up for grabs – two days without drills, kit inspection and the deadly Ulster fry. We've got every kind of act you can imagine and plenty of others you couldn't. We've got judges, too, so put your hands together for Station Commander Thornton, Squadron Leader Price and WAAF co-ordinator Sergeant O'Dwyer.'

When the applause died down he went on: 'We've twelve acts and they've drawn lots to determine the running order. First up is a maestro of the mouth organ, navigator Alan Hardman.'

Alan was sitting near the front and his friends clapped and cheered and slapped him on the back as he stood up. Once on stage, he stood there grinning from ear to ear before someone shouted, 'Get a move on, mate, we ain't got all night.' He pulled the mouth organ from his trouser pocket, blew the dust off it and played a rousing medley of tunes that had everyone singing along. Next up was a gunner telling the sort of jokes that made everyone groan, followed by a WAAF, still in uniform, who sang 'We'll Meet Again'.

Sheila leaned across to whisper to Jessica, 'She sang that really well, didn't she?'

'Yes, she did, but it lacked something and the uniform was a mistake.'

The acts came and went and, as the audience grew more raucous, Gerry struggled to get them to be quiet as each new act was introduced. Then once they began to perform it wasn't long before someone would make a wisecrack and they'd all be laughing again. The act before Sheila consisted of three airmen in full makeup dressed as WAAFs right down to the lisle stockings and beetle crusher shoes. They ran on to the stage blowing kisses to the audience and went straight into the Andrews Sisters' big hit 'Don't Sit Under the Apple Tree'.

The room erupted and Sheila rocked with laughter at the sight of what looked like a ludicrous version of the Golden Sisters. They even got one hapless airman up on the stage to dance, just like the

Golden Sisters used to do, while his friends roared them on. At the end they left the audience helpless with laughter by lifting up their skirts to jump off the stage showing their regulation 'blackout' knickers, which came down to their knees.

Sheila was still laughing when the compère returned to introduce her. 'And now a complete change in mood, so settle down for a song from a genuine WAAF – Sheila Goulding from the ops room.'

Sheila slipped the cardigan from her shoulders and there were audible gasps and a few whistles from the men behind her as the off-the-shoulder sheath dress was revealed.

She took a deep breath and walked confidently on to the stage to stand at the microphone looking out over the audience. Meanwhile, Jessica settled herself at the piano and seconds later began the introduction. Sheila, smiling as she waited for her cue, swayed to the beat and began to sing 'Blue Moon'. At first there was some cheering and clapping, but the audience quickly settled down to listen. Sheila could see them swaying, some with their eyes closed, others smiling, and she reached deep within herself to convey the emotion of the lyrics through her voice. She held the final note and raised her hands in the air. A moment's silence and she swept her hands back into a final bow.

The audience were on their feet clapping, cheering, whistling and shouting for an encore. Sheila swept the room with a delighted smile and blew them a kiss. She returned to her seat accompanied by warm applause and as she sat down she felt a hand touch her shoulder and a familiar voice whisper, '*Ma chérie*, you were wonderful.'

There were just three more acts after Sheila, and then the judges went away to decide on the winner of the two-day pass. The girls from the hut were so excited about the fact that one of their friends could sing so well that they bombarded her with questions about how she had learned to sing and whether she was a professional. After a few minutes a movement at the door caught Sheila's eye and she looked to see Philippe beckoning her over. She excused herself and followed him out outside.

'You were wonderful,' he said. 'I couldn't believe it was you.'

'Well, it was.' She laughed.

'I know that, but do you remember when we first met and I said I thought I knew you?'

'Yes, but that was just a joke, wasn't it?'

'No, it wasn't. When you were singing tonight I realised that you're one of the Golden Sisters. I saw you at RAF Aldergrove months ago, couldn't take my eyes off you that night.' He laughed. 'And here you are. I've found you again.'

'Philippe, what are you talking about? You haven't found me; I've been here all the time.'

'But now I know you're her. The Golden Sister, the one I dreamt about for weeks.'

'Come on, that's silly. I'm just Sheila. You know, the WAAF?'

'Sheila … yes, I know that,' he said, and before she knew what was happening she was in his arms and being kissed with such tenderness.

She had no idea how long the kiss lasted, but at the sound of the compère at the microphone calling for order, she stepped back, her head still tilted upwards, her eyes closed.

Philippe reached for her again. 'Oh, Sheila …'

She looked at him, eyes wide with wonder. 'I have to go now,' she said.

The results were announced in reverse order. 'The act in third place is the trio of WAAFs also known as Bill, John and Ian. In second place, wireless operator and amazing tap dancer Jim Maguire. Finally, unanimously voted the best act and winner of the coveted two-day pass – Miss Sheila Goulding!'

While Sheila celebrated with the girls, Philippe stood at the bar with some of his crew. Maybe he too felt a bit awkward about their kiss. After such an intimate moment, she was unsure how to behave towards him.

The girls were in high spirits and singing 'Blue Moon' at the tops of their voices as they left the NAAFI. Philippe was waiting outside.

'Hello Sheila, can I speak to you?'

There was an 'Oooh!' sound from the girls and plenty of suppressed giggles.

Sheila went to him, her heart beating fast.

'Come on, girls,' said Jessica, 'let's leave these two to have their little chat.'

'And the rest!' shouted someone and, as the girls marched off into the darkness, a line from the song came again: 'Now I'm no longer alone'.

He came towards her, his arms open. She stepped back.

'What's the matter?' he said.

She didn't look at him. 'It's not right.'

'Not right? You don't mean that, Sheila. What happened between us before was meant to happen. You know that you felt the same way I did.' He took another step towards her.

'I made a mistake.' Sheila's voice was strained. 'I forgot for a moment that I'm engaged. I shouldn't have let you ...'

'But it wasn't a mistake – you know that. You let me kiss you and you kissed me back.' He held out his arms. 'Come here. I can't let you go now I've found you.'

'I'm sorry, Philippe. It's not me you've found, is it? It's the Golden Sister, that's who you kissed. You wouldn't have kissed me, Sheila the WAAF, would you?'

The slight hesitation before he spoke sealed his fate. 'You're Sheila, my friend, and it was you I held in my arms.'

'But don't you see that things won't be the same between us now. I don't know who you think I am? I can't explain it but ...'

'Sheila, you kissed me and I know you felt the same as I did.'

'Philippe, I don't know how I feel about you.'

He touched her arm and again she stepped back.

'Look,' he said. 'Let's forget tonight ever happened, okay? We'll be just the same as before. What do you say?'

'I don't know,' said Sheila. 'I'm tired now and I need to get some sleep.'

'I'll see you tomorrow, then?' he said. 'We'll talk like we always do.'

'Maybe,' said Sheila, and she turned and walked away.

Chapter 27

On the morning of Christmas Eve there were plenty of people on the streets of Belfast despite the fact that the temperature had plummeted overnight and there wasn't a great deal in the shops. Nevertheless, Martha, Irene and baby Alexander wrapped up warm and were determined to enjoy the festive atmosphere down the town.

Their first stop was the toy department in Sinclair's to see the decorations and Christmas tree and to find a suitable toy for a nine-month-old boy. The little wooden car painted blue and red was just the right size to fit in Alexander's hand so he could push it over the oilcloth.

On Royal Avenue they walked past carol singers and sang 'In the Bleak Midwinter' along with them until they reached the Salvation Army silver band further along the street, where they switched to 'Good King Wenceslas'. That took them as far as Goldstein's music shop where they called in to say hello. Peggy and Esther's squeals of delight when they saw the pram being pushed into the shop brought Goldstein out of his office.

'Oh, such a boy you have, Irene,' he said, and lifted the child out of the pram. 'A strong child too – see how his legs are wanting to run.

Ah, look at him, he sees the lights reflecting off the instruments.' Goldstein carried him over to the brass and silver section. 'You like these? That is because you are musical, like your family. I can see it in your eyes.' He took a flute from the shelf and Alexander reached out and held it fast. Goldstein declared, 'A good choice,' and he took the child and his flute to the counter. 'Esther, wrap this up for Alexander.'

'Oh, Mr Goldstein, thank you so much. It's such a beautiful gift.'

'Not at all. It's my pleasure,' and he lifted Alexander up into the air. 'Remember this, my boy, when you are seven years old, you come to Mr Goldstein's shop and he will teach you to play your flute.'

They left the music shop and headed for Robb's, braving the biting wind that swirled round Castle Place. There were crowds of children and their parents on the pavement, looking at the beautiful window displays. Irene took Alexander from his pram and held him up to see Cinderella in a sparkling blue ballgown crossing the cotton-wool snow in her glass slippers to get to her cardboard coach. On to the next window, where a gingerbread cottage, lit from within, was surrounded by painted trees and right at the front of the window lying on the ground were Hansel and Gretel, under a quilt of russet leaves, surrounded by stuffed woodland creatures. Each window a different fairy tale, and when they came to the entrance door there was a large sign: 'Rocket Ride to the North Pole'.

'Oh Mammy, is he too young to see Santa?'

A huge smile lit up Martha's face. 'You're never too young to see Santa, Irene, and never too old either.'

On the first floor they bought their tickets and followed the 'North Pole' signpost down a corridor decorated with pictures of toys until they came to a closed door. Several people were already waiting their turn to travel in the rocket. The door swung open and a rather large elf emerged and asked them to have their tickets ready. One by one they filed into a dimly lit space and, as their eyes adjusted to the light, they could see rows of oddly shaped chairs. When everyone was seated, the door closed, and boards of flashing lights and dials lit up and revealed metallic walls and portholes. There was the sound of something like an engine starting up, and Irene leaned towards her mother and whispered, 'I'm not sure about this. I hope Alexander doesn't start screaming.'

A sudden crackling sound made everyone jump and a tinny voice in a broad Belfast accent began the countdown. 'Ten, nine, eight ...'

'Mercy me!' said Martha. 'What on earth?'

The roar of the engine got louder and louder and a child screamed. Alexander was making whimpering sounds.

'... two, one , zero, BLAST OFF!'

Their seats began to shake and Martha grabbed Irene's arm. 'They didn't say it was a real rocket!' she screamed.

At that moment the portholes lit up and they watched in amazement as the moon and the stars went rushing past. There were gasps, then everyone was laughing and pointing and their fear evaporated in a chorus of oohs and aahs.

All too soon they were instructed to get ready for a landing at the North Pole. The night sky disappeared from the porthole windows, the lights dimmed and the engine faded away with a soft whine. The elf stood at the front. 'Welcome to the North Pole. Please follow the signs to Santa's workshop.' Then he pulled back a curtain to reveal another door through which they all disembarked in high excitement.

After the rocket trip, meeting Santa in his wooden hut was a bit of a disappointment for the adults, but for the children it was the highlight of their trip to the North Pole. Alexander took it all in his stride. He sat on Santa's knee and had his photo taken and, when he was given his gift from the sack, he shook it and threw it away and Santa laughed a special 'Ho! Ho! Ho!' just for him.

Before they left Robb's they paid a visit to the ladies' department to see Grace McCracken. Martha had told Irene about Grace walking out with the manager of the shoe department and how her brother John had forbidden her to see him.

'I feel so sorry for her,' said Martha. 'Aggie and Grace don't have much in their lives to cheer them, so I thought I'd invite them round for our Christmas get-together tomorrow night.'

Grace was just serving a customer who was buying evening gloves so they wandered round the department looking at the clothes until she was free. 'They're awful dear in here, aren't they?' said Martha.

'Aye, but they're good quality, they'd last you a lifetime, so they would.'

A candlewick dressing gown caught Irene's eye, soft green with swirls of pink roses. 'Here, Mammy, why don't you try this on?'

'Sure, I have my felt dressing gown.'

'You've worn that for as long as I can remember and I don't think it was yours to begin with, was it?' Irene slipped the dressing gown off the hanger and made her mother try it on.

'Right enough, it's lovely and thick to keep the heat in, and so soft,' said Martha as she stroked the material.

'Well, that's your Christmas present from me sorted.'

'You can't buy me this – it's far too dear.'

'Mammy, I've been away for months and I've not spent any money or used any clothing coupons. So I'm buying you this and that's an end to it.'

'But you—'

'But me no buts – I'm buying it.'

They took the dressing gown over to Grace and she wrapped it, then put the notes in a little cylinder which she fed into a pipe above the counter. There was a sucking sound and Grace said, 'That's it away to accounts. The change'll be back in a minute.' While they waited, Martha told Grace about the 'wee bit of a party' she was having. 'Will you come and bring Aggie and John?'

'That's really kind of you, Martha, but I'm not sure John could be persuaded.'

'Well, if he wants to stay at home that's up to him, but I hope you and Aggie will come.'

Grace smiled. 'I'll do my best.'

Their last bit of shopping was at St George's Market to see if there were any bargains to be had for the party. On the butcher's stall there was one small piece of ham left. 'I can let you have it for three shillings. Finest Galway ham, you'll not get better.' But Martha hesitated – would it be enough for the sandwiches? 'Ach missus, call it half a crown – what d'ye say?'

Alexander slept soundly on the bus back home, and Martha felt her eyes closing too. It had been a lovely day, the three of them together, and it was surely going to be the best Christmas ever.

Sheila came off the night shift early on Christmas Eve morning and went straight to Command HQ to collect her two-day pass. There would be just enough time to walk to Ballykelly Station to catch the Londonderry to Belfast train when it stopped there at nine o'clock.

Nell from her hut was on duty and she checked the in-tray. 'Here it is, Sheila. Oh—'

'Is something wrong?'

'I don't believe it,' said Nell. 'It's been cancelled – look.'

And Sheila saw the red ink scrawled across her precious pass. 'But that can't be right. I won the pass, didn't I, so I'm going home for Christmas.'

Nell was nearly in tears. 'Oh Sheila, I'm so sorry, but somebody's stopped it. You can't go.'

'Who stopped it?'

Nell lowered her voice. 'I shouldn't tell you, but it's got Sergeant O'Dwyer's initials on it.'

Sheila's heart sank. She needed to get it sorted quickly, if she was to catch the train. 'There must have been some mistake. What can I do?'

'I heard O'Dwyer say she was going to the NAAFI for a fag. Why don't you go and speak to her?'

Sheila ran all the way there, but as she pushed open the door, she was met by a wall of sound and a room packed with air crews who had been out on patrol overnight. She pushed her way through the crowd, searching for the sergeant. At one point she caught sight of Philippe. She wasn't surprised to see him there – she had plotted his plane all the way back to Ballykelly and knew it had landed half an hour earlier. She hadn't spoken to him since the night of the concert three days before and she had no intention of seeking him out. She just needed to find O'Dwyer as quickly as possible. She spotted her sitting alone on the far side of the room smoking a cigarette and, without any thought of how to manage the situation, she walked straight up to her, saluted and said, 'Permission to speak, Sergeant.'

O'Dwyer nodded her consent.

'My pass has been cancelled,' Sheila explained, 'and I need you to sort it out for me or I'll miss my train to Belfast.'

O'Dwyer narrowed her eyes and blew out a stream of smoke. 'You won't be going to Belfast.'

Sheila felt as though she had been slapped in the face. 'But I won the pass and I need it to get home for Christmas.'

O'Dwyer leaned forward and stubbed out the cigarette in an ashtray. 'Not today you're not. I've a plotter in the sick bay doubled up with food poisoning. You'll be working her shift tonight in the ops room.'

'That's not fair. I was promised the pass.' Sheila's voice was bordering on the shrill and the buzz of conversation around them ceased.

'Of course it's not fair. Nothing's fair when there's a war on,' said O'Dwyer, 'and you need to watch how you're speaking to a superior officer, Airwoman Goulding, or you could find yourself on a charge.'

'I apologise,' said Sheila. 'It's just that I thought I was going to see my family.'

O'Dwyer shrugged her shoulders. 'If she's any better in the morning you can have the pass.'

'But that's no good. There's no train tomorrow and I'll be stuck here.' Sheila was close to tears.

'Just like the rest of us, then.'

Sheila wanted to tell her how desperate she was to see her family and how cruel it was to dash her hopes at the last minute, but the sneering look on the sergeant's face told her there was no chance the pass would be authorised. So she bit her tongue, saluted smartly, wheeled round and marched across the room and out of the door.

Back at the hut some of the WAAFs were getting ready to go on duty. Jessica was sitting on her bed rolling her hair and pinning it above her collar. She put the end of a kirby grip in her mouth and eased it open. 'Are you off?' she asked as she secured the final piece.

'Yes,' said Sheila and she grabbed her bag and greatcoat. 'I'll see you on Boxing Day,' she said, and she ran out of the hut and all the way to Ballykelly Station.

Several people were waiting on the platform. At the ticket office there was a small queue and the wait gave her time to get her breath back and with it came some semblance of calm. She bought her ticket and went to stand on the platform. She wasn't the kind of girl to cause trouble, she told herself, but it was a matter of principle. She was entitled to the pass and Sergeant O'Dwyer was wrong to say she couldn't go to Belfast to see her family. In any event, there would be time enough when she came back to sit down and persuade Sergeant O'Dwyer that she was right. The signal had changed to show the train was approaching and within a minute the sound of it was audible. As it drew closer, she became aware of the conflicting voices in her head. She was certainly entitled to leave, but now there was another opinion vying to be heard. She had joined up to do something worthwhile, to be part of that vast force working together to bring an end to the war. Was she not obliged to stay and do her duty?

The train came into view and the sound of it braking filled her head, drowning out the shouts from someone on the road beyond the station. She moved closer to the edge of the platform and the train slowed to a stop. Her hand was on the carriage door when a sudden shout made her hesitate. It came again. 'Sheila, Sheila! Where are you?' There was the sound of movement behind her. She hesitated a moment and suddenly strong arms were around her, preventing her from moving. She looked down at the sleeves of a flying jacket.

'Philippe, is it you? Let me go.'

He was behind her and when he spoke she felt his breath on her ear. 'No Sheila, you can't leave. I won't let you.'

'I'm going home for Christmas. It's nothing to do with you. So don't try and stop me.'

He turned her towards him, but his grip was just as tight. 'You think this is about me and how I feel about you? Don't you realise, if you leave the base and go AWOL, you'll be court-martialled.'

'Don't be ridiculous. I'll get my knuckles rapped when I come back, but I'm in the right here.' She struggled to free herself from his arms.

'Stop behaving like a silly girl. So you want to see your family? We all want to see our families, Sheila, but what really matters is those convoys and the boys who risk their lives out there to protect them. Tonight you're needed in that ops room to bring them home safely – to bring me home safely.'

She lowered her eyes and the fight left her. People were pushing past them to get into the carriages, but still he held her. 'Look at me.' His voice was fierce. She raised her eyes and flinched at the hurt in his face.

The passengers were all on board, the stationmaster blew his whistle and lowered his flag and the train chugged slowly out of the station, leaving the two figures locked in a fierce embrace, wreathed in billowing clouds of steam.

When Pat had attended the now annual children's party at the American Red Cross Services Club on the Sunday before Christmas, Joe Walters had invited both her and Peggy to join their Christmas Eve celebration. At first Pat had dismissed the idea, but Peggy, who was disappointed that Archie had not been in touch for several weeks, was determined not to sit at home moping.

'Oh come on, Pat, don't be so miserable. I tell you, a Christmas Eve with the Americans is something not to be missed.'

In the end Pat gave in to her nagging. 'I'll go for an hour to show my face, that's all,' she said, knowing that would be time enough to get the latest news on the Italian Campaign from Joe.

From the first day it opened, Pat had loved the atmosphere in the club. Of course, it helped that she and Tony had created it together – it was where they fell in love and where he proposed – but it was more than that. It was the Americans themselves. She loved their optimism and generosity of spirit, their informal ways and straight talking.

When they got to the club, Joe was in the foyer greeting everyone as they arrived. As soon as he saw the girls his face lit up. 'Hi Patti, glad you could come. And Peggy too – gee, it's good to see you again.' He shook their hands warmly. 'Go on in and get yourself a drink. You'll find I've put you on a table with some friends of mine. I'll come join you when I've finished out here.'

The ballroom was festooned with decorations and the Christmas tree, strung with coloured lights, went all the way up to the ceiling. But it was the sight of so many immaculate GI uniforms that impressed Peggy. 'Oh my,' she said, 'and they're all so handsome, aren't they?'

Joe's friends made them welcome and brought them Coca Cola from the bar. There was a six-piece band playing Christmas music – some couples were already on the floor and it wasn't long before the girls were asked to dance.

Later, Joe joined them and danced a quickstep with Peggy and a slow waltz with Pat. Then the band took a break while the buffet was served and Pat saw her chance to ask Joe if he had any more news about the Italian Campaign.

'It's pretty much as I told you at the kids' party – they've marched north and west and they seem to be dug in somewhere near a town called Cassino. It's cold and it's Christmas so I guess the Germans are keeping their heads down too.'

Pat tried to imagine the scene: dark and cold; soldiers out in open country; huddled in tents or trenches; the enemy over the next hill. She shuddered and Joe, who had been watching her intently, covered her hand with his. 'Easy now,' he said. 'They're okay. I doubt if anything will happen there for quite a while. It could be spring before there's another advance.'

Pat didn't seem to register his touch. 'I'm sitting here, warm and safe, listening to Christmas music' – her voice was soft, almost a whisper, and Joe leaned closer to catch her words – 'while somewhere thousands of miles away … It doesn't seem right.' She stood up. 'I shouldn't have come tonight.'

Joe sighed. 'Patti, the last thing I wanted to do was upset you. But I can tell you, if I was Tony, I'd be happy to know that tonight you're right here with us – his own people. He'd want us to look after you.'

'Maybe he would, Joe, but I think I'd like to go home now.'

'I understand. Would you like me to drive you? The jeep's right outside.'

Pat saw the concern in his face and realised what a good friend he had become. He had helped her make things better for the children and was the one person she could talk to about what was happening with Tony.

'No, you need to be here,' she told him. 'Peggy and I can get home easily enough.' Then a sudden thought occurred to her. 'Joe, what are you doing tomorrow evening?'

'I'm not on duty – haven't decided what to do yet.'

'How would you like to come to our house? My mother's having a bit of a party.'

His smile was lovely. 'Gee that'd be swell, thank you, Patti.'

Chapter 28

On Christmas morning Sheila came off the night shift, went straight to the hut and got into bed. Clemmie had tried to coax her to have breakfast. 'You've got to eat something and after that we'll go to the church service in the village. It'll be lovely singing carols.' But as far as Sheila was concerned Christmas wasn't happening and she didn't want to see or speak to anyone. Yes, she was upset that she wouldn't be with her family for Christmas but, added to that, she was ashamed that she had almost left the base without permission. Where was her loyalty to her friends and the Air Force? What had got into her? She slept for a while and awoke to the sound of shouting.

'Sheila, get up, get up!' Clemmie pulled the blanket off her. 'The plotter who was sick? I've just seen her tucking into a bacon sandwich. She'll be as right as rain for her shift tonight.'

'So what?' Sheila yawned and pulled the blanket back up.

'Don't you see? They've got to authorise your pass now.'

'Oh, that'll be great,' said Sheila, 'because then I'll be able to spend my two days sleeping through Christmas and when I wake up it'll all be over.'

'But don't you want to go to Belfast?'

'And how would I get there, Clemmie? By flying carpet?'

'Sheila, all I want you to do is to get up because there might just be a chance you could be home for Christmas dinner, but if we don't go right now and get the pass there's no hope.'

Sheila sat up and looked, really looked, at Clemmie's face. She was serious. Maybe she should go and see if her pass had been authorised, even though there was no point. No point in lying in bed either, or missing out on breakfast and a good dinner.

'I look like a scarecrow,' said Sheila as she smoothed her uniform in front of the mirror. 'Where's my comb?'

'There's no time for all that – just stick your cap on and bring your coat and bag.'

They raced to the headquarters building and Nell was there, smiling. 'It's been authorised,' she said. 'Sergeant O'Dwyer signed it this morning when she heard the plotter had recovered.'

They went back to the NAAFI where Brad was waiting for them. 'We think we can get you some transport. Philippe's out there now trying to organise it and he'll come for you if it's on.'

'What transport?' asked Sheila. 'I don't understand.'

'Philippe's pulled a few strings. He's trying to hitch a lift for you' – Brad tapped the side of his nose – 'hush, hush you know.'

Sheila didn't get her hopes up. Who would be travelling all the way to Belfast on Christmas Day and how many hours was that going to take? Even if she did get a lift, they'd have had their dinner by the time she got home.

The door opened and they turned to see Philippe coming towards them. He looked tense, hardly the expression of someone who had managed to 'pull strings'.

He spoke quickly to Sheila. 'Get your bag. We're going for a walk. Don't ask any questions – I'll explain when we get there.'

They left the NAAFI and skirted round the buildings and eventually came round the side of a hangar close to the runway.

Philippe explained. 'In a few minutes, a Liberator will taxi out on to the runway. When I say go, run as fast as you can towards it and someone will help you into the plane. You'll fly to RAF Aldergrove, where the Liberator's based, then a friend of mine will take you the rest of the way on his motorbike.'

'I don't understand. How come the plane is here? Why would they take me?'

Philippe smiled. 'The pilot's a buddy of mine from Aldergrove. I saw him in the mess this morning and he told me he was out on patrol last night and landed here because he was low on fuel. Soon as I heard the plotter was A1, I asked him if he could do me a favour.'

'Why would you do this for me?'

Philippe shook his head. 'You know why.'

There was the roar of an engine and the plane emerged from the hard standing and turned towards the runway. Philippe gripped her arm. They waited. The door to the plane was open. Sheila turned to Philippe, tears in her eyes. 'Thank you so much,' she shouted over the deafening noise.

'Go!' shouted Philippe and he pushed her towards the plane.

She ran as fast as she could, her kit bag bouncing against her shoulder, but she seemed no closer to the plane. An airman stood at its open door, his hand outstretched, urging her to run faster. She fixed her eyes on him and drew on all her strength. Time seemed to slow as the gap between them closed. Now she could hear the airman's voice. 'Keep going! You can do it!' he shouted. Almost there and she reached for his, missed it, tried again. He grabbed her and her feet left the ground. There were two of them now, hauling her upwards into the body of the plane where she lay on the floor, cold metal against her face.

The smiling airmen set her on her feet. 'There you are, love. Next stop, Aldergrove.'

In the seconds it took them to close the aircraft's door, Sheila marvelled at the sight of Ballykelly growing smaller and smaller. Somewhere below Philippe was watching her and somewhere ahead her family waited.

Martha had almost completed her annual juggling trick of immaculate timing, combined with making three kitchen pans do the work of six, whilst ensuring that not a mouthful of food would be anything less than piping hot. She had only to carve the splendid

Dungannon goose and get everything as quickly as possible on to the heated plates. The meat was falling off the bone and she was just about to pop a little piece into her mouth when she heard the gate at the side of the house rattle. Before she could think, 'Who on earth?' a figure in uniform appeared at the window. She screamed in delight and Pat rushed into the kitchen to see what was going on. By that time, Sheila had come through the back door and was standing with her bag at her feet, her coat over her arm and a smile that seemed to light up the entire room.

'God bless us, look who it is,' said Martha. She was half-laughing, half-crying as she put her arms around her daughter, and by this time the kitchen was full of sisters jostling, hugging and talking over one another in their excitement.

'Dinner,' said Martha, and Pat set an extra place for Sheila. In no time at all Martha was bringing the plates to the table. She took off her apron and sat down, all eyes upon her. They didn't usually say grace, but Christmas Day was different – with a feast in front of them, all daughters present and correct and a wee grandson, she had to say something.

'Dear God, we thank you for keeping us all safe this year. Thank you too for the precious gift of Alexander. We're grateful for the goose and all the lovely presents, but especially for Sheila, back home at last. Amen.'

Round the table the chat and craic was nineteen to the dozen. 'How is it they gave you leave? I thought you had to be there six months for that,' said Martha.

'It's a long story,' said Sheila and she told them about the talent show and they cheered when they heard that she had won.

'I'm not surprised,' said Peggy. 'Sure, aren't you practically a professional.'

And when Sheila explained that the sergeant stopped her going home, the woman was roundly disparaged. 'I only got my pass this morning when there was no way of getting here anyway.'

'So how did you get here?' asked Irene.

'You'll never believe it,' Sheila grinned. 'I flew here in an aeroplane.'

Her sisters laughed in delight and Martha let out a little gasp.

'Mercy me,' she said. 'I'm glad I didn't know anything about that,' and she turned to the girls. 'I never heard it land, did you?' And that set them all laughing.

'What was it like in the plane?' asked Peggy.

'It was the scariest and the best ever experience I've ever had. I thought the noise when we took off was going to burst my eardrums. We had to be strapped in – it was a bumpy ride and so cold. You could see all the little fields and houses down below. I've never seen anything like it. Then we flew into clouds and they were lumpy like snow. We'd only been up there a wee while and I could feel the aeroplane rolling a bit on its side. The land was coming up towards us then we were level again only much lower, skimming over the hedges, then it was bump, bump, bump and we were on the ground.' Sheila was silent, filled again with the awe of it all and her family, amazed that one of their own had experienced such a thing, were momentarily struck dumb.

'Well, if I'd known you were up there, I'd have gone out and waved,' said Martha and that set them off again.

When the meal was over Peggy said, 'Irene, you and Sheila should do the dishes; you've both missed a lot of turns since you've been away, haven't they Pat?'

And they did do the dishes; it was a good opportunity for them to catch up. Irene washed and Sheila dried and they talked about Alexander. 'What made you call him Alexander?' asked Sheila and Irene told her about the brave pilot and the American doctor.

'What about you and Charles?' said Irene. 'That was a surprise.'

'Yes it was.' Sheila turned away to put the dishes in the cupboard.

'So you'll be going to see him now you're home? Invite him round – I'd love to meet him.'

Sheila shrugged. 'I don't think there'll be time. I'll have to catch the train tomorrow afternoon. Anyway, he's probably gone to his parents in Armagh.'

Irene paused, dish mop in her hand. 'If I didn't know better, I'd say you've gone a bit cool on him.'

There was no answer. Irene tried again. 'It's difficult when you're separated for months on end, I know that, but once you see him again it'll be like you've never been apart.'

'I'm not sure it will,' said Sheila.

Irene pursed her lips, considering whether or not she should say what she thought. 'Have you met someone else?'

'Sort of … he's a friend.'

'And you like him?'

'I do, but I'm not sure …'

'Does he like you?'

Sheila nodded.

Irene wasn't sure what she could say to her sister. She'd been torn between two men once – Sandy and Sean O'Hara, her friend's brother, and could have ended up with either. 'Look Sheila, don't do anything drastic, give yourself time to get to know him better and, when it comes to making a decision, you'll know.'

They spent the afternoon relaxing and catching up with the rest of their news and everyone took turns at nursing or playing with Alexander. When he finally succumbed to sleep, Martha announced that she would start to get things ready for the party.

'What?' said Sheila. 'A party? Mammy, we've never had a party.'

'Ach, it's just like we usually do on Christmas night.'

'How many's coming?'

Martha reeled off the guest list. 'Just Betty, Jack, Mr Goldstein, Esther … oh, and the McCrackens.'

'Counting us that's twelve people, Mammy. That's quite a party,' said Sheila.

Then Pat remembered. 'I forgot to tell you, I've invited Captain Walters from the club.'

'Dear God, you've invited an American? Sure, he'll be expecting one of those cocktail parties.'

'No he won't, Mammy, lots of people invite the GIs into their homes, especially at this time of year. They get lonely, you know.'

Martha counted the guests on her fingers again and looked at them in horror. 'Thirteen. We can't have thirteen – it's bad luck.'

'And which one of them do you want to send away?' said Peggy.

'There's not really thirteen,' said Pat. 'You can't count Alexander, he's too young.'

'Oh, for heaven's sake.' Martha's face was a picture of dismay.

222

'The worst of it is, I haven't enough food.'

'Come on, Mammy,' said Irene, 'let's see if we can turn five loaves and two fishes into a party for the five thousand.'

They made sandwiches with the ham they had bought in the market. Martha insisted on slicing it. 'It'll need to be very thin to go a long way.'

There was a good-sized piece of cheese with water biscuits and pickles and a Dundee cake with glacé cherries on the top. Finally, they opened two cans of fruit and poured them into a big glass dish and emptied a can of condensed milk into a jug. They stood back and surveyed the table. 'Not much there, is there?' said Irene.

'Oh, I forgot,' said Martha, and she went out into the back hall and came in with four bottles of ginger beer and a blackcurrant cordial and put them on the table. 'Sure, most people will want tea, won't they?'

'And let's hope they've had a big dinner,' said Irene.

Betty and Jack from next door were the first to arrive, bringing a bottle of sherry with them. 'There'll be a few more people coming round tonight,' Martha told them. 'Would you be able to bring over a few extra glasses and plates, Betty?'

'Of course – I'll away and get them.'

Goldstein and Esther arrived with a box of latkes and a jar of apple sauce. 'Potato pancakes, very good,' said Esther and Irene added them to the table. The McCrackens brought corned beef sandwiches and a Victoria sponge and the spread looked a bit better.

They brought chairs in from the kitchen to the front room and everyone sat around chatting. Pat had just made sure everyone had a drink when there was a knock at the door. It was Joe Walters. As soon as he walked in, the atmosphere was somehow charged. His height, the uniform, his broad smile revealing perfect, white teeth – the sort of man they would expect to see on the silver screen. He was clearly delighted to be there and shook hands with everyone and said 'Hi' and made a point of listening carefully so he could remember all their names despite the Belfast accents. He'd brought some beer and a platter of doughnuts, fruit and chocolate from the club.

Peggy organised a game of charades and soon they were shrieking with laughter and shouting out the answers. After a while Martha slipped away into the kitchen to put the kettle on and looked at the table with all the lovely things to eat. Yes, there was a war on, but tonight everyone would be sharing what they had in the company of friends.

No Christmas at the Gouldings' home was complete without a sing-song round the piano. They sang carols and Christmas songs and some of the guests were persuaded to sing.

Then Martha said, 'Sing us something American, Joe.'

He was a bit taken aback. 'Never sung to an audience before. Not sure what to sing.'

But Peggy came to his rescue by playing the opening to 'The Star-Spangled Banner' and Joe bravely sang the first two verses. He blushed at the applause and went back to his seat next to Pat. Leaning across to her he whispered something that made her throw back her head and laugh. Irene caught the look in his eyes as he watched her. Oh my goodness, she thought. He's in love with her.

Martha thought she heard someone at the door and slipped out of the room. She didn't turn on the light, but called out, 'Who's there?'

'Major Dewer, Coldstream Guards. I'm looking for the home of Peggy Goulding?'

Martha opened the door and he stepped inside. When she turned on the light she found herself staring into a face she had seen before – in a photograph. So this was the so-called 'sugar daddy' she had feared.

'I wondered if Peggy might like to come to the Grand Hotel with me this evening.'

'We've got guests,' said Martha, then added, 'it's a party.'

At that moment Peggy came into the hallway. She looked startled to see Archie and her mother standing there, but recovered quickly. 'Archie, what are you doing here? Mammy, this is Major Archie Dewer.'

They shook hands. 'How lovely to meet you, Mrs Goulding. Strangest thing,' he said, turning to Peggy. 'I was supposed to be on duty tonight, but turns out I'm not. Thought I'd pop along here and see if you'd like to come out for a drink with me.'

Peggy looked at her mother, who shrugged her shoulders. 'Come and meet everyone then I'll go and get changed,' said Peggy.

The appearance of another officer, British this time, in the small front room was a surprise. Betty gazed at him with a wistful smile on her lips and Aggie and Grace were wide-eyed as Peggy introduced him. Of course, the sisters knew him, as did Goldstein and Esther, and they greeted him pleasantly enough. The conversation in the room resumed and Archie sat next to Joe and Pat went to get him a drink.

As usual with Peggy, it took her a good while to decide what to wear and to apply her makeup. When she returned, she and Archie said goodbye and went out to his car.

It was as if the evening had fallen a bit flat with Peggy leaving, but Pat said, 'Mammy, why don't you play a few tunes on the piano and we'll have another sing-song?'

The last thing Martha felt like doing was playing the piano, but Pat was right, their guests were what mattered. She sat at the piano and played the opening of 'We'll Meet Again' but before they'd sung the first line there was a noise outside, raised voices and what sounded like a scream. Joe was the first on his feet and out the door, Pat close behind him.

Outside, the scene lit by a full moon, were two men in uniform squaring up to each other and Peggy between them screaming, 'Stop it! Stop it!'

'Who the hell's this, Peggy?' A Belfast accent.

The man had his back to her, but Pat recognised the voice immediately. Harry Ferguson. Joe had already pulled him back. 'Take it easy, buddy,' he said. 'We don't want any trouble, do we?'

Harry shrugged Joe off. 'What's the bloody Yank doing here?'

'Hey mister, you've sure had too much to drink.' Joe's voice had the ring of authority. 'Now why don't you calm down and we can settle this all peaceable like.'

Archie took Peggy's arm. 'Come on, get into the car,' he said, but Harry pushed past Joe and lunged at them, grabbing Peggy's other arm. For a moment she was pulled back and forth like a rag doll.

'Harry, please …' Peggy was pleading.

Pat stood next to Archie and in a calm, measured voice said, 'Major Dewer, I think it would be best if you stepped to one side for a moment. We don't want Peggy hurt.' With only a moment's hesitation Archie nodded and let go of her.

Joe spoke again to Harry. 'Why don't you let Peggy go as well and maybe we can sort this thing out?'

'There's nothing to sort out, Yank. Peggy's my girl and this fella isn't getting his hands on her!' And Harry launched himself at Archie, throwing a wild right hook. Archie grabbed the arm with one hand and gripped Harry's throat with the other. 'I could have you court-martialled for that, soldier, but you know as well as I do that very soon we're going to need scum like you as cannon fodder. So I'm not going to give you a cosy billet in the glass house, I'm going to let you go. But know this – if I hear that you've come anywhere near Peggy Goulding, or so much as sent her a snivelling letter, I'll find you wherever you are and you'll be sorry.' And he pushed him away.

Harry rubbed his throat and glared at Archie, then turned to Peggy, his face contorted with anger. 'How could you do this? I trusted you. I'm on embarkation leave, getting posted overseas, God knows where. Came straight off the boat to see you.' He shook his head. 'To think I was going to ask you to marry me.' He backed away from her and gave a humourless laugh. 'Thought if I was going to fight, going to die, I wanted to ...' He let out a growl of frustration.

'Hey buddy,' said Joe, 'you need to go home and sleep this off. In the morning, things'll look different. You can talk to Peggy with a clear head. I'm sure she'll listen to what you want to say.'

'You don't know anything, you stupid Yank.' Harry took one more anguished look at Peggy before turning away, walking at first then breaking into a run and disappearing down the street.

Archie straightened his tunic, took the car keys from his pocket and addressed himself to Peggy. 'If you will forgive me, my dear, I feel the evening has lost its appeal. I fancy the officers' mess and a glass of single malt will provide a more convivial atmosphere.' And without a backward glance he got in his car and drove away.

Peggy was trembling and Pat put her arm round her and together with Joe they walked back up the path. Martha stood at the door, visibly shaken, Goldstein just behind her, his hand on her shoulder. In the hallway, Martha took Peggy upstairs and Pat and Joe went in to face the guests. But Goldstein was already there, standing by the piano. 'These things happen ... a misunderstanding,' he was saying. 'Harry is a decent young man, but he has been away in the Forces for so long and maybe he expected things to be just the same as they ever were. He has gone home now and no doubt he will wake up in the morning and regret that he broke the Christmas cheer. It was only a storm in a teacup – speaking of which, I think a cup of tea and a slice of that splendid Dundee cake might be a good way to end our evening.'

At that point, Joe stood up. 'I'll take a rain check on the cake, if you don't mind. I need to get back to base. Sure was nice to meet you folks and thanks for your hospitality.' He shook everyone's hand, remembering their names, and his smile never wavered.

'I'll see you out,' said Pat.

In the hallway Joe turned to her. 'Gee, Patti, can't thank you enough for inviting me into your home.'

She shook his outstretched hand. 'No Joe, I'm the one who needs to thank you. If you hadn't been out there tonight I don't know what would have happened.'

'Who was the young guy, a boyfriend?'

Pat nodded. 'He and Peggy went out together for quite a while, there was talk of them getting married, but then he enlisted. Peggy wrote to him a lot, but he hardly ever replied.' Pat bit her lip. 'It can be lonely – the waiting. I suppose when the major came along she was flattered. He's a good-looking man, I suppose, and in a position of some power, but from what I've seen tonight, he's frightening too.'

'Tough situation ... one girl, two guys ... happens all the time,' said Joe. 'Well, thanks again for the food and the company. Don't forget to call in when you're passing.'

When he had gone Pat went upstairs to check on her sister and mother. Peggy was lying facing the wall and Martha was sitting on the bed.

'Everyone's having some tea and cake,' said Pat. 'Are you coming down?'

'I suppose I'd better,' said Martha. 'You stay here if you want to, Peggy.'

Peggy said nothing.

On the landing Pat tried to reassure her mother. 'Don't worry – they all understand that these things happen.'

Martha's voice was grim. 'It's not them I'm worried about. It's all those neighbours standing in dark rooms looking out at that carry-on in the street. I've never felt so ashamed in all my life.'

Chapter 29

Sheila arrived back at Ballykelly around teatime on Boxing Day and went straight to the NAAFI. When she came in some wag began singing 'Blue Moon' at the top of his voice and she acknowledged him with a bow. She spotted Philippe and Brad sitting together and went to join them.

'Well, how was it?' asked Brad.

'It was wonderful. I didn't want to come back.'

'Good job you have, the U-boats have been a bit lively. Anyway, I'll go and meet Clemmie off her shift, leave you two to chat.'

On the long train journey Sheila had gone over in her mind what she wanted to say to Philippe. She owed him a lot, not least because he was the one who had got her to Belfast when it had seemed impossible. But it was more than that; he was one of the people who made life on the base enjoyable. The last thing she wanted was to lose his friendship.

'Philippe, I wouldn't have seen my family at all if it wasn't for you. You could have been on a charge if they'd found out.'

'Yeah, you, me and the entire crew of the Liberator.' He didn't meet her eye and that jokey tone he often used when he spoke to her had gone.

'I just wanted to say thank you for what you did.'

There was the merest shrug of his shoulders in acknowledgement.

They sat a while in silence until Sheila could bear it no longer. 'Philippe, about what happened at the talent contest. I'm sorry about the way I spoke to you. I had no idea that ...' She couldn't finish the sentence. How could she begin to discuss the feelings he had spoken of that night?

'Listen to me, Sheila. I don't know why I said the things I did. Maybe I'd had too much to drink, who knows. It was as if you were a different person when you were singing. As you said, it wasn't you I thought I was kissing.' He laughed and tried to make a joke out of it. 'In fact whatever you do, don't sing again in front of me or I'll end up kissing you – again.'

Sheila blushed to the roots of her hair. 'So, you didn't mean the things you said?'

'I was out of line and I'm sorry if I embarrassed you. You know you and I are ... best buddies, right? Nothing's changed there. That night you said I didn't know who you were. But I do know you – you're Sheila the WAAF, you're my best friend.' He laughed again. 'No idea who that singer was!'

Clemmie came through the door and squealed when she saw Sheila was back and proceeded to bombard her with questions about her trip home. She asked about Alexander and Sheila showed her the photo of him Irene had given her, taken in a studio in Belfast. 'Isn't he cute,' she cooed. 'And how are your mom and sisters? Were they pleased to see you?'

'They're all well,' said Sheila. 'They couldn't believe it when I walked in – just in time for Christmas dinner.'

'And what did Charles say?'

'Nothing ... he wasn't there. I think he went to his parents in Armagh.'

'You think? You didn't go and see if he was home?' said Clemmie.

'Well, no, there wasn't enough time to go looking for him.'

Philippe looked at her strangely. 'You should write to him, Sheila, and explain what happened. If you don't, he'll be really upset when he finds out that you were home and you didn't tell him.'

'I might,' she said. 'Well, I think I'll go and have a look at the roster, see what shifts I've got for the rest of the week.' She stood up.

'I'll come with you, get a bit of fresh air,' said Philippe.

They walked to headquarters and Philippe talked about Christmas on the base. 'We didn't get much time off, sang a few carols, drank a few beers; seemed like most people were homesick a lot of the time.'

They checked the rosters and found they were both on duty at the same time.

'Hey, Lucky' – he touched her hair – 'I like it that you're in the ops room watching over me when I'm flying.'

January was a month that Martha, Pat and Peggy would be glad to see the back of. Low clouds hung over Belfast for days on end, obscuring Cave Hill, and the damp seemed to penetrate everywhere. Driving rain came through the ill-fitting windows leaving puddles on the window sills and the wind blew down the chimney, dampening the meagre fire.

Martha had been glad to have Sheila home for Christmas, even for so short a visit, but she was deeply disappointed that she had made no attempt to see Charles. However, if she'd learned one thing in the past year it was that interfering had no effect on her children's actions, save making them all the more determined to plough their own furrow.

Irene and Alexander went back to Fermanagh even before the Christmas decorations had been taken down. It was a wrench to see them go. Shortly afterwards Martha caught a chill and took to her bed, wracked by a cough that settled on her chest and that no end of bread poultices could shift.

Peggy had been badly shaken by the row between Archie Dewer and Harry Ferguson. She had gone to Harry's house the day after the party, hoping to talk to him, but his mother came to the door and said he wasn't there and she had no idea where he was. Peggy suspected he was inside and, when she returned the next day and no one came to the door at all, she pushed her carefully written letter through the letter box. In it she begged him to see her before he left. She told him she thought he had forgotten about her because he hadn't written to her in months. She swore the major was just an acquaintance and she hardly ever saw him. But the days slipped by and she never heard from him.

As for Archie, he did his usual disappearing act, but this time she didn't care. She couldn't believe the aggressive way he had attacked Harry and she hated the way he had spoken to him. There was a time when she found his confidence and power very attractive, but now they just frightened her.

Pat had continued to follow the reports on the wireless about the Italian Campaign and when, towards the end of the month, the area round Cassino was mentioned, her fears for Tony's safety grew. Joe Walters was usually well informed about what was happening on the ground with US troops, but she was reluctant to bother him, partly because of the embarrassing incident at the Christmas party. Then one evening there was a knock at the door and there was Joe, chocolate bars in his hand and a shy smile on his lips. 'Just thought I'd visit to see how y'all are,' he said.

Peggy was out at the pictures with Esther and Martha was ironing in the kitchen. At the sound of voices, she came through to the front room.

'Nice to see you again, Captain Walters.'

'And you, Mrs Goulding.'

'Pull that chair up to the fire and get warm,' she told him, 'and Pat, throw a wee bit more coal on there,' and she went off to finish her ironing.

There was an awkward moment when neither Pat or Joe spoke but then he remembered the chocolate in his hand.

'I brought you this,' he said.

'Thank you – that's a treat for us.'

'I thought you might have called into the club …' He hesitated. 'You know, with all the reports about the fighting near Cassino?'

'Oh, I know you're busy with all the troops that have been arriving. I didn't want to bother you.'

'Aw, Patti, don't ever think that. You know I'm always there if you need to talk.'

Pat sat on the sofa opposite him. 'Well, I have to say it's very worrying at the moment. I really thought I'd have heard from Tony at Christmas. That somehow they'd try to get letters to family and sweethearts. But there was nothing.' She picked up the atlas she had been studying when Joe had knocked on the door. 'Now there's all these reports of fierce fighting …' She began to leaf through the pages. 'I keep staring at the map of Italy, see here … But I can't find Cassino. I've looked and looked.' There was desperation in her voice. 'I've no idea where he is.'

'Let me see.' Joe gently took the atlas from her and studied it a moment. Then he knelt down beside her and put his finger on the position of the town, too small to be named on the map. 'They're here,' he said, 'surrounding a high hill. On the top of it there's an abbey where the German Forces are holed up. There are thousands of American and Allied troops in the area and it's only a matter of time before the enemy is ousted.'

'And what then?' asked Pat.

He traced the route northwards. 'They push on to Rome.'

Pat's anxiety drained away. 'It's the not knowing that's hard to deal with,' she said, 'but I understand now, thank you.'

'Look, if you get worried you gotta come and see me and I'll tell you what I know. Promise me you'll do that.'

'I promise,' she said and with a twinkle in her eye she asked: 'What about all these troops training in Northern Ireland? We've been giving concerts to bigger and bigger audiences at camps we've never been to before. What's that all about?'

He grinned. 'Now that's something I can't talk about.'

Towards the end of January, Ted Grimes called round to the house to tell Martha that Vera had passed away and to let her know the funeral arrangements. The following Tuesday she walked to Oldpark Presbyterian Church and joined the half-dozen mourners. After the service she offered Ted her condolences and explained that she would not be going on to the graveyard. He thanked her for coming and added, 'I'd be grateful if ye would call round to the house tomorrow afternoon, Martha.' She gave him an uncertain look, but he went on, 'I'd like to talk to ye. It's to do with Vera's will.'

Martha didn't tell the girls she was going to Ted's house. They would have thought it strange and questioned her about it. Truth was she didn't want to go, but how could she have said no, right there outside the church and the woman on her way to be buried.

He showed her into the cold parlour. The curtains were open and Vera's bed had gone, but the air was still stale. Ted was in the suit he had worn for the funeral. He cleared his throat. 'Vera was very grateful for the times ye called to see her when she was ill. She liked to hear ye talk.'

'Sure, I just dropped by a few times when I was passing,' said Martha.

'I know that she talked to ye about me.' He stared at her, unblinking.

'Ach, not really, only that you were busy with your work.' Martha could feel the sweat on her upper lip and wiped it away.

'You and I used to be friends, Martha.'

She started to speak. 'I don't want—'

He held up his hand like he was stopping traffic. 'Hear me out, please. We were friends and after your Robert died, I like to think I supported ye.'

The clamminess had spread to Martha's forehead, but she didn't move.

'Then there was all that trouble with Irene and those republicans. Now, in my book, I was only doin' me duty, but I'll hold me hands up and say I was … quick to judge.' He ran a finger round his starched collar as though it was so tight he couldn't get his words out. 'Vera wanted us to be friends,' he said, and nodded at her as though expecting her to agree with him. 'And I was hoping that in time … we might … ' Martha looked away, shocked at what he was suggesting.

Ted cleared his throat. 'Well, something to think about.' Still Martha didn't look at him. Ted went on, 'Anyway, Vera wanted to leave ye something in her will, to thank ye.' He took a small box from the mantelpiece and handed it to Martha. She opened it – a gold cameo brooch on ivory satin. 'It was an engagement present,' he said. 'She wanted ye to have it.' Martha stared at the brooch. Was she reading this right? How had she got herself into this? Trapped in the parlour with a man she despised standing over her, his wife's jewellery in her hand.

In a flash she was back in Dungannon, Bridie was reading the tea leaves and her words were crystal clear. 'I see a friend, no an acquaintance, and death surrounds this person. They need your help.'

Dear God, this isn't possible, she thought. I should never have come here. Then she remembered the rest of Bridie's prediction. 'Trust your instincts.' She thrust the cameo at him. 'No, never! I'll have nothing more to do with you.'

Chapter 30

'Do you think if the weather's miserable, it makes you feel miserable too?' asked Peggy as she took off her wet shoes and set them in front of the one-bar electric fire in Goldstein's office.

Esther laid her shoes next to Peggy's. 'Yes, it's a fact of life.'

Peggy leaned back in Goldstein's chair. 'But maybe you're just miserable because you miss Reuben now he's away at music school in London.'

'That's true as well, so I'm twice as miserable as you.'

Peggy thought for a moment. 'But if a handsome young fellow were to come in the shop this morning and invite me out on a date, I would probably be very happy even though it was still raining.'

'Well, that's not going to happen to me, is it?'

'Why not? Esther, you're very pretty and you're a brilliant musician. You'll be snapped up before long.'

'I don't know. I waited all that time for Reuben to take an interest in me, but our only dates were in front of an audience playing duets.' She sighed. 'And now he's gone.'

'Don't mope, Esther. The love of your life could walk in here at any minute.'

Not thirty seconds later the shop bell rang. 'See?' said Peggy.

'He's here.' They went out into the shop and an elderly gentleman in a mackintosh raised his hat to them and called out, 'Good morning, ladies, I wonder if you can help me?' And Esther and Peggy dissolved into fits of laughter.

When the elderly suitor had gone, Peggy said, 'You know what I miss most about dates?' and she ticked them off on her fingers. 'Number one: having something to dress up for. Number two: having someone who wants to please me. Number three: having someone to make me laugh.'

'What about Archie? Do you think you'll see him again after what happened with Harry?'

'I doubt it. You should have seen how angry he was. No, I won't be going out with him again, but sure there's plenty more fish in the sea.'

A few nights later, just as Peggy left the shop, the heavens opened. She ran as fast as she could through puddles in the pitch dark, towards the bus stop, but the bus roared past her, drenching her from head to toe. She was so angry she stood there and screamed in fury, totally unaware of the car that had pulled up at the kerb alongside her. She did not see the man get out of the car or come towards her and when he said, 'Goodness me, you're drenched,' she jumped. He took her arm and she pulled away shouting, 'Leave me alone!'

'Don't be a silly girl, Peggy. I'll take you home.' Archie put his arm around her waist and when he pulled her towards the car she let him.

Inside, the car was warm and Archie passed her a blanket from the back seat. 'You're shivering, put this round you.'

They drove in silence a while, until Archie said, 'Giving me the cold shoulder, are you?' Peggy ignored him. 'Well, have it your own way,' he said, and he put his foot down and drove at speed out of the city centre. At Joanmount Gardens, he parked a few doors down from her house and turned off the engine. Peggy searched for the handle to open the door. 'It's locked,' he said.

'Let me out,' she demanded.

'In a minute. I just want to talk to you.'

'I don't want to talk to you.'

'Is this about your squaddie sweetheart?' said Archie.

'Don't call him that. He used to be my boyfriend and I thought it was all over between us … anyway it is now.'

'And what about you and me, Peggy?'

She thought for a moment. 'I don't know … sometimes I think you're not a very nice person.'

Archie threw back his head and laughed. 'But you like my company, don't you, and the places I take you. You like to be seen with an officer and a gentleman.'

'Maybe I do, but there's something about you … something dangerous … and I know when it's time to walk away.'

'Well, that's a pity, Peggy, because I was thinking the best is yet to come for you and me.' He reached out and pushed back a strand of damp hair that hung over her eye. 'Remember that day in the Botanic Gardens? A flame was lit and it smoulders still between us.' He laughed and ran the back of his hand down the side of her face and cupped her chin. 'We have unfinished business, you and I.'

She pulled away from him. 'Don't talk like that.'

'Why not? We could have such fun together, you know that.'

Peggy struggled to explain. 'Look, you're good company, I'll give you that, but it just feels wrong.'

It was as if he hadn't heard her. 'I was watching for you tonight, hoping to see you.' His voice was soft, regretful. 'I had a surprise for you, something I knew you would love, but now …' He paused.

Peggy waited.

He started the engine.

'What is it?' she asked.

'It would have been a great night, the cream of Belfast society and the military top brass. The tickets cost an arm and a leg, but never mind.' He leaned over and unlocked the door on Peggy's side.

'Tickets?' she said. 'Tickets for what?'

'You don't want to know.'

'Maybe I do.'

Archie rubbed his hand over his jaw, first one side then the other, as if considering. 'You've heard of the film *In the Army Now*?'

There was disappointment in her voice. 'Yes, I saw it at the pictures.'

'But that's not the same thing. I've got tickets for the Grand Opera House for the stage show: a huge cast, wonderful score and a special appearance by the greatest composer of modern music, Irving Berlin himself.'

Peggy let out a gasp. 'You're joking. Really, they're coming here? But it's the most successful musical in the entire world …' She almost screamed with excitement. 'Let me get this right: you have two tickets for the show and you were going to take me to it?'

'No,' said Archie, 'I have four tickets to the show, seats in the front stalls and an invitation to the party afterwards.'

And this time Peggy really did scream and when she calmed down she asked, 'Why four tickets?'

'Because my subaltern, a very nice Jewish boy, is the son of a West End theatre impresario and he was able to get the tickets. In return, I thought that your friend Esther might like to make up the party.'

For half a second after Peggy heard about the tickets she had thought she ought to refuse the invitation, but the mention of Esther and the fact that she would meet a well-connected Jewish boy, made her pause. Had she the right to refuse to go, if that meant ruining Esther's chance of finding romance?

The following Saturday at exactly seven o'clock there was a knock on Goldstein's front door and he opened it to see two British officers in their dress uniforms. 'Come in, come in,' he said and shook their hands.

'Allow me to introduce Jacob Weinberg, my subaltern,' said Archie. 'And Jacob, this is Mr Goldstein who has made quite a name for himself as an impresario in this city.'

'It's a pleasure to meet you, sir,' said Jacob.

Goldstein was impressed with the demeanour of the young man; quietly spoken, but with a firm handshake. 'Can I offer you both a drink?'

'Maybe not,' said Archie, 'we came through quite a bit of fog on our way here. It might take us a bit longer than expected to get to the Opera House.'

'Let me see if I can hurry the young ladies along.'

When Esther and Peggy swept into the room the two men smiled broadly at the sight of them. They looked like debutantes. Peggy wore the kingfisher blue shot-silk cocktail dress that had been worn by all of the sisters on stage at some point. Esther's dress was new, her first evening gown, dusky pink taffeta in a simple design, beautifully tailored, made by a seamstress from the Malone Road. Archie introduced them. 'Jacob, this is Esther and this is Peggy. Ladies, this is Jacob.'

He stepped forward, shook their hands and all the time his gaze never left Esther's face.

'Right, let's get going,' said Archie.

'I'll expect Esther back home before midnight,' said Goldstein as he waved them off.

In the foyer of the Grand Opera House the anticipation was tangible and the chatter of excited people filled the space. Everywhere Peggy looked she was thrilled by what she saw: handsome men in dinner jackets; elegant women in dresses the like of which she had only seen in American films. She glanced up at Archie and felt her heart leap at the smile he gave her. A smile that could be saying all the things she wanted to hear from a man. This is going to be the most important night of my life, she told herself, and I'm going to enjoy every moment.

They had seats half a dozen rows from the front and, as they waited for the overture to begin, Archie pointed out the great Irving Berlin himself sitting next to the aisle at the end of their row. She studied him, an unassuming-looking man with olive skin, dark hair and heavy eyebrows. Was this really the man who had written all those wonderful songs?

The overture began and Archie squeezed her hand. 'You look beautiful,' he whispered, 'and that flame we talked about is now a roaring fire.'

The first half was the best entertainment that Peggy had ever seen and she was still humming the tunes in her head in the bar at the interval. It was clear that Esther and Jacob were getting on well together. She hung on his every word. He teased her about being a violinist. 'The only stringed instrument to command respect is the cello,' he told her and added, 'especially when I'm playing it!'

When they returned to the auditorium, Peggy was surprised to see that Irving Berlin's seat was empty. How strange that he wasn't there to see the rest of his own show.

She soon forgot about him when the stage filled with what looked like two hundred GIs marching and singing loud enough to make the heart thump and the ears ring. Then they disappeared, revealing a row of tents with the American flag flying above them. The stage was silent and then there came a single bugle call – the Reveille – and a lone figure in uniform came to the front of the stage and the entire audience were suddenly on their feet cheering, shouting, whistling. A few piano chords and the audience sat down, waiting quietly, knowing what was going to happen. Irving Berlin, the middle-aged song writer, was unable to resist the opportunity to sing the famous comic song, 'Oh How I Hate to Get Up in the Morning'. His voice might have been thin and reedy, but he delivered it with perfect comic timing. At the end of the first verse, several other soldiers came on stage and they, along with everyone in the audience, joined in the chorus. 'You gotta get up!' they sang. 'You gotta get up!'

The finale of the show was breathtaking. The stage was packed with all the soldiers singing 'On our Way to France'. Then there was a call, 'Quick … march!' and to the amazement of the audience the front line of soldiers marched down the steps from the stage and up the aisle through the audience, singing as they went. Row after row of soldiers filed off the stage and the audience clapped and cheered them out of the auditorium and those nearest the aisle slapped them on the back, shook their hands. Peggy was swept away by the rousing singing and the emotion of seeing the soldiers pouring past her and when she saw some of the women in the audience reaching out and hugging them, she couldn't resist doing the same. By the time the last soldiers had passed by, tears were running down her face. After four years of war, she finally understood what it was like for men to march off to fight and, more than that, she felt the pride of seeing them go and the unbelievable ache of knowing that they might never return.

The after-show party was in an oak-panelled private room at the Grand Hotel and was for the main performers and invited guests only. Jacob's father had staged the show in London and saw to it that his son and friends would be on the list. There was a sound of a tinkling piano in the background and someone singing 'I'll Take Romance'. A waiter appeared with a tray of champagne. 'Now, girls,' said Archie, 'only one glass for you tonight – we don't want you tipsy,' and he winked at Peggy. Esther giggled and looked up at Jacob and Peggy noticed they were holding hands. When did that happen, she wondered?

'Would you like to meet Irving Berlin?' asked Jacob. 'He's just over there.'

Esther and Peggy looked at each other in amazement. 'Oh yes, please,' they chorused.

Close up the famous composer looked taller and thinner than he had looked on stage. Jacob introduced himself as the son of Solomon Weinberg and Mr Berlin smiled broadly. 'Good to meet you, Jacob. I had dinner with your father in London a few weeks ago.'

'I promised the girls here that they could meet you – hope that's okay,' said Jacob.

'Sure it is,' he said, and shook their hands.

'They're both members of ENSA, the British organisation for performers who entertain the troops.'

'Is that so?' said Berlin. 'We're all in the same business then, and what do you both do?'

'I'm a violinist,' said Esther.

'And I sing with my sisters, in close harmony, similar to the Andrews Sisters.'

'Well, that's swell, girls,' he said, 'I wish you luck with that,' and then the next guests were at his shoulder waiting to speak to him.

'I can't believe we met him.' Esther was so excited. 'I can't wait to tell my uncle.'

Jacob and Esther went off to speak to a friend of his father's who had travelled with the show to Belfast, leaving Archie and Peggy alone.

'They make a lovely couple, don't you think?' said Archie.

Peggy watched them. She had styled Esther's dark hair, sweeping it back from her face in a French pleat, and had done her makeup with a light touch to add just enough sophistication not to lose her girlish complexion. 'Yes,' she said, 'it's time for her to fall in love.'

'And what about you? Is it not time you fell in love?'

Peggy looked up into his handsome face. 'Maybe,' she said and Archie laughed.

'Tell me,' he said. 'What was the best bit of the show for you?'

Peggy didn't need to think about it. 'I loved it all, but the best bit was the ending. It sent shivers up my spine.'

'Was that because you got to kiss some GIs?'

'Well, that was fun, but it was just so moving imagining all those boys going off to war, so sad and happy at the same time. I never thought it was like that.'

He took her hand and when he spoke his voice was serious. 'And will you kiss me like that when I go?'

She caught her breath. She had never thought about such a parting and only now did she have any understanding of the emotions it would bring.

'You're going?' she said.

'We're all going, Peggy – it's time.'

'When?'

'My company is moving out in two weeks.'

'Where are you going?'

'To England first for special training and then …' He could say no more about the final destination, but she could guess.

She wanted to cry. How could this happen just as she had realised that Archie meant so much to her, allowed herself to hope they had a future together – her dashing major. How she ached for him.

'Oh Peggy, I can't bear to think of leaving you. Tell me you feel the same.'

'Yes I do,' she whispered, 'I do.'

He put his arm around her, stroking her back. 'Why are we here with all these people? I long to kiss you.'

Peggy's eyes closed and all that mattered in the world was Archie's hand caressing her.

'Are you ready to go yet?' Jacob and Esther stood in front of them.

'So soon?' said Archie.

'It's almost midnight,' said Jacob.

'Of course. Why don't you take Esther home in the car and I'll see that Peggy gets home.'

Esther looked at Peggy. 'Are you sure you want to stay?'

'Of course she does,' said Archie. 'The night's still young, isn't it, Peggy?'

And Peggy nodded. 'Yes, I'd like to stay.'

When Esther and Jacob had gone, the room seemed to thin out a bit and there were couples dancing to the sound of the piano. Archie took Peggy in his arms and they danced to the languid, late-night music and the longer they danced the more she clung to him. When there were only a few couples left on the floor, Archie suggested that they go down to the hotel lounge for a nightcap.

There were a few people having coffee and drinks but they easily found a cosy corner on their own, and Archie ordered whiskey and a port and lemon. Peggy snuggled up to him and he put an arm around her shoulders and a hand on her knee.

'It's so lovely to be with you. I'm going to miss you so much,' he said. 'I've never met a girl like you before, so talented, such fun.' He kissed her softly. 'I want to remember everything about you: your hair, your face, the shape of you.' He ran his hand over her body as though memorising every curve.

'Oh Archie.'

'I wanted tonight to be so special for you.'

'I've loved every moment of it. I never want it to end.'

His kiss was long and lingering and Peggy felt her whole body weaken under his passion. His lips left hers, she opened her eyes and she was sure there was love in his face. 'Did you like that?' he whispered.

'Mmm …'

'Peggy, do you remember when I said I'd always do what you wanted me to?'

She nodded.

'But I don't dare ask you what you want, my darling.'

'Ask me,' she said.

'Do you want me to be with you tonight, all night, so I can love you?'

Peggy's eyes were closed and a smile played round her lips. 'Yes ... oh yes, Archie.'

He hugged her close. 'I'll go and sort out a room for us here in the hotel. I won't be long.'

The evening had been full of delights and soon it would change her life for ever. Archie loved her and she would give herself to him and when the war was over they would be together.

'Excuse me, miss ...'

They'd live in his big house in London overlooking the park. There would be a drawing room with a baby grand. Mammy would come to visit her and she'd be so proud.

There was sharp cough and she looked up. A man in a dinner suit with a gold badge in his lapel spoke to her. 'Excuse me, miss. We do not allow unaccompanied women in the hotel lounge after midnight.'

'I beg your pardon? Who are you?'

'The night manager, miss, and I'm sorry to tell you single women are not allowed in here. I must ask you to leave.'

'But I'm with someone, a gentleman—'

'Come on, now, out you go,' he said, and reached out to take her arm.

'Don't you touch me! I'm with a major in the British Army – he's just gone to the desk.'

The manager threw out an arm and pointed to the lobby, then swept his other arm in the same direction as though he was sweeping a bit of rubbish into the street.

'All right I'm going, but only to find Major Dewer and when he finds out how you've treated me, you'll be the one getting your marching orders.'

Archie was nowhere to be seen. Peggy felt the beginnings of panic – where could he be? The manager was probably watching her to make sure she went out the door but, if she did that, she'd not get back in. And then she heard Archie's laugh, from somewhere across the lobby ... caught sight of his broad uniformed shoulders leaning against a pillar. His back was to her, but she could hear the elderly officer talking to him in the loud voice of someone used to giving orders. She held her head high and began to walk across the marble floor.

'Lovely to see your wife again, Dewer. Not enough of our women have the gumption to get on a boat and come to see their husbands off. Pity she couldn't stay longer.'

Peggy's steps slowed.

'Indeed, sir, but unfortunately my mother-in-law was taken ill.'

'What!' Peggy shouted the word and marched towards Archie. His face froze in horror as he turned to see her storming towards him, followed by the manager, who grabbed Peggy just before she reached the two officers. 'How could you? How could you?' she shouted as she struggled to escape from the man's grasp.

'Do either of you gentlemen know this young lady?' asked the manager.

'Certainly not,' bellowed the elderly officer.

'And you, sir?'

Archie looked straight at Peggy, his eyes hard as flint, his face expressionless. 'Never seen her before in my life,' he said.

The manager tried to pull her away, but Peggy said calmly, 'I'm going to leave, there's no need to frogmarch me out the door, so please let go of my arm.'

The manager stepped back and Peggy turned to Archie. 'Archie Dewer, you are a deceitful man. You made me believe you loved me. You tried to seduce me, not once but twice.' The manager tried again to pull her away, but she stood her ground and her voice echoed around the lobby. 'You never told me you were married. You're a British Army officer, but you're a disgrace to your uniform and your country. I wish I'd met your wife so that I could tell her how worthless you are.'

The silence that had descended on the lobby, the lounge and the bar was broken only by the sound of Peggy's heels on the marble floor before she disappeared though the revolving door into the night.

Outside, the fog swirled around her and she momentarily lost her bearings. Behind her the hotel had ceased to exist, enveloped as it was in the blackout made denser by the fog. She stood a minute to calm her racing heart and rising temper, half-expecting, despite herself, that Archie would come after her to talk her round or at the very least to apologise. Not that she wanted him to. She was so angry with him, but worse than that, she was furious with herself for not trusting her instincts about him and she shuddered at what she had almost done.

With her back to the hotel she turned left to walk up Royal Avenue. It must be close to one o'clock, she thought. There would be nobody on the streets at all, and she knew it could take her the best part of an hour to walk home, assuming she could find her way – she cursed the fact that she hadn't a torch, for she could barely see the hand in front of her.

She walked on the wide pavements and kept her hands outstretched to avoid bumping into anything; she'd heard so many stories of people walking into lamp posts in fog or blackout. A car went slowly past, its headlights shaded, then once again she was all alone.

Soon she came to a kerb and crossed the junction, turning left out of the city. The ground began to rise beneath her feet as she headed north, but the fog was worse than ever and her eyes began to sting. The fear that she might already have taken a wrong turn began to gnaw at her, and her confidence that she could find the next turning was beginning to desert her.

After about fifteen minutes' walk, an eerie sound penetrated the darkness, but she was so disoriented that she couldn't pinpoint its direction. Now her fear was real. Did she want to come across the sort of people who would be out at this hour? The noise came again and she realised it was laughter, and coming from somewhere ahead of her. Relieved, she reached sideways and touched a wall, then followed it – muffled voices now, a man and a woman, close by. She inched forward and ran her hand along the wall, felt it slip on to wood, a handle, a door and, behind it, voices. She knocked.

'Who is it?'

'I'm sorry, but I think I'm lost,' Peggy called.

The door opened a crack and a hand reached out and guided her inside. The light was switched on and she shaded her eyes to make out where she was: a small room with a table and chairs, posters on the wall, tin hats on the table.

'God bless us, what's a young woman like you doing out on a night like this?' said the man.

'Welcome to Peter's Hill ARP post,' said the woman. 'Come and sit by the heater. Would you like a wee cup of tea?'

Peggy warmed herself by the heater and explained that she had become separated from her friend.

'Where are ye headin'?' the man asked.

'Top of the Oldpark.'

'What? You'll never find your way there; you're already on the wrong road.'

Peggy's shoulders sagged. 'How will I get home?'

'Never you worry, love,' said the woman. 'Sure, Sammy's off duty in half an hour, he'll see ye get home safe.'

Chapter 31

Martha just loved her paraffin heater for those bitter mornings. She would light it as soon as she came downstairs, even before she put the kettle on, and would stand in front of it as it slowly warmed the room. On this February morning the fog was lying thick and it would be a few hours before any daylight broke through.

She had just finished her porridge when she heard a knock at the front door. She was immediately unsettled; no one ever called this early in the morning. She went to the door and opened it and there stood Mr Goldstein. She caught her breath at the sight of his face. He was trying to speak but, although his lips moved, no sound emerged and his eyes were full of tears.

'God save us,' whispered Martha, 'come in, please, come in.'

In the kitchen, Goldstein looked around him as if uncertain where he was.

'Mr Goldstein' – Martha touched his elbow – 'what's the matter? Tell me.'

His eyes flitted around the room, came back to Martha's face and for a moment she thought he didn't know her. 'Esther' was all he said.

'Esther? What about Esther?'

His voice was no more than a whisper. 'Esther is dead.'

Martha gasped and covered her mouth. 'No! How? When did this happen?'

Goldstein shook his head slowly as if to rid it of the words he had spoken. 'I didn't know where else to go. So I came here.'

Martha took his arm. 'Here, sit down. Take your time and tell me what's happened.' She pulled a chair up and sat next to him. Then suddenly her heart was beating wildly in her chest. 'Just a minute,' she said and ran out of the room and up the stairs. In the middle of the night, something had woken her and she had assumed that it was Peggy home from the show. But maybe it wasn't, maybe she had dreamt it? She burst into Peggy's room and there was her daughter, sound asleep. 'Oh, thank God, thank God,' she whispered, but her joy was gone in an instant. She shook her awake. 'Get up, Peggy,' she said. Even half in sleep, Peggy heard the urgency in her mother's voice.

'What is it?'

'Oh, God help us.' Martha began to weep. 'It's Esther ...'

Peggy sat up, frightened now. 'What about Esther? What's happened?'

Martha reached out and hugged her. 'Esther's dead, love.'

Peggy's eyes were wild with fright and shock. 'Esther? How?' And then she was shaking and crying.

'I don't know how. Not yet. Get yourself dressed – Mr Goldstein's downstairs.'

Pat, woken by all the noise, had come out on to the landing. 'Mammy, what's going on?'

Martha rubbed the tears from her face and repeated the awful words: 'Esther's dead.'

When Martha returned to the kitchen Goldstein was staring at the floor. 'I've asked Peggy to come down,' she told him.

Peggy was shaking when she came into the kitchen, closely followed by Pat. Goldstein looked up. 'You weren't with her, Peggy,' he said. A statement only, not an accusation.

'No, she wanted to be home before twelve and Jacob said he'd drive her.'

Goldstein nodded. 'I do not know everything, but it seems they drove up the Antrim Road, where the fog was so thick it would have been well-nigh impossible to see where they were going. The young man, Jacob, must have strayed into the middle of the road. An army lorry was coming down the hill, too fast probably, and it ploughed into the car. They were killed instantly.'

They sat, all four of them, in stunned silence until Martha said, 'Where is Esther now?'

'She's at the Mater Hospital. The police came to tell me about the accident. They didn't know who she was at first, but Jacob had identification on him and they contacted his regiment. His superior officer' – he looked at Peggy – 'Major Dewer was able to give them Esther's name and address.' Goldstein frowned. 'You weren't with them, Peggy.'

'No,' she said softly, 'I wanted to stay for the dancing with Major Dewer.'

Goldstein nodded. 'How lucky you are, Peggy.'

The sudden thought that she might well have been in the car terrified her, and at the same moment the realisation that Esther was gone struck her to her core. She put her head in her hands and wept great sobs of anguish. Pat comforted her as best she could and through her own tears she said, 'Peggy, come on, we'll go upstairs and leave Mr Goldstein to talk to Mammy. Mr Goldstein, I'm so sorry about Esther. We all loved her.'

When they'd gone, Martha asked him, 'When did you last have something to eat?'

'Oh, I do not know, yesterday sometime.'

'I'll make you something,' she said, and she let him sit quietly with his thoughts.

He ate the poached egg and soda farl she cooked him, and when he had finished, Martha thought it best to talk of practical things. She learned that Mr Goldstein would go to schul, his church, where there were people who would see to Esther. The funeral would be as soon as possible – that was their custom. Martha asked if they could send flowers. No, that was not their way, and they should not attend the funeral.

Seeing that Martha was upset by this, he tried to reassure her. 'I will be in mourning for seven days, during which I will stay at home. That is when people visit and it would be an honour if you and the girls would come to see me.'

'Yes, we will, thank you,' said Martha, 'and perhaps we could help in another way. Would you like Peggy to go to the shop and put a notice in the window to tell customers the shop will be shut for seven days?'

'Ah, yes that would be a great help to me,' he said and he took a set of keys from his pocket. 'You can bring them back to me when you come to the house.' He eased himself out of the chair. 'Thank you, Martha, you have steadied my nerves.'

She went with him to the door and shook his hand. 'I'm so very sorry about Esther; she was a lovely girl and a credit to you. If we can do anything at all to help you, you know you've only to ask.'

Goldstein nodded and turned away. Martha watched him walk down the path and her heart went out to him at the loss of the child.

Peggy cried all day. Martha tried to comfort her, but all she would say was, 'You don't understand. I spent every day in the shop with her. I taught her how to speak English. I showed her how to put on makeup. I did her hair for her. And now I'll never see her again.'

And Pat came and sat with her, just as Peggy had sat with her when William died, trying her best to look after her sister in her distress. 'It's all my fault,' said Peggy. 'I should have gone with her, not stayed behind with that horrible man.'

'What difference would that have made?'

'They might have dropped me off at home first. Then she wouldn't have been on that road at that time.'

Pat lay down on the bed beside her sister. 'You can't blame yourself. When William died I thought it was the end of the world. I think about him all the time. The hurt never goes away, but in the end you live with it.' She smiled. 'He's still with me every day.'

Martha and the girls went to Goldstein's home one evening a few days after the funeral. He was sitting in the dark on his own when they arrived. He'd had some visitors in the afternoon and they had brought a meal to share with him.

'People have been very kind,' he said, 'but they have to get on with their own lives, I understand that.'

'And what about you?' said Martha. 'Are you going back to the shop next week?'

'I'm not sure, maybe not.'

'It might be a good idea to get out of the house,' Martha suggested.

'Perhaps ...' He attempted a smile. 'Peggy, you see over there on the sideboard, there is something I want you to have.'

Peggy went to look. 'You mean Esther's dressing table set?'

'Yes, lovely is it not? Solid silver, beautifully engraved. I bought it for her for her birthday soon after she came to Belfast. I think she would want you to have it.'

Peggy could barely speak. 'Thank you so much.'

At home in her bedroom Peggy cleared her dressing table of all its clutter and set out Esther's mirror, comb and hair brush. Then on a sudden impulse she picked up the brush again, intending to brush her hair when she caught sight of a single long, dark hair, tangled in the bristles. She carefully removed it and wound it around her finger to form a little lock that she placed in a neatly folded handkerchief.

When the seven days of mourning had ended, Peggy went back to the music shop. She let herself in with Goldstein's keys, intending to place another notice in the window saying that the shop would be closed for the coming week but, once there, she felt reluctant to leave. It was as though she and Esther were there together again, starting their day's work. She fetched the duster and went round the shop dusting the wirelesses and the instruments as they always did. After that she chose a record to play – 'With a Song in My Heart' – while she tidied up the sheet music, a job she usually hated.

The shop bell rang, startling her, and she looked up to see a woman in a camel hair coat and a green felt hat. 'Can you help me?' she said. 'I'm looking for a present for my daughter ... a gramophone record, but I've no idea what she would like, maybe something modern.'

'There's a new Inkspots' song called "Smoke Gets in your Eyes" that's selling very well. Would you like to hear it?'

The morning wore on and Peggy served other customers. She didn't stop for dinner or a tea break and when it grew dark outside and there were no more customers she sat at the piano, picking out the notes of Esther's favourite piece of music, from Vivaldi's *Four Seasons*. At six o'clock she closed the piano lid, fetched her coat and locked up. She didn't leave a sign in the window, there was no need. She would be back again tomorrow.

Martha called round to see Goldstein the following day to explain to him that Peggy had been in the shop serving customers and, if he agreed, she would keep the shop going.

'The thing is,' Martha explained, 'she would rather be working than sitting at home. I think she wants to feel useful.'

Goldstein seemed uncertain about her being there. 'It is too much for one person; it gets busy in the afternoon.'

'But it'll only be for a week, maybe two at the most, and then I'm sure you'll be ready to go back, won't you?'

'I was thinking about selling the shop. I cannot see myself going back there.'

Martha tried to hide her dismay. 'I understand why you would feel like that. When you lose someone nothing else seems worthwhile any more. I know you can only focus on Esther now and that's how it should be. It's not for me to give advice, but it might be easier for you to leave important decisions about the shop until you're strong enough to deal with them.'

Goldstein sat a while considering. Eventually, he said, 'Nearly twenty years I've had the shop, all those pianos, instruments, wirelesses. Then, when Peggy arrived, there were the gramophone records. She knew her modern music, all right.' He smiled at the memories. 'I would be grateful if Peggy would continue in the shop a while. That will give me time to find the strength to sort out what needs to be done.'

Martha wasn't sure whether he meant he would sell the shop or not, but Peggy owed it to him to keep it open until he decided.

When Martha explained the situation that night, Peggy was upset. 'How could he even think about selling the shop? Esther loved it there … and I'll never get another job like that.'

'He's devastated,' explained Martha. 'He just sits there all day and I don't think he's eating properly. He can't face the world, never mind his shop. We have to help him.'

'Can you manage in the shop on your own, Peggy?' asked Pat.

'It really needs two people and I wouldn't have the time to order new stock and then there's the concerts for the troops … Oh, I don't know.'

'Maybe it would be best to cancel the concerts for the time being,' said Pat. 'Then if Mr Goldstein comes back to work he could re-book them. But I've got a feeling that slowly but surely the Forces are beginning to leave Northern Ireland.'

'Could you manage if you had someone to help you?' asked Martha.

'Yes, but how would I get someone? Mr Goldstein won't be putting an advertisement for an experienced shop assistant in the *Belfast Telegraph*, will he?'

'He doesn't need to,' said Martha. 'I'll do it.'

'What, place an advertisement?'

'Of course not,' she said. 'I mean I'll work in the shop with you.'

Peggy looked sceptical. 'You can't work in a music shop.'

'Why not? I have experience in a butcher's and a grocery shop. I can add up and give change. I play the piano and have some knowledge of classical and popular music. I have a pleasant manner and a very nice navy woollen dress. And if that's not enough I can also use a bacon slicer.'

'Oh Mammy, you do make me laugh,' said Pat. 'What do you think, Peggy? Has she got the job?'

Peggy smiled in spite of herself. 'I'll give you a week's trial.'

Martha was soon into the routine of visiting Goldstein for an hour or two each morning and they'd sit and talk until it was time for her to go and work in the shop.

In the beginning, they talked about Esther – sad things mostly. He couldn't reconcile the fact that she had escaped Warsaw only to die in Belfast. He talked about the rest of his family in Poland and how the letters from his sister had ceased once the Nazis had occupied the city. But before Martha left each day, she tried to bring him round to thinking about happy memories of Esther and his family.

There were some awful mornings when he couldn't speak at all and she sat with him in silence. Other times, he was content to listen to her talk and she chatted about anything that came into her head. She would tell him about the happenings in the shop, but he never commented. It was as if it didn't exist any more.

One bright morning in early March, Martha arrived at Goldstein's and announced that it was time he got out of the house. 'Get wrapped up,' she told him. 'We don't want you catching a chill because you haven't been over the door for weeks. We'll not go too far today – end of the street and back'll do.'

Every day for a fortnight they went walking, further and further each time. 'It'll build up your strength and put fresh air in your lungs,' she told him, and it was true. He seemed brighter and more willing to talk. One morning in late March, there was a real sense of spring in the air and Martha suggested they should walk up the hill behind his house on a path that led to the castle.

The trees were covered in buds and there were primroses on the edge of the lane. They walked in comfortable silence broken only by the sound of birdsong in the air. The path skirted the castle itself and took them to a higher vantage point from where they had a panoramic view of the city far below them to the right. They stood a while, each with their own thoughts, and it was Goldstein who broke the silence. 'Esther loved Belfast, you know. She would always say, "I was lucky I had an uncle here or I could have ended up anywhere." She loved the shop too. It would have been hers …'

The wind was getting up – it was time to go. Back on lower ground, Goldstein seemed in the mood to talk. 'I was wrong to sit there in the house all this time. You can mourn anywhere and sometimes different surroundings give you a clearer view of what you have lost and what you still have.'

Martha left him to his door. 'Same again tomorrow?' she said.

'Indeed, Martha.'

'I'll see you then, Mr Goldstein.' She turned to go.

'Martha.'

She looked back. 'Yes?'

'Please call me Isaac.'

The following day, when Martha arrived at Goldstein's house she could see that everywhere was neat and tidy and the windows were open to let in the fresh air. His voice was brighter too. 'I have been up since seven, went for a walk then came back and sorted out some things in the house.'

'I'm impressed,' said Martha.

'I was thinking maybe I might go into the shop, just for an hour or two, to see how Peggy is getting on.'

'That's a good idea, Isaac.'

He hesitated. 'I wonder … whether you would accompany me?'

Chapter 32

'Hurry up, Jessica, or we'll be late,' shouted Sheila.

'Calm down, they won't go without us.' Jessica buttoned up her tunic and placed her WAAF cap at a jaunty angle. 'Can't see why we have to wear our uniforms when strictly speaking we're off duty. I ask you, how the hell can we roller skate in a skirt? I'll end up showing everyone my knickers.'

'Well, you'd better make sure you stay on your feet then,' said Sheila.

The lorry was outside the NAAFI with its engine running and, as soon as Sheila and Jessica had been hauled inside to join their dozen or so friends, they were away. 'First stop, Londonderry!' shouted Clemmie to cheers.

The lorry pulled up outside what looked like a very large church hall and they all bailed out and joined the queue to pay their money and collect a pair of battered roller skates. Inside the hall it was mayhem. There was music playing loudly, accompanying the rattle of skates on the parquet floor and the skaters themselves shouting to be heard or squealing with excitement. Sheila had never donned a pair of roller skates and once she had strapped them on she teetered at the very edge of the floor, uncertain of what to do.

People were flying past her, all in the same direction. She stepped out into the flow and pushed one leg forward, but when she tried to lift the other leg she found that the skate on the floor had rolled ahead and she fell backwards, legs in the air, and put her hands out to save herself. The skaters veered round her, but one was unable to avoid her and ran over her hand. Worse was to come as she tried to push herself on to her feet; the skates kept slipping forward and she panicked, thinking she would never be able to right herself. Suddenly someone grabbed her under the arms and lifted her on to her feet. 'Stand straight. Stand straight.' And the hands shifted to her waist and steered her to the side. Only then did she take her eyes off the floor and look up at her rescuer. Philippe was laughing. 'So, Sheila, I take it you've never learned to roller skate?'

'No,' she admitted, 'but I thought it would be easy – look at all these people whizzing around.'

'It is easy, once you know how.' He shook his head at her and smiled. 'Come on, I'll show you – soon have you waltzing round the floor.' And with one hand firmly round her waist and the other holding her hand, he took her slowly round while he explained how to push one foot in front of the other and to glide rather than step. And each time she slipped he held her upright until she was steady again. After a couple of circuits, he let go of her waist and hand in hand they went round the floor and before long she skated off on her own. She caught sight of him a bit later and this time he was with Jessica. She wasn't very good, slipping and clinging on to him and giggling all the time instead of concentrating.

Sheila was getting into her stride and had managed to go a whole circuit without stopping, when someone came up behind her and she felt an arm round her waist again. She turned, smiling, expecting to see Philippe, but it was a sailor, tall and slim with curly, blond hair. 'You skate with me, yes?'

'I'm not very good,' she told him, but it was too late, he was already rushing her on at a speed far faster than she had skated before. It was hair-raising and exhilarating. She hardly knew what her feet were doing, but it didn't matter because he had such a firm hold of her that, even when she stumbled, he held her upright and carried on until she regained her rhythm.

When they had completed half a dozen circuits he steered them towards the side. Sheila was laughing and her face was flushed with the excitement of it all.

'You like to skate fast?' said the handsome sailor.

She tried to catch her breath. 'Yes … yes … but I could never do that on my own.'

'Never mind, I will hold you up always.'

Sheila was puzzled and not a little embarrassed. 'Thank you,' she said.

'I am Jan … Dutch. What is your name?'

'I'm Sheila. You're a very good skater, Jan.'

'Not so good on these,' – he pointed to the roller skates – 'but I am very good ice skater, far faster than on floor. You want to do more?'

'Oh no, I think I'll have a rest now.'

'I will rest also,' he said. 'Come with me, I buy you very bad cup of tea.' And Sheila went with him to a smaller room where some ladies were serving tea for tuppence a mug.

They sat at a table and Jan just stared at her. Sheila began to wonder if he had used up all the English words he knew. She smiled nervously. 'You're right, this is very bad tea.'

'I like your face,' he said.

She didn't know what to say to that, so she asked, 'Is your ship in port for long?'

'My ship? No, I leave tonight.' The silence stretched between them. Then he held out his hand. 'Come, skate again.'

As they left the tea room, Philippe and Jessica were coming in. Jessica was looking up at him, flushed and laughing, and his arm was still around her as though she might fall again. Sheila managed to smile at them, but her heart lurched at the look on Philippe's face when he realised the sailor was holding her hand.

Jan raced faster than ever over the wooden floor, holding on to her, and sometimes her skates were on the floor and sometimes she was suspended above it. In the end, he went slower and slower until they came to smooth stop.

'I go now to ship,' he said, and he bent his head and kissed her lightly on the lips as though she was his sweetheart and they were saying goodbye.

In the lorry going back to base, Sheila had Clemmie and Brad next to her and Jessica and Philippe opposite. None of them seemed to notice she was there. Jessica's flirting was embarrassing; she reminded her of Peggy, full of giggles and wide eyes. Once, Philippe glanced in her direction, but she looked away and the next minute he was telling some story about flying and Jessica was hanging on his every word.

'Are you all right, Sheila?' Clemmie asked when they left the lorry.

'Yes, why wouldn't I be?'

'I don't know. It's not like you to be so quiet. Are you coming with us to the NAAFI?'

'No,' said Sheila, 'I'm a bit tired. Think I'll go back to the hut and maybe write a letter to Charles.'

Sheila had never been more miserable or confused. Her mind was racing with wild thoughts breaking free and crashing into one another, each one making her more and more agitated.

Philippe called her his 'best buddy', but somehow in the course of a few hours all that had changed. Now she hated him. And Jessica had been her friend. She hated her too. Why did she ever join the WAAFs? She should have stayed at home … She wished she was there now. How she missed Mammy … If only she could talk to Pat about how she felt, Pat would know what to do.

Then there was Charles, who loved her. She wished she was in his arms again … She imagined his touch so gentle and his kisses so fierce. So different to Jan's lips, and she smiled at the memory of the sailor's handsome face and sweet kiss.

She pretended to be asleep when Clemmie and the other girls came back and soon the hut was dark and quiet. In the small hours she was woken by the sound of movement close by. She heard someone undressing, the bed next to her creaking and, finally, a soft sigh. Jessica had returned.

Over the next few weeks it became clear that Jessica and Philippe were spending time together when they were off duty. It was hard for Sheila to avoid them so she volunteered for extra duties and that in turn gave her an excuse to plead tiredness and spend her free time in the hut.

One evening Clemmie tried to persuade her to go to the village dance. 'Come on, we haven't been to a dance for ages.'

'No, I can't be bothered,' she said.

Clemmie gave her a long, hard stare. 'Sheila, what's going on with you? You can't carry on avoiding Philippe.'

'I'm not—'

'Yes, you are and I know why. You and he were always together, the best of friends and everybody could see where it would end up – everybody except the two of you.'

Sheila's face flushed.

'I thought after that night at the talent show, you might have realised you were falling in love with him.'

'Clemmie, I'm engaged to Charles. I admit Philippe means a lot to me, but we'll only ever be friends, not sweethearts.'

'So how would you explain the way you feel, now that he's been seeing Jessica?'

Sheila had no answer, except that the thought of them together made her miserable.

The following evening when she and Clemmie came off duty, they nipped into the NAAFI for something to eat. They had just finished when Philippe came in.

'Hi girls, you okay'? Hey, Sheila, haven't seen you in a while.' He sat across the table from her.

'I've been really busy,' she said.

'Thought maybe you're avoiding me.'

'No, I'm not.'

Clemmie stood up to go. 'I've got some stuff to do back at the hut. I'll see you later.'

'I'll come with you,' said Sheila.

Clemmie turned her head away from Philippe and gave Sheila a fierce look. 'No, you stay here. You two need to catch up.'

When Clemmie had gone, Philippe leaned across the table. 'I've missed your company, you know.'

Sheila didn't look at him. 'I doubt that. From what I've heard you don't lack company.'

He was taken aback. 'Ah, is this about Jessica and me?'

Sheila didn't answer.

'It is, isn't it? You're not jealous, are you?'

She wanted to deny it, but the words wouldn't come. The look on her face, though, was enough for Philippe to reach out and touch her hand.

'I'm sorry, Sheila, I shouldn't have said that. Look, Jessica and I meet up sometimes. I like her, she's good fun.'

She pulled her hand away.

'I'm not involved with her, you know.' Then he smiled. 'Any more than you were involved with that sailor.'

She stared at him in disbelief.

'Hell, I shouldn't have said that either. The thing is, you don't understand about Jessica and me.'

'I understand that if she's out till two in the morning with you, she certainly thinks you're involved,' she said, and without another word she stood up and left the NAAFI.

Back in the hut Clemmie eagerly awaited her return, but one look at Sheila's tear-stained face and her heart sank. 'Aw, Sheila, what happened?'

'It was awful. He said I was jealous and he likes Jessica because she's good fun.'

'That's terrible,' said Clemmie.

'No, no it's true. I see that now. It's not his fault, he's done nothing wrong. It's me. I am jealous and there's nothing I can do about it.'

'But do you love him?'

Sheila put her head in her hands. 'I think so, but it's too late.'

Pat could make neither head nor tail of the news reports about the Italian Campaign, particularly the fighting around Monte Cassino. One minute the Americans were dug in for the winter and the next the fighting was the fiercest ever seen. She was desperate to know if Tony's division was involved and decided that she would call at the American Services Club on her way home from work in the hope that Joe might be able to give her the facts. The sergeant on the desk told her that he was in a meeting and would be tied up for at least an hour. 'Can I wait?' she asked.

'Of course. I'll show you into his office.'

The room was just as she remembered it when she and Tony had worked there together. She closed her eyes and imagined the scene: the two of them talking, laughing, and making plans. Those were the best of days.

As soon as Joe arrived, she could see by his face that something was wrong. 'Patti, I'm glad you've come,' he said. 'I was going to call at your home at the weekend to see you.'

Joe pulled up a chair and sat beside her. 'I know what you're going to ask me.'

Her heart was beating fast. 'I'd be grateful for anything you can tell me,' she said. 'Just so I can understand what's going on.'

Joe appeared to be choosing his words carefully. 'The 34th attacked Monte Cassino in … difficult conditions. No one can remember a finer feat of war by any infantry division, anywhere, but they didn't capture the position. I won't lie to you, there were casualties. The division was eventually pulled back and replaced by British and other Allied troops.'

Casualties. The word reverberated in Pat's head. She had always known at some point that Tony would be in the thick of the fighting. In North Africa he had probably been in danger, but that was a vast area and she had no way of knowing exactly where he was. This was different, specific; his division had obviously sustained casualties, and if the fighting was described as a 'fine feat of war' it must have been desperate.

'When was this?' she asked.

'I'm not sure. Mid-February maybe.'

Pat's eyes opened wide. 'That long ago? What happened after that?'

'They would've been moved back, maybe to another area altogether.'

'And the men who died?' Her voice was no more than a whisper.

'The families will be informed, but that could take a while.'

'But they must know who—'

'Patti, this is war.'

Pat held her hand over her mouth as if to trap her emotions inside.

Joe gently pulled her hand away and took it in his. 'Aw, Patti, Tony's a hell of a fine soldier. He'll have come through, you'll see.'

Martha was waiting for Pat when she arrived home. 'There's two letters for you from US Forces mail. That'll cheer you up, won't it?'

Pat's heart stopped. 'Where are they?'

'In the front room, on the mantelpiece. What's the matter?' but Pat was already through the door, Joe's words ringing in her ears: 'Families will be informed.' Both letters in her hand, she could hardly bear to look … Then relief washed over her. There was her name, in Tony's handwriting, on both envelopes. 'Thank God,' she whispered.

'Are you all right, Pat?' Her mother stood at the door.

'Yes, I'm just … just happy to hear from Tony at last,' she said, and went upstairs to read the letters.

The envelopes bore the evidence of having passed through several hands. She opened the first one and saw it was dated in early October. Six months ago. She cast her eyes over it then quickly ripped open the second envelope, searching for a date. Nothing. But then she caught sight of a line at the end of the page where Tony had written, 'I'll be thinking of you over Christmas, my darling.' The letter had been written four months before. She lay on her bed and closed her eyes, and the cold hand of fear tightened its grip on her heart.

It was midnight, with no more than a sliver of moon in the sky, when Sheila and Clemmie came off duty. They linked arms and set off towards the hut with Sheila carrying her torch to light their way. They hadn't gone far when someone called Clemmie's name. Sheila shone the torch in the direction of the sound and in that split second saw what looked like two figures, before Brad stepped into the light.

'Hello,' said Clemmie. 'What are you doing here? I thought you were on patrol at six.'

'I need to talk to you,' he said.

'I'll just go on then,' said Sheila. She was coming round the back of the quartermaster's stores on to the path that would take her to the hut when she heard a slight crunch on the gravel. She called out, 'Who's there?' There was no answer and nothing to be seen in the sweep of the torch down the path. She quickened her pace, but within yards she caught her breath. A figure had stepped into the torchlight.

'Philippe!'

He came towards her. 'Sheila, I had to see you before I leave.'

No, she thought, not Philippe as well … not now when she had only just … 'Where are you going?' she said.

'I can't tell you, I'm sorry. I leave at six and I don't know when I'll be back. I just wanted to say I'm sorry I upset you. You know you're very special to me.'

She could bear it no longer and flung her arms around him, burying her face in the soft fleece of his flying jacket. His arms encircled her and held her tight. Moments passed and the beating of his heart soothed her until he slowly drew back.

'I have to go,' he whispered. He kissed the top of her head, touched her cheek lightly – tenderly – with his hand, and was gone.

In the hut, only the soft sounds of sleeping girls could be heard. Sheila undressed quickly and got into bed; she would give the ablutions block a miss tonight. She noted that Jessica was fast asleep. It had been two weeks since she had last been out late at night and, although Sheila would never admit it, she was pleased that her escapades seemed to have stopped. She was just dropping off to sleep when Clemmie crept in and felt her way in the darkness to sit on her bed, next to Sheila's.

'Are you awake?' Clemmie whispered.

'Yes.'

'Oh Sheila, you'll never believe it.' Her voice cracked with emotion. 'Brad's being posted.'

Sheila sat up. 'I know, I saw Philippe, he told me he was leaving.'

'What else did he tell you?'

'Nothing more.'

Clemmie explained. 'They're to fly to RAF Aldergrove for further orders. He doesn't know where they'll end up. It's all very hush hush. You know that Liberator pilots are trained in low-level flying – well, they're needed for some special mission.'

'He told you that?' asked Sheila.

'Yes, but don't breathe a word. He shouldn't have told me, but I made him. Anyway, everybody knows something big is going to happen any day now.'

'Oh Clemmie, will they be away for long?'

'I don't know, but there's something else.' Sheila could tell even in the darkness that Clemmie was smiling. 'He's asked me to marry him.'

'That's wonderful. I'm so pleased for you,' Sheila said, and she meant it, but inside she envied her friend's happiness.

At breakfast, Sheila and Clemmie were talking about the departure of Brad and Philippe when Jessica joined them. 'I've just heard about the boys being sent to Aldergrove,' she said. 'What's going on?'

'I don't know,' said Clemmie, 'it's to do with the Liberators being needed elsewhere, I think.'

'Oh, it'll be something to do with the landings in France probably,' said Jessica, knowingly.

'You think that's really going to happen?' asked Sheila.

'Of course. I hear plenty of talk when I'm driving the top brass around. It's just a matter of time. How else will they win the war? They need to land a huge force somewhere on the French coast and push the Germans all the way back to Berlin where they came from.'

'And you think it's going to happen soon?' asked Clemmie.

Jessica lowered her voice. 'I drove our CO to a US camp last week for a meeting and he stayed to watch the GIs, hundreds of them, gathered on a hillside somewhere in the Sperrins, being addressed before they shipped out.' Sheila and Clemmie hung on her every word. 'And do you know who it was rallying them?' They shook their heads. 'None other than General Patton himself.'

'Oh no, Brad could be gone for months. That puts the tin hat on an early wedding,' said Clemmie.

'A wedding?' said Jessica.

'Yes, he asked me last night when he told me he was being posted.'

'That's wonderful, congratulations!' said Jessica and she turned to Sheila. 'Did you see Philippe before he left?'

Sheila nodded.

Jessica chewed her lip and appeared to come to a conclusion. 'Look Sheila, I know that you and Philippe have always been good friends, but that's all you ever were. Philippe liked me in a different way, if you know what I mean. But I think we both know that he wasn't the sort to make any kind of commitment. All he really cared about was his plane and his crew and I doubt whether either of us will ever hear from him again.'

Pat knew straight away that something was wrong when her mother handed her the blue airmail letter bearing a row of strange-looking stamps. She stared at it, noted the US post mark, turned it over to see the sender's address and stared at that.

'Are you not going to open it?' said Martha.

'I can't,' said Pat.

Her mother's voice was calm. 'I think you need to.'

'I can't.'

'Do you want me to open it?'

'No,' said Pat, and the clock high on the mantelpiece ticked off the time between not knowing and knowing. Without a word, Pat gave the letter to her mother and Martha opened it and read it.

'It's from Tony's sister. She's writing to say that Tony has been reported as missing in action.' Martha put her arms around her daughter and they stood a long time, each with their own thoughts. At last, Pat let go of her mother and when she spoke her voice was strong. 'I don't believe it. Tony isn't dead.'

Time and again Joe had told Pat, 'If there's anything I can do, just let me know.' Well, now there was something he could do. He could find Tony.

Pat went to see Joe the following day and they sat together in his office. He looked at the letter. 'I see,' he said, 'they wrote to his family of course. You understand that you're not his next of kin?'

'I know that.' Pat rushed on, 'Now tell me this, missing in action doesn't necessarily mean he's dead, does it?'

'Well no,' said Joe, 'but, Patti, you mustn't get your hopes up. Most times it turns out that—'

'He could be wounded, couldn't he?'

'That's a possibility, but—'

'You said there was so much fighting going on and troops were being moved. He could've been separated from his company. He could be anywhere.'

He touched her arm. 'Patti, please, you need accept that he's missing.'

'Missing, yes, because nobody knows where he is, but I know he isn't dead. Joe, I want you to speak to your contacts. Find out if he's in a field station somewhere or been left behind. Somebody must know where he is. Will you do that, please?'

Joe looked at her face so full of emotion and nodded. 'I'll see what I can do, but it's unlikely that I'll get any information. A lot of men were killed and those left from the division will already have regrouped; they could be anywhere in Italy.'

'Thank you, Joe, you're a good friend.'

Chapter 33

Martha enjoyed working in the music shop for a few hours every day – it got her out of the house and she could keep an eye on Peggy and Mr Goldstein at the same time. Both of them tried to put on a brave face, but it was clear to her that, under the surface, they were lost in their grief for Esther. Peggy should have been easy to read and in some ways she was, but Martha sensed that there was something hidden beneath the sorrow. She had tried to coax it out of her, but Peggy had shrugged off the suggestion that there was something else troubling her.

As for Mr Goldstein, his sadness was like a badge pinned to his heart. Shortly after he had returned to work, he announced that he would not be arranging any further Barnstormers' concerts. Peggy, Martha noted, accepted his decision without comment when previously she had always made a fuss at the slightest suggestion that concerts might be cancelled. Before Martha left the shop each afternoon, she and Isaac would have a cup of tea together in his office and over time there evolved a rhythm to their conversation. First the latest news about the war was discussed and then Martha would ask, 'And how are you today, Isaac?' and he'd talk about Esther and his feelings and his fears. Martha never dreamt a man would talk about such things, but she put it down to him being musical and a foreigner and liked him all the more for it.

And then there was Pat. After the awful news that Tony was missing in action, Martha held her breath, expecting Pat to be devastated. The days went by and Pat continued to believe that he had simply gone missing, never contemplating the reality behind the military term. She had even written back to Tony's sister thanking her for letting her know about Tony and telling her she was certain that he was still alive.

One sunny Sunday morning towards the end of April, Martha, Pat and Peggy went together to church. Inside there were daffodils on every surface wide enough to hold a vase and shafts of sunlight fell on the congregation. Even the hymns were full of joy and Martha watched her daughters sing with gusto in the choir.

The minister was in the porch shaking hands as usual when they left. He shook Pat's hand and held on to it. 'Ah Pat,' he said, 'any word yet about your young man?'

'No, not yet,' said Pat.

'Well, you know we are praying for him and for you. Take comfort in knowing that the death of a soldier serving his country is a glorious thing.'

Pat withdrew her hand. 'My young man is not dead and even if he were no one should ever call his death glorious.'

Martha waited until after dinner when Peggy was in the kitchen washing the dishes, before she spoke to Pat. 'I know that you won't want to hear this, but there'll come a time when you might have to accept that Tony is not coming back.'

Pat opened her mouth to speak, but Martha held up her hand. 'No, hear me out, please.' Pat shook her head as if dismissing the whole conversation. 'I'm your mother and I worry about you and you know why, don't you?'

'Because of what happened with William, but this isn't the same thing at all.'

'Oh, but it is,' said Martha. 'Only this time you're being told what's likely to happen. Do you not see that you need to prepare yourself, to get used to the idea that he might not come back?'

'What a terrible thing to say. I'm telling you now, he's not dead. I know he isn't.'

'Pat love, you can't know that.'

Pat spoke with absolute certainty. 'I do. He isn't dead. He promised me he wouldn't die.'

On the following Sunday, there was a knock at the door and when Pat opened it Joe Walters was standing there. She tried to calm herself, took a deep breath and said, 'Have you found him?'

Joe looked a little embarrassed. 'I'm sorry, Patti – I haven't. I've tried but—'

'Who's that?' shouted Martha.

'It's Joe.'

'Well, bring him in, for goodness sake.'

He came into the sitting room and held up a brown paper bag. 'I brought you some doughnuts and Coca Cola.'

'Thank you,' said Pat, but there was no expression in her voice or her face.

At that moment Peggy came through from the kitchen. 'Did I hear someone say "Coca Cola"?'

'Yeah,' said Joe. 'Here you are.'

'Sit yourself down, Joe,' said Martha.

'No, I can't stay,' he said, and hesitated. 'I don't know if you heard about all the ships gathering on the lough?'

'Yes, there was a picture on the front of the *Telegraph*,' said Peggy.

'Well, I need to take a trip down to Bangor where the battleships are.' He looked at Pat. 'Wondered if you ladies would like to come with me?'

Peggy was just about to say 'Yes, please' when Martha intervened. 'Pat, why don't you go? Peggy and I have some washing and ironing to do. Haven't we, Peggy?'

Peggy caught the narrowing of her mother's eyes. 'Yes, that's right. I'll just stay here and eat doughnuts and drink Coca Cola.'

'There you are now, Pat, away and get your bag. Oh, and take a cardigan with you. There might be a breeze off the sea.'

On the one hand Pat was annoyed with her mother, but the trip would give her a chance to question Joe about what he'd actually done to try to find Tony. It turned out he had contacted what he called 'buddies', but although they double-checked casualty records and military hospitals they found no trace of Tony. 'The problem is,' explained Joe, 'that it's just not possible for me to contact anyone in that combat zone.'

It was a beautiful May afternoon and they were soon driving out of the city in the open jeep, following the south side of the lough. In spite of her disappointment that there was no news about Tony, Pat felt the tightness across her shoulders, that she had been carrying for weeks, melt away.

They drove to Holywood and Joe turned down towards the esplanade. The sight in front of them was breathtaking. The lough was packed with ships of every shape and size: destroyers, cruisers, and other fighting craft alongside trawlers and all kinds of merchant vessels. And everywhere there were fluttering flags: Stars and Stripes, Union Jacks and signal flags of all colours.

'It's an armada,' said Pat. 'Oh Joe, it's really going to happen, isn't it? They're heading for France.'

'They sure are,' said Joe. 'Forces are gathering all round the British Isles. On every airfield the planes are waiting too. From every barracks men are already on the move. I don't think there's ever been anything like this in the history of warfare. Gotta make you feel proud.' He turned and smiled at her and saw the tears on her cheeks. 'Aw gee, Patti!' he said, and put his arms around her, 'don't cry, please.'

She stepped back from him, wiped away the tears and almost laughed. 'It's fine,' she said. 'It's just the sight of all this … it takes your breath away. After all that's happened …' her voice faltered. She watched the ships and Joe watched her and after a few minutes she spoke again. 'We were on the road not far from here when the city was first bombed. We'd been singing at a concert at Palace Barracks. It was very late and we were on our way back to Belfast. First there was the noise, a droning sound that came up the lough, louder and louder, then the black shapes in the sky above us. We watched it all … the flares lighting up the sky, the incendiaries to start fires, and last of all the high explosives to flatten buildings and kill people.'

'I can't imagine what that must have been like for you and your family,' said Joe.

'People carry on, you have to, but you think the war will last forever. Ordinary people have no way of knowing how such a mess could ever be put right.' She looked up at him. 'But look at all this, Joe … surely this'll put an end to it all, won't it?'

'Yeah, it will. It sure will, Patti.'

They drove on to Bangor and parked the jeep at the North Pier, and if Pat thought the ships on the upper part of the lough were impressive, she was stunned by the battleships anchored at its mouth, waiting for the order to lead the flotilla out into the open sea.

Joe explained, 'Next week, General Eisenhower will come here to inspect the ships before they leave. I've been asked to organise a small group of local dignitaries on the quayside so that he can thank them, and the community, for their support. Then he'll go in a launch to the battleship *Tuscaloosa* where he'll address the men.'

They walked along the pier, Joe considering the placing of the dignitaries, the area where the public would be permitted to stand and where the launch would be tied up. Pat walked alongside him, lost in her own thoughts.

'What do you think?' asked Joe.

'I'm sorry,' said Pat, 'I was miles away. What do I think about …?'

'I thought you might like to have a drink or something. There's a hotel we passed just up the road.'

'Well … yes, that would be nice.'

They went through the revolving doors of the Royal Hotel to the lounge, found a quiet corner, and Joe ordered a beer and some coffee for Pat.

'Things are happening so quickly now,' she said. 'Soon there'll be hardly any Americans left in Northern Ireland.'

'And will you miss us when we go?'

'Of course, but you won't be going will you?'

'Yeah, we'll all go.'

'But what about the American Services Club?'

'They'll lock it up, maybe sell it. It was a dancehall once, wasn't it?'

274

'Yes, the Plaza. I'll be sad if they close it.'

'And will you be sad when I'm gone?'

Pat put her head on one side and pretended to study him. She had grown used to his face – the pale green eyes and strong features, and the way he always listened.

'Yes, I think I will,' she said.

He laughed. 'You had me worried there, lady!'

'Joe, can I ask you something?'

'Ask away.'

'When Eisenhower comes here next week, would it be possible for me to speak to him?'

'Patti, if this is about Tony I have to be honest with you, Eisenhower can't take his eye off the ball. The stakes are too high. Yes, he's the man responsible for every soldier, airman and sailor, but he's not gonna be in a position to find out what's happened to Tony.'

'But if he could send a message or something to his commanders he might be found, Joe. I think Tony's ended up with the wrong battalion in all the confusion after the fighting.'

Joe leaned towards her and spoke softly. 'Eisenhower is in supreme command of this whole operation. You must see that he can't start looking for one lost GI when he's busy putting an end to the war.'

In that moment, Pat knew that it was all over. Tony was lost and her certainty that he would come back to her disappeared in a wave of black despair.

Joe tried to console her, but she seemed not to hear him and when he put his arm around her to comfort her it made no difference. They drove back to Belfast in silence and outside her house Joe asked if he should come inside with her. She shook her head, stepped out of the jeep and never looked back.

Martha was all smiles when Pat came in. 'Well, did you have a good time?'

'No,' said Pat, 'I felt sick in the car, I don't want any tea,' and she went straight to her room.

She lay awake half the night thinking about Tony and every time the thought that he had been killed crept into her mind she pushed it away. 'Please be all right. Please be all right,' she repeated over

275

and over. When she awoke, tired and groggy, an echo of her words came to her, miraculously transformed: 'I am all right. I am all right,' as though Tony was right there with her.

On the day of Eisenhower's visit Pat took a day's leave and caught the train to Bangor. The weather was so good that she hired a deck chair at Pickie Pool in the morning, had her dinner at the Jubilee Café, and then walked to the North Pier. A small crowd had already gathered and she could see Joe further along the pier with his group of dignitaries. She got herself on the front line where she'd get a good view of Eisenhower when he arrived. There was a holiday atmosphere among the people around her, and excitement at being part of history. 'Now, ye see yer man Eisenhower,' said the woman next to her, 'he'll be the one in charge of this enterprise, nobody else, not yer Churchills, nor yer Montgomerys.'

Then a man added, 'Aye, and it was Eisenhower who chose Belfast to be the start of all this. Sure, there's half the whole Allied fleet out there in the lough.'

'Where's the other half?' asked the woman.

'Who cares?' said the man. 'Belfast's the place that matters.'

At that moment there were shouts of 'He's here!' Pat quickly opened her bag and took out her piece of paper, but too late she realised that the crowd had surged and people had pushed in front of her. She panicked and tried to squeeze through them. 'Please let me through.' She caught sight of the general's head and shoulders above the men and women who crowded round him; she saw him smile and wave. But she was hemmed in, people pressed against her and all she could see was the back of his head as he walked away. In seconds he would be gone. She had to do something. If only she could attract his attention. Her eyes widened. There was something …

She took a deep breath and began to sing 'Dove Sono' from The Marriage of Figaro, the lament of lost love, the same aria she had sung for Eisenhower all those months ago.

The crowd was momentarily hushed by the sound as it floated over their heads and Eisenhower, no more than twenty feet away, slowed down, stopped, turned. Pat sang on. Eisenhower listened, smiled and spoke to an aide.

The young officer came into the crowd, which parted to allow him to see Pat. He asked her to come with him and together they walked to where Eisenhower was standing. He recognised her, shook her hand warmly. 'We met at Stormont, didn't we?'

'Yes sir,' she said.

'I wasn't expecting to be serenaded on the quayside.'

'I have to confess, I sang in the hope of attracting your attention.'

'Is that so? Well, you've got me.'

'My fiancé Tony Farrelly of the 34th is reported MIA after the battle at Monte Cassino. I thought maybe you …' She suddenly saw how foolish she had been. On the eve of this huge military endeavour why would anyone care about one lost GI? 'I'm sorry,' she said, 'I shouldn't have come,' and she turned to walk away.

'What's that in your hand?' asked Eisenhower.

'His name, rank and serial number.'

Eisenhower took it from her, put it in his breast pocket and saluted.

On 2 June, the fleet set sail from Belfast Lough with thirty thousand mariners on board. Four days later, Martha and her girls listened to the wireless reports of the D-Day landings on the Normandy beaches. 'Praise be to God,' said Martha.

Chapter 34

Goldstein had been out to lunch at his club and when he returned to the shop it was clear that something had upset him. His face bore that haunted look that Martha remembered from those awful weeks after Esther died.

'Is something the matter?' she asked.

He handed her the early edition of the *Belfast Telegraph* and she read the headline: 'Plane Crashes on Cave Hill'.

'Oh no,' said Martha. 'What happened?'

'An American plane, one of those Flying Fortresses, was on its descent into Nutts Corner, but …'

'Oh, don't tell me it was the fog.' Martha shook her head in despair.

'Yes, it seems the pilot couldn't see the hill, or didn't know how high it was and flew straight into the side of it. The plane came down somewhere near the Floral Hall.'

Peggy, who had been listening, suddenly burst into tears and ran into the office.

Goldstein watched her go, a look of anguish on his face. 'It's just brought it all back. Seven crew members, boys really, lost just like Esther in the fog. Their poor families …'

'I'll go and speak to her,' said Martha.

But Peggy wouldn't listen; she just kept repeating, 'It's all my fault that Esther died, it's all my fault,' and getting more and more distraught.

'You can't keep blaming yourself,' Martha told her.

'But it's true,' she said, and covered her face with her hands.

Goldstein appeared in the doorway and said, 'Let me speak to her,' but Martha looked uncertain.

'Please …' he said. 'Let me.'

When Martha left, Goldstein went and sat next to Peggy. He waited until she took her hands from her face and looked at him.

'When people lose someone close to them,' he began, 'they sometimes blame themselves. They say things like, "If only I had done this" or "I should not have done that". We feel guilty and, believe me, that is normal.'

'But it is my fault.'

'How so?' said Goldstein. 'Tell me.'

'If I hadn't let myself be taken in by Archie Dewer, we wouldn't have been out that night and Esther would still be here. I shouldn't have had anything to do with him after the way he treated Harry at Christmas.'

'I know why you feel like that,' said Goldstein. 'I could blame myself too.'

'How could it be your fault?' said Peggy.

'Because if I had told Esther that I disapproved of her mixing socially with Major Dewer, as I should have done, she would still be here.'

'Then why didn't you stop her?'

'I keep asking myself that question but, you know, it was because I wanted her to go to the show, something she would really enjoy, and when I heard she would be going with a Jewish boy …' He shook his head sadly. 'To cap it all, I was the one who said she should be home by midnight …'

'Oh no,' said Peggy, 'you can't, you really can't blame yourself.'

'You are right, Peggy, it has taken me a while, but I know now that it is nobody's fault. Not yours, not mine – it just happened. Esther could have died in Poland, but she escaped and came to us and she loved every minute of her life here, especially with you as her friend. It was an accident. We are not to blame.'

And Peggy saw the certainty in his face. 'I think I understand,' she said.

Pat had just come out of a meeting to discuss Emergency Factory Made houses – prefabs. How many they could apply for and where in the bomb-damaged city they should be erected. What with that, and the new proposals for free meals for school pupils, she felt that at last the families who had suffered most in the bombings could look forward to a better life. She had just returned to her desk when one of the Stormont doormen appeared in the office.

He took a moment to catch his breath. 'There's somebody wants to see you downstairs,' he said, and added, with a roll of his eyes, 'a Yank.'

Pat's heart skipped a beat. 'Who is he?'

'How would I know? An officer.'

Pat straightened her skirt and ran her fingers through her hair. Could it be news about Tony? She ran down the stairs and along the corridor to the main entrance. There was nobody waiting. Then she caught sight of the uniform outside, a tall officer with his back to her. He turned as she came through the door.

Joe.

'Hello Patti,' was all he said. There was no smile.

'What's happened? Is it Tony? Tell me.'

Joe shook his head. 'I don't have any news about Tony. I've come to say goodbye. I'm shipping out.'

Pat felt the relief rush through her – no news was good news – but this was followed by another powerful emotion, a feeling of impending loss.

She touched his arm. 'Oh Joe, I'm going to miss you.'

He looked at her hand resting on his arm. 'Do you think we could take a walk?'

'Of course,' said Pat. 'We could wander down the avenue a bit, if you like.'

Pat was glad to be out of doors in the warm sunshine, walking the long driveway that ran from Stormont Buildings on the hill.

'That was some stunt you pulled on Eisenhower,' said Joe.

Pat looked at him, surprised by his tone. 'I had to do something. I couldn't let an opportunity like that pass me by.'

'But it's come to nothing.'

'Well, not yet.'

Joe pressed on. 'What will you do if he doesn't come back?'

'I don't want to think about that, Joe. I'll always believe he's alive until somebody tells me he isn't.'

That seemed to put an end to the conversation and they walked in silence for a while until Joe caught her arm and they stopped. 'Patti, forgive me, I can't leave without telling you …'

She saw the anguish in his face. 'Telling me what?'

'That I love you.'

Pat's eyes widened.

'You didn't know?'

She shook her head.

'That's good. I never wanted to make you feel uncomfortable. I knew it was hopeless, of course, you were engaged to Tony. I would never have told you how I felt. Gee, I'm only telling you now because …' He seemed to struggle to find the words. 'I've prayed so much these last few days since the orders came through and I know we're on our way to France …' His voice cracked. 'But Patti, I can't die without telling you that I love you.'

Pat stared at him. 'I don't know what to say.'

'You don't need to say anything. I just want you to know I've loved you ever since that morning at your aunt's school when we marched in with all those kids and there you were – with your beautiful smile – and you shook my hand and thanked me. I'd never met anyone like you before.'

If only she could take away the hurt in his eyes. 'Oh Joe …'

She loved his kindness, his honesty, the way he had supported her. Given another time and place, she might well have fallen in love with him.

Joe seemed to sense her thoughts. 'Maybe if things had been different …'

She wanted to touch him, but knew instinctively that he wouldn't want that. 'Joe, you mean so much to me. You've always been there, soothing my fears and taking care of me. What will I do without you?'

They retraced their steps until they stood again in front of the grand portico. Pat held out her hand to him. 'You've been the best of friends, Joe. Take care of yourself.'

He took her hand, held it a moment. 'Goodbye, Patti,' he said, then walked to his jeep and drove away.

When Pat arrived home that evening she was surprised to hear the sound of Peggy's high-pitched laughter as she came through the door. She followed the sound to the sitting room to see Peggy waving a letter in the air and her mother smiling broadly.

'Oh Pat, you'll never believe it. Harry Ferguson has written to me.'

'Really? I thought he had fallen out with you after that row at Christmas with Archie Dewer.'

'He had, but after all this time he's got in touch with me.'

'What does he say?'

'Well, the letter must've been written just before the D-Day landings because he says he'll be leaving England to go and fight and he hopes this is the beginning of the end of the war. He says he thinks about me all the time and he's sorry that he didn't see me before he left. He should have answered the letter I left with his mother, but he was angry.' Peggy's voice was faltering and she swallowed hard before reading from the letter. 'At the end he says, "You know I've always loved you and, when the war is over, I'll come and find you and I hope you'll forgive me." Isn't that lovely?'

'It is, Peggy. That'll be something to look forward to.'

For days after Joe's confession of love, Pat was plunged into a deep melancholy. She was the sole cause of his sadness and, although in a way she did love him, it was not the same kind of love she had for Tony. Now Joe too was gone and soon there would be no American troops in Belfast at all. Their good humour, generosity and just the sight of them in their uniforms – she would miss all of it.

Chapter 35

'What is it?' asked Sheila, looking at the vast expanse of material spread across several beds in the hut.

'Can you not guess?' said Clemmie. 'Here, feel it.'

Sheila touched the soft material and rubbed it between her fingers. 'Oh, I know, it's silk, like my sister's orange sari from India.'

'Yes it's silk, but what's it used for?'

'Ah – a parachute.' Sheila laughed. 'Where did you get it?'

'Let's just say it was damaged in transit and no longer fit for its original purpose so I requisitioned it.'

'What are you talking about?'

'Knickers!' said Clemmie. 'We're going turn it into silk knickers.'

'How?'

'With precision, skill and teamwork. Oh yes, and a bit luck that we don't get caught.'

'There's a lot of material there,' said Sheila. 'We'll have to hide it somewhere when we have kit inspections.'

Thought of that,' said Clemmie. 'It's over sixty yards, but it's so fine we can store it in a kit bag under the floor boards. There's a loose plank in that far corner.'

The following day was a Sunday, and most of the girls were in the hut first thing, getting ready to go to the mess for breakfast. Clemmie gathered them round and explained her plan. Everyone was excited at the idea, but they asked a lot of questions.

'So all of us will get silk knickers?'

'Well, one pair each I think,' said Clemmie.

'Who's going to make them?'

'I am,' she said. 'I'm a good needle woman; used to make patchwork quilts before the war. If anyone else is good at sewing, they can make them too.'

'What will they look like?'

Jessica held up a pair of her beautiful French silk knickers and told them, 'We're going to use these as the pattern, except there won't be any lace. They don't have lace on parachutes. Sheila will be in charge of measuring and adapting the pattern if you're a different size from me. I'll do the cutting out.'

Barbara put her hand up. 'Is it a German parachute or one of ours?'

'Does that make a difference?' said Jessica, and everyone laughed.

It was agreed that Clemmie would make the first pair for herself as part of her trousseau and if they turned out all right she would make two pairs a week. They then drew lots for the order in which their knickers would be made.

It was usual for Jessica to drive the Commanding Officer to Londonderry every week for a meeting and, on her first trip after the parachute came into their possession, she sought out a draper's shop that sold fine thread, needles, dressmaking pins and a tape measure. While she was there she spotted some lace, but the sales girl could only let her have a couple of yards. 'Now if you need a lot more, I could get that for you – cash only and no coupons needed.'

Within a few days, Clemmie had made the first pair of French knickers, which she christened 'Boudoirs'. There were squeals of delight from the girls when she removed her skirt to reveal her exquisite silk underwear, trimmed with lace. Then with great excitement, one by one, each WAAF stood in front of Sheila to have her measurements taken.

Before long other girls who had the skills joined in Clemmie's Sunday morning 'sewing bee', and Jessica was soon bringing back spools of lace smuggled from over the border. The girls would gather after breakfast, the parachute would be on the floor, with Sheila making patterns and Jessica cutting out, and the stitchers would sit on their beds sewing while everyone else sat around and chatted.

Then one Sunday, when the Boudoir production line was in full flow, the door quietly opened and someone slipped inside. No one noticed the intruder until she bellowed, 'Stand by your beds!'

Sergeant O'Dwyer.

They dropped everything and rushed to their places. She walked the length of the hut, stopping to look at the knicker-shaped cut-outs on the parachute. She took the sewing from one girl and held it up. There was no mistaking what it was. When she reached the far end of the hut, having glared at every WAAF on the way, she demanded, 'Who's responsible for this?'

'We all are,' said Jessica.

'Where did you get the parachute?'

'We found it,' said Clemmie.

'Where have you been hiding all this?'

'Under the floorboards,' said Sheila.

'Are you making money out of it?'

They shook their heads.

'Hmm,' said O'Dwyer. 'I could have you all on a charge. You could be peeling spuds and mopping out ablution blocks for months.' The girls stared straight ahead.

'But maybe we could come to a different arrangement.' She walked back the way she had come and turned to face them.

'I will require three pairs of these silk and lace undergarments and I'll have them by the end of the week.'

Sheila raised her hand. 'What is it?' snapped O'Dwyer.

'We'll need to know your measurements, Sergeant.'

She glared at Sheila. 'Is that a tape measure round your neck?'

Sheila nodded and without a second thought O'Dwyer removed her skirt and stood before them with her blue 'blackout' bloomers down to her knees and rolls of fat escaping from every piece of elastic.

A year had passed since Sheila had last seen Charles. Their letters had continued, but inevitably they became shorter and shorter. Charles wrote about happenings at school, talking about members of staff that Sheila barely remembered, and always he would dwell on how much he missed her. Sheila found it difficult to write about her life on the base; it was always the same routine and, anyway, she wasn't permitted to write about what went on in the operations room. She couldn't possibly tell him that she thought about him less and less, nor could she lie and say that she missed him. She found it strange that other girls pined for their sweethearts and time spent apart seemed to strengthen their love.

Towards the end of August, she received a letter from Charles that sent her into a panic. 'Oh Clemmie, what am I going to do?' she said.

'You're going to do what he asks. There's no getting out of it. He's off school for the holidays, so he has plenty of time to come up here to see his fiancée. You know what they say: if the mountain won't come to Mohammed, then Mohammed must come to the mountain.'

'Ach, that's the sort of thing my mother would say.'

'Well, there you are – moms are always right.'

'But what will I do with him? He'll get off the train at Ballykelly, where there's not exactly a lot to do, and I can't bring him on to the base.'

'It's simple, you're on the night shift so you'll have most of the day with him. What about you get on his train when it arrives here and the two of you go on together to Londonderry? There's a bit more to do there.'

Sheila thought about it. 'Clemmie, to be honest, I don't know if I want to see him at all. It seems so long ago that I said I'd marry him. I'm scared that when I meet him again he'll be like a stranger.'

'Isn't that exactly why you need to see him? If you don't want to marry him, you've got to do the decent thing and tell him.'

'Oh, I don't know.'

Clemmie leaned over, her eyes twinkling. 'Look at it the other way. You could meet him and fall in love with him all over again. Is he good-looking?'

Sheila smiled. 'Yes, yes he is: tall and dark. And he says the most lovely things.'

'There you are, girl. Answer his letter and tell him to come.'

Less than a week later, Sheila stood on the station platform in full WAAF uniform, twisting her engagement ring round her finger. How odd it felt to be wearing it after all this time. The sound of the train grew louder and, as it rounded the bend, the smoke billowed, obscuring the carriages. By the time it drew up alongside her, there were only wisps of steam swirling round the platform and she spotted Charles looking anxiously out of the window. Her heart was thumping as she waved and ran towards him. He opened the carriage door and pulled her inside. She had only seconds to take him in – to recognise his face and realise the memory of it she had carried all these months had been a poor copy. He was much more handsome than she remembered.

The train was one without a corridor and the carriage itself was empty. She was therefore alone with Charles. He was so happy to see her, words tumbling out of him about how he had missed her, taking her hand and holding it fast. By the time the train gave a little jolt and began to move slowly forwards, she was wrapped in his arms and between the kisses he told her about his plans for their future.

'I've been saving up,' he said. 'We should be able to rent a decent wee house when we get married. Of course, when I qualify I'll look to buy somewhere, get us established, you know?'

Sheila nodded. He raised her chin and looked into her eyes. 'You're a picture,' he said. 'In the time you've been away you've grown into a beautiful woman. Your face, your figure … you delight me.' Sheila lowered her eyes, embarrassed but pleased by his words.

Charles hardly noticed her response as he rushed on with his plans. 'They say the war will soon be over, now that the Allies are pushing back the Germans. I was thinking, if you could leave the

Forces, say by the end of the year, you could come back to Belfast and even get your old job back.'

'But Charles, I've signed up until the end of the war. I'm not allowed to leave before then.'

'But you're not a conscript and anyway you're a girl. I'm sure if you made a fuss about wanting to leave they'd let you go. You could tell them you're getting married. It's not as if they'll need you.'

Sheila extricated herself from his arms and gave him a hard stare. 'A girl? A fuss? Charles, the work I've been trained to do is important. Lives depend on it.'

He wasn't listening. 'I never should've agreed to you joining up in the first place. My parents couldn't believe it when I told them.'

'It wasn't anything to do with you agreeing,' said Sheila. 'It was something I wanted to do.'

'But look how it's turned out.' Charles' tone had changed. 'I'm left on my own for a whole year. You're away here, surrounded by pilots and tail-end Charlies and everybody knows what they're like when it comes to chasing the girls.'

Sheila's eyes blazed. 'How dare you suggest such a thing. What kind of girl do you think I am?'

'I'm not getting into all that now. I'm telling you, you need to come home.'

'And I'm telling you that I can't.'

Charles shook his head as if he was searching for the final word. 'I suppose I'll have to accept that you can't get yourself out of this mess. But that ring on your finger means that you're mine and you'd better promise me that you'll get demobbed as soon as you can and come straight back to Belfast where I can keep an eye on you.'

Sheila was on her feet, glaring at him, but she couldn't find the words to show her anger. 'You can't speak to me like that … I …'

Sheila sensed the train was slowing down as it approached a station and turned away from Charles to look out the window. On the platform, a woman was blowing kisses to an unseen passenger and a man in a corduroy cap was standing beside a large trunk, pointing at the train and trying to attract the attention of a passing porter. Ordinary people leading ordinary lives. Sheila knew in that moment what she wanted – and more importantly, what she didn't want.

The brakes squealed and Sheila, shaking with anger and indignation, found herself yelling at Charles, 'I'm going back to the base! A ring doesn't mean you can tell me what to do.' And she wrenched it off her finger and threw it at him.

The train juddered to a stop. Charles came towards her, arms outstretched. 'Sheila, you can't do this. Don't go, we'll talk about it … get things sorted.' The carriage door swung open behind Sheila and she turned to see the man in the corduroy cap trying to get in. She slipped past him and ran, turning only to see if Charles was following her, but the man in the cap was dragging his trunk through the carriage door and there was no sign of Charles.

Sheila set off walking back to the base, her head full of the confrontation with Charles. It was like he owned her, the way he was making decisions about her life. She thought about when they were together before she joined the WAAF. He had been a bit like that then and she had just gone along with everything he said. Even the engagement was rushed; she had been in two minds about it, but his words had charmed her. She didn't doubt he loved her, but the truth was she was older and wiser, and she knew for certain that Charles was not the one she loved.

By the time Sheila got back to the base she was hot and thirsty and went straight to the NAAFI for something to eat and drink. Clemmie and Jessica were there, along with some of the other girls from their hut, and she went to join them.

'I thought you'd be in Londonderry by now with that handsome fiancé of yours,' said Clemmie.

'And I thought you'd be in the hut sewing knickers the size of barrage balloons for Sergeant O'Dwyer,' said Sheila.

'No, I've had quite enough for one day.'

'I know how you feel …' said Sheila.

'Uh-oh,' said Barbara. 'Did he not live up to your expectations?'

'More like I didn't live up to his,' she said, and gave them a word by word account of their short train journey.

Clemmie was outraged. 'Sounds like he thinks he owns you and you have to ask him his permission to breathe.'

Nell chipped in, 'Did he actually say he wanted to keep his eye on you?'

'I wish I'd seen him,' said Jessica. 'I'd have given him a piece of my mind. "Only a girl" indeed. I hope you let him have it right between the eyes.'

'I did,' said Sheila, 'I threw the ring at him.' There were hoots of laughter.

'You know what I think?' said Jessica. 'This world is changing, has been since the war began and these men have no idea of the revolution taking place in women's heads. This war will be won because of women like us. We know our worth and none of us will ever again be just a man's possession.' And the girls cheered and clapped.

'Very well put,' said O'Dwyer, who had come into the NAAFI just as Jessica started to speak. She turned to Sheila. 'Now then, Goulding, there's a man at the gate, says he's your fiancé and he needs to speak to you urgently. You know the rules – no visitors allowed – especially if they have a face like thunder and look like they're spoiling for a fight.'

'She's broken up with him, Sergeant,' said Clemmie. 'That's why he's turned up here. She doesn't want to see him, do you Sheila?'

Sheila shook her head.

'Right, I'll send him packing,' said O'Dwyer and she headed for the door.

'Wait!' Sheila called after her. 'I think I should tell him I don't want to see him again. It should come from me.'

'Fine, if that's what you want to do. He's at the gate, but if you need help the guards are there – just give them a shout. I'll be close by, too.'

Charles was pacing up and down outside the gate. He caught sight of her and waited, hands in his pockets, grim expression on his face. Sheila slipped through the gate and faced him.

'Sheila, I can't go home leaving it like this. We need to decide what to do.'

'There's nothing to decide, Charles. It's over and, to be blunt, I don't want to see you ever again.'

His face was paralysed with shock and it was a moment before he collected himself. 'Look Sheila, I'll apologise. I shouldn't have spoken to you the way I did. It's just that I love you and I want to marry you and take care of you.'

'But I don't want to be taken care of. I want to have the freedom to do what I want. Not what a man tells me.'

He reached out and grabbed her arm. 'You don't know what you're saying. I'm offering to make something of you. You'll be marrying a professional man, with his own house.'

She stared at his hand on her arm. 'Let me go.'

'Sheila, you've got to listen to me.'

'No, she doesn't.' Sheila recognised the booming voice and turned to see Sergeant O'Dwyer at her shoulder. 'She's told you it's finished and I'm telling you it's time you went on your way before I call the guards.'

Charles ignored her and spoke to Sheila. 'I've wasted a year of my life on you. And you needn't think you can come crawling back to me.' His voice was low and the look in his eyes frightened her. 'I'm glad to be rid of you,' he said, and without another word he walked away.

Sheila was trembling and Sergeant O'Dwyer immediately put her arm round her shoulder and led her back to the NAAFI. When they came in the girls were eager to hear what had happened. 'He's gone for good,' said Sheila, 'Sergeant O'Dwyer made sure of that.'

'I'll not have a fella like that upset one of my WAAFs,' she said, and the girls gave her a hearty cheer.

As September faded and the October nights drew in, Clemmie waited anxiously to hear from Brad. There had been talk on the base of Liberators supporting the push through Belgium as part of Operation Market Garden and it seemed pretty certain that Brad and Philippe would have been involved. Sheila tried hard to keep Clemmie's spirits up by listening to her fears and reassuring her that Brad would come through unscathed. Never once did she mention her own anxiety about Philippe.

Sheila was leaving the admin block one morning after collecting her weekly letter from her mother, when Nell called after her. 'Do you want to take Clemmie's post as well? It's Canadian Air Force mail. She's been waiting for this, hasn't she?'

'Oh yes – I'll take it to her right away.'

Clemmie was fast asleep, having just come off a busy night shift, but Sheila didn't hesitate to shake her awake.

'Wake up, it's come.'

Bleary-eyed and yawning, Clemmie tried to focus on whatever Sheila was waving in front of her face. 'I can't see – what is it?'

'It's a letter. It must be Brad.'

Clemmie sat up, took the envelope and tried to open it. 'Oh, my fingers won't work,' she said, and handed it back to Sheila who carefully opened it.

'Here you are.' She gave Clemmie the single sheet of paper. 'What does it say?'

Clemmie skimmed through the first side. 'He's well, he misses me … oh my goodness, he's coming back to Northern Ireland. Only for a few days … his plane needs some repairs and modifications at Langford Lodge.' She turned the paper over, her eyes darting backwards and forwards as she read. Then she screamed and jumped out of bed and ran halfway down the hut and back.

'What is it?' shouted Sheila. 'Tell me.'

Clemmie grabbed her friend by the shoulders and laughed. 'We're going to get married when he comes back. In Belfast … I need to arrange everything … Oh, what will I do about a wedding dress?'

Clemmie's excitement was infectious and Sheila was so pleased for her that it was a good fifteen minutes before she felt able to ask, 'Does he mention Philippe at all?'

'Of course he does. His plane needs the modifications as well and not only that, Philippe's going to be his best man.'

'It'll be nice for you to see him again, too.'

Clemmie tilted her head. 'Nice for me? You do realise I'm going to need a bridesmaid and, hey girl, that's you.'

'Me?' Sheila's face lit up.

'And you know what they say about the bridesmaid and the best man?'

Sheila blushed. 'I don't think there'll be anything like that going on.'

Clemmie hugged her. 'We'll see,' she said. 'In the meantime we're going to have to sweet-talk our new best friend Sergeant O'Dwyer.'

Chapter 36

On a frosty November morning Sheila and Clemmie boarded the train for Belfast.

'Three whole days in the big city,' said Clemmie.

'Three days and a wedding.'

'Three days, a wedding and visiting your family – it'll be great to meet them, after all the things you've told me about them. And, just think, Brad and Philippe will have flown to Langford Lodge already. I can't wait to see them both tomorrow.'

Clemmie caught Sheila's poor attempt at a smile. 'You're not still worrying about seeing Philippe again? I'm telling you, he'll be so pleased to see you.'

'Hmm,' said Sheila.

Clemmie laughed and nudged her in the ribs. 'He knows you're not engaged to Charles any more.'

'Oh, you didn't tell him that, did you? He'll think there's some matchmaking going on. How embarrassing.'

They came out of York Street Station and walked in the direction of the City Hall. 'First up, the church,' said Clemmie. 'Let's hope the minister has sorted the special licence. I gave him all the details when I wrote to him to arrange the wedding.'

May Street Presbyterian was a red-brick building, made to look more grand by the addition of four impressive plaster pillars, and close by was the minister's house. He checked Clemmie's birth certificate, read the letter from the church she had attended in Ballykelly and signed the licence.

Outside, Clemmie breathed a sigh of relief. 'Just need to check the hotel booking and buy the posies.'

Sheila linked her friend's arm. 'Then we'll hop on a trolley-bus and be home in time for our dinner.'

They came into the kitchen to the smell of baked bread and the table set with the best cloth and china, then through into the front room all neat and tidy, warmed by the paraffin heater. Sheila went to the hall and called upstairs, 'Mammy, we're here.'

Martha appeared in the doorway, all smiles, in her smart navy dress and, in that brief moment, Sheila thought she looked smaller somehow.

'Mammy, this is Clemmie.'

'Gee, Mrs Goulding, it's great to meet you at last. Sheila always tells me your news when you write her.'

Martha blushed with pleasure. 'Thank you – Sheila's told me all about you. And tomorrow's your wedding day, isn't that grand.'

'I hope it will be, if everything goes to plan. Oh, did a package come for me?'

'Package?' Martha looked from girl to girl. 'What sort of package?'

'Oh no, don't tell me …'

'It's a wedding dress,' explained Sheila. 'WAAF headquarters have a dress they lend to WAAFs getting married – it was donated by the people of Toronto – and Clemmie arranged to have it sent here. They promised it would arrive in time.'

Clemmie was close to tears. 'What will I do? I'll have to get married in my uniform. I've nothing else.'

'Now don't be worrying,' said Martha. 'Maybe we can sort something out. Come and have something to eat – you must be famished – and then we'll have a wee think.'

They ate the soda bread and boiled eggs and Martha said to Clemmie, 'You'll know that Sheila has a bridesmaid dress that she wore at Irene's wedding and she'll wear that tomorrow.' Clemmie nodded. 'Well, we've also got the dress Irene wore for her wedding although it's not really a wedding dress. We couldn't get the right material you see and it's not white, but if it comes to it …'

They went upstairs and laid the two dresses out on Martha's bed: Sheila's primrose yellow and Irene's flax blue.

'They're lovely,' said Clemmie, 'but I doubt if either of them would fit me. You Irish girls are so slim.'

Martha laughed. 'That's because we've been on rations for a good few years.'

Sheila gathered up the dresses. 'Here, Clemmie, take them into our bedroom and try them on. We might be able to alter one of them.'

When she had gone, Sheila nodded towards the open wardrobe door, and Pat's lavender wedding dress with its trim of pearls and embroidery. Martha shook her head. 'I don't think that's a good idea, do you?'

'Clemmie is more like Pat's size,' said Sheila.

'Yes, but—'

'We could just ask her when she comes home.'

For Martha, it was like old times with four girls in the house again and their excitement over the wedding the next day. She thought Clemmie was a lovely girl and was glad Sheila had made such a good friend.

They all got on like a house on fire, swapping stories about life on the RAF base and in Belfast. Clemmie told them all about her home in Canada and got a bit teary because her parents and her brother had never met Brad and wouldn't see her marry. 'That's why I'm so happy that you're all going to be there tomorrow,' she told them. 'Although it'll be a very short ceremony, I think. Only one hymn and we'll hardly raise the roof, will we?'

'You never know,' said Peggy, 'we've been singing in the church choir since we were children.'

Later, Pat went to make them some supper and Sheila followed her into the kitchen. 'Pat can I ask you a favour?' she said. 'You can say no if you like and that'll be fine.'

'Well, there's no harm in asking,' said Pat.

Sheila explained about the missing wedding dress and the dresses from Irene's wedding being too small.

'I'll just stop you there,' said Pat. 'You're going to ask me if she can wear my dress, aren't you?'

'Well …' Sheila was a little embarrassed. 'I just thought …'

Pat closed her eyes and for a long moment didn't say anything. Sheila waited. There was the sound of laughter from the front room. Pat sighed and opened her eyes. 'I never wore it, there was no wedding. It's waiting for a bride and the bride is waiting for her groom. I know it's just a dress. Maybe there is no groom and I'll never wear it, but sometimes I go into Mammy's room … just to touch it and to imagine what it would be like.'

Sheila put her arms around her sister. 'I understand, I should never have asked,' she said, and they stood there together until the kettle whistled and Sheila went and made a pot of tea.

When the girls were in bed, Martha set about altering the blue dress that had been Irene's. She remembered she had a scrap of the original material and it was just enough to insert as an extra panel in the back and all she had to do then was move the buttons. It was close to two in the morning when she finished sewing and damp-pressing the dress. She got into bed and felt the room spin round her. 'For goodness sake, Martha,' she chided herself. 'All that time bending over the sewing. What age do you think you are?'

The ceremony was at two and Mr Goldstein had offered to collect Sheila and Clemmie and run them down to the church. Martha, Peggy and Pat would make their own way there.

It was cold in the church and there were no flowers. 'Bit miserable, isn't it,' Peggy whispered to Pat. 'I feel a bit sorry for her.' She nodded in the direction of the piano. 'Wonder if someone's going to play for her coming down the aisle?'

At that moment the minister came through from the vestry. 'Go and ask him,' said Pat.

Peggy didn't need telling twice. As Pat watched, quite a long conversation ensued. The minister listened, nodding his head, smiling at Peggy. They went over to the piano where she played a few scales, a snatch of a hymn and some opening bars that made Pat wonder what she was up to.

'There you are, all settled,' said Peggy when she returned, looking pleased with herself. 'There was no pianist so I told the minister that I'll play Clemmie in and out, and there'll be the hymn and a solo.'

'A solo is it? And what are you singing?' asked Pat, knowing full well what Peggy had just done.

'Ach Pat, we need to brighten the day a bit. It wouldn't hurt you to sing Mozart's "Alleluia", would it? You've sung it in church plenty of times before.'

'Yes, but it would have been nice to be consulted.'

But Peggy wasn't listening; she was too busy looking to see who had just come in the door.

Her eyes widened at the sight of the two men in the uniform of the Royal Canadian Air Force, and she went to greet them. 'Hello, one of you must be Brad,' she said. 'I'm Peggy, Sheila's sister.'

'Yeah, I'm Brad, good to meet you and this here's my buddy and best man, Philippe.'

'Enchanté,' said Philippe.

Peggy couldn't catch what he had said and was momentarily lost for words as she studied his dark eyes and olive skin.

Then he smiled and she smiled back. 'Come and meet my mother and sister,' she said.

Peggy introduced them and Brad looked from face to face. 'Gee, you sure do look like Sheila. So glad you could come, we were thinking it might be a lonely wedding.'

'Are you both pilots?' Peggy directed her question at Philippe, but Brad answered.

'Yeah, been flyin' missions over Belgium but we're back here at Langford getting some repairs to our planes – they were getting pretty weary!'

Just then Peggy caught sight of Sheila beyond at the door. 'Just

298

excuse me for a moment, I think we'll be starting shortly,' she said, and made her way over.

'Are the boys here yet?' asked Sheila.

'Yes,' said Peggy. 'Why didn't you mention his best man was such an eyeful?'

'Oh, for goodness sake, Peggy. Now listen. Goldstein has volunteered to give Clemmie away. They're outside in the car so I'll go and get them now.'

'Tell her there'll be a bit more music, starting with the "Wedding March".'

'That's great. I'll give you the nod when we're ready.'

To the sound of Mendelssohn, Clemmie swept up the aisle on the arm of Goldstein wearing not Irene's dress, but a beautiful, white satin gown and veil and long white gloves. The ceremony was short and when the register was signed, Pat sang 'Alleluia', accompanied on the piano by Peggy.

After the ceremony, they gathered on the steps of the church chatting. Clemmie and Brad were so pleased that everything had turned out better than they hoped. 'The dress arrived just before we were due to leave for the church. I couldn't believe it,' said Clemmie. 'Mrs Goulding, I hope you don't mind that I wore it instead of the dress you altered for me.'

'Of course not,' said Martha. 'It's such a lovely dress.'

Philippe and Sheila, having walked down the aisle behind their friends, stood side by side.

'It's great to see you again, Sheila,' he said.

'And you, Philippe.'

'How are things with you?'

'I'm fine,' she said, but before she could ask how he was, Brad appeared at her side.

'Hey, Sheila, you look beautiful,' he said, and kissed her cheek. 'Come on you two, time for some photographs.'

After that, the wedding party walked the short distance to the hotel and Sheila couldn't help but wonder how Peggy had so easily fallen into step with Philippe. In the hotel lounge bar there were glasses of sherry and a small buffet and they sat around a coffee table chatting, Peggy next to Philippe and Sheila opposite. The longer they sat, the more agitated Sheila became. All she wanted was to have Philippe next to her.

Philippe stood and made a short speech and they toasted the bride and groom. Then, out of the blue, Clemmie said, 'You know what would be lovely to end the day – a song from Sheila.'

Sheila shook her head. 'No, I couldn't, really.'

There were shouts of encouragement and some cajoling – and Sheila still looked uncomfortable. Then Peggy said, 'There's a piano in the corner. Come on, Sheila – something romantic would be good.'

But still Sheila looked doubtful, until Pat took her hand and pulled her to her feet. 'Why don't we make it the three of us? It's a while since we've sung together.'

Peggy sat at the piano and played the opening bars. Pat and Sheila swayed to the beat and on cue they sang 'I'll Take Romance'. It was as if they had never had a break from singing together; their voices blended in close harmony, and Brad and Clemmie danced together in the tiny space round the piano for the first time as man and wife.

The afternoon wore on and it was time to go home. They were saying their goodbyes when Philippe touched Sheila's arm and whispered, 'Don't go. I need to talk to you.'

Her family were at the door when her mother said, 'Come on, Sheila.'

Sheila looked up at Philippe and saw something in his eyes. It was enough. She called out, 'Go on without me, I'm staying a bit longer.'

'What about your tea?' said Martha.

And without taking her eyes off Philippe, she called, 'I'm not hungry.'

Philippe pulled her gently towards him and fastened the buttons on her coat. 'There now,' he said, 'all warm and cosy,' and he drew her arm through his. 'Let's see if we can find a quiet bar where we can talk.'

Philippe took a drink of his Guinness and shook his head. 'You've no idea how much I've missed you, Sheila. I've been doing a lot of thinking since I left Ballykelly … about you and me. Then when I knew I'd get to see you again at the wedding … well to be honest, I didn't know who I'd see.'

Sheila frowned. 'I'm not sure what you mean.'

'I wondered whether I'd see my friend or the woman I've grown to love?'

Sheila's heart stopped. 'Who did you see?'

He took her hand in his and smiled. 'Standing there in church today, I saw the girl who made me laugh in the NAAFI when I returned exhausted from those long missions. I saw the girl who understood when I told her about my fears and who wept when she thought I was lost. I so wanted it to be you.'

Sheila could feel the tears well up in her eyes. 'So you saw your friend, Sheila the WAAF?'

Philippe's smile grew wider. 'Yes, but more than that, I knew right then that I loved you. And when I saw you sing again, I understood that was just another part of you and I loved that Sheila too.'

Sheila blinked and tears were on her cheeks and Philippe wiped them away and searched her face. 'I don't know why you're crying,' he said. 'I'm sorry if I've said the wrong thing again and upset you.'

Sheila shook her head and tried to speak. 'No … no, I'm not upset. I'm so happy. I thought I'd lost you …'

He took her in his arms. 'Hush,' he whispered.

She lifted her head and smiled at him. 'Philippe?'

'*Ma chérie?*'

'I didn't understand my feelings. I was confused, but now I know what you mean to me and I feel the same as you.'

'You love me?'

Sheila nodded. 'I think I've always loved you.' And she looked into his handsome face and felt her heart melt. 'There's something else,' she said.

'What is it?'

She laughed. 'You said if I ever sang again you'd have to kiss me.'

Then Philippe was laughing too. 'I did, didn't I!' And he kissed her with the same passion as that night after the talent contest only, this time, she knew that he loved her for herself.

They walked back through the empty streets in the bitter wind and now and again Philippe pulled her into a shop doorway to share their warmth and kisses and the whispering of their love. The motorbike Brad and Philippe had borrowed from the base was parked outside the hotel.

'It's late,' said Philippe. 'Let's get you home.'

When they turned into Joanmount Gardens, Sheila called out, 'Stop here and I'll walk the rest of the way, otherwise people will hear the bike and they'll peek through their curtains at us.' She climbed off the bike and Philippe pulled her towards him. 'I don't want to leave you,' he said.

'I don't want you to go,' said Sheila. 'When am I going to see you again?'

'I don't know. There's still a lot to do before we can say this war is over. I reckon we could be flying over Europe for months yet, but I promise I'll—'

Sheila put her finger to his lips. 'No, Philippe, I know how you feel about making a commitment when there's still dangerous work to be done. You don't need to promise me anything. What will be, will be – I learned that from you pilots at Ballykelly and, for now, it's enough that we love each other.'

He nodded. 'That's what really matters, but I'll be careful, don't worry.'

She looked into his dark eyes and did something she always said she would never do. 'Give me your hands,' she said, and Philippe held them out and she took them in hers and closed her eyes.

He laughed nervously. 'What are you doing?'

'Sssh,' she said and all at once she was back in Bridie McManus' kitchen and she remembered her words. 'Sit quietly and let your mind empty and, when something comes to you, just speak it aloud.'

She held his hands and a minute passed, then two, and nothing came to her mind. A moment longer and she heard a high-pitched whine and the crackling of a wireless, and black smoke engulfed her. Her eyes opened wide.

'What is it, Sheila, what is it?'

'Nothing … nothing at all. Just follow your training and you'll be fine.'

And Philippe lifted a strand of her hair and let it fall. 'Okay, Lucky.' He held her face in his hands. 'I love you,' he said and kissed her goodbye.

Chapter 37

With Christmas fast approaching Goldstein noticed a sharp increase in sales, not just of records and sheet music, but of wirelesses, gramophones and musical instruments. 'I tell you, Peggy, every advance by the Allies makes people more optimistic about their own lives. Mark my words, this will be the last Christmas of the war.'

'That's great, Mr Goldstein, but there are times when I'm run off my feet. Mammy's only here for a few hours a day and you know sometimes I'm left on my own.'

'Maybe your mother might like to work full time, just up to Christmas?'

'That's really not a good idea,' said Peggy. 'Haven't you noticed, she's not been able to shake off that chesty cough and it's making her tired.'

Goldstein looked surprised. 'I did not notice. That won't do at all.'

'What we need,' said Peggy, 'is a full-time assistant. That way we can look after the customers better.'

'You are absolutely right,' said Goldstein. 'I too have been thinking about making some changes.'

Peggy was intrigued. 'What kind of changes?'

'There are a lot of things I would like to do in my life, but the shop takes up so much of my time. So I have been thinking that in the New Year I will step back a little from the shop.'

'How would that help? In the end, I'd still be the only full-time assistant.'

'Ah, but what if you weren't an assistant?'

'What do you mean?'

'My idea is to promote you to shop manager, with an increase in pay, of course. At the same time I will advertise for a full-time assistant and, if your mother would rather not carry on, I will find another person to work part time.'

Peggy was astonished. 'Me? The shop manager?'

Goldstein smiled broadly. 'Why not? You have a wide knowledge of music, you are young, enthusiastic and an excellent saleswoman. I would have to go a long way to find anyone more suitable.'

'I can't believe it,' said Peggy. 'I never thought I'd be a manager.' Her face fell. 'But I don't know anything about ordering stock or banking the takings.'

'That is not an obstacle. I will train you to do those things. They are not difficult. Now what do you say?'

'Mr Goldstein, more than anything in the world I would love to be the manager of this shop,' she said, and then Peggy did something she had never done before. She hugged Mr Goldstein. 'Thank you so much, I won't let you down.'

He was a little flustered and patted her arm. 'I know you won't, Peggy. In fact, under your management, I'm expecting Goldstein's music shop to go from strength to strength.'

By the time Martha arrived in the shop just before midday, there was a notice in the window advertising the position of sales assistant and inviting those interested to enquire within.

'Goodness me,' said Martha, 'what's going on?'

Peggy couldn't stop smiling. 'Such changes, Mammy, you'll never believe it. Not only are we getting a new assistant, but Mr Goldstein's going to make me shop manager.'

'Ach, away on with you.'

'Imagine me in charge of all of this. Anyway, Mr Goldstein'll tell you all about it. He said you're to go straight into his office when you arrive.'

Martha put her head round the office door. 'Did you want to see me, Isaac?'

'Come in, Martha, sit down. Did Peggy tell you about my plans?'

'Indeed she did. I don't know to thank you for giving her such an opportunity. She'll not let you down.'

'I know that. She has a good brain.' He leaned back in his chair and made a tent of his hands. 'You know, when Esther died I wanted nothing more to do with the shop. It was Peggy who kept it going and there was you supporting both her and me. I might have sold it, but I couldn't come to terms with a stranger owning it, not after all these years. And yet, I knew I did not have the energy or the inclination to go on.' He leaned forward, searching Martha's face. 'Do you ever think, Martha, that there comes a time when you have to take stock of your life? I'm not far off sixty and I've been asking myself, what do I really want in the time I have left? Yes, I know I want to organise concerts, but there's so much more: reading, walking, going for a drive and there are always talks on such interesting topics.' He smiled at the prospect and Martha smiled back.

'Yes,' she said. 'I think it's about waking up every morning with the whole day ahead of you to do whatever you fancy.'

'That's it exactly.'

'Are you thinking that Peggy will start managing the shop after Christmas?'

'Indeed. By that time I hope to have employed a new assistant in Peggy's current role. Now, I hope you will not think it indelicate of me to ask you whether you would like to continue working in the shop. You have been marvellous and I would be very happy for you to carry on if you wish.'

Martha had certainly enjoyed working in the shop, but she had never intended to stay there so long. The truth was that it had taken more out of her than she expected, coming in and out of town every day, especially in the bad weather, and more recently she found herself exhausted by the time she got home.

'In a way, I feel like you do, Isaac. I was happy to be useful by helping in the shop, but it's time to take some joy from the world, isn't it? After these lost war years, we owe it to ourselves to make the most of the time we have left. So, if you could manage without me after Christmas ...'

Goldstein looked thoughtful. 'Well said, Martha. If that's the case, I think I will employ a second young person full time. That will be three of them to make a go of it, while you and I enjoy our retirement from commerce.'

When Martha arrived home, she was delighted to see a letter from Irene behind the door. She took it upstairs with her when she went to change, then lay on the bed to read it. It was a bit shorter than Irene's usual chatty letters, but the content was just what she wanted to hear. By the time Pat and Peggy arrived home together, she had already cleaned her bedroom from the top of the wardrobe to the oilcloth on the floor and everywhere in between.

'It's a quick tea tonight,' she told them, 'spam fritters with bread and butter.'

'Ach Mammy, I hate spam, so I do,' said Peggy.

'Never mind, when you're shop manager you can have black-market roast beef every night,' said Pat.

'I might just do that.'

'So Peggy told you her good news, then?'

'She did and I'm very pleased for her,' said Pat. 'Maybe now she won't keep pinching my clothes.'

'I never pinch your clothes. Sure, they wouldn't fit me anyway.'

'Will you two stop bickering? Now then, I have some news too,' said Martha. 'Irene, Sandy and Alexander are coming home.'

'Really? All of them?'

'For how long?'

'Irene and Alexander will be staying with us for a good while, but Sandy's being posted to India, so he'll only be here for a few days.'

'He was in India before wasn't he? Remember, when he sent Irene the orange sari,' said Pat.

'Why's he going to India?' asked Peggy.

Pat explained. 'Because the Allies are trying to retake Burma from the Japanese and the RAF will be based over the border in India giving them air support.'

'I just can't keep up with all these different places where they're fighting,' said Peggy. 'So, when will they be here?'

'Saturday,' said Martha, 'and I'd better get a move on if I'm to get this house shipshape.'

'There's nothing wrong with the house, Mammy, don't be killing yourself. Irene won't notice anyway.'

'Well, I'll notice,' said Martha and she put the plates of spam in front of them.

Martha went round the house for the umpteenth time making sure everything was neat and tidy. She had aired the sheets and put an extra blanket at the bottom of the bed because the temperature was set to drop, according to the wireless. The neck-end stew was in the oven, although it was mostly vegetables; she would have to make sure she gave the bits of lamb to the visitors, especially the wee boy.

She stood in the front bedroom from where she would see them as they turned the corner into the street. The nights drew in early in December and it would soon be dark. She should have gone to meet them, for they would surely have a lot to carry. Even now she could walk down to the bus stop. She rushed to put on her shoes and coat, tied a scarf over her head and went quickly down the stairs. She was almost at the back door when it opened and there they were, coming into her kitchen.

'Bless us, look at you all,' she said and she hugged Irene and Sandy and touched Alexander's head. The toddler buried his face in his mother's coat.

'He's a bit shy, Mammy. He'll be fine when he gets used to you again.' Irene looked around the kitchen. 'Just the same as it always was – I can't believe we're here.'

'It's great,' said Martha, 'just in time for Christmas and, Sandy, I'm so pleased you're here too – it's such a while since I last saw you.'

'Aye, good to see you again, Martha.'

'Now do you want take your bags and everything up to the front bedroom? I've put you in there where there's more room. I'll make you a bit to eat now because we won't have our tea until Pat and Peggy get home.'

'That reminds me,' said Irene, and she took a brown paper parcel out of her bag. 'It's a piece of pork from Davey – you remember him, don't you? He picked you up in Enniskillen when you came to visit.'

'I do indeed,' said Martha. 'How nice of him. I'll find somewhere cold to put it for now. It'll be lovely on Christmas Day with the goose Bridie McManus sent us.'

By the time Pat and Peggy arrived home from work, Alexander had got over his shyness. Peggy made a fuss of him and taught him to roll his ball over the oilcloth and chase after it.

'Isn't he the handsomest wee boy you'd ever see, with his dark hair and blue eyes?' said Peggy. 'And the noisiest.'

After tea, they sat in the front room swapping news and catching up.

'And what's all this I hear about you being the manager of Mr Goldstein's shop?' asked Irene.

Peggy didn't hide her pride. 'Yes, I'll be the one in charge after Christmas and I've got new staff. Bernadette's a great singer and Lizzie is a pianist, so they'll fit in right away. I've got lots of ideas to liven things up and drum up trade.'

'What about Mr Goldstein? Has he retired?' asked Irene.

'Not completely – there'll still be Barnstormers' concerts.'

Irene pulled a sad face. 'But no Golden Sisters and no Macy.'

'I know,' said Peggy. 'Macy came into the shop to say goodbye. She really thinks she can make it in America and I think she will too, especially if she can get in with Bob Hope. He was so impressed with her.'

'She wrote to me saying it was the right time to go back home,' said Irene. 'As soon as the war finishes she needs to be right there when work in the theatres and films picks up.'

Alexander had fallen asleep in Irene's arms and she put him to bed. Martha said she was tired too and wished them goodnight and to make sure the fire was safe before they went to bed. When she had gone Irene said, 'Mammy looks thinner.'

'Ach, I don't think she eats enough,' said Pat. 'That's part of the reason she gets tired, that and all the cooking and cleaning.'

'Well, I'll be here every day to help. I could do the cooking and housework for her, give her a rest.'

'You could … if she'd let you,' said Pat.

'So are you home for good?' asked Peggy.

'I'll stay until Sandy comes back from India.' Irene glanced at him. 'After that it'll depend where your next posting is I suppose.'

'How long do you think you'll be away, Sandy?' asked Pat.

'Och, I don't know. Months certainly.' Sandy's voice was a rich Scottish burr and when he spoke it was with a quiet authority. 'Never underestimate the Japanese. It'll take powerful force to get them to surrender.'

The following evening, Irene and Sandy went out together for the first time since before Alexander was born. They caught the early house at the Ritz to see *Champagne Charlie* and they were still smiling and buoyed up by the fun of it when they reached White's Tavern. There was a decent fire in the grate and the hot toddies warmed them up.

'Are you happy now you're back home?' asked Sandy.

'I'm glad to see everybody again, but I'm sad that you won't be here.'

'I know, but when the war is over we'll be together all the time.'

'But will we? You could get posted anywhere and who's to say Alexander and I will be able to go to every new base. We're not going to India this time, are we? We were really lucky to find lodgings with Dorothy at Castle Archdale. It might not be so easy next time and what about when Alexander's old enough to go to school?'

'Irene, who knows what's going to happen? The thing is, I need to concentrate now on the job I've got to do. There'll be time enough to sort out the rest of our lives when I get back.'

'I'm not so sure. It seems to me we always end up doing something in a rush. Maybe this isn't the right time to ask, but when do you think you'll leave the RAF?'

'You're right, Irene. This isn't the time to ask.'

★

On Christmas Day, Irene cooked the dinner, having persuaded her mother that she wanted to do it as a sort of Christmas present to her.

'Mammy, how many dinners have you cooked us all these years?'

'Thousands,' said Martha, 'but this is different. It's not easy to cook a Christmas dinner, you know.'

'But I want you to have a day off doing nothing except playing with Alexander and eating that chocolate we brought you.'

'Do you know how to cook a goose?' said Martha.

'It can't be that difficult.'

'Irene, I'll help you with it,' said Pat and the two of them took charge of the kitchen.

The sounds from the kitchen ranged from hysterical laughter to screams of frustration with the chopping of vegetables and the clatter of pans in between. The goose was taken out at one point and put back in half-cooked. The gravy went lumpy and was saved by a sieve. The roast potatoes took an age to go brown. Eventually, Pat appeared in the front room to announce that dinner was served. The girls had taken longer than Martha would have done, but there were no complaints. Both the table and the food looked wonderful. Martha, sitting at the top of the table, said grace. 'Lord, thank you for this fine dinner in a time of rationing. Thank you too for keeping us safe in dangerous times. We pray for the poor people in London who were bombed last night and our servicemen and women risking their lives today and every day to bring an end to the war. Amen.'

The dinner was praised by everyone and Irene and Pat bathed in the glory. 'I'll have to get you ones to cook more often,' said Martha.

'We'll never be as good as you, Mammy,' said Pat.

'And we could never have made anything like this,' said Irene as she set the Christmas pudding on the table.

'It's one of Gert and Daisy's recipes I got off the wireless,' said Martha, 'but don't ask me to tell you what's in it.'

Irene and Peggy washed the dishes while everyone listened to the King's speech. Sandy knelt on the floor with Alexander and put together the toy train set, a present from Santa, and by the time the child was ready for bed, everyone had spent time on their knees playing with him.

It had been a quiet Christmas night. The usual visitors, Betty and Jack, had gone to visit some friends and Goldstein too was missing. Martha explained that to visit them would bring back memories of that first Christmas he had spent with them when Esther had arrived from Poland. 'He just said he didn't want to bring his sadness into our home and I couldn't get him to change his mind.'

They awoke on Boxing Day to a world transformed. The snow made a satisfying crump when walked on and everyone, even Martha, went out into the garden. Sandy built a snowman for Alexander and lifted him up so he could add the coal eyes, mouth and buttons and a carrot for his nose. The girls were throwing snowballs and Martha took Alexander inside to watch through the window. The battle was fierce and Sandy, who threw bigger snowballs faster and harder, was soon set upon by the sisters and defeated. Suddenly everyone was shivering at once and ran indoors to warm their hands and toes around the fire, laughing and arguing about unfair odds, while Martha delivered dire warnings about chilblains.

That night as Irene lay in Sandy's arms, she thought that this Christmas was the best she had ever experienced because it was the first one with Sandy and Alexander and they'd shared it with Pat, Peggy and Mammy.

As if he had read her thoughts, Sandy pulled her closer. 'You know, this is the first family Christmas I've had since I was seventeen when I joined the RAF. Mind you, Christmases were good fun in the mess, even during those years in India when the cooks somehow managed to cobble together a Christmas dinner.' Irene could tell that he was smiling at the memory.

Sandy went on, 'But these last few days have been better than I could ever have imagined. I don't think I've felt this relaxed and contented since before the war. To be in a proper home with family … there's nothing like it, is there? And our wee boy, isn't he just a wonder? Loved his train, didn't he? Playing with him on the floor

312

was … was … I don't know how to say it.'

Irene could hear the emotion in his voice. 'I understand,' she said.

He kissed her tenderly and when he spoke again his voice was so gentle. 'I never knew my father so I don't really know what fathers do. I'll teach him to swim and play football and I'll read to him … but there's a lot more to bringing up a child than that. I want him to be strong and brave and kind. We've fought a long, hard war and lost so many good men and it's not over yet, but I'm sure we've won a future for our children.'

Sandy closed his eyes and sighed deeply. 'Sometimes I feel like the days of Alexander's childhood are slipping through my fingers. I understand what you said about leaving the RAF but, Irene, I've still got work to do.'

'Sandy, don't be upset. I know that in the end we'll be together as a family.'

'But when?'

Irene held him tight. 'Soon, soon,' she whispered.

The next day Sandy left for India.

Over the coming weeks Irene insisted on pulling her weight as far as household chores were concerned and she and Martha settled into a comfortable domestic routine that suited them both. Irene was grateful for her mother's help with Alexander and repaid her by taking on some of the cooking and most of the cleaning. It wasn't long before she began to see an improvement in her mother's health; her cough cleared up and she felt less tired. Best of all, Irene came to realise that motherhood and the time she spent away from home had helped her see her mother in a different light.

On a bright Sunday afternoon, Pat and Irene went for a walk up the road with Alexander in his pram, and the talk turned to their upbringing. 'I understand now why she worried about us all the time,' said Irene. 'We were so precious to her that she was frightened something would happen to us. All she wanted was for us to grow up, not just happy, but as decent people.'

'She still worries, doesn't she?' said Pat. 'She'd wrap us in cotton wool if she could, even though she's mellowed quite a bit.' They walked in silence a while then Pat said, 'She wants me to accept that Tony has died; thinks I should be grieving, not waiting.'

'And what do you say to her?'

'I tell her "not yet".'

'Is there still hope, do you think?' asked Irene.

Pat shrugged her shoulders. 'I don't know any more. I was so certain he was alive and now … it's been so long.'

'Do you remember Theresa's brother, Sean?' asked Irene.

'Vaguely. Didn't Ted Grimes think he was involved with the IRA?'

'Yes, but he wasn't,' said Irene. 'I had a letter from Theresa a while ago telling me that Sean had been killed in the D-Day landings. I felt very sad. I loved him once, but I was just a girl. It felt strange to know he'd been killed. I hadn't seen him for so long that he had faded into a memory.'

'It won't be like that for me,' said Pat.

When they arrived home, Martha was standing in the hallway in front of the mirror, dressed in her Sunday best, securing her hat with a large hat pin.

'Where are you going, Mammy?'

'Oh, did I not mention I was going to a recital at the Ulster Hall?'

They eyed her suspiciously. 'No, you didn't,' said Irene.

'Who are you going with?' asked Pat.

'With Isaac – I won't be late.' She picked up her handbag, opened the door and shouted over her shoulder, 'And go easy on that coal, there's precious little left.'

Chapter 38

It was almost time to go home and Pat had just finished the list of families who would be allocated one of the new prefabs, when a messenger appeared at her desk. 'You're wanted in the Prime Minister's office right away,' he said.

The corridor leading to the most elegant part of Stormont was long and thickly carpeted and at the end of it was the general office of the Prime Minister. She went straight to his secretary, an attractive, dark-haired girl with a ready smile, and gave her name.

'Wait here,' said the girl.

Pat had seen less and less of Sir Basil Brooke since he became Prime Minister; her work was usually overseen by senior civil servants. As she waited, she went over in her mind the most recent reports for which she had been responsible. Had she overstepped the mark with her recommendations? She was only trying to get things done and that's what she would tell him.

'The Prime Minister will see you now. Follow me.'

She was shown into a grand room with oil paintings on the walls and a large mahogany desk, but Sir Basil was standing next to the fireplace holding a piece of paper.

'Good afternoon, Miss Goulding. Please sit down.' He indicated an ox-blood leather armchair. He remained standing.

'Oddest thing,' he said. 'Had a message come through from an aide at Headquarters, Supreme Allied Command. Thought it was concerning the excellent aircraft production rate at Short Brothers & Harland. Surprised to find it was concerning you.' He looked at the paper and handed it to her. Pat could hardly breathe. Her hand shook as she took the paper and scanned it. She gasped and she felt her eyes fill with tears.

'Captain Farrelly is your fiancé, I believe.'

Pat nodded.

'I won't ask how General Eisenhower comes to be involved, but ...' He hesitated. 'Please don't cry,' he said softly.

Pat took a deep breath and wiped her eyes. 'I'm fine,' she said and looked up at him and smiled.

'Sometimes there are happy endings,' he said. 'He's one lucky soldier your Captain Farrelly.'

Pat was shaking. 'Yes sir, he is. How can I say thank you to General Eisenhower?'

'I'll tell him you are very grateful for what he's done.'

She stood up and steadied herself. 'Thank you so much.'

'Good luck to you both,' said Sir Basil and he shook her hand.

All the way home on the bus, Pat couldn't keep the smile off her face – it was as though she was glowing with happiness. Once or twice she opened her handbag to check she really did have a piece of paper that said Tony was alive. She hopped off the bus and ran up the street, round the side of the house and into the kitchen.

'Tony's alive!' she shouted and burst into tears.

Martha and Irene stared at her.

'He is, he's alive; they found him in Italy, look ...' She took the paper from her handbag and gave it to Irene to read.

'My goodness,' said Irene, 'it's a miracle.'

Martha went to Pat and put her arms around her. 'Thank the Lord. Who would have thought it, after all this time?'

'I thought it, Mammy. He promised me he wouldn't leave me and I believed him.'

'If you read this, he's been incredibly lucky,' said Irene. 'It sounds a bit confused, but it seems he was in an advanced position when his unit was pulled back … He was caught in heavy shelling and wounded. A German patrol found him and carried him behind their lines and then he was evacuated to an Italian hospital under German control as a prisoner of war … He wasn't liberated until the Allies finally broke through the line and the Germans were routed. It says he's being repatriated.'

'They tried so hard to find him,' said Pat. 'Eisenhower himself sent Tony's details to all battalions thinking he might have become separated from his division. Someone recognised his name when he was liberated. That's why they sent me word that he'd been found.'

'Just a minute,' said Irene. 'Eisenhower did all that?'

'Yes,' said Pat, smiling. 'It's a long story.'

Irene gave her sister a look and laughed. 'Pat, it doesn't matter how he was found, it's simply the best, most unbelievable news.'

When Peggy came home, the story was retold and the excitement shared again. All evening they marvelled that Tony, missing for so long, had been found. The talk had turned to the wedding that had been postponed when Peggy suddenly said, 'If Tony's being repatriated does that mean they'll take him back to America?'

Irene was always up early with Alexander and she would take him downstairs so as not to wake her sisters and mother. She would light the paraffin heater in the kitchen then change him and give him his bottle. By the time Pat and Peggy got up, the pot of porridge would be simmering on the range ready for their breakfast. Usually, Martha came down as soon as she heard the girls leave the house, but Irene began to notice that she was spending longer in bed and when she came down for her breakfast she still looked tired. When Irene asked her if she was all right Martha replied, 'Ach, I'm fine.'

A week later Martha slept till noon and came downstairs in a temper, complaining that Irene should not have let her sleep the day away. 'But, Mammy, you look so weary these days I thought it was best to let you sleep. Is there something the matter with you?'

Martha looked away. 'I don't know. To tell you the truth I could sleep for a week.'

'Will you go to the doctor?'

'Not at all, sure what's he going to do? He'll just say it's my age.'

'I could get you a tonic,' Irene teased her, 'Get my own back on you for all those times you made me swallow that disgusting stuff.'

Martha managed a smile. 'I'll see how I am in a couple of days.'

That night, when Martha went to bed, Irene talked to Pat and Peggy about her.

'She's been like this a few times before and then she's all right again,' said Peggy.

Irene wasn't so sure. 'I try to do most of the work in the house, so you'd think she'd have more energy, not less.'

'Let's give her a week,' said Pat, 'and if there's no improvement we'll get the doctor out.'

The following day Martha complained of a sore throat and added, 'I'm not myself, you know.' Irene looked at her mother's drained face, devoid of expression, and immediately wrapped Alexander up warm, put her coat on and walked down the road to fetch the doctor.

He came in the afternoon, looked down Martha's throat, sounded and tapped her chest, took her temperature. 'Hmmm,' he said. 'You have an infection, Mrs Goulding, and your body is busy fighting it. Your temperature is not that high so I'd say the body is winning. There's a bit of crackling in your lungs, but that's probably left over from the bad chest you had a while ago.'

He turned to Irene. 'Plenty of water, keep the room aired, and send for me if her temperature rises.'

Overnight Martha's temperature rose rapidly and the doctor, when he saw her, arranged for her to be taken into hospital. The girls decided that, because only one visitor was allowed, Pat would be the one to visit their mother and to talk to the doctor. Meanwhile, Irene and Peggy waited at home.

'Mammy's never been in the hospital before, has she?' asked Peggy.

'I don't think so; she's never mentioned it anyway.'

'I can't believe she's ill.'

'She'll be fine, don't worry,' said Irene.

'She looked terrible ... so old.'

They heard Pat in the hallway and were standing up when she came in to the room. They could see right away that all was not well. 'She had a chest X-ray,' said Pat. 'They told me it's pneumonia.'

'That doesn't sound good,' said Peggy. 'Can they make her better?'

'They're giving her some tablets to help with the infection. The doctor said we'll have to wait and see what happens.'

'What's that supposed to mean?' said Peggy, her voice rising. 'Surely they should be able to say whether tablets work or not.'

'There's no point in getting angry, Peggy. The doctors will do their best.'

'Is that so? Well, I'll be the one doing the visiting tomorrow night and that doctor had better have some answers,' she said, and stomped out of the room.

'What is she like?' said Pat.

'Ach, she's just upset.'

'Irene, we're all upset but there was no need to shout at me as if it was my fault.'

'Pat, do you think we should write to Sheila?'

'I don't know. It would only worry her and the chances are she wouldn't get any leave unless ... Let's wait to see what happens with these tablets, aye?'

Peggy's visit turned out to be quieter than expected, because when she got there her mother was propped up in bed, still looking pale and drained, but brighter in herself.

Peggy had brought her some flowers. 'They're from Mr Goldstein and I'm to say he's thinking about you and he sends his best wishes for your full recovery.'

'That's kind of him, they're lovely aren't they?'

'He wants to come and see you,' said Peggy.

'Oh no, no, no.' Martha was horrified. 'Absolutely not, tell him it's family visitors only. Do you hear me?'

'Aye, I hear you. It seems like you're better today – will they let you home soon?'

'I've asked them, but they've said it'll be a week maybe, just to make sure.'

Six days later, Martha was brought home in an ambulance, with strict instructions to stay in bed for another week at least until she had finished the tablets. The ambulancemen wanted to carry her into the house on a stretcher, but she insisted on walking.

She finished the tablets a week later and by the end of the following day her condition had deteriorated again. The doctor wanted to send her back to hospital. 'They can make you more comfortable there,' he said.

'But can they cure me?' asked Martha.

'I can't promise anything. The tablets didn't work, but maybe a bigger dose might do it.'

'You can prescribe the bigger dose tablets and I'll take them, but I'll stay in my own bed, if you don't mind.'

Irene was beside herself. 'Mammy, you have to go to hospital. Please.'

'I'm not going back there, Irene. It was awful. The woman in the next bed died, for goodness sake.'

The doctor tried again. 'Mrs Goulding, I think you're making a mistake. You will be well looked after.'

But Martha had exhausted herself. 'No' was all she said and then closed her eyes.

That night Pat and Peggy each went to sit with their mother to try to persuade her to go into hospital. Martha listened to them, but when they had said all that could be said she just shook her head. Later, the girls discussed what should be done. They agreed Sheila should be told.

'But what will we tell her?' asked Peggy.

'The truth,' said Pat. 'Mammy's ill with pneumonia and the tablets they've given her aren't working. She's getting worse and she won't go to hospital.'

'That's awful blunt, writing that in a letter,' said Irene.

'How else can you put it? If you say "Mammy's not very well" she's not going to come, is she? And where will we be then if Mammy—'

'All right,' said Irene, 'I'll send her a letter tomorrow.'

Over the next few days the neighbours, Betty and Mrs McKee, helped Irene by minding Alexander or sitting with Martha. The doctor prescribed aspirin for the pain in her chest and suggested honey in warm water for her cough. Irene sat with her and bathed her hands and face with cold water to reduce her temperature and they talked as they hadn't done for so long until Martha fell asleep.

Goldstein visited every morning, walking all the way from the Antrim Road, to inquire about Martha. Irene gave him the latest news and he asked her to pass on his best wishes for a full recovery. Each time, Irene invited him to come in, but he always declined.

By the time Sheila arrived, Martha was fading.

'Where is she?' said Sheila as soon as she came into the house. 'Upstairs?' She dropped her kitbag on the floor.

Irene stepped in front of her. 'Just a minute, Sheila. Mammy's sleeping, don't wake her.'

Sheila's eyes were wide with panic. 'I want to see her.'

'In a while, come and sit down.'

'Is she any better?' asked Sheila.

'Not really. I have to say she's getting worse.' Irene had gone over this conversation so many times waiting for Sheila to come home and every time she had cried just thinking about it. She knew her sister's reaction would depend on how calmly she could explain the inevitable. 'They've given her the medicine for pneumonia and it hasn't got rid of it. She's fighting so hard, but ... Sheila, it looks like she might lose the fight.'

Sheila took a series of quick, shallow breaths and began to shake, as the shock hit. The first sob was heart-wrenching for Irene and the ones that followed, heartbreaking. She stumbled towards the door and went out into the garden. Irene let her go, but watched her through the window. Sheila stood for a long while, wiping away her tears with the cuff of her tunic, before retracing her steps to the kitchen. Irene could see she was shivering and she went to her and rubbed her arms vigorously. 'Come and sit by the fire now,' she said, and she made her a cup of hot sweet tea. 'Drink this. We knew it would be a shock.'

'We can't just sit here and let her go,' Sheila said quietly. 'What

321

can we do?'

'You could speak to her about going into hospital, maybe she'd listen to you, but I don't think it would make any difference. She's just not strong enough.'

'I'll go up now to see if she's awake and I'll talk to her about it.'

Martha brightened up a little when she saw Sheila, but she still wouldn't agree to go into hospital. 'I'd rather be at home with my girls than in a hospital ward with strangers,' was all she said.

Later that evening her cousins the McCrackens visited Martha. John had brought his Bible and they prayed together and he read to Martha until she fell asleep. After that they sat a while with the girls in the front room.

'When Martha was a girl, you know, she was that lively you never knew what she'd be up to next,' Aggie told them. 'She played the piano in church and the minister would put up the hymn numbers and if she didn't like his choice she would play what she thought was more suitable and, of course, that's what we would sing.'

'That sounds familiar,' said Pat, looking at Peggy.

'We looked forward to her coming to see us every Saturday. She'd always make us laugh, always great craic,' said Grace.

When the McCrackens had gone, Pat went upstairs to watch over her mother a while, but when the sound of laughter filtered upstairs she went back down to see what was going on.

Betty and Jack were there and Peggy was telling the story of Martha and the Christmas turkey. 'How was I to know she'd bought a live turkey and left it in the bathroom? I came home from work and went straight to the toilet and the beast flew at me – frightened the life out of me.'

Irene took up the story. 'We were helpless, couldn't stop laughing, but then none of us would go near the bathroom. It would still be there now if Harry Ferguson hadn't shown up – looking for you, Peggy.'

Later, when the girls were alone, Pat said, 'I was thinking that we need to tell Aunt Anna about Mammy. I know she doesn't see her sister very much, but … well, I think we should. I'll leave work a bit early tomorrow and go and see her. And when I've been there I'll go and tell Aunt Kathleen.'

That night Martha found breathing difficult. 'Stay with me,' she said between the rapid, shallow breaths and Irene held her hand and told her not to worry.

Pat was not looking forward to seeing her aunt Anna. They really should have told her about their mother's illness sooner and Anna would no doubt make a fuss. She left Stormont early and was walking down the driveway, when a car drew up beside her and she turned to see a grand, highly polished vehicle driven by a chauffeur. The rear window was wound down and someone called her name. It was Sir Basil Brooke. 'Can I offer you a lift, Miss Goulding?' She was about to decline, but the chauffeur was already out of the car and opening the door for her.

'You've finished work early today,' he said.

Pat blushed. 'I was given permission to leave early, because my mother is ill and I need to tell her sister what's happened.'

'I'm very sorry to hear about your mother. Is it serious?'

'She has pneumonia. She's been in hospital and the treatment didn't kill the infection. We have her at home now ... she's very ill.'

'That's a worry for you,' he said. 'The same thing happened to Winston Churchill, you know. Yes, he was in Cairo at the time, planning the D-Day landings with the Allied commanders – my uncle is Chief of the General Staff, as you may know.'

'What happened?' asked Pat.

'He nearly died.'

'How did he—'

'There was a new drug, just been developed. They managed to get hold of it, flew it out to Cairo. He took it with a shot of brandy, joked afterwards it was the brandy that cured him.'

'Well, I don't think they had any of that to give my mother.'

'It was over a year ago that Churchill was treated, it must be available somewhere. Tell you what, I'll speak to my physician, see what he knows about it. Where do you live?'

Sir Basil Brooke was as good as his word and, by the time Pat arrived home, there was a car parked outside their house and a tall thin man with a moustache in an old-fashioned suit was talking to Irene in the front room. 'Pat, this is Dr Craig, he came to see

Mammy.'

Pat shook his thin, bony hand. 'You're Sir Basil's doctor?'

'Yes, he asked me to call because I have one or two connections with pharmaceutical companies in England.' His English accent was not dissimilar to the King's when he spoke on the wireless. 'I've started your mother on a course of the very latest drugs, not generally available. You must make sure she takes them all, even if she feels better, and most importantly ensure she has a high fluid intake.'

'I don't know what to say.' Pat glanced at Irene who looked close to tears. 'We are so grateful. We can't thank you enough.'

'Not at all, there's no need, I'm happy to help. Here is my card – contact me if she isn't showing signs of improvement in the next few days.'

And he took his bag and hat and bid them good day.

By the end of the week Martha was on the mend and Irene made sure she got the best of the rations to build her up. Within a fortnight she was downstairs and happy to receive visitors and Goldstein was first there, with flowers and oranges. Irene took Alexander out in his pram in the spring sunshine, leaving them to catch up.

'My dear Martha, I am glad to see you looking so well. You had us worried.'

'Ach, it was a lot of fussing. I'm stronger than they think. Now tell me, how are you, Isaac?'

'No doubt you've heard all about Peggy's plans for the shop: the painting; the parquet floor; the new counter and cash register.'

'And what do you think about it all?'

Goldstein shrugged his shoulders and lifted his hands, palms up. 'She is right, of course, the shop is just as it was when I bought it in the twenties. She has so many ideas to make it modern and that is what people will expect in the new era of peace and prosperity – out with the old and in with the new.'

'Aye, we're the old ones now.' Martha smiled. 'We'll be strangers in this new world.'

'Do you remember that conversation we had a while ago, Martha, when we agreed you have to make the most of the days you are given? Well, that kept coming back to me when you were ill.'

Martha waited for him to continue, but instead he went and stared out of the window. A minute or two later he came back and sat opposite her and continued with his train of thought.

'I was struck by how sad I was that your days might be slipping away and I thought that if you recovered I would like to …' He paused and changed tack. 'I am a bachelor by nature, but I enjoy good company.' He moved forward in his seat and Martha thought for a moment that he was about to go to the window again, but he went on, 'May I suggest that you and I, as friends, could enjoy each other's company as we did when we went to the Ulster Hall recital … only more frequently.' And he sat back in his chair to await her response.

Martha was dumbfounded. What sort of proposition was this? Thankfully, nothing like Ted Grimes had had the cheek to suggest after Vera's death. She recalled the advice Bridie had given her about trusting her instincts. Over the years she had come to admire Isaac Goldstein; he was a man of principle, as well as good company.

'Are we talking about companionship?' she asked.

Isaac smiled broadly. 'The very thing – pleasant outings and good conversation. I think that would suit us well, don't you?'

Chapter 39

It was still dark and eerily quiet when Pat arrived at the docks. A few people waited on the quayside, their backs against the cold wind that blew up the lough. Pat stamped her feet, blew into her cupped hands and wished she had worn an extra jumper under her coat.

The Liverpool boat was late, but she had waited all these months, so what was an hour or two more? It gave her time to think about what it would be like to see Tony again. What would she say to him? Would he be the same after all he'd been through? Would he still love her?

By the time the boat docked the grey sky was streaked pink with early morning light. The passengers crowded along the rails, jostling to disembark, and Pat searched for Tony among them. There was no sign of him. The gangplank was manoeuvred into place and the passengers, laden with bags and suitcases, descended. Just when it seemed that everyone had left the ship, and she was beginning to worry, he appeared at the top of the gangplank in his cap and greatcoat, with his kit bag balancing on his shoulder. She watched as he slowly descended, leaning on a cane, and her heart went out to him. He caught sight of her and smiled, his eyes never leaving her face until he stepped ashore and took her in his arms.

No words were needed. He was just the same. He loved her still.

They walked to the American Red Cross Services Club where Tony would be staying and dropped off his kit bag. They ate breakfast – eggs over easy, crispy bacon and hash browns – and sitting across the table from him, Pat was surprised to see how well he looked. His skin was tanned and the blue of his eyes more intense. He was maybe a little thinner and there was a pale scar on his right temple.

'Gee, Patti, it's so good to be back here. You and me together again, just like it was when we got this whole club started. Every day I was in that hospital and then the camp, I imagined myself right here with you.' He looked as though he would say more, but instead he stared into space and Pat saw a haunted look come into his eyes. Then suddenly he was aware of her again. 'I'd remember us pouring over the plans to turn this old building into a home from home for the GIs. Every day we were together overseeing the work, choosing the colours of the walls, ordering furniture, everything to make the club a reality. Hey, remember the day the dance hall floor was finished?'

Pat smiled. '"The Blue Danube" was playing on the gramophone and we waltzed, just the two of us, in the empty hall.'

Tony reached out and took her hand. 'That was when I realised how much I loved you.'

Pat blushed and lowered her eyes. She wanted to tell him she had loved him weeks before that day they danced the waltz, when she had unexpectedly found herself studying him: his dark crew cut; the cleft in his chin; his kind eyes …

Tony squeezed her hand. 'And what about the night Glenn Miller played here? The night I proposed.'

'It was wonderful,' she whispered.

Tony put his head to one side and looked at her. 'Patti, we've been a long time apart, far longer than we were together. I've done a lot of thinking about us. Like I said in my letter, I've two weeks furlough before I go back to England then I have to decide whether to take the desk job they've offered me at headquarters

– or, with this injury, I could leave the army altogether.' He gave a nervous smile. 'It seems to me we should maybe take that time to get reacquainted.'

Pat tried to hide her surprise. She had thought Tony was coming back to marry her. How foolish she had been to assume such a thing, but Tony saw the look on her face and when he spoke his voice was gentle. 'Patti, my darling, believe me – I love you with all my heart. The thing is, I just need to adjust, to spend time with you. I might not be the same as I was and I want you to be sure about us.'

Pat looked into his handsome face and saw how anxious he was. It was odd, she thought, but she was feeling a little awkward, a little shy in his company. Was it possible that he felt the same? 'If that's what you want …' she said.

A smile lit up his face. 'It'll be sorta like when we first met, when we didn't really know each other. All I want is to make you fall in love with me all over again.' And Pat thrilled at the thought of being wooed by this wonderful man who made her heart sing every time she looked at him.

Later they went out into the sunny Saturday morning and Tony offered her his arm.

'Is your leg very painful?' she asked.

'No, not any more. It hurt like hell when it happened and I could've lost it if they hadn't found me. Now it's stiff and it aches a bit. The doc says it'll take a while to build up the muscles, and even then I'll never see active service again.'

'If you left the army, what would you do?'

'I've a buddy back home, known him for years; his family own a construction company.' Tony was suddenly animated. 'We always said we'd do something together after the war. Now he's got this crazy idea about building new homes for returning GIs, wants me to manage the construction workers. We'll turn potato fields in Long Island into a town of lovely homes. Never mind home from home, it will be "homes at home" for the guys.' He laughed. 'You know, Patti, I was never happier than when we made the whole American Services Club thing happen and this'll be the same kind of thing.'

They walked towards the City Hall and Pat told him about the parade on the first anniversary of the arrival of American troops in Northern Ireland and showed him the monument to mark the occasion.

'Yeah, I got that letter you wrote me about the parade and that other time when Eisenhower got stranded here and you sang for him. I was real proud of you. Then when I was liberated, the officer in charge recognised my name, said Eisenhower had put out a call after I was reported MIA to say he wanted me found – heard you had something to do with that, as well.'

When she explained her visit to Bangor to ask Eisenhower for help, Tony stopped walking and looked at her in amazement. 'Wow, Patti, you did that for me … ain't that something.'

They sat on a bench a while and Tony put his arm around her and she laid her head on his shoulder, both of them content to be together at last.

They went to the Pam-Pam for lunch and Pat wasn't surprised to see heads turn at the sight of a US Army captain in his immaculate uniform. At one time the city had been full of GIs, but since the D-Day landings they had been few and far between.

'I see the ration situation hasn't improved much,' said Tony when a plate of curled-up cheese sandwiches appeared on the table. 'And still the worst coffee in the Western Hemisphere, I guess.' He took a sip and shuddered. 'Tell me about your family. How're they doin'?'

'They're fine now. My mother was very ill with pneumonia and it was touch-and-go for a while.'

'I'm sorry to hear that. Is she better now?'

'Almost back to her feisty self, getting stronger every day, thank goodness. I've strict instructions to invite you round to the house tomorrow for Sunday dinner. Will you come?'

'Sure will. It'll be good to catch up with them all.'

'You'll meet Alexander as well. He's a lovely wee boy.' Pat's face lit up just thinking about her nephew. She caught the look on Tony's face. 'What is it?' she said.

He shook his head.

'Tell me.'

329

'I know I said we should kinda pretend that we're just getting to know each other but, Patti, I have to say, you're so lovely when you smile.' And both of them laughed at the strangeness of it all.

They sat talking into the afternoon, ordered tea and cake, and all the time the conversation never flagged. The diners in the restaurant glanced now and again at the redhead and the handsome American, heard their laughter and saw quite plainly that they were in love.

As soon as Pat arrived home she was bombarded with questions.

'Well, how did you get on?' asked Martha.

'Where is he?' asked Irene.

'When are you getting married?' asked Peggy.

Pat pretended to be annoyed. 'Can I not even get my coat off before you all start poking your noses into other people's business?'

'We want to hear all about it.'

Pat hung up her coat, took her shoes off and settled herself in the armchair by the side of the fire. 'We got on really well. We've been talking all day. He's staying at the American Services Club and I've invited him for his Sunday dinner tomorrow.'

'And?' said Irene.

'He's asked me out on a date tonight and we're going to the Imperial Hotel. I've to meet him there at seven o'clock.'

'A date?' said Peggy. 'That sounds a bit odd.'

'Well, it's like this,' said Pat. 'We're getting to know each other again. We've been apart for so long and we don't want to rush into things ...' She looked at the faces around her. 'What?'

'But the wedding ...' said Martha.

'There's no hurry, we'll see what happens.'

'I've never heard the like,' said Martha. 'You've been through all those months and months of worry, not knowing whether he was alive or dead – and now he's here, you're back to square one and going on a date.'

'Ach, Mammy, you don't understand,' said Pat and she stood up. 'I'm away to have a bath now and wash my hair.'

'Well, I never,' said Martha. 'I just don't know any more, I can't fathom you girls at all.'

After their tea, Pat went to get ready and Irene left it a few minutes before she put her head round the bedroom door. 'Are you all right?' she asked.

'Of course I am. Why wouldn't I be?'

Irene settled herself on the bed and watched Pat put on her grey dress with the black scalloped collar and shiny buttons. 'You look nice in that,' she said. Pat sat at the dressing table to put on her makeup and Irene asked, 'How did Tony look?'

'He looked well. It seems there was enough food and they were out of doors a lot. His leg is still troubling him though, and he's using a cane.'

'And how was he in himself?'

Pat stopped, the lipstick in mid-air. 'I think maybe he was … not exactly shy, but sort of nervous about meeting me.' She gave a half-laugh. 'Sure, I was a bit the same.'

'And he didn't mention the wedding?'

'Not in so many words.' Pat saw Irene's expression change and she rushed to explain. 'No, it's all right, don't worry. He said he loved me with all his heart, but he wants me to be sure. He said I might find him changed and we needed to get to know each other again.'

'And was he changed?'

Pat shook her head. 'I don't think so. It's more like he's just feeling his way back into the world.'

'But how do you feel about him now?'

'Oh Irene, I love him so much and I don't mind that we'll take our time, if that's what he wants. Today was lovely and I'm so excited about meeting him tonight.'

Irene took the brush from the dressing table. 'Well, finish your lipstick and I'll do your hair for you. When he sees you tonight, he'll think he's died and gone to heaven.'

Tony was waiting for her outside the Imperial Hotel and he kissed her softly on her cheek. 'Gee, Patti, you look stunning,' he said, and held out a small box. 'I brought you something.' She opened it to see a corsage of tiny white narcissi and violets.

'I've never had a corsage before. It's beautiful.'

He pinned it to her dress. 'It's something we do in the States – for a special girl.'

The lounge bar was warm and comfortable, there was a three-piece band playing and a few couples were dancing. Tony went to the bar and Pat looked around at the people enjoying their Saturday night. Soon, when the war was won, it would be like this all over the country. Normal life would resume, but she would never forget the last time she had been in this hotel. It was Irene's wedding, the day after the Easter bombing in 1941, when roads were closed, buildings lay in ruins, and people were still buried in the rubble. She couldn't help but recall the anguish she had felt waiting in church for William Kennedy. They were to sing a duet, but she was convinced he had been killed in the bombing. The opening bars had already begun when suddenly there he was walking up the aisle to join her. Afterwards, they had danced in in this very room ...

'Are you okay, Patti?' asked Tony and he set their drinks on the table.

'Yes of course, I was just thinking of Irene's wedding reception here. It all seems so long ago now.'

He held out his hand. 'Would you like to dance?'

'Oh, I thought with your leg ...'

'Aw gee, I can manage a shuffle round the floor to the slow numbers, but don't be expecting any lindy hopping or jitterbugging.'

It felt wonderful to be in his arms, to feel the nearness of him ... to trail her fingers across the back of his neck ... look up and see him smile.

The evening flew by and when the last waltz was announced they were surprised to find that it was nearly midnight. Their waltz was slow and languid and, when the final note faded away, everyone applauded the band and Tony gently raised her chin and kissed her until they were alone on the dance floor.

'Well, Tony,' said Martha as they sat down to Sunday dinner, 'I'm sure they serve up far better than this where you've been staying, but sure you'll take us as you find us, won't you?'

'Mrs Goulding, it's a real pleasure to be here. My mom always said it's not the food, it's the company that makes the meal, but even so this sure looks appetising to me.'

For dessert, Tony had brought a kind of chewy chocolate cake – a 'brownie' – as his contribution to the meal. He cut it into squares and the conversation round the table ceased as soon as it passed their lips …

'My, my,' said Martha when she had finished. 'That's some cake.'

'The most delicious thing I've ever eaten,' said Peggy.

'Mmmm,' said Irene. 'We've a lot to thank the Americans for.'

Tony looked at their faces and laughed. 'If you think that's good, just wait'll you taste our cheesecake.'

'Cheese cake?'

He looked at their puzzled faces. 'Well, maybe not,' he said.

After dinner Tony and Pat went for a walk up the lane towards Carr's Glen. There were forget-me-nots in the hedgerows and the sound of a blackbird singing its heart out close by. They sat on bank beneath a blackthorn covered in delicate, snow white flowers.

'A day like this makes you glad to be alive, doesn't it?' said Tony.

Pat nodded. 'We used to play up here when we were small.'

'I bet you were the bossy sister, weren't you?'

She laughed. 'For a while, until Peggy got into her stride.'

They sat in silence, each with their own thoughts. After a few minutes Tony turned to her and his face was troubled.

'I have to tell you something.' He hesitated, searching for the right words. 'Truth is, I found it so hard to come back here to you.' The shock must have registered on Pat's face. 'Oh, please don't look so sad, Patti, it wasn't because I didn't love you. It's just that I can't stop thinking that I don't have any right to be happy, to marry the girl I love, to make a new life.'

'Why would you think that?'

He closed his eyes a moment and when he opened them Pat could see his anguish.

'Ever since I was captured I've been going over and over what happened to me. That terrible battle, all those men, good men, killed. And I'm still here. I should've died with them.'

Pat reached out to him. 'Don't say that. You can't blame yourself. You were lucky, that's all.'

'Yeah, but why me?' Tony shook his head. 'Why did I get a second shot at life?'

'Nobody can answer that question,' said Pat. 'You should be thankful. You're here with your whole life in front of you.'

'You know, I never stopped thinking about you when I was in the hospital and later in the camp. In a way you kept me going. I asked them to ship me back to England, but when I arrived ... I don't know, somehow it didn't feel right to rush off and get married. The days went by and I was desperate just to see you again. That's when I decided to take it one step at a time ...'

'And now you're here and we're doing all right, aren't we?' said Pat.

'God, Patti, who am I trying to kid? As soon as I got off the boat I knew I didn't need time to think about whether I wanted to marry you. I love you so much – you're everything to me. But I can't get rid of this feeling that I don't deserve to be alive ...'

Pat put her arms around him and in her desperation the words poured out of her. 'Listen, you promised me you wouldn't die, do you remember? You said you'd never leave me and that I had to trust you. And I did trust you even when people were saying you were dead. I knew you wouldn't let me down. Can't you see, you and I are meant to be together? I've never doubted that and neither must you. We're bound together you and I. Remember, before you went away and we couldn't marry, we said it didn't matter because you are my husband and I am your wife? That's the pledge we made and God spared us both because that's how it was meant to be. Tony, I love you and I want to marry you and every day of our lives we'll be thankful that you were spared.'

Tony looked into her eyes and knew she was right. He held her tightly in his arms and kissed her.

In the time it took to walk back to the house, the shape of their future was planned. They would marry on 8 May, less than a month away but enough time to post the banns and gain the permission of Tony's commanding officer. Tony would write to his friend agreeing to join him in the homes for GIs project and suggesting that his new wife, who had all the relevant experience and skills, would be an asset to the business.

Chapter 40

Martha woke early and pulled back the curtains to see a clear sky that promised a bright and sunny day. Even after last night's celebrations she found it hard to believe that the war was over. News that the Armistice had been signed had brought people out on to the streets. In Joanmount Gardens they had danced the conga and sung all those songs that had sustained them through the darkest days, about bluebirds and white cliffs and meeting again some sunny day. Bonfires had been lit in the streets off the Oldpark Road giving the sky an amber glow, and the sound of Belfast in celebration had lasted into the small hours.

Now it was 8 May, VE Day, and Pat and Tony were getting married. They could never have known a month before that they had chosen such an auspicious date and time. The service of thanksgiving in the cathedral would be over in time for their wedding and after the reception at the Imperial Hotel they would be able join the crowds outside the City Hall to hear the live broadcast of Winston Churchill's speech.

One by one the girls came down to the kitchen for their breakfast. Pat was the first. 'Did you sleep?' asked Martha.

'Hardly at all after the craic last night and heaven only knows what today will be like.' She laughed. 'The two biggest events of my life in one day, I won't know what's hit me.'

A sleepy Peggy was the next one down. 'How far did you go with that conga?' asked Pat.

'Halfway to the City Hall, I think. My feet are killing me. There were so many on the streets and we were in and out of people's houses.'

Irene and Alexander were the last up and the wee boy went straight to his gran and held his hands out to be lifted up. She balanced him on her hip and fetched his breakfast of mashed-up egg in a cup and while she fed him she watched the girls round the table, full of excitement and fun. She had never been so proud or so happy.

Sheila and Clemmie caught the early morning milk train from Londonderry and arrived in a city waking up to a new world. A two-day holiday had been declared and at that time of the morning the streets were deserted, although they bore the littered evidence of the huge crowds that had thronged there the night before. Sheila bought the *Belfast News Letter* with the banner headline, 'A City Without Strangers', to catch up on the news.

'Looks like they had a hell of a party last night,' said Clemmie.

'And can you imagine what it's going to be like today?'

'Hope the boys made it here. Bet you can't wait to see Philippe.' She winked and Sheila thumped her on the arm.

'Don't you start all that again.'

By the time they arrived at the house, the preparations for four women and a little boy to get washed and dressed were well underway.

'There'll be a room for you two to get changed shortly,' Martha told them.

'We'll just need a wash, Mammy. We've decided we're going to wear our uniforms to the wedding.' Martha looked surprised and Clemmie explained, 'We figured it was the right thing to do, especially today. We're proud to be in uniform and to remember all those who fought.'

Martha nodded. 'It's a lovely idea, so it is.'

Peggy had already changed into her bridesmaid's dress and was upstairs helping Pat do her hair. 'I think you made the right decision not to have a veil,' she said. 'The little spray matches your posy and shows off your hair.' She fastened it with clips and arranged Pat's hair on her shoulders. 'You look so beautiful,' she said.

Pat, sitting at the dressing table, looked up and smiled at Peggy in the mirror, but there was no smile on her sister's face, only sadness.

'What is it? What's the matter?'

'Nothing, I'm being silly.'

'Tell me, Peggy, please.'

'It's just that I'm going to miss you so much when you go to America.' Peggy bit her lip and there were tears brimming in her eyes.

Pat stood up and put her arms around her sister. 'I know … I know. I feel the same. Over these last few weeks since Tony came back I've wondered how I could possibly leave you all. What will I do without you?' She tried to laugh, but it turned into a sob. 'Who am I going to argue with about everything? Who'll pinch my clothes now? And the music – oh, Peggy, the music …'

Peggy's eyes opened wide in alarm at what she had provoked, and she gripped Pat's arms. 'Listen to me. We've had the best of it these last few years. Now there's something even more wonderful that's happening to you and you have to grab it with both hands. You'll have a new life in the most exciting country in the world. Just think of it … America, like we've seen in the films – and the music we love will be all around you.'

Pat swallowed hard. 'You're right, Peggy, and the most important thing is that I love Tony so much. If it had turned out that he had died … Well, I don't think I could have carried on without him.'

Peggy let go of her arms. 'You have to go, Pat, it was meant to be.'

'But will Mammy be all right?'

'Of course she will. We'll all look after her, don't worry. She wants you to go. She told me, as long as you're happy that's the most important thing.'

337

'Maybe I'll be able to come back and see you all before too long. I'll work hard and save up the money, so I will.'

'Maybe,' said Peggy.

'I have something for you,' said Pat and she handed her sister a thin leather box. 'For being my bridesmaid.'

Inside was a gold locket. 'Oh, I love it Pat, thank you so much.'

'Wear it now, then,' said Pat.

'I will, I just have to do something first,' she said, and from a drawer she took a handkerchief in the folds of which was a curled strand of hair, and she placed it inside the locket. 'Esther' was all she said.

Everyone was waiting for them in the front room and, when Pat came in followed by Peggy, everyone clapped. They loved the dress and the posies and everyone said how beautiful Pat looked.

Betty and Jack arrived with their camera and suggested a photograph before they left for the church and they went into the garden and arranged themselves in a group. Pat in the centre in her lavender wedding dress with a posy of violets and paper-white narcissi. Peggy next to her in the dress Irene had worn for her wedding, altered again, at Peggy's insistence, to give it more style. Sheila and Clemmie in their uniforms on the other side of Peggy, and Martha in her Sunday-best coat and a hat that was a testimony to the ingenuity of Make Do and Mend, next to Pat with Betty beside her. The two men – John McCracken, who was to give Pat away, and Goldstein, an unlikely but willing best man – stood in the back row behind Pat and Peggy.

Pat, Peggy and John were the last to leave the house and, as the wedding car came closer to the town, people were crowding the pavements. 'It's like the Twelfth of July,' said John.

'There'll be plenty more than that when we get a bit closer,' said Peggy. 'VE Day – everybody'll be on the streets.'

Further on, people were strolling down the road in the holiday sunshine and the car slowed to a crawl. Pat became increasingly anxious. 'I'm going to be so late,' she said, and moments later she gathered up her dress and, posy in hand, she was out of the car and weaving through the crowds. Peggy and John stared at each other in amazement, then Peggy too was out of the car. 'Come on,' she shouted, 'we need to catch up with her.'

The sight of a bride in the midst of the already excited crowd brought an immediate response. People parted to let her through, some clapping, others shouting their congratulations. Someone called out, 'All the best to ye, love. Ye've picked a quare day for it!'

The crowds were thicker now as they came towards York Street, and their progress slowed. Then from behind them they heard singing, and the crowds parted to reveal dozens of marching children, each waving a Union Jack, all singing in defiance: 'Hitler thought he had us with his Ja Ja Ja.'

'Quick, tag on behind them,' shouted Peggy, and they followed in the wake of the procession all the way to the cathedral.

Pat stood at the end of the long aisle. The sublime organ music began and John patted her arm. 'Are you ready?' She nodded and stepped out with her right foot for luck. Faces turned towards her: there were her friends from the Barnstormers' troupe and, further on, colleagues from the office at Stormont. She passed the spot where Captain Joe Walters had reassured her that Tony would be safe, and she sent a silent prayer that Joe too had come through the war. There was her family: Irene, Sheila, Aunt Kathleen, Aunt Anna, Grace and Aggie. And there was Mammy wiping her eyes and the smile on her face made Pat's heart ache.

Tony stood with his back to her. She fixed her eyes on him: the smart uniform, broad shoulders and neatly-cut dark hair. She was within touching distance when he sensed her there and turned towards her. She saw the love in his eyes and her heart leapt. She would never be parted from him again …

They came out of the cathedral to the sound of bells ringing and a sizeable crowd, attracted by the noise, had gathered to see the wedding party as though it was part of the day's tapestry of rejoicing. Jack took pictures of the guests and the bride and groom before they set out to walk up Royal Avenue to the hotel.

Union Jacks and Stars and Stripes were everywhere: in people's hands, hanging from windows or as bunting strung across buildings or fluttering from lamp post to lamp post. In the carnival atmosphere the relief and joy was there in every smiling face. Factory, shop and office girls in their summer dresses linked arms with friends or sweethearts, elderly couples strolled along as though it was a Sunday afternoon, even the babies' prams sported red, white and blue ribbons.

Pat and Tony, followed by the rest of the wedding party, made their way through the crowds and people turned to look at them in surprise and delight. Sheila and Philippe, and Clemmie and Brad walked behind the others catching up and enjoying each other's company.

'It's great to see you again.' Philippe took Sheila's hand.

'I was so worried you wouldn't be able to come,' said Sheila.

'Are you kidding? I'd have gone through hell or high water to get back here to see you – and it very nearly came to that.' He gave a half-laugh and she could see he was thinking whether or not to go on.

'Why, what happened?'

'Took some flak coming back from a raid in Germany a couple of weeks ago – engine on fire – but I thought I might just limp home.' He shook his head. 'I knew I was pushing my luck, but then the strangest thing …'

'What happened, Philippe?'

'I was trying really hard to keep the plane in the air when out of the blue I remembered the last words you said to me …'

Sheila stopped walking and looked up at him. 'Just remember your training and you'll be fine,' she said.

'*Oui*, that's it exactly.' His eyes were wide with the memory. 'Right then, I knew I had to bail out.' He shook his head. 'You know, Sheila, I always thought you brought me luck, but that was the tightest spot I'd ever been in and it was like your voice just cut through all the noise in my head and told me what I had to do.'

He touched her hair as he always did for luck, then kissed her. 'See, I always said we were connected and now I've found you, I'll never let you go.' And he kissed her again, slowly this time, until Brad called out, 'Hey, you guys, time for that later, now we gotta eat.'

★

Irene walked up and down in the lobby of the Imperial Hotel rocking Alexander in her arms and watching the guests sipping sweet sherry. It was over four years since she and Sandy had been here on their wedding day. The city had been bombed the night before and her journey to the church had taken her through horrific sights that would stay with her for the rest of her days. In this very place she had heard the news that her friend Myrtle had been killed in the bombing. Now the war was over and she had a child in her arms. Soon Sandy would come home and they would start a new life together. Her mother had told her once that being married was like making soda bread. 'You make it every day and some days it tastes better than others. You'll find your own recipe.' She hadn't quite understood that advice at the time, but she did now.

'Penny for them.' Peggy was at her side. 'Why don't you have a sherry and be in the company for a while? I'll look after Alexander.'

'No, it's all right, he's nodded off. I'll go and sit over there with him, he won't sleep for long.' They sat in two oversized armchairs in the lobby. 'I was just thinking about my wedding reception here,' said Irene. 'What a strange day that was; it all seems so long ago.'

Peggy nodded. 'That was the day Harry left me to join the army.'

'Do you still think about him?'

'Sometimes.'

'Will he come back do you think?'

Peggy sighed. 'You never know with Harry. He sent me that letter, after the row at Christmas, saying that he loved me and how he'd come and find me when the war was over. Well, I'm not holding my breath. Anyway, I'm happy as I am, managing the shop and being Mr Goldstein's Assistant Director for the Barnstormers' shows. That's plenty to be going on with.' She smiled. 'There again, if I met a very handsome and very wealthy man ...'

The dining room of the Imperial Hotel was impressive, with its rich red velvet curtains, Art Deco mirrors and lights. The tables were set with silver cutlery, crystal glasses and vases of narcissi on white linen. After the meal Goldstein, as best man, rose to speak.

'Ladies and gentlemen, on such an auspicious day the future

341

of the newly married couple must be doubly blessed. They begin married life with a world at peace and the excitement of making their home in America. A new business enterprise awaits them and I am certain their skills, determination and experience of working together will ensure its success.

I would like to say something also about my dear friend Martha and her girls. They have enriched my life beyond measure.' Goldstein paused and looked down, as though composing himself, before going on. 'When Peggy came to work in my shop, I never dreamt that soon my life would be bound up with the Goulding family. It was hearing the girls sing that led me to form a troupe of entertainers that changed the lives of many of you here.'

There was applause and cheering from the Barnstormers at the back of the room.

'Pat was a stalwart of the troupe, not only singing with her sisters but also bringing a classical repertoire to our shows.' He turned to Pat and said simply, 'I will miss her voice. Now I ask you to raise your glasses to toast Pat and Tony!'

After the toast Goldstein produced a telegram. 'Speaking of the USA, I am delighted to read a message from Macy who, as you know, returned home after her "Stirling" work in the aircraft factory. She says, "Wish you guys all the best STOP See you in New York STOP Begin filming next month with Bob Hope STOP ".'

There was a spontaneous eruption of applause at Macy's news and when it died down, Goldstein spoke again. 'Incredible to think that one of our friends will soon grace the silver screen. Now, finally, it is highly unusual for a bride to sing at her wedding, but I've asked Pat to sing one last song for us before she leaves.'

Peggy was already seated at the baby grand in the corner of the room and Pat joined her there.

'This is for Tony,' she said and the dramatic opening bars began. She sang of her joy at seeing his face, hearing his voice and living her life 'With a song in my heart for you'.

When the final note faded, the guests were on their feet clapping and when Tony took her in his arms and kissed her, they cheered.

'I've never seen anything so romantic,' said Sheila.

'Later, will you sing like that for me?' asked Philippe.

'I might, if you ask me nicely.'

'*S'il te plaît, ma chérie,*' he whispered and Sheila threw back her head and laughed.

Peggy, still at the piano, began to play a familiar introduction. 'Don't sit down, Pat,' she said. 'Come on Irene, Sheila, we'll have one last song from the Golden Sisters!' And they took up their positions beside the piano, smiled and swayed and caught the note and swung into 'Don't Sit Under the Apple Tree'. It was as if every concert and every song had culminated in this performance to bring them out of the dark days of war into the sunshine of peace.

They took their final bow, but within seconds the clapping and cheering had been drowned out by a cacophony of sounds: church bells, factory hooters, ships' sirens.

All at once people were hurrying out of the room and into the street. It was time for Churchill's broadcast. The scene that met them outside was beyond belief. The crowds they had seen on the way to the hotel had multiplied to thousands. There was a sea of people all the way to the City Hall and, in the opposite direction, thousands more down Royal Avenue and beyond as far as the eye could see.

At three o'clock precisely, the loud speakers crackled and the crowd fell silent as Churchill's speech to the nation was transmitted. The slow and sonorous voice weighed every syllable and when he declared, 'The German war is therefore at an end,' the noise was deafening. 'We may allow ourselves a brief period of rejoicing …' Waves of cheering and laughter up and down the streets. Churchill's closing words – 'Long live the cause of freedom. God save the King!' – were the cue for celebrations that would last well into the night.

'You know, Martha,' said Goldstein. 'There were times when I thought I'd never see this day, but the spirit of this place and its people is indestructible.'

'Sure, it's about looking after each other,' said Martha. 'Family, friends, neighbours, strangers.'

'Is that how you see the world, Martha?'

She smiled. 'Indeed it is, Isaac, indeed it is.'